THE WANDERING PRINCE

Jean Plaidy

The
Wandering
Prince

G. P. Putnam's Sons
New York

AUTHOR'S NOTE

My plan is to write the story of Charles II, and as he was a King to whom women were of great importance, I propose to do so through the lives of those few women – among so many – who played the most significant parts, not only in his life, but in history.

It is in his dealings with women that Charles is usually seen at his best, for, rake though he was, he was invariably courteous and kind. He loved women, so naturally women loved him – a universal corollary, since the misogynist is always unpopular with women, while their constant admirer, even if he be as profligate as Charles himself, is treated with indulgence. People – men or women – are generally predisposed to love those who love them. That is why – certainly among women – England's Merry Monarch is England's most popular King.

The Wandering Prince, complete in itself, deals with the early life of Charles II as it is reflected in the lives of two women who were to have a far-reaching effect not only on Charles' life but on the history of these islands – his sister, 'Minette' (Duchesse d'Orléans), and his mistress, Lucy Water.

Among the many books I have read in the course of my research I should like to acknowledge my debt to the following:

History of France. M. Guizot. Translated by Robert Black, M.A.

Madame. Memoirs of Henrietta, daughter of Charles I, and Duchess of Orléans. Julia Cartwright (Mrs Henry Ady).

Diary of John Evelyn. Edited by William Bray, Prefatory Notes by George W. E. Russell.

Diary and Correspondence of Samuel Pepys.

Early Life of Louis XIV. Henri Carré. Translated by Dorothy Bolton.

Political History of England, 1603–1660. F. C. Montague, M.A.

History of England. William Hickman Smith Aubrey.

King Charles II. Arthur Bryant.

The Gay King. Dorothy Senior.
Old Paris. Its Courts and Literary Salons. Catherine Charlotte Lady Jackson.
Lives of the Queens of England. Agnes Strickland.
British History. John Wade.

J.P.

HENRIETTE D'ORLEANS
AND
LUCY WATER

"... I think that no joys are above
The pleasures of love."

CHARLES STUART

CHAPTER ONE

IT WAS LATE afternoon on a July day in the fourth year of the Great Rebellion. The sun was hot; the grass banks were brown; and the purple nettle-flowers and the petals of the woundwort were peppered with fine dust.

A small party – two men and two women – trudged slowly along the road, looking neither to right nor to left, their eyes fixed on the ground. One of the women was a hunchback, and it was this deformed one who carried a sleeping child.

Sweat ran down her face; she caught her breath as she saved herself from tripping over a stone and going head-long into one of the numerous pot-holes which were a feature of the road. She wiped the sweat from her face but did not lift her eyes from the ground.

After a while she spoke. 'How far from the inn, Tom?'

'We'll be there within the hour.'

'There's time before dark,' said the other woman. 'Let's stop for a rest. The boy's heavy.'

Tom nodded. 'A few minutes will do no harm,' he said.

The hunchback spoke again. 'Only let us rest if you are sure there's time, Tom. Don't let the dark overtake us. There'll be robbers on the road at twilight.'

'There are four of us,' answered Tom, 'and we look too poor to rob. But Nell's right. There's time for a rest.'

They sat on the bank. Nell took off her boots and grim-aced at her swollen feet while the hunchback laid the child gently on the grass. The others would have helped, but she waved them aside; she seemed determined that none but herself should touch the child.

'Here's the best spot for you,' said Tom to the hunch-back. 'The bush makes a good support.' But the hunchback shook her head and looked at him with some reproach. He smiled and sat down at the spot he had chosen as the best. 'We should be in Dover long before this time tomor-row,' he added.

'Call me Nan,' said the hunchback.

'Yes . . . Nan . . . I will.'

'You must remember to call me Nan. It is short for Nanette. Ask my husband. Is that not so, Gaston?'

'Yes . . . that is so. Nan . . . it is short for Nanette.'

'And that is my name.'

'Yes, Nan,' said Tom.

'There is someone coming,' said Nell quickly.

They were silent, listening to the sound of footsteps on the road. A man and a woman came into sight, and the hunchback's eyes went to the sleeping child beside her; her right hand moved out and rested on its ragged clothes.

The man and woman who were approaching carried bundles, and their dress proclaimed them to be of slightly higher social standing than the group on the bank. The man who wore his hair cut short so that his pink and rather prominent ears could be seen, might have been a tradesman. The woman was plump and puffing with exertion; it was clear that she was finding the heat uncomfortable.

'Here's sensible people,' she was grumbling, 'taking a rest by the roadside. I declare I'll do the same, for my feet won't carry me a step farther until I give them a short rest.'

'Now come along, Kitty,' said the man. 'If we're to be in Tonbridge in time for the waggon there's no time for dallying.'

'There's time enough, and my feet won't go a step further.' The fat woman was smiling as she plumped herself down on the bank, and her husband had no choice but to do the same, for it was too hot to stand and argue.

'God be with you,' said the fat woman.

'God be with you,' murmured Tom and his companions, but they did not look at the newcomers; they kept their eyes fixed on the opposite bank. Unlike the fat woman they did not wish for roadside chatter; but the fat woman was one who usually achieved that which she desired.

'A pretty child . . .' she began.

The hunchback smiled and bowed her head in acknowledgement of the compliment.

'I've a weakness for little girls ...'

'This ... is a little boy,' said Nan, and her accent was unmistakably foreign.

'You sound like a foreigner,' said the woman.

'I am French, Madame.'

'French?' The man shot a suspicious glance at the party. 'We don't like the French much here.'

His wife continued to smile. 'Lee says that when our King went and got married to a French wife the trouble started, and now look what she's brought him to. That's what you say, eh, Lee?'

'Where is she now?' demanded Lee. 'In France ... kicking up her heels and dancing the new dances, I'll warrant. A fine wife she's been to our King Charles and a fine brewing of trouble she's brought him!'

'I'm sorry that the Queen should be French,' said Nan. 'For myself I am a poor woman. My husband here and my child ... with these two fellow servants, go to join our master. The poor in France are much like the poor in England.'

'There's truth in that, I'll swear,' said the woman.

'A master or a mistress says "Go here ... Go there ..." and their servants must go ... even if it is to service in another country. My husband is a valet to a gentleman. That is so, is it not, Gaston?'

Gaston agreed that it was so, in English slightly less fluent than that of the hunchback.

'And we all serve in the same household,' put in Nell.

'Ah,' said the man Lee, 'there's going to be a turnabout in this country ere long. Things will be different for some of us when the Parliament is victorious. We're for the Parliament ... as all the poor should be. Are you for the Parliament?'

'Please?' said the hunchback.

'For the Parliament,' said Lee in a louder tone.

'I do not always understand. I am not English. You will forgive me.'

Lee turned to Tom. 'Are you French too?'

'No, I am English.'

'Then you'll think as I do.'

'How old is the child?' interrupted Lee's wife.

11

'He has two years,' said the hunchback. She had unconsciously laid her hand on the child.

'What a fine-shaped hand you've got,' said the woman. She studied her own gnarled one and its broken nails with a distasteful grimace.

'She's a lady's maid,' explained Nell.

'What! Dressing and curling the hair and sewing on ruffles. You'll be used to high-life.'

'High-life?' said the hunchback. 'What is that?'

'High society, balls and masques,' said Tom.

'Fine ladies and gentlemen making merry while the poor starves,' said Lee.

'I am sorry that that should be so,' said the hunchback gravely.

' 'Tis no fault of yours. The poor stands together ... times like these. Where are you making for?'

'We are joining our master's household at Dover.'

'And all on foot!' cried Lee, 'with a child to carry!'

'That's how the rich look after their servants,' added his wife.

'We have to be there tomorrow,' said Tom, 'to set the house in order. We've little time to lose.'

'A nice way to treat you!' the woman went on grumbling. 'Walking all the way! Where have you come from?'

'Well ...' began Tom; but the hunchback said quickly: 'From London.'

'And carrying a child all that way!'

'The child is mine ... mine and my husband's,' said the hunchback. 'We are glad to be able to have him with us.'

'Why,' said Lee, 'you ought to get the stage waggon. That's where we're going now. To Tonbridge to catch the waggon.'

'Lee's a much travelled man,' said his wife admiringly.

'Yes. I don't mind telling you it's not the first time I've travelled on the stage waggon. Once I went from Holborn to Chester ... travelling the whole of six days. Two miles the hour and a halfpenny the mile, a waggoner to hold the horses and lead them all the way while you sat on the floor of the waggon like a lord. 'Tis a wondrous thing to travel. Hist! I think I hear riders coming this way.'

The hunchback shrank nearer to her friends as once

12

again her hand hovered over the sleeping child. They were all silent for some seconds while the sound of horses' hoofs grew louder; and soon a party of riders came into sight. They were soberly dressed and their hair scarcely covered their ears, thus proclaiming them to be soldiers of the Parliamentary forces.

'God go with you!' called Lee.

'God be with you, friend,' answered the rider at the head of the cavalcade.

The dust raised by the horses' hoofs made the hunchback cough; the child started to whimper. 'All is well,' murmured the hunchback. 'All is well. Sleep on.'

'I heard,' said Lee's wife, 'that the King won't hold out much longer. They say he's gone to Scotland. He hadn't a chance after Naseby. Best thing he could do would be to join the Frenchwoman in France.'

'Mayhap he would not wish to leave his country,' said Tom.

'Better for him to leave for France than the next world,' put in Lee with a laugh.

The child sat up and gazed at the Lees with an expression of candid distaste.

'All is well,' said the hunchback hastily. She put her arm round the child and pressed its little face against her.

'No, no, *no!*' cried the child wriggling away.

'A fine temper,' said Lee's wife.

'It's so hot,' replied the hunchback.

'I see you spoil him,' said Lee.

'Let's have a look at the little 'un,' said his wife. She took hold of the child's ragged sleeve. The child tried to shake her off, but she only laughed, and that seemed to enrage the little creature. 'You're a spoiled baby, you are,' went on the woman. 'You'll never grow into a fine soldier to fight for General Fairfax, you won't. What's your name?'

'Princess,' said the child haughtily.

'Princess!' cried Lee. 'That's a strange name for a little boy.'

'It is Pierre, Monsieur,' said the hunchback quickly.

'That in English is Peter,' added Gaston.

'He does not speak the very good English,' went on the

hunchback. 'His words are not very clear. We talk to him sometimes in our own tongue ... sometimes in English ... and our English, as you see, Madame, is sometimes not very good.'

'Princess!' repeated the child. '*Me* ... Princess!'

There was silence while all looked at the child. The Lees in puzzlement; the four companions of the child as though they had been struck temporarily lifeless. In the distance could be heard the sound of retreating horses' hoofs. Then the hunchback seemed to come to a decision; she rose and took the child firmly by the hand.

'We must go,' she said. 'We shall not reach our lodging by nightfall if we stay longer. Come, my friends. And good day to both of you. A pleasant journey and thank you for your company.'

The other three had risen with her. They closed about the child.

'Good day to you,' murmured the Lees.

The child turned to take a last look at them, and the big black eyes showed an angry defiance as the lips formed the words: 'Princess. *Me* ... Princess!'

*

They did not speak until they had put some distance between themselves and the man and woman on the bank. The hunchback had picked up the child so that they might more quickly escape.

At length Nell said: 'For the moment I was ready to run.'

'That would have been unwise,' said the hunchback. 'That would have been the worst thing we could have done.'

'If we could only make ... the boy understand!'

'I have often been relieved because he is so young ... too young to understand; and yet if only we could explain. ... But how could one so young be expected to understand?'

The child, knowing itself to be the subject of discussion, was listening eagerly. The hunchback noticed this and said: 'What will there be to eat at this inn of yours, Tom?' 'Mayhap a little duck or snipe ... peacock, kid, venison. Mayhap lampreys and sturgeon ...'

'We must remember our stations,' said the hunchback.

The child wished to bring the conversation back to itself. The little hands beat the hunchback. 'Nan ... Nan ...' said the child. '*Dirty* Nan! Don't like dirty Nan.'

'Hush, dearest, hush!' said the hunchback.

'Want to go home. Want clean Nan ... not dirty Nan.'

'Dearest, be good. Only a little while longer. Remember you are Pierre ... my little boy.'

'Little *girl*!' said the child.

'No, dearest, no! You are Pierre ... Pierre for Peter.'

'No Pierre! No Pierre!' chanted the child. 'Dirty Nan! Black lady! Want to get down.'

'Try to sleep, my darling.'

'No sleep! No sleep!'

Two soldiers had rounded the bend and were coming towards the party, who immediately fell silent; but just as the two men drew level with them, the child called to them: 'Me ... Princess. Dirty frock ... not mine ... Me ... Princess!'

They stopped. The hunchback smiled, but beneath the grime and dust her face grew a shade paler.

'What was it the little one said?' asked one of the soldiers.

It was the hunchback who answered. 'Your pardon, Messieurs. I and my husband do not speak the English very well. Nor does our son. He is telling you his name is Pierre. That is Peter in English.'

One of the soldiers said: 'I thought the boy said he was a Princess.'

The child smiled dazzlingly and chanted: 'Princess! Princess! Don't like black lady. Want clean Nan.'

The soldiers looked at each other and exchanged smiles. One of them brought his face near to that of the child. 'So you're a Princess, eh, young fellow?' he said. 'I'll tell you something.' He nodded his head in the direction of his companion. 'He's Oliver Cromwell and I'm Prince Charley.'

'Forgive, Monsieur,' said the hunchback quickly. 'We mean no harm. We are walking to Dover to the house of our master.'

'To Dover, eh!' said the soldier. 'You're on the right road

but you've many hours journey before you yet.'

'Then we must hasten.'

The second soldier was smiling at the child. 'Listen to me, little 'un,' he said. ' 'Tis better in these days to be the son of a hunchback than the daughter of a King.'

'Ah, Messieurs!' cried the hunchback. 'You speak truly. I thank God these days that I am a poor hunchback, for I remember there are others in worse case.'

'God's will be done,' said the soldier.

'God be with you,' said the hunchback.

'And with you, woman. And with you all. Farewell, Princess Peter.'

The child began to wail as they continued along the road. 'Me Princess. Want my gown. Don't like dirty Nan.'

Again that silence; again that tension.

Nell said: 'Can it go on? Shall we be so lucky every time?'

'We must be,' replied the hunchback grimly.

*

It was dusk when they came to the inn. They were glad of that, for the daylight was disturbing; moreover the child slept.

Tom went across the inn yard and found the landlord. He was a long time gone. The rest of the party waited uneasily beneath the hanging sign.

'Mayhap we should not have come here,' said Nell. 'Mayhap we should have made beds for ourselves under the hedges.'

'We shall be safe enough,' murmured the hunchback. 'And we'll leave at daybreak.'

At length Tom called to them to come forward. The landlord was with him.

'So this is the party,' said the landlord. 'Two women and two men and a young boy. I don't make a practice of taking foot passengers . . . nor those that come on the stage waggon. My inn is an inn for the quality.'

'We can pay,' said Tom quickly.

'There's comings and goings these days,' said the landlord. 'We had a troop of soldiers in here only this day.'

Tom took out his purse and showed it to the innkeeper.

'We'll pay in advance,' he said. 'We're tired and hungry.
Let us make a bargain here and now.'

'Very well, very well,' said the landlord. 'What'll you
eat? It'll be at the common table, I reckon, and that'll cost
you sixpence a-piece.'

Tom looked at the hunchback, who said: 'Could we
have the meal served for us alone? Mayhap we could have
a room to ourselves.'

The innkeeper scratched his head and looked at them.

'We'll pay,' said Tom.

'Well then . . . it could be arranged. Please to wait in
the inn parlour, and you'll be called to table in good
time.'

He led the way into the parlour, and Tom went out with
him to settle where they would sleep, what they would eat,
and to pay the innkeeper what he asked.

There were several people in the inn parlour. The hunchback noticed this with dismay and she hesitated, but only
for a second; then she went boldly forward holding the
sleeping child in her arms, with Nell and Gaston on either
side of her.

Several people, who sat at the tables and in the window
seat, and who were talking together, called a good day to
them. The eyes of a plump lady bedecked with ribbons
went to the child.

'Looks worn out,' she commented. 'Poor little mite! She
fast asleep?'

'It's a little boy.'

'There now! So he is! Have you come far?'

'From London.'

The rest of the people went on talking about the war;
they were sighing for the good old days of peace and blam-
ing 'The French Woman' for all their troubles. There was
one large man with short hair who had taken upon himself the task of mentor to the rest. He was explaining to
the company why it had been necessary to wage war
against the Royalists. His knowledge of affairs was imperfect, but those present who might have corrected him
dared not do so.

'The Queen would make us all Catholic if she could,' he
was declaring. 'You, Sir, and you, Madam, and you, my

17

comely wench. Aye, and you who have just come in ...
the hunchback woman and the boy there ... she'd make
us all Catholic if she dared.'

'We'd die rather,' said another man.

'Why,' went on the first, 'on St James' day this Queen
of ours walked afoot to Tyburn to honour Catholics who
had died there. And I tell you, friends, by the gleam in her
eyes it was clear she'd like to see done to some of us good
Christians what was done to idolators at Tyburn gallows.
If I'd been at Exeter I'd not have let her give *me* the slip.
I'd have found her. I'd have carried her to London ... aye,
that I would. I'd have made her walk to Tyburn gallows
... and it wouldn't have been to honour idolators!'

'She's a very wicked woman,' volunteered one of the
women. 'They say the French are all wicked.'

'It won't be long,' said the large talkative man, 'before
we've done with kings and queens in England. Kings and
queens have no place in England today.'

'If the King was to be killed in battle ... or after,' said
a short fat man, 'there'd still be his children to make
trouble.'

'I saw the Prince of Wales once,' said the beribboned
woman.

'An ugly fellow!'

'Well, that's as may be,' said the woman with a smile.

'And what would you mean by that?'

'Oh ... he was dark ... dark to swarthiness ... He had
a big nose and a big mouth ... He was a boy and yet ...'

'Sounds as if you're a Royalist, madam,' said the large
man accusingly.

'Oh no, I wouldn't say that. He was naught but a boy
... Prince Charles ... and he was riding through our town
with his brother, young James. It would have been just
before Edgehill, I reckon.'

'We nearly got those boys at Edgehill,' grumbled the
man. 'If I'd have been there ...'

The woman was wistful. 'No, he wasn't really ugly ...
not when he smiled. And he smiled at me ... straight at me
and doffed his hat as though I were a lady of the Court.
There was a woman with me who declared the smile and
the hat-doffing was for her ...'

'You're bedazzled by royalty!' sneered the man.

'Not me! It was only the Prince himself. There were others there. Gentlemen ... dukes ... lords ... Handsome they might be called, but it was the Prince ... that boy ... that dark and ugly boy ... Mayhap it was because he *was* just a boy ...'

'Tush!' said the man. 'His Royal Highness! He'll not be Highness much longer. It won't be long before he'll want to forget he was Prince of Wales and once heir to a kingdom that will have none of him. People will be ashamed to talk of kings and queens, I tell you. We'll choose our Lord Protector and if he doesn't please us we'll rid ourselves of him and choose another. Royalty! I'd have the heads off the lot of them!'

'Except the prince of Wales ...' murmured the woman.

Tom looked in at the door and beckoned to his party; gladly they followed him out of the parlour.

He whispered as the door shut on them: 'We're to have an attic to ourselves to sleep in. The landlord is having straw put up there now. Food is being prepared for us, and that we can have by ourselves in one of the small rooms. I have paid him well. I think he is a little suspicious of how we can pay for what we want; but his eyes glistened at the sight of the money.'

'Then let us eat quickly and retire to our attic,' said the hunchback.

As they walked across the hall they heard a man's voice, shouting to a groom. It was a loud and arrogant voice. They were all straining their ears to listen.

'Come, boy! Where's mine host? I'm famished. And I want a room ... the best room you have ...'

The innkeeper was bustling into the yard; they could hear the rise and fall of his voice as he obsequiously placated the newcomer.

'Come along,' said the hunchback; and they went into a small room where a meal of duck and boar was laid out for them, with ale to drink. The child awakened and sleepily partook of the meal. They spoke little while they ate, and before the others had finished – as the child had fallen asleep again – the hunchback said she would go up to the attic room with him and there she would stay till morning; for the two of them must not be separated.

'I'll show you the way,' said Tom. ' 'Tis right at the top under the eaves.'

As they came out into the hall the arrogant newcomer was leaning against the wall shouting instructions and looking with distaste at his surroundings. His eyes flickered over the hunchback and the child; he paused for a second and then gave them a look of distaste. The hunchback hastily followed Tom up the stairs and, as she did so, she heard the drawling voice: 'God's Body! This is no inn! 'Tis an ale house. This is no place for the quality. Hunchback beggars and their brats stay here. Plague take you! Why did you not tell me, man?'

The hunchback did not look round as she followed Tom up the narrow staircase. Tom indicated a door and they went in. It was a long, low-ceilinged room; a dark room, and the thatch showed through a small unglazed window. On the floor were two piles of straw which would serve as beds. It was rough but it would do for a night.

'Go back to your food,' said the hunchback. 'I will stay here with the child. All of you join me when you have finished, but first eat your fill.'

Tom bowed and when he had left her she laid the child on one of the heaps of straw and gently put her lips to the small forehead. Then she threw herself down beside the child. She was worn out with the day's exertion. She laid her hand over her fast-beating heart. It should beat more peacefully now; here they would be safe until morning, and there were only a few more miles to Dover. Here they could sleep and refresh themselves, and at daybreak they would be on their journey again.

Suddenly the door opened and a groom came in. He hesitated. 'Ah ... I did not know there was anyone here. I have brought more straw.'

'I thank you.'

'There are four of you and the little girl?'

'Little boy,' she corrected him.

As she spoke she had laid her hand on the child; it was as though when anyone spoke of it she had to touch it, fearing that someone might try to snatch it from her. The man came over and looked down at the sleeping child. He stared, and she remembered how the woman on the bank had noticed her finely-shaped hands.

'A little boy,' said the groom, 'with the looks of a girl.'

'He is young yet, and I am told that he resembles his mother rather than his father.'

'He has an air,' said the groom. 'He might be the child of someone of high degree.'

He was watching the hunchback in a manner which brought the flush to her cheeks, and in that instant, as the rich blood showed beneath the dirt, she was young and comely.

He lowered his voice. 'Lady,' he said, 'there are some hereabouts who would be loyal to His Majesty.'

She did not answer; her grip tightened on the child.

'Your hands are too fine, madam,' he said. 'They betray you. You should keep them hidden.'

'My hands? I am a lady's maid.'

'That would account for it, mayhap.'

'Mayhap! It does account for it!'

'Your hump has slipped a little, lady. If you'll forgive my saying so, it is a bit too high. And you should bend over more.'

The hunchback tried to speak, but she could not; her mouth was dry and she was trembling.

'I was with the King's army at Edgehill,' went on the groom. 'I was with the little Prince Charles and his brother James. There was that about him – Charles, I mean – which made me want to serve him. Boy as he was, I'll never forget him. Tall for his age and dark for an Englishman, and so ready to give a smile to a man that he didn't seem like a king's son. Just one of ourselves ... and yet with a difference ... He came near to capture at Edgehill ... God bless him! God bless the Prince of Wales!'

'You're a bold man to speak thus before a stranger.'

'These are days for bold deeds, madam. But you may trust me. I wish you God speed and a safe trip across the water.'

'Across the water?'

'You go to Dover, madam. You will cross the water with the child and join the Queen.'

'I have said nothing that should make you think this.'

'They say the Queen is the cause of the King's troubles, madam. That may be so, but the Queen is devoted to the King's cause. Poor lady! It must be two years since she fled from England. It was a few weeks after the birth of her youngest, the little Princess Henrietta.'

'This makes uneasy talk,' said the hunchback.

'You may trust me, madam. And if there is anything I can do to serve you . . .'

'Thank you, but I am only a poor woman who, with her husband and fellow-servants, goes to join her master's household.'

He bowed and went from the room; and when he had gone she was still unable to move, for a numbness had seized her limbs. On the road, passing the soldiers of the King's enemies, she had been less frightened than now. The walls of the attic became to her like prison walls.

When the others joined her, they found her sitting on the straw holding the child in her arms.

She said: 'I am afraid. One of the grooms came to bring straw, and I am sure he knows who we are. And I . . . I cannot be sure whether or not we can trust him.'

*

The night was full of terrors. She shifted from side to side on her straw. The hump of linen hurt her back, but she dared not unstrap it. What if the hunchback were surprised without her hump! Had she been foolish in attempting this great adventure? What if she failed now? That virago, Queen Henrietta Maria, would never forgive her for exposing her youngest child to such dangers of the road. And yet there were times when it was necessary to take a bold action. The Queen herself had acted boldly, and because of that was at this moment in her native country where she might work for the King, her husband, instead of being – as she most certainly would have been, had she been less bold – the prisoner of the King's enemies.

Anne Douglas, Lady Dalkeith, had had to find some way of disguising her tall and graceful figure, and the hump had seemed as good a way as any; and to assume French nationality had seemed imperative since the little Princess could prattle and her lisping 'Princess' sounded more like

Pierre than any other name. If it had only been possible to make the child understand the danger she was in, how much easier would this task have been! But she was too young to realize why she must be hurried from her comfortable palace, why she must be dressed as a beggar's child, and that she must be called Pierre. If she had been younger – or older – the journey might have been less dangerous.

Anne Douglas had scarcely slept since she had left the Palace of Oatlands; she was exhausted now, but even with the others at hand, she dared not sleep. The groom had made her very uneasy. He had said she could trust him, but whom could one trust in a country engaged in a great civil war?

It would have seemed incredible a few years ago that she, Anne Villiers, wife of Robert Douglas who was the heir of the Earl of Morton, should be lying in such a place as this. But times had changed; and it occurred to her to wonder where the King slept this night or where the Prince of Wales had his lodging.

She had made the decision suddenly.

It was two years since the little Princess had been born. The Queen had been very weak at the time, and before she had risen from her bed news had come that Lord Essex – who was on the side of the Parliament – was marching to Exeter with the intention of besieging the city. Henrietta Maria had written to him asking for permission to leave for Bath with her child; Essex's reply had been that if the Queen went anywhere with his consent it would be to London, where she would be called before the Parliament to answer a charge of making civil war in England.

There had been only one course open to her – flight to France. How she had wept, that emotional woman! She had cried to Anne: 'I must leave this country. If the Parliament make me their prisoner, my husband will come to my aid; he will risk all for my sake. It is better that my miserable life should be risked than that he should be in peril through me. I have written to him telling him this; and by the time he receives my letter I hope to be in France. The Queen of France is my own sister-in-law, and she will not turn me away.'

She was all emotion; her heart was ever ready to govern her head, and this, Anne knew, was in a large measure to be blamed for the King's disasters; for, oddly enough, although the marriage of Charles and Henrietta Maria had begun stormily, they had quickly understood each other, and with understanding had come passionate affection. The Queen was passionate by nature; frivolous she seemed at times, yet how singlemindedly she could cling to a cause; and the cause to which she now gave her passionate energy was that of her husband.

'Take care of my little one, Anne,' she had said. 'Guard her with your life. If ill befall her, Anne Douglas, you shall suffer a thousand times more than she does.' Those black eyes had snapped with fury as she had railed against a fate which demanded she leave her child; they softened with love for the baby and gratitude to Anne Douglas, even while she threatened her. Then, having made these threats, she had taken Anne in her arms and kissed her. 'I know you will take care of my child ... Protestant though you are. And if you should ever see the light, foolish woman, and come to the true religion, you must instruct my daughter as I would have her instructed. Oh, but you are a Protestant, you say! And the King will have his children brought up in the religion of their own country! And I am a poor desolate mother who must give up her new-born babe to a Protestant! A Protestant!' She had become incoherent, for she had never bothered to learn the English language properly. Anne knelt to her and swore that, apart from her religion, she would serve the Queen and obey her in all things.

Poor sad Henrietta Maria, who had come to England as a girl of sixteen, very lovely and determined to have her own way, was now an exile, parted from her husband and children. But with God's help, there should be one child restored to her.

To Exeter the King had come, for he had not received his wife's letter and believed her to be still there in childbed; he had fought his way through the Parliamentary forces to reach her. It had been Anne's unhappy task to tell him that he was too late. Her eyes filled with tears now as she remembered him – handsome, even with the stains of battle on him, noble of countenance as he always would be, for he was a man of ideals; and if there was a weakness in that face, it but endeared him to a woman such as Anne Douglas. He was too ready to listen to the wrong advice; he was weak when he should have been strong, and obstinate when to give way would have been wise. He believed too firmly in that Divine Right of Kings which had grown out of date since the reign of Henry VIII; he lacked the common touch of Henry's daughter, Elizabeth, who had been able to adjust her rule to meet a more modern way of life. Weak though he might have been, a ruler unfit to rule, he was a man of handsome presence and of great personal charm; and it was moving to see his devotion to his family.

With him to Exeter had come the young Prince of Wales, a boy of fourteen then, who had none of his father's good looks, but already more than his father's charm. He was rather shy and sweet-tempered. It had been moving to see him take the baby in his arms and marvel at the smallness of her.

Anne wept afresh; she wept for the handsome King who was losing his kingdom, for the Prince, who would be heir to his father's lost throne, for the baby – the youngest of a tragic family.

'Poor little daughter,' the King had said, 'you have been born into a sorry world. You must be baptized at once.'

'What name shall she be given, Your Majesty?'

'Let us call her Henrietta after my wife. But she must be baptized according to the rites of the Church of England.'

And so the ceremony had taken place in the Cathedral of Exeter on a warm July day two years ago; then the King had left for Cornwall where he pursued the war with some success.

Later, when the baby was three months old, he returned to Bedford House in the city of Exeter where she was caring for the child, but only for a brief visit, and Anne had not seen him since. The Prince came to see his little sister a year later. The child, fifteen months old, was not too young to notice the tall dark boy who made so much of her; she was old enough to crow with pleasure when she saw him, and weep bitterly when he went away. The

Prince had had to leave in a hurry because once more the Roundheads were marching on Exeter. Remembering Henrietta Maria's words, Anne had done her utmost to escape with the child to Cornwall, but her attempt to do so had been foiled. She had been surrounded by spies, and there had been nothing she could do on that occasion but shut herself and her servants up in the security of Bedford House and remain at the side of the Princess day and night.

From her exile in France an angry Queen, knowing that her precious child was in Exeter and that the town was being besieged by her enemies, had raved with fury against fate, the Parliament and that slothful traitress, Anne Douglas.

That was a cruel charge and Anne had suffered deeply. In vain did those about her tell her that she was foolish to attach such importance to the Queen's reproaches. Did she not know the Queen!

It was said of Henrietta Maria that she regarded unfortunate friends blameworthy, even as traitors were. Anne tried to understand. Henrietta Maria was beside herself with grief, wondering what was happening to her child in a besieged city where there would be little to eat, where death stalked the streets and there would be constant dangers. Henrietta Maria was like a child; when she was hurt she stamped her foot and struck out at those nearest.

Anne had told herself she must remember the Queen's grief and bear with her.

Sir John Berkeley, who had held the city for the Royalists, deciding they could hold out no longer, had surrendered the city on the condition that the little Princess and certain of her household should be allowed to leave Exeter; so they went, by the Parliament's order, to the Palace of Oatlands, and there they had been living for the last months at Anne's expense as the Parliament refused to grant money for the Princess's upkeep.

Oatlands, that royal pleasure house built by Henry VIII, had proved a refuge as pleasant as could be hoped for in the circumstances. But, since the day civil war had broken out in England, there had been no lasting peace for any member of the royal family; and there came that day

when, leaving the garden and coming through the court-
yard to the quadrangle with the machicolated gateway,
Anne had met a messenger who brought her a letter from
the House of Commons telling her that the Princess must
be made ready to leave for London; there she was to join
her sister, the Princess Elizabeth, and her brothers, Prince
James and Prince Henry, in St James's Palace, where they
would be placed in the care of the Earl and Countess of
Northumberland.

Then Anne had made her decision. She would not again
incur the anger of her mistress. She had long determined
that she would never give up the child to any but the Queen
or her family. The wild plan had come to her then. Henrietta Maria had fled to France; why should she not follow
her? Surely she could disguise herself more successfully
than the Queen had done. A woman with a child . . . a
beggar woman? No! For beggars were sometimes set upon
and treated badly. A humble servant and her child would
be better; and for company she would take with her
French Gaston, who would pretend to be her valet husband; and Elinor Dykes and Thomas Lambert, servants of
the household, should come with her.

They would slip out of Oatlands Palace and none should
know that they had gone. She would write a letter which
should be sent back to the palace by another of her servants whom she would take with her for this purpose, informing certain members of her household whom she
believed she could trust; she would give them permission
to share the Princess's clothes and some of her possessions among themselves, and warn them that they must
give her three clear days before informing the Parliament
that she and the Princess were missing. If they obeyed her,
none would know of her flight until the fourth day; and by
that time she should be safely on the water on her way
to France.

It had not seemed so difficult; but how could she have
foreseen the weariness of a gently nurtured lady after
tramping the roads for three days; how could she have
guessed that the little Princess herself, not understanding
the danger, would insist on telling those whom she met on
the road that the clothes she wore were not the fine

garments to which she was accustomed, that her name was not Pierre nor Peter; but that she was the Princess?

Another day, thought Anne feverishly, and we shall be at sea. Only another day . . . but here we are in this attic, and the attic walls are like prison walls, for suspicion has been born in the mind of a groom.

*

They were awakened by a clatter of hoofs in the court-yard. It was dark in the attic; but Anne, starting up, saw a patch of starry sky through the window.

'Tom . . . Nell! Are you awake?'

'Yes, my lady.'

'Hush, Tom!'

'Yes, Nan; we're awake,' said Nell.

'What was that noise?'

'Only newcomers arriving, I doubt not.'

'It's late . . . very late.'

'Can you not sleep?'

'I am thinking of that groom.'

'But he said he was loyal to His Majesty.'

'How can we know whether he was speaking the truth?'

'Do you think he suspected who the child is?'

'I am not sure. But if she had awakened and called her-self "Princess" we should certainly have been betrayed.'

They were silent for a while. Then Anne started up again. 'Listen! Steps on the stairs!'

' 'Tis new arrivals at the inn,' said Tom.

'But they are on the attic staircase. It leads only to us. I am sure they are there. It is the groom. He has betrayed us.'

The next seconds seemed like minutes. Anne held the Princess close against her. Little Henrietta began to whim-per in her sleep. Tom was on his feet; the footsteps had stopped and they knew that someone was standing on the other side of the door.

Then there was a sudden nerve-shattering hammering against the wood.

Tom threw his weight against it. 'Who's there?' he demanded.

'It is your landlord.'

28

'What do you want of us at this hour?'

'Soldiers are here. They demand quarters. I have no room for them all.'

'Open the door to him,' said Anne, and Tom obeyed.

'Listen here,' said the landlord. 'I've got to find room for the soldiers. I told them that the inn was full, but they wouldn't have it. They demand shelter. Some of them have been drinking. Now there's an outhouse you can have for the rest of the night. I often let it to passengers from the waggon. It would serve you well.'

'Cannot the soldiers use the outhouse?' asked Tom.

'I don't want trouble at my inn. There's a war raging in this country. In wartime we're in the hands of the soldiery.'

Anne said quickly: 'Let us go to this outhouse. I doubt not that it will suit us well.'

'Thank you. You are a wise woman. Come quickly. The soldiers are drinking in the parlour.'

He held his candle aloft and, gathering the sleeping child in her arms Anne, with Tom leading and Nell and Gaston taking up the rear, followed the man down the staircase. When they were on the lower landing, a door opened, and there stood the elegant man who had made such a commotion earlier that night.

'By God's body!' he cried. 'Cannot a gentleman be allowed to sleep? Comings and goings the whole night through! What is happening now, man?'

'Your pardon, your honour. It's the soldiers. They've just come in. That's how it is these days, sir. There's nothing a poor innkeeper can do.'

He quizzed the party. 'These hardly look like soldiers.'

'Nay, sir. Some poor travellers I took in, sir, and let them have the attic. Now the soldiers want it and . . .'

'So you're turning them out into the night, eh?'

'No . . . no, your honour. They've paid for shelter and they shall have it. I am giving them an outhouse. 'Tis warm and comfortable and will seem cosy to such as they are, I'll swear.'

With an oath the man shut his door and the party continued their descent. The landlord took them through the kitchens where, setting down his candle, he took up a lanthorn, and conducted them to the outhouse.

'You'll pass the rest of the night in peace and comfort here,' he said. 'You could not be more snug. See, there's straw for you all and 'tis a warm night.'

'Can the door be barred?' asked Tom.

'Aye. You can lock it from the inside if you wish to.'

'This will suit us for the rest of the night,' said Anne quickly.

The landlord left them; and as soon as he had gone Tom turned the heavy key in the lock.

'I feel a little safer here,' said Anne; but she was still trembling.

*

They left early next morning as soon as the first sign of dawn was in the sky. All through the morning they walked, and in the afternoon they came into the town of Dover. Anne felt great relief as, looking out to sea, she caught sight of the Dover Packet-boat lying at anchor; the weather was undoubtedly favourable. Very soon her ordeal must be ended.

Henrietta was lively; she had ridden all the morning on Anne's back, and if Anne was tired, she was not.

'Water!' she cried.

'It is the sea, my precious one,' Anne told her.

'Nan . . . want my own gown . . .'

'Soon you shall have it, little Pierre.'

'No Pierre! No Pierre!'

'Just a little while longer, dearest.'

'No Pierre!' chanted Henrietta. 'Me . . . Princess. No Pierre! No Peter!'

'Let's pretend for a little longer. Let it be our secret, eh?'

Tom said: 'I wish the Princess would sleep.'

'She cannot sleep all the time.'

'No sleep! No sleep!' chanted the Princess.

' 'Twould please me better if she slept as we passed through the town,' persisted Tom.

A man passed them. He gave no sign of having recognized them, but he was the elegant gentleman whom they had seen at the inn and who had opened his door as they had passed along the corridor.

None of them spoke, but each was aware of him. He turned slowly and followed them. At the water's edge he called to a boatman in his arrogant manner. 'Is that the Dover Packet lying there, fellow?'

'Yes, milord.'

'Then row me out to her, will you? These people will go with us.'

'Milord . . .?' began Tom.

The man shook his head impatiently.

When they were in the boat the baby Princess showed clearly her appreciation of the elegant gentleman, but he did not glance at her as he gave orders to the boatman in his cool arrogant manner.

'How's the wind?'

'Set fair for France, milord.'

'Then the Packet will be leaving soon, I'll swear.'

'Waiting but for the turn of the tide, milord.'

Now they were alongside and the party stepped aboard, obediently following the man who led the way.

He signed to Anne and led her and the child into a cabin. When they were alone, he bowed to her, taking her hand and kissing it. 'You have done a marvellous thing, Anne,' he said. 'The Queen will love you for ever.'

'It was a great comfort to know that you were with us . . . though not of the party.'

'There were some uneasy moments. The worst was last night when I opened my door and saw you being marched down the stairs. Well, that is over. Stay in your cabin during the crossing, and remain disguised until you are safely on French soil. I must go now. Assure Her Majesty of my untiring devotion.'

'I will, John.'

'Tell her the Berkeleys will hold the West against any number of Roundhead oafs.'

'I'll tell her, John.'

'Goodbye and good luck.'

Sir John Berkeley kissed her hand and that of the Princess. Then he quickly returned to the boat and was rowed ashore.

Not long after, the Packet slipped away from the white cliffs on its way to Calais.

CHAPTER TWO

THE PRINCESS WAS happy. No sooner had she and her
faithful little party set foot on French soil at Calais than
her dear Nan discarded her hump, kissed her rapturously
and called her Beloved Princess. The indignity she had
suffered was now over; there was no need to remind people
now that she was a princess. There were fine clothes to be
worn, there were many to kiss her hand and pay her the
homage she had missed when dressed as the child of a
servant. The crowds welcomed her. They called to her that
she was the granddaughter of great Henri, and therefore
France was her home and all French men and women
were ready to love her.

How she crowed and waved her little hands! How she
smiled as she smoothed down the folds of her dress! Occasionally she would turn to Nan and look with happy pleasure at the tall and beautiful governess whom it seemed
she had sought in vain to revive from those dirty rags.
Henrietta was happy; she did not know that she came to
France as a suppliant; that she was a beggar far more than
she had appeared to be on the road to Dover.

'You are going to see your mother, the Queen,' Anne told
her.

The child was wide-eyed with wonder. Her mother, the
Queen, was just a name to her. Nan, during the Princess's
two years of life, had been the only mother she had known.

'You must love her very dearly,' Anne explained. She
will be so happy to see you, and you will be the only one
of all your brothers and sisters who may be with her to
make her happy.'

'Why?' she asked.

'Because the others cannot be with her.'

'Why not?'

'Because your brothers, James and Henry, must stay
with your sister Elizabeth; and your big brother, Charles,
cannot stay with his mother in France because he has
other matters to which he must attend. Your big sister,

Mary, is the Princess of Holland, so she cannot be with your mother either.'

But Henrietta did not understand. She only knew that she was happy again, that she had bright clothes to wear and that people called her Princess.

So she was escorted from Calais to Saint-Germain.

The news had spread that her infant daughter was about to be restored to the poor sad Queen. There was a romantic story of a brave governess who had brought the child out of a war-torn country under the very eyes of the King's enemies. The story was one to delight the warm-hearted French. They wanted to see the little Princess; they wanted to cheer the brave governess. So they gathered along the route from Calais that they might cry 'Good Luck' to the little girl, and let her know that as granddaughter of their greatest King, they were ready to welcome her to their country.

The people cheered her. 'Long live the little Princess from England! Long live the granddaughter of our great Henri! Long live the brave governess!'

And the Princess smiled and took this ovation as her right; she had already forgotten her uncomfortable journey. Anne was worn out with fatigue, and now that her anxiety had lifted, she felt lightheaded; she could not believe that the people of France were cheering her; and while she smiled she felt as though she were not really there in France but sitting on a bank while the Princess betrayed their secret, or that she was in an attic, terrified while a groom told her that her hump was slipping.

When they came to the château on the edge of the forest, Henrietta Maria was waiting to greet them. She had been granted the use of the château at Saint-Germain-en-Laye and she had her own apartments in the Louvre; she had been given a pension by her royal relatives of France, and at the time of Henrietta's arrival she lived at Court with all the state of a visiting Queen.

She was waiting in her salon – surrounded by her attendants and some of the exiles from England who visited her from time to time – magnificently dressed in blue brocade decorated with frills of fine lace and pearls; her black eyes were filled with tears, and her usually sallow cheeks were aflame. This was the happiest moment of her life since she had left England, she declared.

When the Princess was brought to her she gave a great cry of joy; she dispensed with all ceremony and swooped on the child, pressing her against her pearl-decorated gown while tears gushed from her eyes. She began to talk in French, which the little girl could not understand.

'So at last, my little one, I have you here with me. Oh, how I have suffered! You, my little one, my baby, whom I had to leave when I fled from those wicked men! But now you are back with me. Now you are here and we shall never be parted as long as we live. Oh see, this is my daughter, my youngest and my most precious. She is returned to me and it is such a miracle that I must give great thanks to God and all the saints. And I do so here in this happy moment.' She turned her tearful yet radiant face to Cyprien de Gamaches, her priest, who stood beside her. 'Père Cyprien shall instruct this child of mine. She shall be brought up in the true faith of Rome. Rejoice, for she is not only snatched from her enemies – those round-headed villains who would destroy her father – she is saved from a subtler enemy; she is saved for Holy Church!'

Henrietta wriggled; the pearls on her mother's gown were hurting her; she turned and held out her hand to Anne who was standing close by.

The Queen's brilliant eyes were now on the governess.

'And here is my dearest Lady Anne ... my dear faithful servant! We shall never forget what you have done. All Paris, all France talks of the wonderful deed. You have behaved with great courage and I shall never forget you.'

The Queen put down the child and would have embraced Anne, but as she was about to do so, Anne, worn out by the terrible fatigue of her long tramp and by all the anxieties of the previous days, sank fainting to the floor.

It seemed that her determination to hand over the Princess to none but the child's mother had kept her going; now that her task was completed she must pay the price of the mental strain and physical hardship she had suffered.

*

Henrietta Maria sat with her niece Mademoiselle de Mont-pensier in her apartments in Saint-Germain. Henrietta Maria was a schemer; when she decided she wanted some-thing, she could be very single-minded. There were several things she wanted very badly; the first was to see an end to the war in England, with her husband victorious; the second was to bring her children up in the Roman Catholic faith; and the third was to arrange suitable marriages for her children.

All of these seemed to her not only natural but virtuous desires. It was a fact that in their marriage contract, the King, her husband, had promised that their children should be instructed in the Catholic faith. In this he had not kept his word; the whole of England would have been against his keeping his word; England still remembered the reign of Bloody Mary, and the people had decided to run no risk of a recurrence of those terrible days.

Henrietta Maria loved her husband and was devoted to her family; but, she told herself, as a staunch Catholic, she loved her religion more. Fate had played into her hands by delivering to her the Princess Henrietta; here was one child who should not be contaminated by wrong teaching; Père Cyprien was already taking matters in hand. He had had a clear run so far, because the Protestant governess, Anne Dalkeith, had been seriously ill since her arrival at Saint-Germain, and had been unable to take a hand in the Princess's upbringing or to remind the Queen of the King's wishes which were those of the majority of the people of England. And she *would* have reminded her, thought Hen-rietta Maria grimly; even though her ears would have been boxed for it, even though she would have to protest to the Queen and the mother of the child, Anne would do what she considered her duty. It would have been a pity to quarrel with Anne so soon after her glorious adventure. Perhaps, as Père Cyprien said, the hand of God was in this; first, in bringing her daughter to France at an early age before the contamination of a hostile Church could be be-gun, and secondly, by striking the Protestant governess with a fever and so preventing her interference. Père Cyprien would go even further; he would say that the Great Rebellion and Civil War in England had doubtless been an act of God calculated to save the soul of the young Princess.

Henrietta Maria could not follow him as far as that, but she was at least satisfied that her young daughter would be safe from heresy and now she could turn her thoughts to the marriages of her children. There was one whose marriage was of the utmost importance: Charles, Prince of Wales.

He was a boy of sixteen, very young to marry; yet Princes married young. Henrietta Maria's illogical mind darted hither and thither, taking up one idea, rejecting it for another, and then returning to the first. If young Charles were to remain an exile, he would need a very rich wife; if he were to be King, he would need a royal wife. But riches were always useful; she had not thought of that until she found herself an exile from her adopted country. What would have happened to her, she wondered, if, instead of being the daughter of the fourth Henri of beloved memory, she had been the daughter of the despised third Henri. Who could say?

Now she studied the young woman before her, for she had decided on Mademoiselle as the most fitting bride for her son Charles, and she had received reports that Charles was on his way to Paris.

Mademoiselle de Montpensier, known throughout France as the Mademoiselle of the French Court, was Henrietta Maria's own niece, being the daughter of her brother, Gaston, Duke of Orléans. Mademoiselle unfortunately had a great opinion of herself. She was the richest heiress in Europe; she was a cousin of the young King Louis XIV; she believed herself to be peerless in charm and beauty and, although she was willing to be wooed by the Prince of Wales through his mother, she would give no assurance that she would even consider his suit.

Now she smoothed the folds of her rich brocade gown about her beautiful figure, and Henrietta Maria knew that she was thinking what a charming picture she made with her pink and white complexion and her abundant fair hair; the Queen knew that she considered herself not only the wealthiest heiress but the most beautiful young woman in France. Henrietta Maria's fingers itched to box

36

her ears; Henrietta Maria's small foot tapped impatiently; there was a great deal of hot temper bottled up in the diminutive body of the Queen of England.

'My son will soon be with us,' said the Queen. 'I live for the day.'

'Ah, my dearest Aunt, it must be wonderful for you – an exile from your country in a foreign land – to have your family escape from those villains.'

'A foreign land!' cried the Queen. 'Mademoiselle, I was born in this country. I am my father's beloved daughter.'

'A pity he died before he could know you,' said the malicious Mademoiselle.

'Aye! His death was the greatest tragedy this country ever suffered. I burn with indignation every time I pass through the Rue de la Ferronnérie where that mad monk pierced him to the heart.'

'My dearest Aunt, you upset yourself for something that happened years ago ... when you have so many present troubles with which to concern yourself.'

Henrietta Maria flashed a look of irritation at her niece. Mademoiselle was clever; she granted her that; she knew how to make those little thrusts in the spots where they hurt most. There she was, the arrogant young beauty, reminding her aunt that she, Mademoiselle, cousin to the King, daughter of Monsieur de France, was really being rather gracious by spending so much of her precious time with her poor exiled aunt.

Henrietta Maria could subdue her anger when great issues were at stake.

'My son is of great height, already a man. They say he bears a striking resemblance to my father.'

'In looks only, I trust, Your Majesty. Your father, our great King, Henri Quatre, was France's greatest King, we all know, but he was also France's greatest lover.'

'My son will love deeply also. There is that charm in him which tells me so.'

'Let us hope, for the sake of the wife he will marry, that in one respect he will not resemble your great father whose mistresses were legion.'

'Ah! He has his father's blood in him as well as that of

my father. There never was a more noble man, nor a more faithful, than my Charles. I, his wife, tell you that, and I know it.'

'Then, dear Aunt, you were indeed fortunate in your husband. When I choose mine, fidelity is one of the qualities I shall look for.'

'Beauty such as yours would keep any man faithful.'

'Such as your father, Madame, would never be faithful to Venus herself. And as your son is so like him . . .'

'Tush! He is but a boy!'

'So very young that he need not think of marriage yet.'

'A Prince is never too young to think of marriage.'

'Mayhap while his affairs are in a state of flux, it would be wise to wait. A great heiress would more readily accept a King whose crown is safe than one who may live through his life with only the hope of regaining it.'

Mademoiselle was smiling absently to herself. Her thoughts were of marriage, but not of one between herself and the young Prince of England. Henrietta Maria fumed silently. She knew what was in the minx's mind. Marriage, yes! And with her royal cousin, the King of France. And Henrietta Maria had already decided that Louis XIV was for her own Henrietta.

*

The Princess Henriette – she had been Henriette from the moment she passed into her mother's care – loved her brother immediately she set eyes on him. He came into the nursery where she was with her governess, poor pale Lady Dalkeith, who had just risen from her sick bed to find herself fêted as the heroine of the year. Lady Dalkeith, serious-minded and conscientious, found little pleasure in the eulogies which came her way; she had discovered the Queen's determination to bring up the child in the Catholic faith, which was against the wishes of the King of England and his people; and this disturbed her so much that she could feel only apprehension in contemplating the fact that she, having successfully conducted the child to her mother, was indirectly responsible.

But the little Henriette was unaware of the storms about

her; all she knew was that she had a brother, and that as soon as she saw him, and he held her in his arms and told her that he had known her when she was a very tiny baby, she loved him.

'Charles!' she would cry in her high-pitched baby voice. 'Dear Charles!'

And he would call her his baby sister. 'But,' he said, 'Henriette is such a long name for such a small person, and now I hear they are to add Anne to it out of respect for King Louis' mother. It is far too long. My little puss . . . my little love, you shall be my Minette.'

'Minette?' she said wonderingly.

'It shall be my name for you. It is something we share, you and I, dear little sister.'

She was pleased. 'Minette!' she said. 'I am Minette, Charles' Minette.'

He kissed her and let her pull his long dark curly hair.

'I wondered when I should see you again, Minette,' he told her. 'I thought mayhap I never should.'

'You are so big to be a brother,' she said.

'That's because I'm the eldest of the family. I was four-teen years old when you were born.'

She did not fully understand, so she laughed and clasped his arm to her little body to show how much she loved him.

He held her tightly. It was wonderful to be with one of his own flesh and blood. He wondered whether all his family would ever be together again. He was only a boy but he had been with his father in battle, and he knew that events were moving against his family. He was quiet and shy; he enjoyed the company of women, but they must not be haughty ladies like his cousin Mademoiselle de Montpensier; he liked humbler girls, girls who liked him because he was young and, although not handsome, had a way with him. He was particularly shy here in France because he knew that they laughed at his French accent; and although he himself was ready to laugh at it – for he knew it to be atrocious, and he never tried to see himself other than the way he was – he was too young, too unsure of himself, to be able to endure the ironic laughter of others. He remembered continually that he was a Prince whose future was in jeopardy, and that made him cautious.

So it was wonderful to be with this affectionate little sister; she was so frail but pretty, and she had the Stuart eyes and the promise of Stuart gaiety. It was good, Charles decided, to have a family.

He had escaped from his companion, his cousin Prince Rupert, who spoke French perfectly and was considered to be a fine soldier in spite of his defeat at Marston Moor. He had escaped from his mother and her continual prodding, her many instructions as to how he must set about wooing his cousin, Mademoiselle of France.

'I love you, little sister,' he whispered, 'oh, so much more than haughty Mademoiselle.'

'Charles,' murmured the little girl, as she pulled his black hair and watched the curls spring back into place, 'will you stay with me, Charles?'

'I shall have to go away soon, Minette.'

'No! Minette says No!'

He touched her cheek. 'And Minette's commands should be obeyed.'

Lady Dalkeith left them together; she was very fond of the Prince and rejoiced to see the signs of affection between the brother and sister. She thought: Perhaps I could speak to him about her religious instruction. He knows the wish of his father. But how could I go against the Queen? How could I carry tales of his mother to the Prince? The child is too young to absorb very much at this stage. I will wait. Who knows what will happen?

'Were you little once?' Henriette asked her brother when they were alone.

'Yes, I was little, and so ugly that our mother was ashamed of me; I was very solemn, so they thought that I was wise. Dear sister, when in ignorance remain silent and look wise. You will then be judged profound.'

Henriette could not understand what he meant, but she laughed with him; her laughter came of contentment.

He talked to her as he could not talk to others. He talked wistfully of his youth. He talked of England, where he had once been the most important of little boys; he told of playing in the gardens of palaces with his brother James and his sister Mary; they had played hide-and-seek on wet days through the great rooms of Hampton Court and Whitehall, and on fine days in the gardens, hiding among the trees, stalking each other through alleys of neatly-trimmed yews. Best of all he loved to watch the ships on the river; so he told her how he used to lie in the grass for hours at Greenwich, watching the ships pass by.

'But, Minette, you do not know of these things, and I am a fool to talk to you, for in talking to you I am really talking to myself, and that is a foolhardy thing to do when such talk brings self-pity; for self-pity is a terrible thing, dear Minette; it is the sword which is thrust against oneself; one turns the blade in the wound; one revels in one's own pain, and that way lies folly.' He stopped, smiling at her.

'More! More!' cried Henriette.

'Ah, my little Minette, what will become of us . . . what will our end be, I wonder?' But it was not in his nature to be sad for long. He did not believe that his father could be victorious, but he still could turn a nonchalant face to the future. He could live in the moment, and at this moment he was discovering what a delightful sister was his; he was discovering the pleasures of family life. 'Dearest Minette, you do not tell me I must go and court the haughty Mademoiselle, do you! You laugh at my maudlin talk as though it were precious wit. Small wonder that I love you, sweet Minette.'

'Minette loves Charles,' she said, putting her arms about his neck.

Then he told her of Mr Fawcett who had instructed him and his brother James in archery. His mind raced on; he thought of his French master and his writing master, and the tutor who had made him read from his horn-book; he remembered, too, his mother, who had smothered him with her affection, and had impressed on him the importance of his position. 'Never forget, Charles, that one day you will be King of England. You must be as great and good a King as your father.' He smiled wryly. Would the people of England now say that his father was a great and good King when they were doing their utmost – at least thousands of them were – to rid themselves of him?

Would they ever welcome young Charles Stuart as their King?

'Poor Mam,' he said softly, 'I have a feeling that she will never be satisfied. She is one of the unlucky ones of this world. It is a comfort to talk to you, sweet sister, because you are too young to understand all I say.' He put his lips against her hair. 'You are lovely, and I love you. Do you know, I would rather be with you than with all the fine ladies of the Court – or with the King and Queen, and Mam . . . all of them.'

Then to amuse her he told her of the piece of wood which he always took to bed with him when he was a boy of her age. 'In vain did they try to take it from me, for I would not let them. I loved my wooden billet, and I confess I kept it until it had to be taken from me by very force – and I knew then that I had long outgrown it. One day, Minette, I will tell you more. I will tell you of the fun we had – my brother and sister and I – and I'll tell you how we thought we should go on for ever and ever, laughing, playing our games; and then, suddenly, we grew up, all of us on the same day. It was worse for them, as they were younger than I; Mary only a year younger, James four years younger, and little Elizabeth five years younger. I was the big brother. Henry was the baby then, and there was no little Minette in our family, for she had not yet put in an appearance.'

'No Minette!'

'You cannot imagine a world without her, can you? Come, Minette, let us play a game together. I weary you with my talk.'

'No. Stay like this!' she said.

And thus it was that Mademoiselle, acccompanied by his cousin Prince Rupert, found them.

'Your mother would not be pleased that you should spend your time playing with a baby in the nursery,' said Mademoiselle coquettishly. She told herself that she had little time to spare for this boy whose fortunes were in the balance, but she was never averse to a light flirtation, and there was something about him – in spite of his youth and inexperience – which interested her more than his cousin Rupert did.

'You must forgive me, Mademoiselle,' said Charles. 'My French is not good enough to answer you in that language.'

She tapped his arm with her fan. 'Are you not ashamed, cousin? You cannot speak French!'

'It is remiss of me. I fear I occupied myself riding and shooting at the butts when I should have been studying French, just as you, Mademoiselle, doubtless indulged in some pastime when you should have been studying English.'

Rupert translated, and Mademoiselle pouted.

'What would you say if I said you might wear my colours, Charles?'

'I should say you are very gracious,' he answered through Rupert.

'I might allow you to hand me into my coach.'

'Mademoiselle is most kind.'

'And perhaps to hold the flambeau while I am at my toilette.'

'Pray tell Mademoiselle that I am overwhelmed by her generosity.'

Mademoiselle turned to Rupert. 'Do not translate this I only do these things because I am sorry for the poor boy. I would never marry him, as his mother hopes I will. I have set my aim higher . . . much higher.'

'I am sure,' said Charles, 'That Mademoiselle is talking sound sense.'

Rupert smiled. He knew that the Prince of Wales understood every word, and that it was only his shyness which prevented his speaking French with Mademoiselle.

'Tell him,' said Mademoiselle, 'that he may come to my apartment and sit at my feet while I am with my women.'

When Rupert translated this, Charles replied: 'Mademoiselle is overwhelmingly generous, but I have a previous engagement with a lady.'

'A lady!' cried Mademoiselle.

'My little sister, Mademoiselle. My friend Minette.'

Henriette guessed that the beautiful Mademoiselle was being unkind to her brother. 'Go away!' she said. 'Minette does not like you.'

Mademoiselle answered: 'I know she is young, but she

43

should be taught how to conduct herself. She should be beaten for that.'

Henriette, recognizing the word 'beaten' put her arms about her brother and buried her face against him.

'No one shall hurt you, Minette,' he told her. 'No one shall hurt you while your brother Charles is here.'

Mademoiselle laughed, and rising, commanded Rupert to lead her away.

'We will leave the boy to play with his sister,' she said; 'for after all, he is but a boy and still concerned, I doubt not, with childish things.'

And when they were alone, Minette and her brother were soon gay again, and she loved him dearly.

*

Each day they were together; each day he talked to her, and although she did not always understand what he said, she knew that he loved her as she loved him.

It had not occurred to her that life could change, until one day he came to her and sadly kissed her. 'Minette,' he said, 'we shall always love one another – you and I.' And the next day he did not come.

Angrily she demanded to know where he was. He had gone away, they told her.

She fretted; she would not eat; she so much longed for him.

Her mother warmly embraced her. 'My dearest child, you are very young, but there are things you have to learn. Your father is fighting wicked men, and your brother must go to help him. Then, when they have beaten those wicked men, we shall all go home, and you will not only have one brother, but three – as well as a dear sister.'

'Don't want three brothers,' sobbed Henriette. 'Minette wants Charles.'

And all through the days which followed she was a sad little figure in the palace of Saint-Germain.

If any asked her what ailed her she would say: 'Want Charles.' And each day she knelt on the window seat watching for him to come again; she waited, so it seemed to her, for years; but she never forgot him.

*

44

In the palace of the Louvre, the Princess Henriette lay in her bed. Her mother sat beside the bed, and about her shoulders were three cloaks, and her hands were protected by thick gloves. It was bitter January weather, and outside the Louvre, in the narrow streets of Paris, Frenchmen were fighting Frenchmen in that civil war which had been called the War of the Fronde.

Little Henriette, who was but four years old, shivered with the cold; her mother shivered also – but not only from cold. As her friend, Madame de Motteville, had said to her: 'This year a terrible star reigns for kings and queens.'

Henrietta Maria was not thinking so much of the blood-curdling shrieks which again and again reached her from the streets; her thoughts were across the Channel in her husband's country, for he was now the prisoner of the Parliament, and awaiting trial. She had begged to be allowed to see him, but this had been denied her. If she came to England, she was told, it would be to stand on trial with him, for the Parliament considered her as guilty as her husband of High Treason.

What was happening in England? She knew little for no messengers could reach her, France having its own civil war with which to contend. She was alternately full of self-reproach and indignation towards others. She accused herself of ruining not only her own life but that of her husband and children; then she would rail against the wicked Cromwell and his Parliamentarians who had brought such suffering to her family.

And here she was – Queen of England – without food and warmth in this vast palace, alone with her child, the child's governess, Père Cyprien and a few servants who were all suffering now as she and her daughter suffered.

Three of her children were prisoners in the hands of the Parliament – James, Elizabeth and Henry. Mary, she thanked God, had been safely married and out of England before the trouble grew beyond control; and Mary at the Court of Holland provided a refuge for her brother Charles and any of those who managed to escape thither. The family relied on Mary in these hard times.

When she had first come to France much honour had been given to Henrietta Maria; but little by little she had shed her pomp, her plate and jewels; her foremost thought had been to send all she possessed to her husband in England. If she was frivolous, if she had been in a large measure responsible for his downfall, at least she was wholehearted in her passionate desire to help him. Only now that she was separated from him did she realize the extent of her love for that good and noble man, the best of husbands and fathers, even if he were not the wisest of kings. And now what assistance could she hope for from her royal relatives of France? They had been forced to leave Paris; the little King, in charge of his mother, the Queen-Regent, had slipped away from Paris to Saint-Germain where they stayed during the siege of Paris. Mademoiselle de Montpensier had decided to place herself on the side of the Frondeurs, which was typical of her; trust Mademoiselle to call attention to herself in some way!

It was an evil star indeed which shone on kings and queens during that year. Henrietta Maria had in vain warned her sister-in-law. Had she herself not suffered so much because she had once believed as Anne believed, behaved as Anne behaved? It was hard to learn that their countries were moving forward, that new ideas had brought a new outlook. The Stuarts would have been as autocratic as the Tudors, but they did not understand the people, and that understanding had been at the very root of the popularity achieved by those great Tudor sovereigns, Henry VIII and Elizabeth. The common people denied the Divine Right of Kings to govern; there were some who remembered the revolt of the barons in an earlier century. The people wished to go back to those conditions when a king's power was limited. How easy it was to see mistakes when one looked back, and to say: 'Had I done this, that would not have happened. Had we not made mistakes, Charles I and Henrietta Maria would be reigning in England now, living happily together.'

And so it was with Anne of Austria, the Queen-Mother of France. The situation was tragically similar. Mazarin and the Queen-Regent had imposed crushing taxes on the people, and the people would have them know that the age when kings and queens could believe they ruled by Divine Right was over. France was divided. Anne, frivolous, as Henrietta Maria had been, and as unrealistic, had laughed in the face of Paul de Gondi, the Coadjuteur of Paris; she had encouraged her friends to laugh at him because he was something of a dandy, and that accorded ill with the *soutane* he wore as a man of the Church. Paul de Gondi was a strong man; he had declared he would be master of Paris and he had prepared himself to bring about that state of affairs.

It was last July, in the heat of summer, when, below that apartment in which the Queen of England and her daughter now shivered, Parisians had barricaded the streets. Great barrels, filled with earth and held in place by chains, were placed at the entrances of narrow streets. Citizens were detailed to guard these streets. This was reminiscent, and indeed inspired by the 'Night of the Barricades' of the previous century.

The War of the Fronde had started. It was typical of Parisian humour that the war should be so named. A law had recently been passed prohibiting young boys from gathering in the streets of Paris and attacking each other with the *fronde* (a sling for stones) then so popular. These games of stone-slinging had on more than one occasion proved fatal and there had been public concern. So it was that, during the heated discussions in the Parliament concerning the taxes about to be imposed by the hated Cardinal Mazarin, the favourite of the Queen-Regent, the President of the Parliament had begged the assembly to consider the terms which Mazarin was proposing. The President's son – he was de Bachaumont and known throughout Paris as a *bel esprit* – had said that when his turn came to speak he would '*frondera bien l'opinions de son père.*' This *bon mot* was taken up and repeated; and *Frondeur* was adopted as the name of those who would criticize and 'sling' rebellion against the Court party.

So, during those months, Paris was in danger; and the French throne seemed about to topple as had that of England. Henrietta Maria's pension had not been paid since the war started; she had run short of food and wood, and now that the winter was upon her suffered acute discomfort;

yet, soothing her little daughter, putting her arms about her and cuddling her in an attempt to keep her warm, she was not thinking of what was happening immediately outside her windows but of her husband who was about to face his trial in London.

'Mam,' said the little Princess, 'I'm cold.'

'Yes, little one, it is cold, but perhaps we shall soon be warm.'

'Cannot we have a fire?'

'My love, we lack the means to light one.'

'I'm hungry, Mam.'

'Yes, we are all hungry, dearest.'

The Princess began to whimper. She could not understand.

'Holy Mother of God,' murmured the Queen, 'what is happening to Charles?'

Anne, who was now Lady Morton as her husband's father had recently died, came into the room. Her lips were blue, her beautiful hands mottled with the cold.

'What is it, Anne?' asked the Queen.

'Madame, Monsieur le Coadjuteur is here to see you.'

'What does he want of me?'

'He asks to be brought into your presence.'

The Coadjuteur was at the door; this was not a time when Queens should be allowed to stand on ceremony, and he was master of Paris.

Henrietta Maria did not rise; she looked at him haughtily.

But Paul de Gondi had not come as an enemy.

He bowed before the Queen, and she looked into the face of the man who was temporarily king of Paris. It was a dissolute face though a strong one. Paul de Gondi, who from childhood had wished to be a great power in the land, had been destined for the Church. His uncle had been Archbishop of Paris, and it was intended that Paul should succeed him. But Paul, having no vocation for the Church, had tried to prove himself unsuitable for the office by riotous living and frequent duelling. Finding himself unable to avoid acceptance of the archbishopric he decided to become a learned man and rule France as Richelieu had done. First he had set about winning the people

48

of Paris, and having done this with some success he found himself in his present position of power.

But when he looked at the poor suffering Queen of England, stoically shivering by the bed of her daughter, and thought of what was happening to her husband and other children, he was filled with pity for her.

'Madame,' he said, 'you suffer much.'

'Monsieur le Coadjuteur,' she replied, 'if you have news for me, pray give it – I mean news from England.'

'That I cannot give, Madame, but I can give some comfort. I can have food sent to you – food and firewood.'

She said: 'Monsieur, if you know anything, I beg of you give me news.'

'I have no news. But it shall not be said that I stood by and allowed the daughter of Henri Quatre to starve.'

Henrietta Maria shrugged her shoulders. 'It is six months since I received my pension, and no one would supply me with food and the means to keep my apartment warm because I could not pay.'

'But this is terrible!'

'I keep my little daughter company. It was too cold for her to rise today.'

'Madame, I shall myself see that your daughter does not have to stay in bed for want of a faggot.'

'What can you do, Monsieur?'

'First I shall have comfort sent to you; then I shall put your case before the Parliament.'

'The Parliament!' Henrietta Maria laughed aloud and bitterly. 'Parliaments do not love kings and queens these days, Monsieur.'

'Madame, the Parliament will not allow it to be said that it denied food and firewood to a daughter and granddaughter of Henri Quatre.'

The Queen wept a little after he had gone.

'Why do you cry, Mam?' asked the little girl. 'Was the man cruel to you?'

'No, my sweetheart. He was not cruel; he was kind.'

'Then why do you cry?'

'There are times, dearest, when unexpected kindness makes us cry. Ah, you look at your poor Mam with those

49

big black eyes and you wonder at my words. But there is much you do not yet know of life. Yet you are learning; you are learning fast for a little one.'

Paul de Gondi was as good as his word. That very day firewood and food were brought to the Louvre, and a few days later, at the instigation of de Gondi, the Parliament ordered that 40,000 livres should be sent to the Queen in memory of Henri Quatre.

In memory of Henri Quatre! Henrietta Maria could not help comparing her father with her husband. She could not remember her father, yet she had heard much of him; she had seen pictures of that great man, depicting the full sensuous mouth, the large nose, the humorous eyes and the lines of debauchery. She remembered stories she had heard of the stormy relationship between her father and mother; she had heard of the continual quarrels and the ravings of her mother whose temper she knew to be violent. She could imagine that angry temper roused to madness by the cynically smiling King; she knew that many times her mother had struck him, and she had heard how such blows reduced him to helpless laughter in spite of the fact that she was, as he himself said, 'terribly robust'. He had been called the ugliest man in France, but people would always add 'and its bravest gentleman'. They had loved him as they had loved no other King; the lecher (who, at the time of his assassination in his fifty-seventh year had been courting Angelique Paulet, a girl of seventeen) had declared, old as he was, that conquest in love pleased him better than conquest in war – and he was the most popular King who had ever ruled France.

This ugly man, this cynic, without any deep religion, ready to turn from the Huguenot faith to the Catholic faith (for 'was not Paris worth a mass?') was the hero of France; and even after his death those who had rebelled against the Court remembered him, and for his sake would not let his daughter starve.

When he had been stabbed by a fanatical monk, all France had mourned him; his assassin had died the horrible death which the nation demanded as the penalty of such a deed. And yet in England a good and noble man, religious, faithful and striving to act in a manner he considered to be right, might die and the people would cry: 'God's will be done.'

*

It was February of that tragic year. There was a little more comfort in the bare rooms of the Louvre than there had been during previous months. But a worse tragedy over-hung the palace; the servants knew of it; Anne knew of it; but there was no one who dared speak of it to the Queen. So they kept her in ignorance.

Henrietta Maria, during those weeks, was subdued yet determined to be hopeful.

'I often wonder why there is no news,' she would say to those about her. 'But good it is that there should be no news. I know the people love the King, my husband. Per-haps they have already released him from captivity. Oh, it is a sad and wicked thing that he should be a captive. So good . . . so noble . . . the best husband any woman ever had. No child ever had a more kindly father. How happy we could have been!'

Towards the middle of February she would wait no longer. Paul de Gondi had shown his goodness to her; he would not deny her in her great need. She would ask that a messenger be sent to Saint-Germain where there would certainly be tidings of her husband.

Then they knew that they could withhold the truth no longer.

Anne asked Lord Jermyn, the Queen's most faithful ad-viser, to break the news to her. 'For,' she said, 'you will do it better than any of us could. You will know how to soothe her.'

He went to Henrietta Maria in her apartments. With her was the little Princess, Anne Morton and Père Cyprien de Gamaches.

Jermyn knelt before the Queen.

She said at once: 'You have news from England?'

He lifted his face to hers; his lips quivered, and she knew, even before he spoke. A blank expression crept over her face; her eyes were mutely pleading with him not to speak, not to say those fateful words.

'Madame, dear Madame, on the 30th of January, the

King, your husband, laid his head upon the block . . .'

She did not speak.

'Madame,' resumed Jermyn, his voice broken with a sob. 'Madame . . . Long live King Charles II.'

Still she did not speak. Anne placed her hand on the shoulder of the little Princess who was looking at her with wondering eyes, and gently pushed her towards her mother. The Queen, putting out her hand, reached for her daughter and held her fast to her side; she still looked blankly before her and said not a word.

*

The little Princess was bewildered. She was five years old; she lived in the great Palace of the Louvre, but the vast rooms were deserted and there was war in the streets. She could not understand her mother's sudden passionate embraces, the great floods of tears and what seemed to her the incoherent ramblings. Her mother had changed. She wore sombre widow's mourning; she was constantly in tears; she referred to herself as *La Reine Malheureuse*; and little Henriette would cry with her, not knowing why she cried.

'Ah, you do well to weep!' the Queen would say. 'Do you know that but for you I should not be here now. I should be with the Carmelite nuns in the Convent of the Faubourg Saint-Jacques; that is where I yearn to be, to pray for strength to help me bear this burden of living. Ah, *ma petite*, I pray that you will never feel as I do. I pray that you will never be beset with doubts as your poor mother is this day. There are many who say I brought him to this – that good and noble man! They say that had he never attempted to arrest the Five Members seven years ago, civil war would have been averted. *I* urged him to do that. I did not believe that any would dare oppose the King to the extent of going to war. I believed that we could govern without a Parliament. Oh, my little Henriette, have I, who loved him, brought him to the scaffold?'

Henriette did not know what to answer; she could only take her little kerchief and wipe away her mother's tears.

And now her mother had gone away to stay with the nuns, and she could only feel relieved because of this. She was left to the care of dear Anne Morton and Père Cyprien. But these two were beginning to cause her some anxiety; and their teachings often seemed to be contradictory. She was conscious of some vague strife between them, of triumphs enjoyed by one to the discomfiture of the other; and in some way, which she herself did not understand, she was involved in their polite warfare.

'I wish my brother would come,' she often said to herself. 'All would be well if he were here.'

She thought of him constantly; he had always been kind and loving; he was so big and clever, yet not too big and clever to make a little girl feel she was of some importance to him.

And then, one day, he came to the Louvre.

He had grown up since she had last seen him; he was a young man of nineteen now. He was taller, but he still had the same luxuriant black hair and humorous eyes.

When he came into the apartment Lady Morton and Père Cyprien both fell on their knees, but Henriette ran to him and flung herself into his arms.

'My child,' said Anne reprovingly, 'you forget the respect due to His Majesty.'

'But it is *Charles*!' cried the little girl.

'Come now. You should kneel to him. He is your King first . . . your brother second.'

'A poor King, my Minette,' he said, as he swung her up that her face might be on a level with his; 'a King without a kingdom, but a brother rich in love. Which will you have?'

She did not understand him, but she had never had need to understand his words; she only knew that he loved her; his eyes told her that, as did his loving arms about her.

His mother, who hearing of his arrival had left the convent and returned to the Louvre, embraced him warmly. She wept afresh for his father. She was *La Reine Malheureuse*, she declared. 'Life has nothing left to give me. I have lost not only a crown but a husband and a friend. I shall never regret enough the loss of that good man – so wise, so just, so worthy of the love of his subjects.'

The young King smiled his melancholy smile. ' 'Tis no use to weep, Mam,' he said. 'We must look forward as he would have had us do. We'll defeat them yet.'

'Amen, my boy, my Charles, my King.'

When the Queen-Mother of France heard that the King of England was at the Louvre, she asked the royal party to join the French Court at Saint-Germain.

'I have warned Queen Anne,' said Henrietta Maria, 'that my husband lost his life because he was never allowed to know the truth, and I have implored her to listen to her advisers before it is too late . . . before the crown of France goes the way of that of England.'

Charles smiled ruefully. 'It is difficult enough to learn through one's own experience, Mam, let alone the experience of others.'

His mother smiled at him sadly. Even when he was a baby – an ugly, solemn little fellow – she had felt he was cleverer than she was. Now she hoped that was true. He would need to be clever. He had to fight his way back to his throne.

She had heard that there were plans afoot, that soon he would be returning to Scotland where he could hope for support which would help him make an onslaught on England.

'May God go with you then, dear son,' she said. 'You will need His help.'

'That's true, Mam,' he answered. 'But 'tis better to die in such an enterprise than wear away one's life in shameful indolence.'

'I heard rumours concerning your visit to The Hague.'

'There will always be rumours concerning our family, Mam.'

'This was concerning a young woman named Lucy Water. You know of such a one?'

'Yes, Mam. I know of such a one.'

'They say she is a foolish little thing . . . though beautiful.'

'I doubt not that they who say it are often foolish – and never beautiful.'

'Now, Charles, this is your mother speaking, your mother who had you beaten when you would not take your physic.'

He made a wry face. 'That physic, Mam; it was no good

54

to any. Lucy is not in the least like a dose of physic.'

'A woman of easy virtue ... too ready with her smiles and caresses, I understand.'

'What should I want of one who was niggardly with the same?'

'You are no longer a boy, Charles. You are a King.'

'You speak truth, Mam. I am a King. Pray thee do not think to make of me a monk. Come! We prepare ourselves for the journey to Saint-Germain. The crowds in the streets are ugly. But never fear. I shall be there to protect you. I must tell Minette that we are going.'

'Henriette is a child. She will not understand.'

He lifted his sister in his arms. 'Minette will wish to know that we are going on a journey. Minette, do you wish to go on a journey?'

'Are you going, Charles?'

'I am taking you and Mam.'

Henriette smiled. 'Yes, please; Minette will go.'

'Dearest, the crowds may shout at us as we pass through the streets. You'll not be afraid, will you, if I am there?'

She shook her head.

'Nobody would dare hurt Minette while King Charles is there to protect her. You know that, don't you?'

She put her arms round his neck and kissed him.

'How much do you love me, Minette?'

'Forty thousand livres,' she answered, remembering that amount which Paul de Gondi had urged the Parliament to grant to her mother.

'Forty thousand livres! That's a lot of money.'

She nodded happily. 'But it's all for you – and something else.'

'What else, Minette?'

'The silver laces in my shoes.'

He kissed her. 'And what shall I give you in return for those you give me, eh?'

She thought awhile, then she said: 'Never go away.'

'Ah, Minette,' he said, 'if only that could be! And if all loved me as you do what a happy man I should be!'

Then he thought of Lucy, charming, gay and very loving; Lucy who had initiated him into delights which he had scarcely been aware existed, and had promised more revelation; Lucy, practised harlot, some said, but nevertheless his love.

He had much love to give; he loved them both – Lucy and Minette; he loved them with all the capacity of a nature deeply concerned with the pleasures of loving.

He continued to think of Lucy, who was now with child.

'Your child, Charles,' she had said. 'Your royal bastard – that is unless you marry me and so make an honest woman of your Lucy ... and your bastard, heir to the throne of England.'

He smiled. Lucy was amusing; Lucy was light, but Lucy was gay; he would look forward to enjoying her amusing and erotic company as soon as he possibly could.

But in the meantime he had his little sister to love, and deeply he loved her.

She sat with him and their mother in the coach which carried them through the dangerous streets of Paris; about them swirled the mob of angry men and women, and among them were those to whom Madame d'Angleterre – as they called Henrietta Maria – owed much money.

Minette felt safe; she did not fear the people, for there was her big brother, one hand on the door of the coach, the other on the hilt of his sword, ready to repulse any who dared come too near.

And so they came to Saint-Germain; and as the little girl observed the homage paid to her brother, she was thrilled with pride and pleasure.

And he, turning suddenly, caught her earnest eyes upon him.

Ah, he thought, if only I could be as sure that Lucy loves me as does my sweet Minette!

CHAPTER THREE

THE FIRST TIME Lucy set eyes on Charles he was merely
Prince of Wales – a boy of eighteen. Lucy was also eighteen; but she seemed older. She was full of wiles and she
had been born with them. There had always been admirers for Lucy from the days when, as a little girl, she had
played in the grounds of Roch Castle. She was brown-
skinned, brown-eyed, and her rippling hair was brown
also; she was plump and indolent. Her father, watching
her even as a girl of twelve, decided to marry her off
quickly. She was a girl who was obviously ripe for marriage.

There were local squires in the neighbourhood of Haver-
fordwest and St David's who would have been ready
enough to link their fortunes with those of the Waters, for
Lucy's mother was a niece of the Earl of Carbery, and her
family was not without fortune. Moreover, Lucy was as
luscious as a ripe peach and wherever she went men's eyes
followed her. Her voice had a soft lilting Welsh accent
and it rose on a note of laughter at the end of her sen-
tences; it was not that Lucy's conversation was so very
amusing and witty; it was merely that she appeared to be
ready to enjoy life. She was aware of her ripe young body;
she was aware of the ripe young bodies of others. Lucy
was longing for amorous adventures; she would lie in the
grass on the mound at the top of which stood Roch Castle,
and dream of lovers.

The war altered life at Roch Castle as it did everywhere
else. Her father went off to fight for the Royalist cause, and
Lucy remained at home – a girl of fourteen, restive, forced
to sit at her needlework during long sunny afternoons,
stitching reluctantly, the despair of her governess.

There was continual talk of the war. Lucy rarely listened
to it with any great attention. She was a fervent Royalist
because the Cavaliers, in their dashing clothes, their curls
falling about their shoulders and their jauntily feathered
hats, pleased her; and the soberly clad soldiers of the

Parliamentary forces, with their round cropped heads and their text-quoting, did not attract her at all.

Lucy was filled with vague longings. She was not sure that she wanted to settle down to a married life. She had watched her mother looking after the servants, working in her still-room, arranging meals, having children. Such a life did not seem very attractive to Lucy. She had noticed at an early age how men's eyes followed her, and that pleased her. She would sit before a mirror tying ribbons in her brown hair, arranging her curls, aware that she was very pretty and remembering how the men looked at her; but she was only vaguely aware of what she wanted. It was more than admiration, more than warm glances; yet she did not want to be the chatelaine of a castle like that of her parents, to have children, a still-room, servants to command.

Lucy was lazy, it was agreed by all. She would not attend to her lessons; she could not even concentrate on her needle-work. Her eyes would wander from her work, and her thoughts would wander too.

Then Lucy suddenly discovered what she wanted from life.

It was when a party of Royalists rode up to the Castle and asked for a night's shelter. There was always food and shelter at Roch Castle for the Cavaliers. The Captain of the troop was young and handsome; he was the most elegant man Lucy had ever seen; his curled moustache was golden; so was his pointed beard; his fair hair fell to his shoulders; he was a dashing figure in his doublet with its wide sleeves and narrow sash; in his wide-brimmed hat was a curling feather. He was the most handsome man she had ever seen, and her eyes told him so.

From the time the Cavaliers entered the house the Captain was aware of Lucy. She must wait on him at table because, said her mother, it was a symbol of loyalty to the cause that the daughter of the house should do this in place of the servants; and as she waited on him he took opportunities of touching her hand. Lucy's large brown eyes glistened. She was ripe and very ready for seduction on that day; and the handsome Cavalier was well aware of this. He was young – not yet twenty – and life was adventurous in wartime. Any day might be his last; he was no canting Puritan to think longingly of the next world; he was a Cavalier determined to make the most of this one.

They would stay the night at Roch Castle, these soldiers of the King, for Roch Castle was at the disposal of His Majesty's friends; and during that evening the handsome Cavalier was not absent from Lucy's mind one moment – nor was Lucy from his. Even in the presence of others he managed to suggest desire, and Lucy, inexperienced as she was, managed to convey her response.

It was a July evening – warm and sultry – and there was an air of unreality in the Castle. Everyone felt that the war had moved closer. If Royalist soldiers were in the neighbourhood, it was probable that Roundheads were not far off. These handsome Cavaliers admitted that they were in retreat, that they had given their pursuers the slip near Brecknock, and that although their scouts had not seen a sign of them for several hours, it did not mean that the enemy had given up the chase.

At any moment there might be the sound of clattering horses' hoofs in the courtyard; at any moment rough soldiers might be demanding to search the Castle in the name of Oliver Cromwell.

It was not yet dark, but it soon would be; yet no one made preparations for settling down for the night. In the great hall the soldiers kept a look-out; there were men posted in the turrets.

Lucy was aware that at any moment this man who so excited her might ride away and never again be seen by her. His burning eyes watched her as she moved about the great dining hall, for once eager to help as she was bid.

With a quick glance at the Cavalier she made her way to the door and slipped out into the grounds. Almost immediately she heard footsteps behind her; she ran down the slope towards the moat and into the copse where as a child she used to hide from her governesses.

There she waited, and she had not long to wait. She stood, tense and breathless. He called her name softly. Then she felt his arms seize her; she was lifted up, violently kissed and quickly laid down among the bracken. She was aware of the urgency of the moment. There was no time for delay; he sensed that, even as she did; and it was she, he reminded himself, who had led the way to the copse.

Her first erotic adventure was all she needed to tell her for what she had been longing. It was not marriage; it was love, physical love, this sort of love – desire which came suddenly and must be swiftly satisfied. Lucy was perfectly contented lying there among the bracken. She was not frightened, though she was but fourteen; she knew that she had been born for this. She had been scolded for carelessness, laziness and stupidity; but in love she could attain perfection. Ignorant in many ways she might be, but now she needed no instruction. Entirely sensual, she was the perfect lover.

The young Cavalier looked at her wonderingly as she lay back in the bracken, her eyes wide and starry, her lips parted. It was he who had to remind her that they might be missed. For Lucy there was only the moment; consequences could not touch her in this mood of ecstasy.

'Which is your room?' he asked.

She told him.

'Tonight, when all is quiet, I will come to you.'

She nodded. But the night was a long way off. She put her arms about his neck and pulled him down to her again.

*

The dusk had turned to darkness but they were unaware of it. They would have remained unaware had not the shouts and screams from the Castle become so insistent.

He started up and sniffed the air. He coughed, for the smoke had drifted into the copse.

'God's Body!' cried Lucy's lover. 'They're here! Cromwell's men are at the Castle!'

Lucy looked at him, but even so she was only vaguely conscious of what he had said; she was dazed, lost in a maze of emotions. She had ceased to be a child; only that morning she had been ignorant and innocent, and in that state, dissatisfied; now she was fulfilled; now she knew herself.

He gripped her arm and drew her with him deeper into the copse.

60

'Don't you understand?' he said. 'Cromwell's men are here. They are burning the Castle!'

*

That was the beginning of a new life for Lucy. Roch Castle was burned down that night, Lucy had lost her home and her family; and she had nothing but her personal attractions.

There was only one course open to her and her lover – they must try to escape from Pembrokeshire. All that night they walked, and before dawn Lucy had led her lover to the house of a neighbour and friend to her family who lent them horses. The next day they began their journey towards London where, said her lover, Lucy could set up house for him, and he would visit her when his duties permitted him to do so.

Sometimes they slept under hedges, sometimes in friendly cottages, occasionally in big houses, the owners of which were faithful to the Royalist cause.

Lucy was a constant surprise to her lover; when he had first seen her he had planned a quick seduction before he passed on; now he found that it was Lucy who was in control of their relationship, Lucy whose big brown eyes rested ardently on other men, Lucy who would have smiled and bidden him a friendly farewell if he had suggested a parting. In vain did he tell her that she was a natural harlot. Lucy did not care. Lucy knew what she wanted, and it was becoming increasingly clear to her that she would never be obliged to go short of lovers.

Lucy was the perfect mistress of a fleeting passion, for her own passions were fleeting. She did not ask for gold or jewels but the slaking of her desire. This quality, added to voluptuous beauty, made her doubly desirable.

They came to London, and London enchanted Lucy. Her lover set her up in lodgings not far from Tower Hill, and she prided herself on being faithful to him when he could come to her. There were times, of course, when he could not visit her, but Lucy was never lonely, never long without a gallant.

London was a merry town at that time, for Puritanism had not yet cast its ugly pall over the city. The people were noisy; brawls were frequent; and opportunity for indulging in pageantry was eagerly seized upon. No one was safe after dark; but by day the streets were crowded. Fiddlers seemed always at hand to play a merry jig for any who cared to dance; ballad-sellers sang samples of their wares in high trebles and deep basses; carriages jingled through the narrow cobbled streets; London was everything but dull. The brothels were flourishing, and girls, scantily clad, painted and patched, talked to each other from the gables of opposite houses which almost met over the narrow streets; nor were these disorderly houses confined to Bankside and Southwark; they were appearing all over London from Turnbull Street at Smithfield to Ratcliff Highway and Catherine Street near the Strand – and, of course, they abounded in Drury Lane.

The most important highway of the city was Paul's Walk – the centre aisle of the old cathedral. This was not so much a part of a church as a promenade and market. All kinds of people gathered there – merchants to sell their wares, prostitutes to offer theirs. The pillars were used to denote the centres for certain trades. If a man wanted a letter-writer he was to be found by the first pillar; horses would be sold at the second pillar; the money-lenders were farther along; and next to them was the marriage-broker, and after that the obliging gentleman who could arrange for a man to spend a night – or an hour – with one of the women he controlled; mercers showed their materials; and those who had something to sell announced the fact by sticking notices on the pillars.

Nor was Paul's Walk the only place where it was possible to mingle with the London world. There was the Royal Exchange and the New Exchange; and in each of these were the galleries where shopkeepers set up their stalls, where pretty young women not only sold trifles but made appointments with the dandies who strolled through the galleries. There were young men in velvet coats carrying swords with jewelled hilts; they wore gold buttons on their coats, brilliant feathers in their wide-brimmed beaver hats; their breeches were trimmed with fine point lace and held in at the knees with ribbons, and their hair was beautifully dressed and hanging in ringlets over their shoulders – the delight of the girls and the envy of every apprentice. The theatres had closed at the beginning of the war, but the London to which Lucy came was a very merry place.

Each day she would wander out into the street, would stroll through the Royal Exchange, buy herself a fan or a ribbon, give her peculiarly inviting smile to the ogling men, and if her lover were away, she would agree that the one she fancied most should come to her lodging.

She found a little maid — Ann Hill — who thought her wonderful and declared she would die rather than leave her service — as she probably would of starvation, being ill-favoured. Lucy was glad to take her in and, in her lazy way, was kind to her.

Lucy would have been content to go on in her pleasant way, but the war brought changes. Each year there was a difference in the London scene. There were more soldiers in the town, and now they were not swaggering Cavaliers; they burned beautiful buildings and praised God as they did so. Beauty had no place in the good life, they believed; they used the churches as sleeping quarters; they took possession of St. Paul's; they stabled their horses in the Cathedral and cut down the beams for firewood; they played ninepins in the aisles and shouted to each other throughout the night. Very few Cavaliers flaunted through the streets now. The King's cause was a lost one, said the people. Noll Cromwell was in command.

Lucy's lover had appeared at her lodgings in a great hurry; he had stayed there for several days and nights, for he dared not face the streets. London was less merry; people were subdued and no longer openly expressed an opinion unless it was favourable to Cromwell.

Lucy went out to buy food during those days, and she was watched, she knew, by a man who always seemed to be lounging in the gallery of the Royal Exchange. For several days she had seen that that man's eyes were on her. She was not sure how, but she knew him to be a Cavalier. His hair was cropped and his clothes were sombre; yet there was that in his face which told her he was no Roundhead.

She liked his appearance; she more than liked it. She thought about him a good deal; if she had not already been harbouring one man at her lodgings she would have invited him there.

Then one day he followed her. Lucy was not frightened so to be followed; she was only exhilarated. She understood the meaning of his glances. He wanted only one thing from her; and she believed she would be very willing to grant that; so what had she to fear?

He caught up with her in a deserted alley whither she had led him. He plucked her sleeve and, as she turned, he released it and bowed as only a Cavalier would bow.

'You would have speech with me?'

'You are Mistress Lucy Water?'

'That's true enough.'

'You are the most beautiful woman in London.'

Lucy smiled complacently. He kept his eyes on her face.

'I wish to know you,' he said, 'very well.'

'You know my name,' she answered. 'Should I know yours?'

'I will tell you . . . in time.'

'And now what would you have of me?'

'You have a lodging near here?'

She nodded.

'And you share it with . . . a friend?'

Her eyes flashed. 'A very good friend.'

He caught her arm; his touch pleased her because it excited her. 'I know him,' he said. 'He served with me. Take me to him. I must have speech with him. Please believe me. There must be no delay.'

To Lucy this was a new method of approach and she enjoyed novelty. 'Come this way,' she said.

When she brought the stranger to her lodgings her lover was over-awed. There was no doubt that the man had spoken the truth.

'Let us talk,' said the newcomer. 'There is little time.'

'Sit down, sir,' said Lucy's lover. 'Lucy, bring a stool.'

Lucy obeyed; she sat at the table watching them, her plump hands supporting her chin, her dreamy eyes on the newcomer. He would be an exciting lover, she was telling herself. He *will* be an exciting lover! She knew that whatever he was implying, that was what he wished to be ere long; and that was what had brought him to their lodging.

He flicked his fingers. 'Your life won't be worth that, if you're caught here, my dear fellow.'

'No, sir, 'tis true.'

'I am leaving this day . . . for The Hague.'

'To join the Prince, sir?'

'Aye! To join the Prince. You would do well to make good your escape while there is yet time.'

'But to journey to The Hague . . . I have not the means.'

'Can you obtain two good horses?'

'I could . . . if I had the money, sir.'

'Then get them. Make for Harwich. The coast is quiet there . . . and I will tell you how you can find a boat to carry you across.'

'But, my lord . . .'

'You have but to tell the Prince that I have sent you, and you will be well received; you will be given a place in the Army there. Here is money.' He turned to look at Lucy. 'We shall meet in The Hague. If you bring Mistress Lucy Water to me safely there, you will not regret it.'

'I will do as you say, sir. You will take a little wine?'

'I have no time. I have certain things that must be done before I leave for The Hague. Wait till dusk, then go. Mistress Water will crop your hair. Don't venture out with your love-locks flowing. Mistress Water . . .' He stood up and Lucy stood up with him; he gripped her arms and looked into her face. 'You and I will meet ere long. I eagerly await our next encounter.'

He was gone and the two looked at each other in amazement.

'Why, my pretty Lucy,' said her lover, 'you have got yourself one of the quality this time. Do you know who that was? It was Algernon Sydney, son of the great Earl of Leicester. Get ready, girl. Don't waste time. We'll be out of this place as soon as night falls. We're going to Court . . . the Prince's Court. We're going to leave the sinking ship, my pretty. Come! Cut my hair. He's right, you know. You've got to make me into one of those ugly Roundhead fellows, and I'm to deliver you to your new protector, Lucy; and when I do my reward will be great.'

But his smile was rueful while he jingled the gold in his silken purse.

*

Lucy lay in bed watching her lover dressing. He was preparing himself to go to the little Court which the Prince had set up in The Hague.

Lucy had seen little of the place as yet. She had arrived after a tedious journey which had taken far longer than her ex-lover had anticipated. The journey to Harwich had been beset by difficulties; one of the horses had gone lame, and they had to procure another; everywhere they went they were under suspicion, as many were in England at that time; and then, when they had been ready to sail, the wind and weather had been against them. Meanwhile, in The Hague, Algernon Sydney eagerly awaited the girl who was being brought to him.

Lucy had discovered that he had paid fifty gold crowns to her lover, and that amused Lucy. He had paid for that which he could have had for nothing, had he waited to court her as a gentleman should. Not that Lucy would have needed much courting. She could quickly decide whether or not a man could appeal to her, and how far that appeal would carry him; Algernon Sydney need not have feared that he would fail to win that which he coveted.

Yet she would always laugh at the way things had turned out. She heard now, from Colonel Robert Sydney, how impatient his brother Algernon had been – watching the tides, riding three miles a day to Scheveningen where the boat was expected to make port, finding no satisfaction in any other woman, so that he had been the laughing stock of the whole Court.

Colonel Robert laughed with her, for after all he had come very well out of the affair.

'God's Body, Lucy!' he told her. 'He almost wept, so vexed was he! He said there wasn't another woman in the world who would do; and worse still he had paid some rogue fifty gold crowns for you.'

'Then he has none but himself to blame,' said Lucy. 'No man should pay another money for me. I'm not that sort of harlot.'

66

Now, watching him dressing for his appointment at Court, she did not regret the way in which matters had turned out. Robert was a satisfactory lover and she doubted his brother could be better. When she thought of arriving from the boat, and being brought to this place, to the comfort of hot food, a warm bed and a lover, she was not sorry. Robert was handsome and bold; he had wasted no time in taking to himself his brother's preserves. 'It is, after all, a family matter!' he had joked.

She had not known that her arrival and the fifty gold pieces had provided the amusing story of the moment. It was the sort which would amuse a band of exiles. They craved other amusement than continual dicing, and all were eager to see the young woman for whom Algernon Sydney had paid his fifty pieces. That he should have been called to join his regiment for service elsewhere and so been deprived of his prize, was a matter for the greatest hilarity.

Robert knew how all at Court were laughing over the affair; he also knew that his brother – whom he had always believed to have been something of a connoisseur where women were concerned – had not been deceived about this one. Robert was anxious to keep her to himself and not eager that she should be seen by the young roués who circulated about the Prince.

Lucy was happy enough; never very energetic she was content to lie about the apartment, eating the sweetmeats which Robert provided, trying on the pretty ribbons which he had procured for her.

So Robert went off to Court and Lucy lay in bed. Soon Ann Hill would come in – for Lucy had insisted on bringing Ann with her to The Hague – and her toilet would be made by the time her lover returned. Later, Lucy would explore the town, but not yet; she needed a few more days to recover from her journey.

Ann came in and sat on the bed and talked in her bright cockney way which was such a contrast to Lucy's musical Welsh accent.

Ann had been out; she had seen something of the flat country and she dismally shook her head over it. There could not be anything more different from London, she assured her mistress. The land was so flat; the wind blew across the sand, forming it into dunes; and these people had built dykes to keep out the sea water. There were small lakes all along the coast, where the sea had defied all attempts to keep it out. The town itself was more interesting although quite different from London. She had seen the palace where the Prince's sister Mary lived; and she had heard that the Prince was with her there; she had seen the arched gateway which led to the prison. But this town was a poor place compared with London, and the fresh wind howled all the time. Yet there were many gallant gentlemen in the streets, and to see them in their fine clothes, and with their fine manners, one might be in London; moreover, these gentlemen were even finer than those they had been wont to see in London recently; yes, there were some who were very fine indeed.

Lucy's eyes shone as she listened. She said: 'I think I shall dress myself and take a walk.'

But as she rose from her bed she and Ann heard a voice singing outside the window; it was a deep, masculine voice and very musical. Lucy put her head to one side, listening, for the singer had stopped beneath her window.

'I loved a lass, a fair one,
As fair as e'er was seen;
She was indeed a rare one,
Another Sheba's Queen!
But fool as then I was,
I thought she loved me too:
But now, alas: she's left me,
Falero, lero, loo.'

Lucy could not refrain from going to the window; she opened the casement wide and leaned out. Below was a very tall young man of about her own age with large brown eyes, the warmest and merriest she had ever seen; he had long dark curly hair, and as she looked down he stopped singing, swept off his beaver hat, and bowed low.

'Good day to you, mistress,' he said.

'Good day,' said Lucy, drawing about her the wrap she had slipped on – and which was all she was wearing – but

68

making sure that it did not cover too much of her magnificently-rounded shoulders.

'I trust you liked my poor song, mistress.'

'It was well rendered, sir.'

'At least it had the desired effect of bringing you to the window.'

'So that is why you are singing there!'

'Why else?'

'Then you know me?'

'Everyone in this town has heard of the beauty of Mistress Lucy Water.'

'You flatter me, sir.'

'Nay, to flatter is to praise unduly. However great the praise accorded to you, it could not be undue. Therefore it would be impossible to flatter you.'

'You must be an Englishman.'

He bowed. 'I am glad you recognize me as such. These Dutchmen are dull fellows. They are not our equals in eating, dicing or loving the ladies.'

'I have no knowledge of your talents at the table, sir, nor with the dice, nor . . .'

'Who knows, I may be able to prove my talents in all three one day, mistress.'

'You are bold.'

'There again we differ from these Dutchmen. Bold they may be on the seas, but it would need an Englishman to be as bold as this.'

Lucy gave a little scream, for he had swung himself up on to the parapet, and his long slender fingers, immaculately white and adorned with several flashing rings, were clinging to the sill.

'You will fall, foolish man!' She reached for him, and, laughing, he managed, with her help, to scramble through the window, which was no easy matter, the window being small and he being six feet in height.

Lucy's wrap had slipped from her shoulders in the effort; this but added to their pleasure in the adventure – his to see so much which was beautiful, hers to show it.

'You might have killed yourself,' she reproved.

'It would take more than a fall from a window to kill one so strong as I.'

'And all for a silly prank!'

'It was worth the slight discomfort. I see rumour has not lied. Mistress Lucy Water *is* the most beautiful woman in The Hague.'

'I must send you away. You should not come here thus. What Colonel Sydney would say if he found you here, I dare not think.'

'I will risk Colonel Sydney's displeasure.'

'You are too bold, young man.'

'I count boldness a virtue. It is a quality which such as I could not do without.'

'I must tell you that Colonel Sydney is a very important man.'

'I know of him, and you are right.'

'Then have you no fear . . .?'

He put his hands on her shoulders and, drawing her swiftly to him, kissed her lips, then her throat, then her breasts.

'This is too much,' she stammered.

'Indeed, it is not enough.'

'It is too much to be suffered!'

'That which cannot be helped must be endured.'

'Sir . . . how dare you come thus to my chamber?'

'How dare I? Because you are beautiful; because I am a man; because I saw you at the window; because you heard my song and helped me in; because I have seen that which makes me long to see more; because I have kissed your lips and tasted that which I would savour to the full.'

'I have a lover.'

'I offer you a better one.'

'You are insolent!'

'I am ardent, I confess.'

Lucy tried to be stern, but how could she be? Colonel Sydney was a lover to her taste, but this young man was different from any she had ever known before. He was tall and strong; he could have overpowered her, and perhaps she would not have been sorry if he had; but he did no such thing, although he was somewhat arrogant and very sure of himself. He was not going to take by force, she realized, that which he knew would not long be denied him. There was a tenderness mingling with the passion

70

she saw in his eyes, and such tenderness she had never before encountered. There was something lazy in his manner which matched her own laziness; his sensuality, she felt, was equal to her own; he was of her age; and yet he was by no means handsome; but Lucy's experience told her that he had more than good looks; he was the most charming person it had ever been her good fortune to meet.

Lucy said: 'You must know that Colonel Sydney will consider it a great offence to force your way in here thus.'

'Are we not to tell him that you helped me in then?'

'I did not mean to help you in. It was but to save your life. I feared you would fall.'

'I thank you for my life, Lucy. How can I repay you?'

'By going quietly before Colonel Sydney returns and finds you here.'

'Is that all I am to get for my pains . . . after risking my life to be near you as I did?'

'Please go. I am afraid the Colonel will arrive.'

'You are beginning to make me fear the Colonel. Are you fond of him, Lucy? Is he good to you?'

'He is good to me and I am fond of him.'

'But not so fond that you cannot spare a smile or two for a passing fancy, eh? Lucy, do you think you could grow as fond and fearful of me as you are of the Colonel?'

'You forget I do not know you. I saw you for the first time only a few minutes ago.'

'We must put that right. From now on we will see a good deal of each other. I will risk Colonel Sydney's displeasure. Will you?'

'I might,' murmured Lucy.

He took her hand and kissed it. 'You are the most beautiful woman I have ever seen,' he said; 'and I have always been a close observer of women. Why, I remember an occasion – in the town of Oxford it was – when I was in church with my father, and he smote me on the head with his staff because, instead of listening to the sermon, I was smiling at the ladies. I am older now, but I have never ceased to smile at the ladies, and no amount of smiting on the head will stop me. So you see I know what I am talking about.'

'I am sure you would always give a good account of yourself to women. There is no need to tell me that. Now go, I beg of you. I will order my maid to take you down by the back staircase. You must go at once.'

'But I will have a kiss before I go.'

'Then . . . you will go?'

'I swear it. But do not imagine we shall not meet again.'

'I would do anything to be rid of you before Colonel Sydney returns.'

'Anything!' His warm brown eyes were alert and hopeful.

'I would kiss you,' she said firmly.

So he took her into his arms and kissed her, not once but many times, and not only on the lips as she pretended to intend. Lucy, flushed and struggling, was nevertheless laughing. It was an amusing adventure with the most fascinating man she had ever met. She hoped he would keep his word and visit her again.

She called Ann Hill.

'Ann,' she said, 'show this man out of the house . . . quickly . . . by way of the back staircase.'

'Yes, mistress,' said Ann.

Lucy watched him go regretfully. At the door he turned and bowed. He bowed more elegantly than any man she had ever known. 'We shall meet again . . . very soon,' he promised. 'But not too soon for me.'

Then he turned and followed Ann.

At the door he looked at Ann. She had lifted her face to his, for Ann too felt the power of his fascination. The warm brown eyes softened. Poor Ann! She was not well-favoured, but she had seen the kiss he had given her mistress. 'Od's Fish! he pondered. She's envious, poor girl!

And because, ever since the days when his father had smitten him for his too-open admiration of the girls in church – and perhaps before then – he had been unable to slight any woman, pretty or plain, lowly or high-born, he stooped quickly and lightly kissed Ann's cheek.

*

Robert announced that Lucy was to be presented to the Prince.

'He has heard much of you,' said Robert. 'The talk of Algy's paying his fifty crowns and then being recalled before you arrived seems amusing to Charles. He says he must see the heroine of the story. So put on the dress I gave you and prepare yourself. You'll have to go to Court some day. In a place like this ... all huddled together ... exiles must necessarily mingle.'

While Ann helped Lucy to dress they were both thinking of the tall dark man.

'Do you think he'll come back, mistress?' asked Ann.

'How can I know? He was too quick, was he not? He had the manners of a practised philanderer.'

'But of a gentleman, too,' murmured Ann.

'They often go together, I believe. Come, girl, my kerchief and my fan.'

Even when she reached the palace in which the Prince had his apartments Lucy was still thinking of the tall dark man. She entered the palace with its wheel windows and gothic towers at either end; she walked up the staircase into the hall where the Prince was waiting to receive her.

She thought she was dreaming as he smiled at her, and kneeling before him she could not help lifting her eyes to look into that dark face with the glowing brown eyes which were now shining with mischief. She felt bewildered and, in that moment when she had knelt, she had not believed that he could really be the Prince. She thought it was some hoax, the sort of game he and his friends would like to play.

All about him were men – some young, some old – but he towered above them all, not only because of his height, but because of that overwhelming charm, that easy grace. It seemed incredible, but it must be true: the young man who had climbed through her window was Charles, Prince of Wales, and no other.

He was laughing merrily. 'So, pretty Lucy,' he said. 'I stand exposed in all my perfidy.'

'Sir ...' she began.

He turned to those about him and said easily: 'Lucy and

I have already met, we find. We also find that we have a fondness for each other.'

'Your Grace, I do not understand,' said Robert.

'Then we must acquaint you with the facts, and as a good soldier, Colonel, I am sure you will know when the moment has come to retreat.'

All those about the Prince began to laugh. Only Robert looked dismayed.

He bowed with dignity. Then he said: 'I understand Your Grace's meaning and realize that I am in a position from which the only possible action is retreat.'

'Wise Robert!' cried Charles. 'And speaking of retreat, that is an order I give to the rest of you gentlemen.'

Much laughter followed, and one by one the gentlemen left the apartment, pausing only to throw appreciative glances at Lucy.

So Lucy was alone with Charles.

And thus she became the willing mistress of the exiled Prince of Wales.

*

She loved him truly; he was more to her than any other lover had been, for he was more than mere lover. It was that tender quality in him which moved Lucy. He was easy-going, full of wit, and if he did not always keep his promises, it was due to sheer kindness of heart which would not allow him to refuse anything which was asked of him.

As Prince's mistress her life changed yet again. It was true that he was a Prince in exile, but he was England's heir for all that. Although his eyes would never fail to light up when they rested on a pretty woman, he became devoted to Lucy; she was his chief love, and was content that this should be so. These weeks, she decided, were the happiest of her life.

She made the acquaintance of men whose names she had heard mentioned with awe; she heard the plots and intrigues which were in motion to win this second civil war, begun this year, and which one of these men – George Villiers, Duke of Buckingham – had helped to bring about. Buckingham had recently joined the Prince and was

his closest companion. Charles told her that he and Buckingham had been brought up together, and when the elder
Villiers died, King Charles I took his children into the royal
household and Lord Francis and Lord George – as this
Buckingham was then – had played with the royal children.

Lord Francis had been killed recently, as many people
were killed in England; and the young Duke had escaped
to join the Prince.

Charles enjoyed unburdening his mind to Lucy. He felt
it was unimportant what he said to her, for Lucy only
half-listened. He would smile on seeing the vague look
which would come into her eyes at times, when she would
nod and express surprise even when she had little notion
about what he was talking.

'Why, Lucy,' he said, 'you'd never betray my secrets to
others, would you, for the simple reason that you have
never heard me betray them to you.'

That amused him. Some might have been angry at her
obtuseness; Charles was rarely angry. If he was inclined
to be, some spirit of mischief would seem to rise within
him and make him see himself partly in the wrong.

'Lucy,' he would say, 'I am like a man with an affliction
of the eyes. They don't focus together; consequently I have
two pictures of every scene – two views, you see, and of
the same affair. That's very disturbing. Then I begin to
wonder whether there are not many versions of the same
picture, and whether the man with whom I have been so
fiercely arguing has not as true a picture as mine. Lucy,
you are not listening. You are wise, my love, for I am sure
I talk much nonsense.'

She wanted to please him; she wanted to show her gratitude. She would not look at other men – or hardly ever.
He noticed this; he had a quick appreciation of such
things, and he thanked her gravely.

He introduced her to his brother James who was not
quite fifteen years old.

James liked to talk to Lucy; he talked often of his recent
escape. To Lucy he would talk of it again and again, for
she did not mind, and would appear to be interested on
every occasion. It was the most exciting thing that had

ever happened to him and he was so very proud of himself.

'To tell the truth, Lucy,' he told her on one occasion, 'I escaped because I dared stay no longer. There were messages from our mother, and she was ashamed of me for not managing to get away. Elizabeth – that is my sister – was also ashamed. She used to say: "If I were a boy I should have found some means to escape." But it was not easy, Lucy. We were at St James's Palace where old Noll Cromwell had set guards to watch everything we did. They said they were going to make apprentices of Elizabeth and me, so that we could earn our living with our hands.'

'So you ran away,' said Lucy.

'Yes, I ran away. How I wish the others could have come with me! It was not possible, though, for the three of us to escape. Elizabeth was not strong enough. She was never strong after she fell and broke her leg. And Harry was not really old enough. He's only nine now. We made plans, but only one of us could get away in safety. So we planned a game of hide-and-seek. I was to run and hide, and so was Henry. Elizabeth would look for us. I ran back to the guard and pretended to hide; then Harry came running out and asked a guard to lift him to the top of one of the porches where Elizabeth would not easily find him. While they were doing this I managed to slip away to where my valet was waiting for me with horses. I changed my clothes and dressed up as a woman, Lucy. I nearly betrayed myself by raising my leg and plucking at my stocking as no woman would. But we got to Gravesend and so I went to Middleburgh and Dort and finally here.'

'It was a wonderful escape,' murmured Lucy.

'I'm glad you think so, Lucy.'

His eyes were admiring; he was almost as fond of the ladies as his brother was; and perhaps, thought Lucy, when he was older he would be quite as fond. But, she decided, although she liked him very much, he would never have his brother's charm.

Yes, she was happy during those warm days of summer, and before September she knew that she was going to have a child.

*

76

Lucy grew large and there was speculation throughout the Court of exiles. Men and women made bets with one another. Whose child is this, they asked – Charles' or Robert's? Who could be sure of Lucy?

Lucy heard the gossip; so did Charles.

'It is your child,' she told him. 'It could not possibly be that of another man.'

He nodded gravely; whether or not he believed it she was not entirely sure. He would never *say* that he doubted her word. He would consider that most ungallant. Moreover she might weep, and there was nothing which distressed Charles more than the tears of women. They could upset him more, it was said, than bad news from England. And what did it matter whose child Lucy carried? The Prince would acknowledge it as his, for, considering his relationship with the mother, he would feel it to be most unchivalrous not to do so.

There were some who remembered his grandfather, Henri Quatre; and they declared that the resemblance between these two – in character, not in appearance, of course – was great. Both were great lovers of women and treasured conquests in love more than those of war; both were blessed, or tormented, by the ability to see many sides to all questions and disputes; both were easygoing and good natured almost to a fault. Henri Quatre had been a great soldier and an even greater King. Those who wished the Royal House of Stuart well, hoped that Charles had inherited more from his maternal grandfather than these qualities.

There were times during those summer months when a deep melancholy would show itself in the Prince's face. The news from England was disastrous. Charles shut himself up with the letters his father sent from England.

He thought of the kindly man who had not, to his cost, possessed that gift of tolerance towards the opinions of others, but who had nevertheless been a loving father. He read the words Charles I had written.

'An advantage of wisdom you have above most Princes, Charles, for you have begun and now spent some years of discretion in the experience of trouble and the exercise of patience. You have already tasted the cup whereof I have liberally drunk, which I look upon as God's physic, having that in healthfulness which it lacks in pleasure . . .'

Charles had to face the truth. He knew that his father was the captive of his enemies. He feared greatly that he would never see his face again.

He thought of his family: little Henry and Elizabeth, prisoners of the Parliament in St James's Palace; James here with him after a miraculous escape; little Henriette – his dear Minette – after an equally miraculous escape, in Paris with his mother; and lastly, Mary, his eldest sister, whose hospitality he now enjoyed.

War was raging in England; war was raging in France; and both these wars were civil wars, the rising of the common people against their royal rulers.

What did the future hold for him – the penniless, exiled Prince? He could not say; and, because he was never one to trick himself with false beliefs, he dared not think.

He would go to Lucy; they would sport and play together. He thanked God for love, which could always enchant him, always make him forget his troubles. Lucy was a delight; he must be thankful for the gifts he had, for though he was a Prince without a kingdom and heir to a throne which would be denied him, he had certain gifts which would always bring him favour with women. So he would plunge into pleasure and try to forget his melancholy state.

*

News came from England which set a gloom over the Prince's Court.

Charles Stuart, King of England, stood convicted, attainted and condemned of high treason; and the penalty for high treason was death.

They would not dare! it was said.

But all knew that Cromwell and his followers had little respect for kings. To them, Charles Stuart was no ruler anointed by the Lord; he was a man guilty of treason to his country.

The Prince had lost his gaiety. He shut himself away from his friends. Even Lucy could not comfort him. His thoughts were all for the noble, kindly man. He thought of

Nottingham, where his father's followers had tried in vain to raise the royal standard, and how the wind blew it down and seemed determined, so fiercely did it rage, that the King's colours should not be unfurled. An evil omen? it had been whispered. He thought of the skirmish at Copredy Bridge which had decided nothing and had led to the disaster of Marston Moor. He remembered the last time he had seen his father; it was in Oxford almost four years before.

And what could he do now to save his father? He was powerless; he depended on others for his very board. He was a beggar in a foreign country; his entire family was reduced to beggary. But at least he was a Prince, heir to a throne, and Cromwell would never feel at peace while he lived.

Impulsively he wrote to the Parliament of England; he sent them a blank sheet of paper which he sealed and signed Charles P. He asked them to fill in on that blank sheet any terms they cared to enforce; he would fulfil them; they might bring about his own disinheritance; they might execute him; but in exchange for his promise to deliver himself into their hands that they might do what they would with him, they must spare his father's life.

He despatched three messengers each with a copy of this document to ensure the message's reaching its destination; and he bade them depart with all speed to England.

Then there was nothing he could do but wait. He had done all that a son could do to save his father.

*

One February day as he left his bedchamber he was met by one of his men, and was struck by the way in which the man looked at him before he fell to his knees and said in a solemn manner: 'May God preserve Your Majesty!'

Then he knew what had happened to that kindly man, his father. He could not speak, but turned abruptly and went back to his bedchamber. There he threw himself upon his bed and gave way to passionate weeping.

Not until several days later could he talk of his father. Then he wished to hear of the heroic way in which he had died. He pictured it so clearly; it was engraved on his

79

mind so that he would never forget it. He visualized his father, handsome and stately, brought to the Palace through St James's Park; he pictured him walking with the guards before him and behind him, the colours flying ahead of him, and drums beating as he passed along. It was all so clear to him. He saw his father take the bread and wine which were brought to him; he saw him break the manchet and drink the claret just as Sir Thomas Herbert, his father's groom of the chamber, described the scene. He saw the crowds assembled; and as the King passed them on his last journey, his son knew that many in the crowds had muttered prayers and called: 'God bless Your Majesty!' Never would Charles I have looked more noble than he did on that last walk to the scaffold; he would be noble to the end, even when he laid his head upon the block.

And ever after that, although the young Prince might be gay – and there were few who could be gayer than he – it seemed to those who observed him closely that a touch of melancholy never completely left him.

*

Now Lucy was no longer the mistress of a Prince; she was a King's mistress; for although the Parliament of England would have none of him, he had been proclaimed King Charles II in Jersey.

Moreover, there came tentative offers to receive him in Scotland and Ireland.

It was a different matter being the mistress of the King from being merely that of a Prince.

Charles kissed her warmly and told her he must leave her. Business called him now – affairs of state. 'Our ranks have risen, Lucy,' he said; 'and with new honours come new responsibilities. I must leave you for a time. I go to Paris to see my mother.'

Then he told her he had another love in Paris. 'Oh, Lucy, now you look hurt. You must not be, and you will not be when you hear who this is. She is not quite five years old, and she is my little sister. I am torn between my melancholy in leaving you and my delight in the prospect of seeing her. Lucy, you will be true to your King?'

Lucy declared she would. He wondered. Then he believed that she might until the child was born.

'Take care of yourself, Lucy, and of our child,' he said.

She kissed him with passion, telling him that she loved him truly; she wept after he had gone.

Lucy knew she might not be faithful; it was not in her nature to be faithful, any more than it was in his; but she also knew that, though her body might demand other lovers, there would never be one to equal Charles Stuart – Prince or King.

*

In a house in the city of Rotterdam, not far from Broad Church Street where Erasmus was born, Lucy lay in childbed. She was vaguely aware of the women about her, for she was quite exhausted by the ordeal through which she had just passed.

It was Ann Hill who held up the child for her to see.

'A boy, mistress. A bonny boy!'

Lucy held out her arms for the child and Ann laid him in them. There was a dark down on his head and he bawled lustily.

'He's one who will want his own way,' said one of the women.

'The son of a King!' said Ann with awe.

Some of those about the bed raised their eyebrows, and their eyes asked a question: 'The son of a King or the son of a Colonel? Who shall say?'

But Lucy did not see them and Ann ignored them.

'I shall call him James,' said Lucy. 'That is a royal Stuart name.'

She bent and kissed the soft downy head.

'Jemmy,' she murmured. 'Little Jemmy – son of a King – what will you do in the world, eh?'

CHAPTER FOUR

THE LITTLE Princess Henriette was bewildered. She sensed tension between two beloved people – her mother and her brother. It had something to do with Father Cyprien's instruction, which occurred daily. Charles was not pleased that it should take place, and her mother was determined that it should. It was Henriette's great desire to please her brother in all things; if he had said to her: 'Do not listen to the teachings of Père Cyprien; listen to the words of Lady Morton!' gladly would she have obeyed. But her brother was careless – he was never really angry – while her mother could be very angry indeed. It was the Queen who put her arms about her little daughter and whispered to her that she was her mother's *'enfant de bénédiction'*, the Queen who told her that God had rescued her from heretics that she might become a good Catholic. Charles merely played with her, told her gay stories and made her laugh. She loved best of all to be with Charles, but it did not seem so imperative to follow his wishes as those of her mother, for if she obeyed her mother, he would merely be wistful and understand that she was by no means to blame; whereas if she obeyed Charles' wishes, her mother would be passionately angry, would rail against her and perhaps punish her. She was only a little girl and she must do that which seemed easiest to her.

So, to please her mother, she tried to become a good Catholic; she believed Père Cyprien when he had said that God had caused a great civil war so that she, Henriette, should escape from her father's country and come to France to learn how to be a good Catholic. She tried sincerely to thank God on her knees – through the saints – for having thousands of men killed, including her father, that her own soul might be saved.

Henrietta Maria had bought a house in Chaillot and thither she had taken several nuns from the Convent of Les Filles de Marie that she might found an order of her own. In this house Henrietta Maria had her own rooms which were always preserved for her, and it was her pleasure to spend a great deal of her time 'in retreat' as she called it. It delighted her to take her little daughter there. Henriette would stand at the windows looking down on the gleaming Seine with the buildings of Paris clustered on either bank; but she knew that she was there for a more important reason than to admire the view; she was there to learn to be a good Catholic.

Lady Morton invariably accompanied her, and would often be present when she received her instruction. Lady Morton was very anxious about this instruction and Henriette was sorry for this. Why could they not all be pleased? What did it matter whether she was brought up in the religion of France or England? To tell the truth, Henriette herself could see little difference in those faiths about which others grew so fierce.

Henrietta Maria declared to Charles that she had been promised on her marriage that all her children should be brought up as Catholics. Again and again Charles reminded her that it would be against the wishes of his father. Then the Queen swore that her husband had promised her that, even if others of the family must follow the teachings of the Church of England, Henriette should become a Catholic.

'I swear it, Charles! I swear it!' she cried, tapping her foot as she did in moments of agitation. 'He could deny me nothing. It was the last time I saw him. I swear to you, Charles. You would not wish to go against your father's wishes, would you?'

'No, Mam,' was Charles' answer. 'That is why I wish you to allow Lady Morton to supervise my sister's religious education in the faith of the Church of England.'

'But it was your father's wish . . .'

The young King smiled gently at his mother. He was always extremely courteous to her, but he was not fond of her and he was too honest to pretend that he was. He loved his little sister dearly; but he also loved peace. A young King with a kingdom yet to be won had too many difficulties to face without making others with a fanatical Catholic such as his mother was. So Charles consoled himself with the thought: Minette is only a child. She will absorb little as yet. Later, something must be done. Perhaps then he could commission someone else to take up the struggle with his mother, and so escape the unpleasantness.

Meanwhile there was much to occupy him. Lucy had come to Paris with their son, and he was delighted with them both. Young Jemmy was a lusty youngster; Charles swore he had the Stuart eyes; he was certain that Robert Sydney could not claim him as his son. He often said: 'If I were not the King, I'd marry Lucy to make the boy my heir.'

He had been alarmed because young Jemmy had already started to cause some trouble at The Hague. It was realized that he was a very important little boy, and there had been a plot to kidnap him which had nearly succeeded. Charles had declared that Lucy must come to Paris and bring the boy with her. This she had been quick to do. Paris suited Lucy better than The Hague – even Paris suffering from the disasters of the Fronde. So Charles, with plans for expeditions to the loyal territories of Jersey, Scotland and Ireland to be considered, and his playmate, Lucy, and his little son to enchant him, found it easy to shelve the problem of his sister's religion.

Henrietta Maria looked on with quiet satisfaction.

Let the boy amuse himself. Soon he would have little time for amusement. It was natural that he should wish to dally with a mistress. Was he not the grandson of Henri Quatre?

So Henrietta Maria kept her daughter with her, and often she would take the child against her knee and, embracing her fiercely, tell her that only by learning all that Père Cyprien had to teach her could her soul be saved.

'And what will happen to those whose souls are not saved?' asked Henriette.

'They burn in the fires of hell eternally.'

'How long is eternally?'

'For ever and ever.'

'And Lady Morton will burn for ever and ever?'

'If she does not become a Catholic.'

Tears filled Henriette's eyes. 'Oh no! Not dear Nan!

84

Please Mam, pray to God and the saints not to burn poor Nan.'

'If she becomes a Catholic she will be safe. You must try to convert her.'

'Oh, Mam, I will . . . I will!'

So Henriette went to her governess and put her arms about her neck crying: 'Do be converted, dear Nan. Dear Lady Morton, you must be a Catholic to be saved. Do be a Catholic, and I will love you more dearly than ever.'

'My dearest, we cannot easily change our convictions,' said Anne Morton.

'But you must be a Catholic . . . you *must*! All those who are not cannot be saved. They are tormented for ever and ever.'

'So they have told you that, have they?'

'I cannot bear that you should be burned, dear Nan.'

'Come, dry your tears. I promise you this: I shall not be burned.'

'Then you will . . .'

'Let us not talk of this, my dearest. Might it not be that there are many ways to salvation?'

'But there is only one. Père Cyprien says so.'

'It may be that he knows only one. Now I will tell you how we came out of England, shall I?'

'Oh yes, please . . . and how I kept telling people that I was the Princess and that the clothes I wore were not my own.'

So she was appeased for the moment, and later she said to her mother: 'I will tell Charles he must be saved, for, Mam, he too may burn eternally.'

'Do not speak of these matters to your brother, *chérie*.'

'But, Mam, he will not be saved if he is not a Catholic.'

Henrietta Maria was more brusque than she usually was with her little daughter. 'Now . . . now . . . you talk too much. It is not for you to save souls. That is for Père Cyprien. You must learn what is told you. You are not yet ready to teach.'

'But if I may try to save dear Lady Morton, why should I not try to save Charles?'

Henrietta Maria pinched the soft cheek affectionately.

'I have said you must learn first. There is so much you do not understand.'

Henriette nodded. She was content not to understand, for understanding, it seemed, could make people disagree, and that had already caused trouble between those whom she loved.

*

It seemed to Henriette that any day might bring news which made her mother weep and declare that she was the most unhappy Queen in the world and that no woman suffered as she did.

The troubles of the Fronde endangered the lives of royal people. It was a long time since Henriette had seen her cousins, Louis the King and his brother Philippe, so that she had forgotten she had ever known them. Her own beloved Charles had left again; he had gone to Jersey where the people were loyal. Henriette quickly learned that it was a sad thing to be an exile in a strange land. And although her mother told her stories of the days when she herself was a little girl and Paris had been her home, still they were looked upon as strangers. When the French were angry with the English government much was made of Henriette and her mother; when they were indifferent to the English government they had nothing but sullen looks for the exiles.

'It is the saddest thing in the world to have no country,' said Henrietta Maria.

'Shall we never have a country?' asked her daughter.

Her mother's eyes, with the dark shadows beneath them, gleamed as she enlarged on one of her favourite topics. 'If you marry, the country of your husband will be your country.'

Henriette nodded slowly; she knew that her mother had a husband in mind for her. It was a boy who would one day be the most important man in France. He was already a King, even as Charles was. He was Louis XIV. She had forgotten what he looked like so she began to picture him looking exactly like her brother Charles, although she knew that he was not so old. But he was a King, and people would kneel and kiss his hands as they kissed

Charles'. She was not displeased at the thought of marriage with Louis since when she thought of him she thought of a boy who looked like Charles, spoke like Charles and indeed *was* another Charles – but instead of being called by that name he was Louis, and King of France instead of King of England.

Now, of course, on account of the Fronde, the little King and his brother did not come to Paris. Henrietta Maria and her daughter stayed there because they were not important and Paul de Gondi allowed them to.

So sometimes they were in the apartments of the Louvre, and sometimes they were in the house on the hills of Chaillot. Henriette studied; she found it easy to study and there were few distractions. She wanted to learn; there was so much to know. She wanted to understand why the people of England had killed her father and would not allow Charles to have his throne; she wanted to know why the people of France were threatening their monarch with the same treatment.

Mademoiselle de Montpensier visited them now and then. 'La Grande Mademoiselle' she was called in Paris, for she was on the side of the Frondeurs; and she hoped to be remembered in the years to come as another Jeanne d'Arc who had saved France. She was very handsome and very anxious that everyone should pay homage to her, the cousin of the King, the richest heiress in Europe, and now . . . the heroine of the Fronde.

Henriette knew that her mother wanted La Grande Mademoiselle to marry Charles, and Henriette thought she was almost worthy of him as she looked at the handsome girl so exquisitely dressed in the fashions inspired by the Fronde – her long hanging sleeves were *frondées*, slung, not looped; her fan, gloves and kerchief were all *à la mode de la Fronde*; on her elaborate hat she wore an ornament which was the shape of a sling. The people cheered as her carriage drove through the streets: '*Vive la grande Mademoiselle!*'

Mademoiselle should, so said Henrietta Maria, look to her actions. Did she think that her attitude endeared her to the Queen Mother? Was this siding with the Queen's enemies a wise thing? It was true that the great Condé was on the side of the Fronde, and that many aristocrats had followed his example, but for a young woman who hoped to marry the little King to side with his mother's enemies, was surely unwise!'

But Mademoiselle was unwise and Mademoiselle was arrogant. She thought herself grand and clever enough to do exactly as she pleased.

She was coquettish; she liked to talk to Henrietta Maria about Charles, for Charles was one of her many suitors, and although Mademoiselle considered him beneath her, she was not averse to hearing of his passion for her.

The little Princess liked to be present at these conversations between her mother and Mademoiselle; she liked to hear their talk of Charles, for, of course, they talked of him differently from the way in which they talked of him to her. There was so much she wanted to know about that most fascinating person, her beloved brother Charles.

'When he regains his kingdom his wife will be the Queen of England,' Henrietta Maria constantly reminded her niece.

'Ah, when, dear Madame! When will that be?'

'Can you doubt that it will be ere long? The people of England will not endure for ever that upstart Cromwell and his miserable rule.'

'They say he has a way of enforcing that which is not palatable.'

'Can you doubt that a young man so strong, so full of courage, so determined, will not soon win back his kingdom?'

'There are some who say he loves the company of women better than that of soldiers and statesmen.'

'So did my father, but that did not prevent his conquering his enemies and bringing an end to civil war in France.'

'But that happy state of affairs did not come about until he was well advanced in years. I should not care to spend the days of my youth an exiled Queen. Moreover, the King of England, even while courting me, brought his mistress to Paris.'

'Bah! A man must have a mistress. What of that?'

'And treats her bastard as though he were a prince.'

'He is at least the bastard of a King.'

'I have heard that there is some doubt of that. This Lucy Water! Who is she? A King's mistress should have some quality, should she not?'

'He but amuses himself. And what ladies of quality were there, do you think, at The Hague where he found her?'

'Madame, she was his mistress in Paris.'

'He is the sweetest natured man in the world. He could not turn her off because he was in Paris. You will see what grand mistresses he will have when he is in his own country.'

'Madame, I would rather my husband were faithful to me than that he should have the grandest mistresses in the world. Your son cannot remain faithful to any woman. Why, even when he courts one, his eyes follow others. I hear now that he is causing some scandal in Jersey. There is a woman's name which is mentioned in connexion with him – Margaret Carteret.'

'Margaret Carteret!' interrupted the Queen. 'She is merely the daughter of the Seigneur of Trinity. She is a young girl. My son stays at Elizabeth Castle which is her father's residence, and because my son is there and a young woman is there ...' Henrietta Maria's hands flew up in a gesture of inevitability.

'Wherever Charles Stuart is, Madame, there will be scandals concerning women.'

'That is because he is so gallant and charming.'

'And such a lover of women!'

'Mademoiselle,' said Henrietta Maria, 'I shall tell my brother to marry you to a monk. I can see that you do not wish for a man.'

And with that Henrietta Maria rose and left her niece, taking short rapid steps which, to her daughter, conveyed her anger.

Little Henriette sat on, quietly thinking of her brother.

*

Lucy, who had been lonely, was lonely no longer.

She had left Paris for The Hague – with her was the King and his little Court – for Charles had returned from Jersey and there were new plans afoot with the Scots. The Marquis of Montrose was awaiting him at The Hague with new propositions to lay before him. England would have none of her King; but Jersey had accepted him, and Scotland was prepared to do so – on terms. All Charles need do was sign the Oath of the Covenant, and he could be crowned at Scone.

Lucy did not understand why the King should be so perplexed. If he could not be King of England he could at least be King of Scotland. To be King of any land was surely better than to be King of none; and even Lucy could see that Charles was King in name only.

'You don't understand, Lucy,' her lover tried to explain. 'The Covenanters of Scotland are Presbyterian, and the Church of Scotland is the enemy of the Church of England, of which my father was head. There was trouble when my father sought to force them to accept the English liturgy. To sign the Covenant is, in a measure, to betray England. But what is the use of explaining, Lucy? You do not care for these matters, and perhaps in that you are wise. Lucy, I often think that if all the world were as careless of so-called great matters, and so absorbed in the pleasure of love, this Earth would be a happier place.'

Lucy smiled; she knew how to turn him from his worries; and he was only too ready to be turned. He hated trouble; when it presented itself he always seemed to be looking for the easiest way out of it.

His friend George Villiers, the Duke of Buckingham, was at his elbow now. 'Why not sign the Covenant?' he asked. 'Better to have a country to rule over – even if it is that bleak and puritanical one – than remain an exile here!'

And so eventually he decided to sign. He knew that his mother would throw up her hands in despair, for the Covenanters' aim was to destroy Popery; he knew that there would be many to say that had he been a nobler man he would have preferred exile to siding with the Covenanters. He explained to Buckingham: 'I am not a man who is so devoted to religion that he cannot set it aside for the sake of peace. My grandfather changed his religion that the wars of France might cease. There are times when I feel that I am my grandfather re-born.'

'It is true you are as careless of religion,' agreed

George. 'You are devoted to women. There is certainly a resemblance. But, Sire, you will have to work harder with the latter if you are to compete with your noble grandsire.'

'Give me time,' murmured the King. 'Give me time.'

The two young men could not be serious for long, and even the prospect of a sojourn in a land of Puritans could not curb their levity.

So Charles left for Scotland, whither obviously he could not take his mistress and little Jemmy. The Scots, said the King, so assiduously loved God that it gave them little time for loving others – even their wives; but he had little doubt that they took time off from their devotions to make love to their wives now and then, though it would be under cover of darkness and, as he had heard, for the sole purpose that more Puritans might be procreated.

Before he left he embraced Lucy and spent as long as he could playing with Jemmy.

'Take care of my boy, Lucy,' he admonished, 'and remember me when I am gone.'

'I will never forget you, Charles,' she told him.

'Nor I you, Lucy.'

He did not promise that he would be faithful; although he broke so many promises, he did not make them callously. He doubted that he would be faithful, though he had heard that the Scottish women were as cold as their climate. There were always exceptions, as he well knew, and if there was one warm-hearted woman in Scotland, he doubted not that he would find her.

So Lucy stood on the shore watching the ship sail away from Holland; then she returned to her apartments where she had so often entertained her royal lover, and declared to Ann Hill that no gentleman should enter her bedroom until her royal lover returned.

'You could not tolerate another after him,' said Ann.

'Indeed I could not!' declared Lucy.

She believed this for two whole days. Then she began to feel lonely. Her big brown eyes would rest wistfully on several handsome men who still remained at The Hague; but always little Ann Hill would be there to remind her of Jemmy's father.

Lucy would sigh, and she and Ann would talk of Charles; and Lucy tried to be contented with that.

*

There was great excitement at The Hague because the Duke of York had arrived. The Duke lacked the gay charm of his brother; he was not unhandsome – and Charles was far from handsome – yet James seemed unattractive when compared with the King. He was solemn and rather obstinate; but in one respect he did resemble his brother – his love of the opposite sex. He did not enjoy his brother's success with women, but he was determined to do so as soon as possible.

Lucy met Sir Henry Bennett soon after the arrival of the Duke. Sir Henry had come to Holland with James, and like James was looking for amusement at the quiet Court. As soon as he set eyes on Lucy he decided she could provide this, and when he learned something of her history, he could not believe – in spite of her association with the King – that she would be unwilling to become his mistress.

He called at her apartments, pretending to bring a message from his master. Ann Hill brought him to her mistress whose big brown eyes were wistful as they rested on his handsome figure, for if he had noticed Lucy, Lucy had also noticed him, and although they had not spoken at their first meeting, their glances told each other a good deal.

'Mistress Water!' said Sir Henry, bowing over her hand.

'Welcome to Holland, Sir Henry.'

'I was loth to leave France for Holland,' he said, his warm eyes full of suggestions, 'but had I known I should find you here, Mistress Lucy, my reluctance would have immediately changed to delight.'

'Men's tongues become sugar-coated at the French Court, I've heard.'

'Nay, Lucy. They learn to appreciate beauty and are not chary of expressing that appreciation.'

Lucy signed to Ann to leave them. Ann was hovering, and Lucy knew that she was trying to remind her of her royal lover. Lucy did not want to remember Charles just now; she had remembered him for four months – an age for Lucy – and none but Charles could have kept her faithful so long.

As soon as they were alone Sir Henry was beside her, taking her hands and covering them with kisses.

'You . . . you move too quickly, sir.'

'Madame, in this world of change, one must move quickly.'

'I would have you know of my position here.'

'Do you think I do not know it? Do you think I did not make it my first business to know it, as soon as I set eyes on you?'

'There is a child in the next room who is the King's child.'

'Poor Lucy! You have been long alone, for indeed it is long since His Majesty left for Scotland.'

'I have been faithful to Charles . . .'

'Dear Lucy! What hardship for you! Come, I will show you that a knight in your arms is a better man than a king across the water.'

'That sounds like treason, sir.'

'Who'd not commit treason for you, Lucy!'

Lucy ran from him and made for the door, hoping he would catch her before she reached it, which he did very neatly. He kissed her with passion.

'How dare you, sir!' cried Lucy.

'Because you are so fair and it is a sin that all these charms should be wasted.'

'You shall pay for this, sir.'

'I'll pay with pleasure, Lucy.'

'You will go at once and not dare come here again.' Lucy's voice faded away; she gasped; she sighed; and she pretended to struggle as she was carried into the bedchamber.

*

So Lucy was no longer alone. Lucy had a lover.

The little Court, amused, looked on. What was Charles doing in Scotland? They wondered; they had heard rumours. Was he thinking wistfully of his exiled Court? From all accounts the Covenanters were keeping a stern eye upon him. He must listen to prayers and sermons each day; he must not walk abroad on Sundays; he must spend long hours on his knees. It was a big price, all decided, to ask of a man such as Charles, even for a kingdom. And what of the women of Scotland? How could he elude his jailors – for it seemed they were no less – to enjoy that company in which he so delighted? It was said that he was not permitted even to play cards, and that he had been seen by a pious lady sitting at an open window doing so, and that she had immediately complained to the Commissioners of the Kirk. The King were sternly reprimanded. Cards on the Sabbath! The Scots would not allow that. One of the Commissioners had come in person to rebuke him and had read a long sermon on the evils of card-playing at all times, assuring him that it was a double sin to play on the Sabbath. But this Commissioner had seemed to be aware of the strain the Scots were imposing on the gay young King, for it was said that he whispered before he left: 'And if Your Majesty must play cards, I beg of you to shut the window before commencing.' From which it might be deduced that Charles had found some in Scotland to understand him a little.

He had not been crowned, and the Duke of Hamilton and the Earl of Lauderdale had been warned that he was not to mingle with the people on the streets, for that easy charm would, it was understood, win them to his side; and because he was such a feckless young man no one could tell what effect this might have. The Scots wished to keep Charles Stuart under their control; he was to be the figurehead they would use when they marched against Cromwell's England.

But, said the exiled Court, if there was an opportunity Charles Stuart would have found a mistress, and there were always women in any country; so it was certain that the warmth of Charles Stuart's charm would have dispersed even the frigid mists of Scotland.

In any case Charles might be hurt when he came back to find Lucy unfaithful, but he would understand. He could always understand. Warm and passionate himself, he would be ready to make allowances for Lucy's warm and passionate nature. It was true, Lucy assured herself, that no one of her temperament – or Charles' – could remain faithful to an absent lover for so long. So, after the first reluctant submission which Lucy liked to imagine had taken place by force, she would make assignations with her lover; she would deck herself with finery; she gave herself up to the arts of loving which she practised so well, and in a month after the day when Sir Henry Bennett called at her apartments she found that she was to have his child.

*

A small and solemn party was riding slowly towards Carisbrooke Castle. There were guards before and behind; there were a few servants and a tutor, and in the centre of the party rode two children, the elder a girl of fifteen, the younger a boy of eleven.

As they rode along the boy would take surreptitious glances at the girl down whose cheeks the tears were quietly falling. The pale face of his sister frightened him; her tears worried him, for he knew that she was now even more unhappy than she had been before.

He had always been afraid of his sister, afraid of her passionate courage as well as her frequent tears. She could not be reconciled to their way of living as he could have been. He could have forgotten that he was a prisoner if she would do so.

'But no!' she cried passionately. 'You must not forget. You always remember who we are, and above all you must remember Papa.'

At the mention of his father's name the little boy was always moved to tears. When he was in bed at night he would make a pact with himself: 'I will not think of Papa!' And to his prayers he added 'Please God guard me this night and do not let me dream of Papa.'

He was Prince Henry, but no one but his sister Elizabeth ever referred to his rank. To the servants and his tutor he was Master Harry, and his sister, instead of being Princess Elizabeth, was Mistress Elizabeth. It was said that they were to be made to forget that they were Royal Stuarts. Elizabeth was to be taught button-making and Henry shoe-making, that they might eventually become useful members of the Protector's Commonwealth.

'I would rather die!' cried Elizabeth, and indeed it

seemed that if grief and melancholy could kill, Elizabeth would soon be dead.

Mr Lovel, the little boy's tutor, whispered to him when they were alone that he was not to be afraid. The Protector's bark was worse than his bite, and he uttered these threats in order to humiliate the little boy's mother and brothers.

So, with Mr Lovel to teach him and to give him comfort in secret, Henry could have borne his lot; but his sister was always there to remind him of what they had lost.

She, who was older than he was, remembered so much more of the glorious days. He scarcely remembered his mother; his father he remembered too well. Charles, James and Mary he had scarcely known, and his youngest sister, Henriette, he had never seen at all. Moreover he was physically stronger than Elizabeth, who had broken her leg when she was eight years old and had remained in delicate health thereafter; she grew paler and thinner, but her spirit of resentment against her family's enemies burned more fiercely every day.

'Elizabeth,' he whispered to her now, 'Elizabeth, do not weep so. Perhaps we shall be happy at Carisbrooke.'

'Happy in prison!'

'Perhaps we shall like it better than Penshurst.'

'Shall we enjoy living in that very place where _he_ lived just before . . . just before . . .'

Henry's lips trembled. It would be impossible to forget Papa in the castle where he too had been a prisoner.

Elizabeth said: 'They took Papa there before they murdered him, and now they take us there.'

Henry was remembering it all so clearly as they rode along. He was sure that he would have more vivid dreams in Carisbrooke Castle. Perhaps he would ask Mr Lovel to sleep in his room. Elizabeth would be angry with him if he did so. 'You are afraid to dream of Papa!' she had cried scornfully, when he had told her of his fears. 'I would I _could_ dream of him all through the days and nights! That would be almost like having him with us again.'

Now the little boy was crying. He remembered it all so vividly, for it had happened only a year ago when he had been ten years old. One day – a bitterly cold January day –

men had come to Syon House, which was the prison of his sister and himself at that time, and they said that the children were to pay a visit to their father.

When Elizabeth had heard this she had burst into bitter weeping, and Henry had asked: 'But why do you cry? Do you not want to see Papa?'

'You are too young to understand,' Elizabeth had sobbed. 'Oh, lucky Henry, to be too young!'

But he was no longer young; he had ceased to be young that very day.

He could remember the sharp frosty air, the ice on the water; he remembered riding beside the frozen river and wondering why Elizabeth was crying since they were going to see their father.

And when they had arrived at the Palace of Whitehall, Henry had felt his father to be a different man from the one he had known before, and in his dreams it was the father he saw on that day who always appeared. Henry remembered vividly every detail of that last meeting. He could see his father's face, lined, sad, yet trying to smile as he took Henry on his knee while the weeping Elizabeth clung to his arm. He could see the velvet doublet, the pointed lace collar, the long hair which hung about his father's shoulders.

'So you have come to see me, my children.' He had kissed them in turn. 'Do not weep, beloved daughter. Come, dry your eyes . . . to please me.'

So Elizabeth had dried her eyes and tried to smile; their father had held her tightly to him and kissed the top of her head. Then he had said: 'I must have a little talk with your brother, Elizabeth. See, he is wondering what all this is about. He says, "Why do you weep, when we are together thus? Is it not a time for rejoicing when we are together?" That's what Henry thinks; is it not, my little son?' Henry nodded gravely. 'We wish to be with you more than anything,' he had said. 'Papa, let us be together now . . . and always.'

His father had not answered that, but Henry remembered how his arms had tightened about him.

'My little son,' he had said, 'grave events are afoot. In these times we cannot say where we shall be from one day to another. I am going to ask you to remember this meeting of ours in the years ahead. I want you to remember what I say to you. Will you try to do that?'

'Yes, Papa.'

'Then listen carefully. These are two things I have to say to you, and although you are but ten years old, you are the son of a King, which means that you have to remember much more than other boys. These are the two things I wish you to remember, and if you are ever tempted to forget them, think of this moment when you sit on my knee and your sister stands there trying not to weep, because she is older than you are. The first: You have two brothers. Never allow any to put you on the throne of England while either of them lives. The second is this: Never renounce the Faith of the Church of England in which Mr Lovel has instructed you. There! That is what your father asks of you. Will you do these things for me, and if any should try to turn you from the wish to obey me, remember this day?'

Henry put his arms about his father's neck. 'Yes, Papa. I will remember.'

And shortly after that time he had grown up. He had begun to understand. He knew that the day after he had sat on his father's knee and made his solemn promise, men had taken the King outside the banqueting hall at Whitehall and there, before the eyes of many people, had cut off his head.

That was the spectre which haunted his dreams – his beloved father, a father no more, but a headless corpse, those kind eyes glassy, staring and smiling no more.

If he could only forget his father's death, if he and Elizabeth could only escape from his father's enemies and join their mother, how happy he might be! He did not mean that he would forget his promise to his father; *that* he would never do. But he would be happy in his love for his mother and his brothers and sisters, and he would then be able to forget that last interview, those brooding eyes, so kind and tender and so heartbreakingly sad.

Perhaps one day Elizabeth would help him to escape as she had helped James. She had reproached James for not escaping before. She had mocked him for his cowardice.

'Were I a boy and strong, I'd not long remain the captive of that beast Cromwell!' she had declared. And at last James had escaped and gone across the sea to their mother and brother Charles, who was the King of England now.

After they had been taken back to Syon House following that last interview, Elizabeth had changed. Then young Henry had seen his sister devoid of all hope.

Then to Penshurst where they had lived with the Earl and Countess of Leicester, who had been kind to them but forced to obey the instructions of the Parliament and treat the two children, not as the son and daughter of a King, but as other children of the household. Henry had not cared; it was Elizabeth who had suffered so cruelly.

And then, when she had heard she was to go to Carisbrooke, she had been stricken with horror. Henry had tried to comfort her. 'It is near the sea, Elizabeth. It is very beautiful, they tell me.'

'Near the sea!' she had cried. 'Very beautiful! *He* was there. There he lived and suffered before they took him away to murder him. Every room is a room in which he has lived . . . and waited for them to come for him. He will have watched from the ramparts . . . walked in the courtyards. Are you blind, Henry? Are you quite callous? Are you completely without sensibility? We are going to our father's prison. One of the last places he was in before he was murdered. I would rather *die* . . . than go to Carisbrooke.'

And so she grew paler every day. She begged that she might not be sent to Carisbrooke, but all her entreaties were in vain. 'Send them to Carisbrooke!' said the Protector, and the Protector ruled England.

'Perhaps we shall escape as James did . . . as Henriette did,' Henry whispered to her as they rode along.

'You may, Henry. You *must!*'

She knew she herself never would. She looked to Carisbrooke Castle as the place whither she would go to die.

If she died, pondered Henry, what of one poor little boy, fatherless and alone, cut off from his family?

Mr Lovel rode up to him and tried to banish his melancholy. Did he not think this island was beautiful? He doubted not that the little boy would enjoy more freedom than he had in Kent. 'For, Master Harry, this is an island and the water separates us from England.' Henry was ready to be beguiled; but Elizabeth just stared straight ahead, seeming unaware of the tears which ran down her face.

Then Mr Lovel began to talk of Carisbrooke, which he said was a British camp at the time when the Romans came to Britain. The land surrounding the castle was then covered with thick yew trees, for the Celtic word 'Caerbroc' meant 'the town of yew trees.'

Mr Lovel discoursed pleasantly of the Castle of Carisbrooke, which had faced the winds and storms of the Channel for so many hundreds of years; he told of Fitz-Osborne, the Norman who held the castle on condition that he defended it and the surrounding lands against all enemies, so that it was called The Honour of Carisbrooke. He told of Montacute, Earl of Salisbury, who had left his mark upon it in the reign of the second Richard, and of Lord Woodville who, years later, had enlarged the place. But Mr Lovel could not continue with the Castle's history for the simple reason that it had played a part in the tragedy of Henry's father. So he came to an abrupt stop and spoke of other things.

Thus it had often been, Henry remembered. There were frequently those sudden terminations of conversation. It was as though people said: 'Ah, now we are coming near to dangerous ground; we are approaching that terrible thing of which this little boy knows nothing.'

At last they reached the Castle, and Henry lifted his eyes to the Keep, high on its artificial mound; the ramparts, the barbican and the battlements seemed impregnable as they looked down in arrogance at the cosier Priory. The walls of the fortress were in the shape of a pentagon with five bastions of defence. The little party crossed the fosse and in a short time were in the Castle Yard, where Henry saw the well with a great wheel turned by a donkey in the same way that a dog laboured in a turnspit.

The servants came out to see them; they did not bow or kiss their hands. They merely nudged each other and made such remarks as: 'Oh, 'tis Mistress Elizabeth and Master Harry come to Carisbrooke.'

Elizabeth looked past them as though they did not exist,

but Henry gave them a forlorn smile, for he understood, since Mr Lovel had told him, that these people did not wish to be disrespectful to the son and daughter of the King; they had to remember that there was now no King and therefore no Prince and Princess; they were all citizens of the Commonwealth, and the Isle of Wight was a part of Cromwell's England.

He dismounted and walked beside Elizabeth who looked small and frail in the big hall of the Castle; the mourning clothes, which she had refused to lay aside since the death of her father, hung loosely on her form. She would not eat the food which had been prepared for them. Henry tried not to eat, but he was so hungry, and Mr Lovel pointed out that he could not help Elizabeth by joining in her fast. And very soon Elizabeth retired to her bed and, when she was there, she asked that she might speak to her brother before she slept.

Henry was frightened more than ever when he looked at the pale face of his sister.

'Henry,' she said, 'I feel I shall not live long. I should not want to . . . in this prison. The happiest thing that could happen to me – since our enemies will not let me join our sister Mary in Holland – would be to join our father in Heaven.'

'You must not talk thus,' said Henry.

'Death is preferable to the lives we lead now, Henry. They are a dishonour to a line of Kings.'

'One day my brother will come to England and drive the Beast Cromwell away.'

Elizabeth turned her face to the wall. 'I fear our brother lacks the strength of our father, Henry.'

'Charles . . . !' stammered the boy. 'But Charles is now the King. All loyal subjects proclaim him such.'

'Our brother is not as our father was, Henry. I fear he will never live as our father lived.'

'Would it not be better so, dear Elizabeth, since our father's way of life led him to the scaffold?'

'Our father's way of life! How can you say such things! It was not our father's way of life which led him there; it was the wickedness of his enemies. Father was a saint and martyr.'

'Then,' said the little boy gravely, 'since our brother is not a saint he will not die as a martyr.'

'It is better to die or live in exile than to do that which is unkingly.'

'But our brother would not do that which is unkingly.'

'He is in Scotland now. He has joined the Covenanters. He has made himself a pawn for the Scots for the sake of a kingdom. But you are too young to understand. I would have lived in poverty and exile . . . yes, I would have been a button-maker, rather than have betrayed our father.'

Henry could not help being glad that his brother was not like his father. He personally knew little of Charles, but he had heard much of him. He had seen the smiles which came on to people's faces when they spoke of him. He had his own picture of Charles – a brother as tall as his father had been, with always a song on his lips and a shrug of the shoulders for trouble. Henry had always thought it would be rather wonderful to be with such a brother. He did not believe he would take him on his knee and talk of solemn promises. Charles was jaunty, a sinner of some sort, yet people loved him; he might not be good, as his father and Elizabeth were good, but he would be a happy person to be with.

Elizabeth put a thin hand on his wrist. 'Henry, your thoughts stray. You do not give your mind to what I am saying. Here we are in this terrible place; here, in this room, our father may have paced up and down thinking of us all . . . our mother and brothers and sisters – all scattered, all exiles from the land we were born to rule! Henry, I cannot live in this Castle, I cannot endure these great rooms, these stone walls and . . . the spirit of our father. I cannot endure it.'

'Elizabeth, perhaps we could escape.'

'I shall soon . . . escape, Henry. I know it. I shall not be here long. This prisoner of Cromwell will soon elude him.'

'Perhaps we could slip away from here. Perhaps there might be a boat to take us to Holland. I should have to dress as a girl, as James did. . . .'

Elizabeth smiled. 'You will do that, Henry. You will do it.'

'I should not go without you. This time you will come too.'

'I have a feeling you will go alone, Henry, for there will be no need for me to go with you.'

Then she turned her face to the wall and he knew that she was crying.

He thought: What good can come of crying? What good can come of grieving? They say Charles is always merry, that he does not let his sorrows interfere with his pleasures.

Henry longed to be with his gay brother.

Then, realizing how callous he was, he took his sister's hand and kissed it. 'I'll never leave you, Elizabeth,' he said. 'I'll stay with you all my life.'

She smiled then. 'May God bless you, Henry,' she said. 'You will always remember what our father said to you, won't you?'

'I will always remember.'

'Even when I am not here to remind you?'

'You will always be with me, for I shall never leave you.'

She shook her head as though she had some special knowledge of the future, and it seemed that she had, for a week after her arrival at Carisbrooke Castle, Elizabeth developed a fever which, mingling with her melancholy and her desire for death, robbed her of her life, and from then on there was only one young prisoner at Carisbrooke Castle. He found a way out of his loneliness in dreams, and those dreams were always of his family. He fancied that his mother came to sit by his bed each night; he could almost feel her good night kiss upon his brow.

One day, he told himself, I shall be with them all.

In reunion he would come to perfect happiness, and looking forward to that happy day he forgot he was a prisoner.

*

In her mother's apartments at the Louvre, Henriette sat with her governess, Lady Morton, who was teaching her to make fine stitches on a piece of tapestry, when Queen Henrietta Maria came into the room. Anne Morton was glad it was a needlework lesson; Henrietta Maria was suspicious of all that was taught the Princess and was apt to fly into a passion if she heard the governess say anything which she might construe as 'heresy'.

Lady Morton often thought of her own children in England who surely needed her; it was four years since, disguised as a servant, she had fled from England with the Princess on her back, and in those four years she had thought constantly of her own family. She knew she was fighting a losing battle against Henrietta Maria and Père Cyprien; they were determined to have this child for their Church, and they were succeeding.

But now Henrietta Maria had not come to talk of religion to her daughter and the governess. She burst in dramatically, for Henrietta Maria was dramatic by nature. Her black eyes were almost closed up with weeping; she was carelessly dressed and her tiny gesticulating hands betrayed her despair even more than the signs of grief on her face.

This was indeed *La Reine Malheureuse*.

She came straight to the Princess and, as little Henriette would have knelt – for the Queen was stricter in her observances of etiquette here in exile than she had ever been in her own Court of Whitehall – she lifted her in her arms and, bursting into bitter weeping, held the child's face against her own.

Henriette remained passively unhappy, patiently waiting for her mother to release her. There was new trouble, she concluded. It seemed to her that there was always trouble. At such times she longed more passionately than ever for her brother Charles, for whatever the trouble he never mourned about it; he would more often laugh at it with a lift of the shoulders; and that was how Henriette wanted to meet trouble when it came to her.

At first she was terrified that this bad news might concern Charles. He was in Scotland, she knew; her mother railed about it at great length; she had sworn that Charles had gone to Scotland without her consent; she was angry because Charles was now a man who could make his own decisions, no longer a boy to be guided by her. 'His father listened to my advice!' she had cried when he had gone to Scotland. 'He never will. Your father was a man with experience of ruling a kingdom. This is a boy who has never been acknowledged King by the English; yet he flouts his mother's advice.'

Henriette began to pray silently that the trouble did not concern Charles.

'My child,' cried Henrietta Maria, 'you have lost your sister Elizabeth. News has come to me that she has died of a fever in Carisbrooke Castle.'

Henriette tried to look concerned, but as she had never seen Elizabeth she could scarcely grieve for her; moreover she was delighted that it was not Charles who was in trouble.

'My daughter ... my little girl!' cried the Queen. 'What will become of us all? There is my son ... my little Henry, left now in that Castle where his father suffered imprisonment before his murder. When shall I see my son Henry? What evil is befalling him in that place with his enemies about him? Oh, I am the unhappiest of women! Where are my children now? Am I to lose them as I lost my husband? My son Charles pays no heed to his mother. He goes to Scotland and makes terms with the Covenanters. He fritters away his time, I hear, in dicing and women ...'

'Mam,' said Henriette quickly, 'what does it mean to fritter away his time with dicing and women?'

The Queen, as though suddenly aware of her daughter, gripped her so firmly that the little girl thought she would be suffocated. 'My little one ... my precious little one! You at least shall be saved for God.'

'But Charles and his dice ... and women?'

'Ah! You hear too much. You must never repeat what you hear. Lady Morton, you stand there weeping. That is for my little Elizabeth ... my little daughter. ... What will become of us all, I wonder? What will become of us ...?'

'Madam, I doubt not that one day King Charles will recover his kingdom. There are many in England who long to see him on the throne.'

'But he has made this pact with the Covenanters.'

'Mayhap they will help him to regain his kingdom.'

'At what cost, at what cost! And my little Elizabeth ...

so young to die. We made plans for her at the time of her birth ... my dearest Charles and I. Oh, I am the most unhappy of women. What would I not give to hear his voice again ... to have him here to share this burden with me!'

'He had too many burdens in life, madam. This would but have added to them.'

Henrietta Maria stamped her foot. 'It would not have happened had he been alive. They have not only killed their King but their King's daughter.'

'Madam, you distress yourself.'

'You speak the truth, Anne. Prepare the Princess for Chaillot. I must go there at once. Only there can I find the comfort I need, the fortitude to bear the blows which God would seem to delight in dealing me.'

The Princess turned to her mother. 'Mam, may I not stay with Nan?'

'My dearest, I want you with me. You too will wish to mourn for your sister.'

'I can mourn here, Mam. Nan and I can mourn together.'

Henrietta Maria forgot her grief for a moment. She looked sharply at Lady Morton. What did she teach the little Henriette when they were alone? Père Cyprien had said that the child asked too many questions. It was perhaps time Lady Morton went home; she had her own children. A mother should not be separated from her own in the service of her Princess.

'Nay, child, you shall come with me to Chaillot. You too, shall have the comfort of those quiet walls.'

'Madam,' said Lady Morton, 'if you would care to leave the Princess in my charge . . .'

Henrietta Maria narrowed her eyes. 'I have declared she shall come with me to Chaillot,' she said firmly. 'Lady Morton, you have been a good and faithful servant. I shall never forget how you brought the Princess to me here in France. The saints will bless you forever for what you did. But I fear we trespass too much on your generosity and your loyalty. I often remind my daughter that you have children of your own.'

Henriette was looking into her governess's face. Lady Morton had flushed slightly. The Queen had touched on a problem which had long given her cause for anxiety. It was four years since she had seen her family and she longed to be with them; yet she had never asked that she should be allowed to go home. She had felt it her duty to stay in France and do battle with Père Cyprien over the religion of the Princess Henriette.

The Queen and Père Cyprien were determined to make a Catholic of her; yet Lady Morton knew that it had been her father's wish that she should be brought up in accordance with the tenets of the Church of England. She could not have understood how Henrietta Maria, who wept so bitterly for her husband, could work against his wishes in this way, had she not understood the nature of the widowed Queen. Henrietta Maria was a Catholic first; and anything else took second place to that. Lady Morton knew that she would have beaten the little girl whom she now fondled so tenderly, if the child had shown any signs of refusing to accept the Catholic faith. Moreover Henrietta Maria had always been able to believe what she wanted to believe, and now she was able to assure herself – in direct contradiction of the facts – that the child's religious teaching had been left in her hands. And as Anne Morton looked at this fervent little woman with the snapping black eyes, she wondered once more whether Charles I might not still be alive had he married, instead of the French woman, the bride from Spain who had at first been intended for him.

Now there was a subtler meaning behind the Queen's words concerning Lady Morton. Was she thinking of dismissing her? It would seem so. She wanted Père Cyprien to take over the education of her daughter completely; she wanted no heretic to have a hand in it. Henrietta Maria would wave aside the valiant part Anne Morton had played in bringing her daughter to France; she would forget that which she had vowed never to forget, for it would be in the name of the Holy Catholic Church. She would forget her gratitude to Anne as she had forgotten the wishes of her husband whom she continued to mourn. Henrietta Maria was a tornado of emotions; and Lady Morton had to make up her mind whether her duty lay with her own children or with the Princess.

Henrietta Maria was watching her slyly, guessing her thoughts. Even in that moment of grief for her daughter Elizabeth, she would not swerve in what she called the battle for the soul of Henriette.

'And now,' the Queen was saying, 'we shall prepare for Chaillot. There we shall mourn together, dearest. Lady Morton, prepare the Princess. You will not accompany us, of course.'

The Princess was led away, thinking sadly of the rigorous life at Chaillot, of the solemn nuns in their black garments, of the hard wood on which she had to kneel for so long, of the cold rooms and the continual ringing of bells. And what if Charles should come while she was there and go away again without seeing her?

She mentioned this to Anne, who said: 'But he is in Scotland. He cannot come so soon. You will doubtless be back in the Louvre before he is again in Paris. Moreover . . .' She paused and Henriette had to urge her to go on. 'It is nothing,' she added. 'I know nothing.'

Henriette stamped her foot – a habit learned of her mother. 'I will not have you start to tell me something and then stop. You do it often. I wish to know. I wish to know.'

Then Anne Morton knelt down so that her face was on a level with that of the Princess. Anne was near crying, Henriette saw; she put her arms about her neck and kissed the governess. 'Anne, are you crying for Elizabeth?' she asked.

'Not only for her, my darling. For us all.'

'Why for us all?'

'Because life has become so hard for us.'

'Are you thinking of your children in England?'

'Of them . . . and of you . . . I pray we shall soon all be in England.'

'Do you think we shall?'

'Well, suppose the Scots helped your brother to regain his throne, and suppose he was crowned in London, and suppose you all went home . . .'

Henriette clasped her hands. 'I will think of that, Anne. All the time I am at Chaillot I will think of that. Then the time will pass quickly perhaps.'

But the time at Chaillot did not pass quickly. There was more bad news.

The Prince of Orange, who was the husband of Henriette's sister Mary, died, and there was more shedding of bitter tears. In vain did little Henriette try to comfort her mother. 'But this is not so bad, dear Mam, is it? Not as bad as Elizabeth's death. Elizabeth was my own sister and your daughter, but the Prince is only the husband of Mary . . .'

'My child, you are but six years old, yet you have already known more sorrow than many know in a lifetime. This is a sad thing . . . in a way it is sadder than the death of Elizabeth for, my love, Elizabeth was but a little girl . . . a prisoner. We loved her dearly and her death hurt us in one way; but the death of your other sister's husband touches us more closely. Now that he is dead, your sister has not the same power, and there are men in her country who wish to be friends with Cromwell.'

'The beast Cromwell?'

'The beast Cromwell!' Henrietta Maria spat out the words, and the Cromwell in the Princess's mind was an ape-like figure with terrible teeth and a crown on his head – her father's crown. 'They are friends of the beast, so they will not offer the hospitality to your brothers that they have received in the Prince's day.'

'Won't there be another Prince, Mam?'

'Yes. We hope that when your sister's child is born he will be the Prince.'

'Then they won't dare be friends with the beast?'

'He will be but a baby. He can do little while he is so young. Oh, was there ever such an unhappy woman as your mother, child? Was there?'

'There was our Lady of Sorrows,' said Henriette.

Then Henrietta Maria swept up her daughter in one of her suffocating embraces. 'You comfort me, my daughter,' she said. 'You must always comfort me. You can, you know. A little girl like you can make up for all I have suffered.

'I will, Mam. I will make you *La Reine Heureuse* instead of *La Reine Malheureuse*.'

There were more close embraces; and Henriette could not understand why that which she had offered as comfort should open the gates to more floods of tears.

*

There was one happy event which pleased the Queen: her daughter Mary gave birth to a son. He was christened William and there was great rejoicing, not only through-out Holland but in the convent of Chaillot. Henriette was delighted. Now there would be no more tears; now they could be gay.

The Queen talked frequently of her grandchild. 'My first grandchild . . . my very first!' She thought fleetingly of that bonny boy whom Charles called Jemmy. If that boy had been the child of Charles' wife instead of that low woman Lucy Water, what a happy woman she would have been! Henriette too was thinking of Jemmy. She reminded her mother of him. 'He is your grandchild too, Mam. And, Mam, it is said that Charles already has more than one son.'

'Then they should have their tongues cut out for say-ing it!'

'Why, Mam? Is it not a matter for rejoicing when a king has many sons?'

'When a king decides to have sons he should first take the precaution of marrying.'

'Why, Mam?'

'Because when a man is a king he should have sons who could follow him as kings.'

Henriette as usual sought excuses for her brother. 'May-hap as he has no crown, he thought he need not have a marriage.'

'He is a gay rogue, your brother.'

Henriette laughed; she did not mind Charles being called that, when it was done in such a manner that 'rogue' was almost a compliment.

'He is the most wonderful person in the world, Mam,' she said. 'How I wish he could be here!'

She looked eagerly at her mother, hoping that her atti-tude had softened towards her eldest son; but there were so many emotions to be seen in the Queen's face that it was impossible to know which train of thought she was following.

'Would the Prince of Orange had lived to see his son!' said Henrietta Maria fervently.

'Still, Mam, it is a good thing that he has left a son, even though he is not here to see him.'

Shortly afterwards they returned to their apartments in the Louvre, and there a shock awaited the Princess, for Anne Morton came to her and told her she was going home to England.

'I have my own children who need me,' she explained.

'But I need you,' said Henriette, her eyes filling with tears.

'My dearest, I must go. I have outlived my usefulness to you.'

'I'll not let you go, Nan. You are my Nan. Did you not bring me here? Nan, do not talk of going. Instead let us talk of the days when we left England and I insisted on telling everyone that I was a Princess.'

'That was long ago, sweetheart. Now you have your mother and Père Cyprien to look after you, and you no longer need your Nan.'

So, thought Henriette, Anne was leaving because of the conflict between her and Père Cyprien. Henriette threw herself into her governess's arms and begged her not to go. But Anne's mind was made up, and so was the Queen's, and beside those overwhelming factors, the tears and entreaties of a little Princess carried no weight.

*

There came a wonderful day in the life of Henriette. It was during the October following her seventh birthday, and her mother and those about her had been more than usually sombre for a long time.

Henriette had tried to discover what it was that saddened them, but no one answered her questions. She was just set to do her lessons under the guidance of Père Cyprien, to read the holy books he brought for her, and so to study how to be a good Catholic.

Then one day her mother said to her: 'My daughter, we are going to meet someone. I want you to ride with me out of Paris to greet this person. Wear your prettiest clothes. You will be glad you have done this when you see who this person is.'

One name trembled on Henriette's lips, but she did not say it; she was afraid that if she said that name her mother might shake her head and say impatiently: 'How can that be! You know he is in Scotland.'

So she waited, wondering who it could be; and on the road between Paris and Fècamp, she was suddenly gloriously happy; for it was Charles himself whom they had ridden out to meet.

She stared at him for some seconds before she recognized him. He had changed so much. His beautiful curls had all been cut off, and his hair was like a thick black cap that did not reach below his ears. He was bearded and seemed even darker than before. He was taller than she remembered, and gaunt; he was no longer a young man. His face was tanned with sun and wind; there were fresh lines about his mouth; his expression was less gentle, more cynical, and the strain of melancholy was more pronounced. But it was Charles. There were the same large eyes ready to twinkle, the mouth so ready to curve into a smile.

And when he saw her his expression became doubly sweet. He cried: 'Why, if it is not my Minette! And growing fast! Almost a young woman.'

She forgot her manners and cried: 'Charles! Dear Charles! This is the happiest day since you went away!'

Then she was aware of her mother's eyes upon her, and hastily she knelt and kissed the hand of her King.

*

They were together often in the apartment of the Louvre. She contrived to be with him whenever possible and he, characteristically, aided her in this. She would curl up at his feet or sit close to him on a window seat; and she would take his hand and hold it firmly between her own small ones as though to imply that if he tried to leave her she would hold him against his will.

'You have been a long time away, Charles,' she scolded. 'I was afraid you would never return.'

' 'Twas no wish of mine, Minette; and constantly I thought of you,' he told her. 'How gladly would I have fled from those dreary Presbyterians to be in Paris!'

'Were they very gloomy, Charles?'

'Deadly. They preached all the time; I was called upon to say my prayers it seemed a hundred times a day.'

'Like Chaillot,' murmured Henriette.

'I'll tell you this, Minette. Presbyterianism is no religion for a gentleman of my tastes.'

'Your tastes are for dicing and women,' she told him.

That made him laugh aloud and she held his hand more tightly than ever. What could be said to Charles of Charles could produce nothing but hilarious laughter, whereas said to others it would bring shocked reproaches. She loved that quality in him.

'So you begin to understand your brother, eh?'

She nodded. 'Tell me about Scotland, Charles.'

'Oh that! It was dull ... dull! You would go to sleep if I told you. No! I will tell you what befell me in England, shall I? That makes a more stirring tale.'

'Yes, please, dear Charles, tell me what befell you in England.'

'It is only due to miraculous providence that you see me here, Minette. There was not only one miracle, but many were required to bring your brother back to you. And the wonder is that those miracles happened.'

'What would have happened if you had not come back?'

'At this hour my head would be on a pike on London Bridge and people passing would point up to it and say: "There is Charles Stuart – the second Charles Stuart – who came to seek his crown and left us his head!" '

'No, no no!' she cried.

'There, Minette, it was but a joke. There is no need for tears. My head is firm on my shoulders. Feel it. See how firm it is. Charles Stuart will never lose his head ... except when dealing with your sex.'

'You must never lose it ... never!'

'But to lose it in that way is not to have it cut off, sweetheart. It is just to love ... so that all else seems of no importance. But I am talking foolishly as, alas, I so often do. No more of heads. I'll tell you what befell me in England,

and you must have no fear of what is past. What's done is done, and here I am beside you. So while you listen to me remember this: I passed under the noses of my enemies and I came back here unharmed. Minette, I have been defeated by my enemies; but perhaps in some sense I have triumphed over them. I sought to win my crown, and in that I failed; they sought to make me their captive, and in that *they* failed. A stalemate, you see, therefore a victory for neither, and one day I will try again. Minette, there is something within me which tells me that I shall one day win my throne, that one day I shall be crowned England's King. 'Tis a fate well worth waiting for, eh? God's Body! 'tis so indeed.'

She listened to him, watching his lips as he talked, looking now and then into those gentle humorous eyes which were momentarily sad, but never for long.

He told her of marching down from Scotland to England, of the fierce battle he and his supporters had fought against the Parliamentary forces. She did not understand all he said; but it seemed to her that he brought a thousand pictures of himself and held them up for her to see, and she believed she would remember them for ever; she would preserve them, and when he was not with her that would, in some measure, serve instead of his exuberant presence.

She saw him, tall and dark, sitting his horse with his men about him; they would be sad and dejected, for they had suffered terrible defeat at Worcester, and many of his friends were in the hands of the enemy. He had escaped by the first of the miracles, and as the few survivors from the battle clustered about him, they would be wondering how they could escape from a hostile country where at any moment, from behind any bush, their enemies might spring upon them.

She pictured him, rising with the Catholic gentleman, Charles Giffard and his servant Yates, whom Charles' devoted supporter, the Earl of Derby, had produced to guide him through the dangerous country to Whiteladies and Boscobel, where there were many places in which a King might hide. She saw him stopping at an inn for a hasty tankard of ale and then riding on through the night, bread and meat in one hand, eating as he rode, because he dared not stay but must journey south since the enemy and their scouts were waiting for him at every turn. She felt she was with him in the saddle as, in the early morning light, he saw in the distance the ruined Cistercian convent of Whiteladies.

He was silent for a while, his face hardened because he was thinking it was a bitter thing that England's King should depend on the bounty of humble Englishmen for a night's lodging.

'Did you stay in the ruined convent, brother?' asked Henriette.

'It is not a convent now. It had been turned into a farmhouse. It was the property of the gentleman, Giffard, who had brought us there. We were not sure whom we could trust, sister. That was why every movement we made was perilous. I remember standing beneath a casement window which was opened suddenly and a man's head appeared. I knew this to be one of the Penderels, a family who had been servants to the Giffards, and who were now tenants of Whiteladies. There were three Penderel brothers living at Whiteladies, and this I guessed to be one of them.

' "Bring you news of Worcester?" cried a voice as the head appeared. It was that of a young man.

'Giffard answered: "Oh, 'tis you, George Penderel. The worst news from Worcester I could bring. The King is defeated!"

' "What happened to His Majesty?" asked George Penderel.

' "He escaped and waits your pleasure below!" I answered.

'Then, my Minette, we were brought into Whiteladies and, to appease my hunger and thirst I was given wine and biscuits; and never, Minette, had food tasted so good as that did. So I sat on the floor with Derby, Shrewsbury, Cleveland, Buckingham and Wilmot about me, and we discussed with Giffard and these Penderels what might next be done.'

She clasped her hands together. 'What wine was it, Charles?'

'Sack . . . the best in the world.'

'It shall always be my favourite.'

'Sister, you say such quaint and charming things that touch my heart and make me love you.'

Then he told her how the Penderel brothers sent a message to Boscobel, and more Penderels came to the aid of the King.

'I changed my clothes, Minette. I wore a green jerkin and breeches, a doublet of doeskin and a hat with a steeple crown – oh, such a dirty hat! I was loth to put it on my head. And when I put on these clothes and my own were buried in the garden, the man under that greasy hat still looked like Charles Stuart and none other – so what do you think? It was Wilmot, merry Wilmot – who could never be serious, even at such a time – who said: "We must shear the sheep, for by his curls shall they know him." And by God's Body, without a by-your-leave, the rogue set about hacking my hair with a knife – and a pretty bad job he made of it – and there were those Penderels and those Yateses and their servants catching my curls as they fell, declaring they would put them away and keep them for ever.'

'I wish you had kept one of your curls for me, Charles.'

'One of my curls! They are all yours, Minette – entirely and for ever yours. And what would you want of one small curl when you have the whole of the man at your command?'

'For when you go away again.'

'You must remind me to give you one when next I depart.'

'I pray you do not talk so soon of parting.'

'Nay, Minette, I shall stay here for as long as I can . . . having nowhere else to go and no money even to buy me a shirt. Here's a pretty pass! Would you believe I was the King of England – a King without a shirt or the wherewithal to buy one?'

'One day you will have as many shirts as you desire.'

'Alas, dear Minette, so many of my desires go beyond shirts. Now I will tell you how Mistress Yates brought me a dish of eggs, milk, sugar and apples, such as I had never tasted before and which seemed good to me; and when I had eaten again, I stood up in my leather doublet and my

116

greasy hat and learned to walk in a loping manner as a rustic would, and Yates taught me how not to betray myself by my speech. I was a sorry failure. I could not rid myself of Charles Stuart. There he was . . . always ready to leap out and betray me . . . in my speech . . . in my walk . . . my very gestures. We heard that a party of Roundheads was not far off, so I went and hid in the woods while they called at the house to ask if Cavaliers had ridden that way; one of the party, they stressed, was a tall, dark, lean man. George Penderel said that such a party had passed that way but had headed away to the north some hour or more since . . . and off they rode; and as soon as dusk fell I went back to the house and nursed little Nan Penderel while her mother cooked eggs and bacon for my supper.'

'What was she like, Nan Penderel? Did you love her?'

'I loved her, Minette, because she reminded me of my own little sister.'

He told her of his arrival at Boscobel, a hunting lodge, and the home of other members of the Penderel family.

'I had walked so far that my feet were sore and bleeding, and Joan Penderel – who was the wife of William and lived with him at Boscobel – washed my feet and put pads of paper between my toes where the skin was rubbed. I rested there and I ate again; but the neighbourhood was full of Roundhead soldiers, and it was certain that soon they would arrive at the house. Staying at Boscobel was a friend and good Royalist, Colonel Carlis, who had escaped from the Battle of Worcester, and was so delighted to see me that he wept – partly with joy to see me alive, partly with sorrow to see me in these straits – and he and I went out and climbed a great oak tree. The leaves were thick and they hid us, but we could peep through and see all that went on below. And while we were up there, we saw the soldiers searching the woods for us; and that was another miracle, Minette. Had we hidden anywhere but in an oak tree we should have been discovered; but who would look for a King in an oak tree? So Colonel Carlis and I waited hidden yet watching, while below us the Roundheads wandered about searching for me.'

'I shall love oak trees for ever,' said Henriette.

Charles kissed her and they fell silent. Henriette was

seeing pictures of Charles on a horse, riding for his life, a piece of bread and meat in his hand; Charles in a greasy hat, and pads of paper between his toes; Charles hidden in an oak, the leaves of which hid him from his enemies.

He was thinking of these things too; but he did not see them as Henriette did. He saw himself an exile, a King without a crown; he had left more than his curls behind him in England; he had left his youth, his lighthearted optimism; he felt jaded, cynical, and at times even careless of his crown.

Now he spent his time dicing and with women, as they had said of him in his little sister's hearing.

He burst into sudden laughter.

It was perhaps a more satisfying way of passing one's time than fighting for lost causes.

*

At her lodgings in The Hague, Lucy heard of the King's return. She stared at her reflection in her mirror as Ann Hill tired her hair. Ann knew what she was thinking, and shook her head sadly. How differently she would have behaved had she been the King's mistress!

Lucy said suddenly: 'Do not look at me thus, girl!'

'I am sorry, madam,' said Ann, lowering her eyes.

'He has been away so long,' said Lucy sullenly. 'It was too long. I was faithful to him for many weeks.'

'A long time for you, madam.'

If it had not required so much effort, Lucy would have boxed the creature's ears.

'You are judging me, Ann Hill,' she contented herself with saying. 'Take care I do not send you back to the gutter.'

'You would not do that. You and I could not do without each other now.'

'Do not deceive yourself. I could find a woman as clever with her fingers as you are, and less impudent with her tongue.'

'But not one that would love you as I do, and it is because I love you that I say what is in my mind.'

'Because you love him, you mean.'

'Madam, he is the King!'

'Oh, do not think of his rank. I have heard that he does not hesitate to take a serving wench, should the fancy move him.'

Ann blushed and turned away.

'There!' cried Lucy. 'You see how you are! It is small wonder that you lack a lover. Men love those who are prepared to adventure anywhere with them. They look at such as myself and say: "Lucy is ready for anything! Lucy is the one for me!" And they are right, for, Ann, I cannot live without a lover. I soon discovered that. I took my first lover when my home was being plundered by Roundhead soldiers, and I had only met him an hour or so before. When you can make love in such circumstances you will be one of whom the men will say: "Ah! she is the one for me!" '

'His Majesty, knowing that while he risked his life at Worcester, you were sporting with another man, will not be likely to say: "She is the one for me!" I promise you that.'

'You promise me? What right have you to promise me anything? But, Ann, you are right. He would not have minded a little falling into temptation – who could understand that more readily than he? – but there is Mary.'

'Ah! There is Mary.'

'Some would have seen to it that the child was never born. I could not do that. I was too tenderhearted.'

'You are too lazy,' said Ann.

'Come nearer, girl, that I may box your ears.'

'Dearest mistress, how will you explain little Mary when His Majesty comes?'

'How can one explain a child? A child explains itself. There is only one way of begetting children. But I could say the child was yours.'

Angry colour rose to Ann's cheeks. 'There is not one person in this town who does not know she is yours and the Colonel's. Did you not start to call yourself Mistress Barlow when you grew large, so that people would think you had gone through the married state at some time?'

'It's true, Ann. You cannot take credit for our little bastard. I believe I can hear her crying now ... Go and see.'

Ann went away and soon came back with the baby. A

boy of two years old, with lively black eyes, followed her into the room.

'Ah!' she said. 'And here is young Jemmy too.'

Jemmy ran to his mother and climbed on to her lap. She laughed at his boisterous ways. He was the spoilt darling of the household, and his flashing dark eyes held a look of confidence that everything he wanted would be his.

Lucy kissed him fondly.

'Mamma,' he said, 'Jemmy wants sweetmeats.'

His greedy little hands were already pilfering sweets from the dish beside her. She watched him, as he crammed them into his mouth.

The son of a King! she mused. And the sight of him brought back memories of Charles which made her a little sad. She was wishing, not that she had been faithful to this boy's father – Lucy was not one to wish for the impossible – but that he had not gone away. She wished that the little girl, whom Ann was soothing, had had the same father as the boy. A sparkle of animation came momentarily to Lucy's face. Would it be possible to pass the girl off as Charles' daughter? Suppose she had arrived a little earlier. . . . But it was impossible. Too many people had noted her arrival, had laughed up their sleeves because Charles' mistress had taken a new lover. No! There was no way of explaining Mary; Charles would have to know.

'More sweeties! More sweeties!' cried the greedy Jemmy.

Lucy caressed the thick curly hair. At least Charles must be grateful for a boy like this one.

Henry came in and sent the children away with Ann, for naturally Henry had not come to see the children. His glowing eyes were appreciative of his plump mistress.

Later she said to him: 'His Majesty is in Paris, Henry.'

'It's true. Soon he will be seeking his Lucy. What then?'

'What then?' echoed Lucy.

'Sydney had to stand aside. I should not care to do that. I rejoice that we have the child to show him.'

'What will the King say to that, think you?'

'He'll understand. Who better? That's Charles' way. He'll not blame us. How can he? He'll see how matters stood. How could he expect you to be faithful for so long?

He knows how easy it is to fall into temptation. He loves us both, so he'll forgive us. You look sad, Lucy. Do you feel regretful for His Royal Highness?' I'll warrant he has nothing I lack . . . apart from his royalty.'

'He is a very kind and tender man.'

'And I am not! Nay! You mean he is the King, and that counts for much. Come, cheer up! Be lighthearted as he will be, I am sure. I'll tell you of a sight I saw outside the town yesterday. 'Tis a statue to a woman who is said to have borne as many children as there are days in the year – and all at one time. What an achievement, eh? What if, instead of one proof of our love, we had 365 to show His Majesty? What do you think he would say to that, eh?'

Lucy began to laugh. She said: 'This is what he would do. He would laugh. He always laughs.'

'There is no need to fear the wrath of a man who is so ready to laugh as is our gracious King. Come, Lucy. Stop fretting. Three hundred and sixty-five all at one birth, eh? What manner of man was he to father such; what manner of woman she to bear them! I'll warrant they were no more skilled than we are, Lucy. How would you like to see a statue raised to you in this town, eh?'

So they laughed, and very soon they were kissing and caressing.

They had nothing to fear from a King who, being so skilled in the arts of loving, understood so much.

*

In Paris Mademoiselle de Montpensier was discovering a new quality in the young King. He now spoke French without embarrassment; he had left his shyness behind him with his luxuriant locks.

He was skilled in the graceful art of paying compliments; even the young French gallants could not do so more graciously than he could, and with the words he spoke went such eloquent looks from those large brown eyes that Mademoiselle was tempted to consider him seriously as a husband.

Charles was certainly seriously considering her as a wife. She was handsome – though not as handsome as she believed herself to be – and she was rich and royal. He could not make a more suitable marriage, he believed, than with the daughter of the King's uncle.

He thought of Lucy now and then. He had little fancy for Lucy now. He was not the inexperienced boy who had been her lover; he had grown up since he had last seen Lucy. Adventures such as he had experienced since he had left the Continent had done much to change him. He had sobered considerably, though this was not outwardly visible; he had lost those wild dreams of easily regaining his kingdom; the defeat at Worcester had marked him deeply; not only had it set shadows beneath his eyes, etched new lines of cynicism about his mouth; it had touched the inner man.

He was indolent; he knew it now, and he blamed himself for his defeat at Worcester. He firmly believed – for his gift of seeing himself without self-bias had been heightened by his misfortunes – that a better man would not have suffered defeat.

He had had a chance and lost it. He did not blame the superior forces of the Parliament, ill-luck, bad weather, or any of the ready-made excuses of defeated generals; it was characteristic of him that he blamed none but Charles Stuart. Somewhere he had failed. He had failed in Scotland; he had failed at Worcester; and he blamed himself because of his inclination to shrug his shoulders and think of dancing, gambling and going to bed with women, rather than starting a new campaign. He often thought: If the first Charles Stuart had had the power of the second Charles to see himself as he really was, and the second Charles had had the noble inclinations of the first Charles, they would, combined, have made one Charles worthy to wear the crown of England. It was a distressing foible to know oneself too well.

He had thought of this when riding with Jane Lane through the Forest of Arden. Dear Jane! So beautiful, so aloof, yet so entirely conscious that she rode pillion with the King. William, she had called him – William Jackson, her humble servant, who must accompany her on a journey. He would never forget that journey, the beautiful girl riding pillion behind him. He had been dressed as a farmer's son in a grey cloak and high black hat; and for a week, Jane – and only Jane – had held his life in her hands. Yet never once had he attempted to make careless love to her, though when he said adieu to Jane, he had ceased to long for Lucy.

Lucy had a child now; he had heard that she was Sir Henry Bennett's mistress. He was fond of Henry – an amusing fellow. He wished Henry luck with Lucy; he wanted to see young Jemmy; but he believed he had finished with Lucy. He wanted a different sort of woman. So he would not seek out Lucy; a meeting between them might provoke an awkward situation, and he had lost none of his desire to avoid such happenings.

No! He would enjoy these weeks in Paris. He would play with his little sister; he would court Mademoiselle who, he could swear, was more inclined to listen to him now than she had ever been.

'My cousin,' she said to him, as they walked through the gardens of the Tuileries, 'you have grown up since you returned from England. You have ceased to be afraid of me.'

'I was never afraid of you, fair cousin,' he answered, 'only afraid of myself.'

'Those are meaningless words,' she countered. 'Afraid of yourself! What do you mean?'

'Afraid of the lengths to which my passion for you might lead me.'

'When you went away you could not speak French. You go to Scotland; you go to England; and you return speaking it fluently. Pray, did they teach you French in those two countries?'

'They taught me much, but not French. I came away not caring what was thought of my French or myself.'

'How was it you acquired such indifference to the opinion of others?'

'I suppose, Mademoiselle, it was because my opinion of myself was so bad that that which others had of me could not be much worse.'

'You sound like a cynical old man. Were the sins you committed in England great?'

'No greater than those committed by others, I dare swear.'

'Am I to conclude that you now have a contempt for the whole world?'

'Never! The world is made up not only of saints and sinners – both of which I have no doubt I should abhor – but also of beautiful women.'

'Could not beautiful women also be saints . . . or sinners?'

'Nay! They are but beautiful women. Beauty is apart. It exonerates them from all charges of sin or saintliness.'

'You are ridiculous, Charles. But you amuse me.'

'You would have been amused far more to see me with servants in the kitchen, posing as a nailer's son from Birmingham. There I sat . . . one of them . . . so sure of myself – William, the nailer's son from Birmingham. God's Body! What a strange world this is, when it is better to be the son of a nailer from Birmingham than the son of a Prince of Scotland and Princess of France!'

Mademoiselle clenched her fists at the thought. She could not bear to contemplate insults to royalty. Charles noticed this and smiled. He was a King, and therefore it was easier to bear such insults than it was for poor Mademoiselle to contemplate them. Mademoiselle would never be a Queen in her own right; though she could achieve a crown mayhap by marrying him. Was this the moment to remind her of this? He doubted it.

He went on: 'Unfortunately for me the meat-jack ran down. "Now, William," cried the cook, "why do you sit there . . . as though you're a lord? Wind up the meat-jack and be quick about it!" I was eager to serve the cook, but although much time and care has been spent on my education, the winding of meat-jacks was never taught me, and I, William, the nailer's son, was exposed in my ignorance and called by that fat cook "the veriest clownish booby in the world!" '

'You should have drawn your sword and run the fellow through.'

'Then, dear lady, I should have left my head behind me on London Bridge. 'Tis better to be called a clownish booby – if you merit the name – than a corpse, to my way of reckoning. Howsoever, I fared better than Wilmot who, hiding in a malthouse, came near to being baked alive, while our enemies looked everywhere but in that spot for him.'

'And this Jane Lane ... doubtless she became your mistress?'

'This is not so.'

'Come, Charles! I know you well.'

'Not well enough, it seems. I was the lady's servant and as such I behaved.'

'Some servants, possessing the necessary qualifications, have been known to lay aside the garments of servitude at certain times.'

'Not such servants as William Jackson when serving such a mistress as Jane Lane. Ah! It is small wonder that you find me changed. You should have seen me trying to squeeze myself into a priest's hole. You should have heard me. That hole was made not only for a smaller man than I, but for one less profane. You should have seen me mingling with the ostlers and the serving men. It is not easy for me to disguise myself. My dark and ugly face seemed known to all. How often was I told that I had a look of that tall, dark, lean man for whom the Parliament was offering a thousand pounds!'

'Yes, assuredly you have had adventures, cousin.'

'And one day, I shall succeed. You know that, dearest lady. One day I shall go to England and not return.'

'Do you mean that you will settle down to a life of servitude with a charming lady – a Mistress Lane?'

'I hope to settle down with a charming lady, but as a king, Mademoiselle. Would you be that charming lady? I should be the happiest man alive if that could be.'

'Ask me later, Charles. Ask me when you have won your crown.'

Charles kissed her fingertips. He was by no means upset. Mademoiselle was too proud a young woman to make a comfortable wife. Moreover, he had caught sight of one of Mademoiselle's ladies-in-waiting, the young Duchesse de Châtillon. She was a lovely creature – calm, serene and so gentle. In some measure she reminded him of Jane Lane; she was warm and tender yet unapproachable, being completely in love with her husband.

The hopelessness of loving her suited the King's present mood.

He was happy to transfer his attentions from the haughty Mademoiselle to charming 'Bablon' as he called the Duchesse.

*

Life suddenly began to change for Henriette. When she was eight years old she renewed her acquaintance with the two most important boys in France. One was Louis, the King, who was fourteen years old; the other, Philippe, his brother, was aged twelve.

The excitement began suddenly. Her mother came to her, and Henriette had begun to know that when those black eyes – embedded in pouches and wrinkles – sparkled and gleamed with speculation, when those plump white hands gesticulated wildly, there were plans in her mother's mind.

'Great events are afoot,' cried Henrietta Maria, and she immediately dismissed all attendants.

The little girl gave her some anxiety; she was so thin and was growing too rapidly; and although she was vivacious and intelligent, she lacked that conventional perfection which was recognized in the Court as beauty.

'What may well be a very important day in your life is approaching, my child!' cried the Queen.

'In *my* life, Mam?'

'You are the daughter of a King – never forget that. My dearest wish is to see you wearing a crown. That alone can compensate me for all I have suffered.'

Henriette was uneasy. Her mother had a habit of imposing unpleasant tasks which had to be done for her sake, because she was *La Reine Malheureuse* who had suffered so much.

'The war of the Fronde is over. The King and his mother and brother are to return victorious to Paris.'

'And this . . . is important to me?'

'Now, child, you are not showing your usual intelligence. Is it not important to all France that those wicked rebels are subdued, that the King returns to his capital?'

'But, Mam, you said for *me* . . .'

'For you in particular. I want you to love the King.'

'All France loves him. Is that not so?'

'You must love him as the King of this land, of course; but you must love him in another way. But more of that later. Louis is the most handsome King that ever lived.'

Henriette set her lips stubbornly. There was only one King who could be that to her.

Henrietta Maria shook her daughter. 'Yes, yes, yes. You love Charles. He is your dear brother. But you cannot marry your brother.'

'I . . . I am to marry King Louis?'

'Hush, hush, hush! What do you think would happen if any overheard such words? How do we know? This is the King of France of whom you speak. Oh yes, he is a boy of fourteen, but nevertheless he is a King. Do not dare talk of marrying him!'

'But you said . . .'

'I said you were only to think of it, stupid one. Only to think of it . . . think of it day and night . . . and never let it be out of your thoughts.'

'A secret?'

'A secret, yes! It is my dearest wish. Mademoiselle, your cousin, hopes to marry him. A girl of her age and a boy of fourteen! It is a comedy! And what does she think will be her reception when the King and his mother come back to their own, eh? What will they say to Mademoiselle, who ordered the guns of the Bastille to fire on the King's soldiers? I will tell you, my child. Monsieur Mazarin declared that the cannon of the Bastille killed Mademoiselle's husband. That is true. When those shots were fired, she lost her chance of marrying her cousin. Foolish girl! And double fool for thinking herself so wise! She thinks she is another Jeanne d'Arc. The foolish one!'

'Mam, you were talking about me, and how important this is.'

'And so I shall talk of you. Let the foolish ways of Mademoiselle be a lesson to you. I'll swear that when the Court returns, Mademoiselle will be requested to leave the Tuileries; she will be retired to the country. There let her toss her pretty head; there let her write in her journal; there let her wonder whether it might not be a good thing to turn to the King of England before it is too late – lest she lose him as she has lost the King of France. The King of France! A woman of her age! Nay, she shall never have Louis. Ah, my little Henriette, how I wish we could plump you up! How thin you are! Bad child! You do not eat enough. I shall have you whipped if you do not eat.'

'Please, Mam, don't do that. I eat very well, but it does not make me fat. It only makes me tall.'

'Louis is tall. Louis is so handsome that all who see him gasp at his beauty. A King ten years . . . and only fourteen now. It is said that he is not mortal, that no one could be as perfect as this boy, and be human.'

'And is he so perfect, Mam?'

'Of course he is. More beautiful than all other boys; taller, more full of health, high spirits and good nature. They say he is the son, not of his father, but of a god.'

Henriette's eyes glistened; she clasped her hands together and listened ecstatically.

The Queen of England caught the child to her and kissed her fiercely. 'No! You must forget you are eight years old. You must conduct yourself as a lady. You must never . . . never forget that, though exiled, you are the daughter of the King of England . . . and that only a daughter of Kings would be worthy to mate with such as Louis. Our dear Mademoiselle is not quite that, eh? For all her airs and so-called beauty . . . for all her wealth . . . she is not quite that. She is the King's cousin, as you are, my little one, but there is a difference. Ah! There is a difference. You are the daughter of the King of England, and your mother is as royal as Louis' own father, for *their* father was one and the same – the great and glorious Henri Quatre of great fame.'

Henriette shifted from one foot to the other; she had heard all this before.

'Now tomorrow His Majesty will ride into his capital, and you will be there to greet him. Beside him will ride your own brother – two young kings side by side.'

'Charles!' cried Henriette gleefully.

Henrietta Maria frowned at her daughter. 'Yes, yes,

brother make you forget your homage to the King of France. It is all very well to love your brother ... but it will be necessary for you one day to love another more than you love Charles.'

Henriette did not tell her mother – for it would have made her angry – that never as long as she lived could she love another as she loved her brother Charles.

'You are eight years old,' repeated the Queen. 'Old enough to put away childish things. Time enough for a princess to think of her future.'

Eight years old! Often Henriette thought of that time as the end of her childhood.

*

The next day the King of France rode into his capital. Along the route from Saint-Cloud to Paris the crowd waited to cheer him. It was a year since he had left Paris, and the people did not forget that, although they had rebelled against the Court, they had never felt any resentment towards this beautiful boy – so tall, so physically perfect, so charming to behold that he only had to show himself to win their applause.

Everywhere was pageantry and colour; the city guards in red and blue velvet led the procession, and following them rode the King, glorious in purple velvet embroidered with golden *fleurs-de-lis*, his plumed hat well back from his handsome face, his brown eyes alight with triumph and loving-kindness towards his people; his beautifully shaped features looked as if they had been carved by a Greek sculptor out of stone, because of their very perfection; yet his clear, bright complexion showed him to be of healthy flesh and blood. Beside him, such an excellent foil to such celestial beauty, was the tall lean figure of the King of England, his dark, saturnine face alight with humour; he seemed ugly in comparison with that pink and white boy, and yet many women in the crowd could not take their eyes from him to look at the beautiful boy-King of France.

From the churches bells pealed forth. The war of the Fronde was over; there was peace in France; and men and women wept and told each other that this handsome King was a gift from Heaven and that he would lead France to prosperity. At the windows groups shouted and cheered; silken streamers hung from those windows; people climbed to roofs to get a better view of their monarch. One woman – ragged and dirty – pushed her way through the crowds that she might kiss the royal foot. The guards tried to prevent her, but the King merely smiled that smile which made the women cry 'God bless him!', and all began to cheer the beggar woman with their King.

Behind the King rode the great Dukes of France – the Duc de Vendôme and Duc de Guise; then followed the Marshall; and after them the Lords in glittering apparel, followed by more guards on horseback.

The Swiss Guards followed just ahead of the Queen's coach. In this Anne of Austria sat back plump and arrogant, displaying her beautiful hands, jewel-covered; the crowds had few cheers for her; they had never liked her and they blamed her – not handsome Louis – for the troubles from which the country had just emerged. With her rode her second son, Philippe – known as Monsieur – who was twelve years old and a little sulky now because of all the fuss which was being made of his brother. It was difficult for a younger son not to resent the fate which had decreed that he should be born after his brother. Philippe lacked the striking beauty of Louis, but he knew himself to be of a sharper intellect, and it was sad to have to take second place on every occasion.

His mother, watching him, reminded him that it was necessary to smile and bow to the people. Did he want them to think he was a sullen fellow, so different from his brother? So Monsieur smiled and bowed and hid his feelings; and the people murmured together that it was a marvellous thing that after twenty-two years God had blessed the union of Louis XIII and Anne of Austria with two such boys.

Now the guns of the Bastille and the salvoes from the Place de Grève roared forth; lamps shone in the windows and bonfires were lighted in the streets of Paris.

The war of the Fronde was over; Louis was back in his Louvre. Now there would be a return of pageantry and gaiety such as the French loved.

So Paris rejoiced.

*

In the great hall of the Louvre the King welcomed his guests.

Henrietta Maria was present with her daughter. Anne of Austria smiled on her sister-in-law, and Henrietta Maria had reason to believe that she was not averse to a match between their children.

That made Henrietta Maria's eyes sparkle; that made her almost happy.

If only one other could be here to see this day! she thought, and the tears gushed to her eyes. None must see them; they were all impatient of her grief, as people always are of the grief of others too long preserved.

If Charles could have the fortune of Mademoiselle, he could begin campaigning for the return of his kingdom. If Anne of Austria would agree to a match between Louis and the little Henriette . . .

All these were dreams; but surely not impossible of fulfilment?

Young Louis had an arrogant air. Would he obey his mother? He was surrounded by sycophants who told him he had been sent by Heaven to govern France; he had been a king from the nursery; none had ever dared deny him what he asked; the most sweet-tempered person in the world could not emerge without a little arrogance from an upbringing such as that which had befallen the boy-King of France. No! He would make his own choice within reason; and was it not likely that he would choose her little Henriette?

Henriette herself felt bewildered by all the pageantry; she had lived so quietly during the war of the Fronde when the Court was not in Paris; she had never in all her life been in such glittering company.

She was excited by it; she loved to see the flashing jewels and the brilliant garments of the men and women. And Charles was here, in a place of honour beside the King of France. That gave her great pleasure. It was wonderful to see the honour paid to him and to remind herself that he was, after all, her dearest brother whose hair she pulled, who tossed her in his arms and was never too much the King to remember that he was Minette's brother.

Now she must go forward and kneel to the King of France. She thought how handsome he was; he was all that she had been led to expect he would be.

She knelt and kissed his hand as she had been told to do.

'My little cousin,' he said, 'it makes me happy to see you here.'

But his gaze flickered over her lightly and, looking up, she caught the eyes of his brother Philippe on her. Philippe studied her languidly and without great interest.

She thought in that moment of her mother's words; she remembered that she had to make this King love her and that she had to love him for the sake of *La Reine Malheureuse* who had suffered so much and must therefore not be allowed to suffer more.

How can I make this magnificent young man love *me!* she thought in panic, and she felt so forlorn and frightened that she hesitated for a moment when she should have passed on.

She was aware of the shocked silence about her. Etiquette was of the utmost importance at the Court of France. She could not think what she must do now. She began to tremble.

Then she turned her eyes to that beloved face; she knew that she could rely on him.

The eyes crinkled up into that well-loved smile; the corners of the mouth turned up. She was appealing mutely to him for help, and, of course, she did not appeal in vain.

He was beside her, dispensing with etiquette, knowing that a breach on the part of the King of England was negligible compared with that of a little girl.

He laid his hand on her shoulder and drew her to one side, that the person who was waiting to kneel before the King of France might proceed.

'This is my own little sister,' he said lightly. 'I hope you will like her well, Louis, for I love her dearly.'

Her hand curled round his finger. She felt safe and comforted. He kept her standing beside him, defiant of raised eyebrows.

I am growing up, thought Henriette, and growing up is

frightening. I need not be afraid though ... if Charles is near.

Charles' eyes sought those of his mother; his glinted with amusement. She was not displeased, and he was glad of that for Minette's sake.

She was thinking: Let all the Court be reminded that this little girl is the beloved sister of the King of England. Let the Queen-Mother also be reminded. Yes ... it is a not unhappy little incident.

God's Body! thought the King of England. Mam is already trying to marry the child to the King of France. So Minette is leaving childhood behind her. My little sister is growing up.

CHAPTER FIVE

THE CARRIAGE of the Queen-Mother of France was turning in at the Palais-Royal. Henrietta Maria was waiting impatiently to receive her, curbing the natural impatience which this flaccid-minded woman inspired in her, cautioning herself to remember that she was dependent on her sister-in-law's hospitality, on her sister-in-law's good will, if that for which she longed above all things was to come to pass.

Into the great reception room swept Anne of Austria, accompanied by her women. Poor creatures! thought Henrietta Maria. They looked worn out – worn out with having to listen to her inanities, having to adjust their minds to hers – quite a feat, for many of them were not only well-born but well-educated women. How relieved they must be at the end of the day after the Queen's *coucher* when they must chatter lightly to her until she had fallen asleep, for then they could escape from their bondage!

It was a great honour that she should condescend to call at the lodging of her exiled sister-in-law. Henrietta Maria's heart leaped with hope in contemplating the cause.

They embraced – the Queen-Mother of France and the

exiled Queen of England. The ready tears came to Henrietta Maria's eyes.

'Such an honour ... such an honour,' she murmured. 'Dearest Majesty, you make me forget I am an exile depending on your bounty.'

Anne smiled. She was generous by nature and she loved to do little kindnesses if they did not involve taking too much trouble. She spent all the morning in bed and after that she prayed in her oratory for hours. She liked to be there alone, while her thoughts flitted lightly from one subject to another. What delicacies would her cooks have prepared for her that day? What new gossip was there in the Court? What new plays were being prepared for her? What was her darling doing at this moment? She must ask him to come to see her. *Ask* now – not command any more. The beloved creature was no longer to be commanded. She could lie back in the sanctity of her oratory and think about his many perfections – her beautiful, beautiful son, of whom she never tired of thinking, whose handsome looks were a delight to her whenever her eyes fell upon him. Every queen in the world envied her her Louis. Any queen who had produced such a one had justified her existence, was entitled to give up her days to idling, gambling, watching plays, gossip ...

She was doubly pleased with herself, for not only had she produced Louis, but Philippe. She laughed to herself sometimes when she thought of her late husband, now no longer here to plague her. Not that she thought of him often; he had been dead for nearly ten years. She was not one to brood on the past. She lightly skimmed over the years of marriage, his dislike for her, the urgent need for a child, which had forced Cardinal Richelieu to bring them together for a brief spell, and themselves to conform to his wishes; and the miracle, the birth of Louis – Louis Dieudonné – and later that of Philippe.

But why think of that other Louis – her husband – the cold, ugly misogynist who, after the first delights of fatherhood, had been irritated by the boisterous manners of his heir. Anne could smile at the memory of the little Prince's distaste when he had first seen his father in his nightcap. He had roared his dislike so that the King had turned furiously on his wife, accusing her of influencing the child against him, and he had even threatened to take the child from her.

Not that he had succeeded in doing that. He had been old; he was enfeebled; it had been clear that he was not long for this world.

It had seemed prophetic when, on the occasion of little Louis' christening at the age of two, his father had taken him on his knee when the ceremony was over and asked him: 'Now what is your name, my child?' and the boy had answered boldly: 'I am Louis XIV, Father.' Then had the bitter mouth curled; then had the ugly eyes narrowed and a faint smile had touched the sallow face. 'Not yet, Louis XIV,' he had said. 'Louis XIII is not dead yet. Aye, but mayhap you speak only a little too soon.'

It was not long after that that the boy was indeed Louis XIV, and new power had come to Anne as Regent. Not that she had ever wished to alter her way of life. Politics bored her and she had her dear Mazarin to do for her what Richelieu had done in a previous reign. She was more concerned with the trivialities of life.

'Dismiss the attendants,' she said now to Henrietta Maria. 'Let us have a sisterly talk.'

'This is an honour and a pleasure,' said Henrietta Maria.

'Ah,' said Anne, when they were alone, 'it is good to be back in Paris. It is good to know that the troubles are over.'

'And to see your son, His Majesty, gives me no less pleasure than it does yourself, I assure you, dear sister,' said Henrietta Maria. 'He grows in beauty. A short while ago it would not have seemed possible for any to be more handsome. But it was so. Louis of today is more beautiful than Louis of yesterday.'

If there was one thing Anne liked better than lying a-bed, gossiping or having her hair combed, displaying her beautiful hands for admiration, partaking of the savoury dishes and sweetmeats prepared for her approval, it was listening to praises of her son.

'You speak truth,' she said now. 'I confess his many perfections amaze me.' She added condescendingly: 'And your little daughter is not without her charm.'

'My little Henriette! I have done my best. It has not been easy. These terrible years . . . I have devoted much time to her education. She is clever. She has also read much and she takes a delight in music. She can sing well; she plays, not only the harpsichord, but the guitar. Her brother, the King, adores her and declares he delights in her company far more than that of many ladies noted for their wit and beauty.'

'He is a good brother to little Henriette. Poor child! Hers has been a hard life. When I think of her fate and compare it with that of my own two darlings . . .'

'Fortune has smiled on you, sister. There are some of us . . .' The ready tears sprang to Henrietta Maria's eyes.

But Anne, who did not care for exhibitions of grief, said quickly: 'Well, the child is here with her family and, now that we have restored peace and order to the land, there will be changes at Court. It is of these matters that I have come to speak to you now. My sons take great pleasure in fêtes and balls . . . and particularly in the ballet. They excel in dancing. Now why should not their little cousin join them in these sports and pleasures? Mademoiselle . . .' Anne's flaccid mouth had hardened a little . . . 'will be staying in the country for a while.'

Henrietta Maria could not hide her satisfaction.

'She was clever at devising these entertainments,' went on Anne, 'but as she will not be here . . . mayhap your daughter could be of some use.'

'This *is* a great pleasure to me. Henriette will be delighted.'

'She may come to the Louvre to help my sons plan an entertainment they wish to give. I am sure she will be very helpful.'

Henrietta Maria almost forgot to be discreet; she wanted to draw her chair closer to that of the Queen-Mother of France; she wanted to chat – as mother to mother – about the charms and achievements of their offspring; she wanted to make delightful plans for linking Henriette and Louis. But her ambition came to her aid and for once she suppressed her impetuosity.

She sat listening while Anne talked, and the talk was of Louis. Louis at seven being reprimanded for using oaths;

Louis at eight, in pink satin trimmed with gold lace and pink ribbons, dancing perfectly, outshining all with his grace and his beauty; Louis with the fever on him, when for fourteen days his mother had done nothing but weep and pray; the sweetness and patience of the sick child; how he had appointed certain boys-in-waiting to share his games; how he had selected one of the serving girls, a country wench, to play with; how he loved her dearly and liked to make her act King while he became the serving maid; how in disputes between the brothers, she had always insisted that Philippe should obey Louis; how he must always be mindful of the great destiny which was his brother's. And so on, until she rose to go.

Then Henrietta Maria sent for her daughter; she embraced her warmly.

'Mam, Mam, what has happened to make you so happy? Is there news of Charles?'

'You think of your brother first on every occasion! There are other people who should concern you now and then. You are to visit the King and his brother; you are to go to the Louvre tomorrow to help them devise a ballet for our entertainment.'

'I . . . Mam!' Henriette shrank from her mother.

'No, no!' scolded the Queen. 'You must not be foolish.' She pinched her daughter's cheek. 'Remember what I have said. Though you must always remember that you are a King's daughter, you should not be insensible of this great honour which is done you. My little daughter, here is great news! Mademoiselle who would wish to marry Louis, is sent to the country in disgrace, and you, my little one, are to take her place in sharing the amusements of Louis and his brother. Now you must agree always with everything Louis says. You must take his side if there is a disagreement between the brothers. You must remember what I have told you.'

'Yes, Mam,' whispered Henriette.

She wished Charles were in Paris that she might tell him how uneasy she felt. He would understand; he would soothe her; but without Charles she was alone and there was no one to whom she could turn.

*

137

The two boys were waiting for their cousin. Louis was impatient.

'A little girl!' he said. 'Here's a pretty pass! So now we must play with little girls! Why should I be asked to play with little girls!'

'Because her brother is the King of England,' Philippe answered wryly.

'King of England! The English have a different tale to tell.'

'As the French might have had, brother . . . not so long ago.'

Louis shook his head in exasperation, but he was used to Philippe's dry comments. Philippe was in a state of continual pique because he was two years younger than his brother and merely Monsieur, Duc d'Orléans, instead of King.

Louis' annoyance did not last long. He was naturally sweet-tempered though often arrogant, for it would have been a miracle if he had been anything else. From the day he was five he had been told he was the most important person in the world. Only a short while ago his tutor had told him that God had given him something that even his illustrious grandfather Henri Quatre had not possessed – a handsome presence, a beauty that was almost unearthly in its perfection, a fine figure, a charm which delighted while it won respect. All through his life it had been the same. His tutors never forced him to learn anything, but allowed him to follow his inclinations; it was a wonder that he had acquired any knowledge at all, considering he loved sports so much. But with all his physical perfections there had been born in him a desire to do what was right, and occasionally this was uppermost. Then he would try to study for a while before his desire to play soldiers – his favourite game – came over him and he could not resist calling his army of young boys together for a mock battle. Alas, only a year ago his Company of Honour had been disbanded, for their exploits had become so realistic that his mother had grown terrified for his safety; and Mazarin had decided to risk the King's displeasure and put an end to these warlike games. Then had Louis turned to dancing and, in particular, the ballet.

He excelled in these, but he never forgot that the praise which came his way might not be entirely genuine; Monsieur de Villeroi his governor, never reproved him; if Louis asked for something, de Villeroi always said: Yes, he might have it, before he even knew for what the boy asked. Yet Louis loved far better his valet, La Porte, who often crossed him and had even on occasion forbidden him to do what he wanted. The most Monsieur de Villeroi would say, if La Porte advised against doing something, was: 'La Porte is right, Sire.' But his governor never actually reproved or forbade, even when the King had turned somersaults on his bed and had ended by falling and getting a most unpleasant bump on the head.

Louis had realized long ago that, surrounded by such sycophants, a great ruler of fourteen must be especially watchful.

'Those who are lenient concerning your faults,' La Porte told him once, 'are not so on your account, but on their own, and their object is merely to make you like them, so that they may receive your favours and grow rich.'

Louis never forgot that warning.

He became very fond of La Porte; he still liked to have the valet read to him when he was in bed at night. The History of France sounded quite exciting when read by La Porte; and Louis always listened gravely to the valet's comments and criticisms of other Kings of France.

But on this day he was by no means pleased that there had been sent to him a little girl, eight or nine years old, to help him and Philippe contrive a ballet.

She came and knelt before him. She was tall for her age and thin – very thin. Louis thought her rather ugly, for he was beginning to be very conscious of the looks of women.

He had grown accustomed to tender looks all his life, but there was one lady of his mother's bedchamber who made him feel very extraordinary when his eyes rested on her. It was an odd sensation, for she had only one eye and was far from comely. She was years older than he was; he assumed she must be at least twenty years old; she was married, and she was fat; yet – he did not understand why – he could not stop himself looking her way.

'So you have come to help us with the ballet, cousin?' said Louis.

'Yes, Sire. On the orders of our mothers.'

'Then rise, and we will tell you what we plan. It is to be a grand ballet which we shall call The Nuptials of Thetis and Peleus.'

Henriette listened as he continued. Philippe, somewhat bored, had wandered away and was looking at himself in the great Venetian mirror, thinking how handsome he was, setting his curls so that they fell more to one side of his head; he was wishing that, instead of this quiet girl, they had asked some of the amusing young men to join them. Philippe smiled at the thought. De Guiche was *so* goodlooking and so understanding.

He turned to his brother who was scowling at him for leaving him to explain to the little girl who, of course, would know nothing of ballets and such things, having just come from the nursery – or so it seemed from the look of her.

But Henriette's face had flushed a little and, listening to the King, she caught his enthusiasm. 'Your Majesty should appear as Apollo in the masque,' she ventured.

'Apollo!' cried the King with interest.

'Yes, Sire. The Sun God. It would be the most enchanting role in the ballet. You would be dressed in gold ... and about your head could be a halo from which light radiated so that all would know that you were the Sun God as soon as they set eyes on you.'

'The Sun God!' murmured Louis. 'You are cleverer than I thought, cousin.'

'I have lived so quietly, Sire, that so much of my time has been spent in study.'

'That is why you are so thin,' said Louis. 'You should have spent more time out of doors. Then you would enjoy more glowing health. Though I'll grant you you would not be so useful in arranging ballets.'

Philippe had come over to them. 'What part is there for me?' he asked. 'I should like the part of a lady. I like wearing ladies' costumes ... jewels in my ears and patches on my face.'

He minced about in a manner which was quite feminine

and which made the King laugh. Henriette, taking her cue from him, laughed also. 'You would make a lovely shepherdess, cousin,' she said.

'A shepherdess! While my brother is the Sun God!'

'Ah, but a shepherdess in silver tissue with ribands the colour of roses ... scented ribands mayhap, and a hat of black and white velvet with sweeping plumes, blue, the colour of the sky on hot summer days. You could carry a gilded crook.'

'I like the costume, but I do not care to be a shepherdess, cousin.'

'Then be a goddess. Be the goddess of love.'

'She has ideas, this cousin of ours,' said Philippe.

'Yes,' admitted Louis, 'that is true.' He looked a little wistful. They were educating her – those old nuns of Chaillot – while he and his brother were allowed to do whatever they wished. This little girl, six years younger than he was, four years younger than Philippe, might be shy and ignorant of great ceremonies, but she had in a few years assimilated more booklearning than he and Philippe had.

'Can you dance, cousin?' asked Louis.

'A little, Sire.'

'Then you shall show us. Dance, Philippe.'

Philippe turned haughtily away. 'I am in no mood to dance, Louis,' he said. 'Why do you not dance with our cousin, the better to test her prowess?'

Louis shook his head impatiently. He was not going to demean himself by dancing with such a thin little girl.

His eyes narrowed slightly as they met his brother's, and Philippe felt waves of resentment rising within him. He was born only two years later and the King was his brother, yet, because of those two years' seniority, he must obey Louis even in their games. His mother had said so. Mazarin had said so.

For a few seconds the two brothers stood glaring at each other. Philippe thought of quarrels they had had. They did not often quarrel, but when they did he had always been the one who must take the blame. He remembered an occasion when the Court was on a journey and Louis had insisted that they share a bedroom. It was such a small room, quite different from those which they usually occupied, and in the morning, on awakening and finding his brother's bed so close to his own, the King had spat on it. Philippe, ever ready to take offence, had immediately spat on Louis' bed; this had enraged the King who immediately spat in his brother's face. Philippe had then jumped on his brother's bed and wetted it. Incensed, the King had repeated this action on his brother's bed. When their attendants rushed in a battle was in progress; the brothers were flinging pillows about and trying to smother each other with the sheets, and it was all poor de Villeroi could do to stop them. Only La Porte had dared separate them and call upon them to realize what little savages they had become; at which Philippe flew into a rage, biting and kicking; but he, Philippe, had been ready to forget the incident in a few hours. Not so Louis. He could not forget. He blamed himself and suffered great remorse because he had conducted himself in a manner disgraceful to a King of France.

He had borne no resentment towards Philippe; he remembered that he had begun the quarrel by spitting on his brother's bed. Within a week, when he was to continue the journey while Philippe stayed behind, he was melancholy at the separation, and during his absence had written notes to Philippe, begging for news of him and reminding him that he was his affectionate and kind little Papa Louis.

But it had not ended there, that quarrel in the bedroom; it was not Louis who had wounded Philippe's *amour propre*. It was his mother and the Cardinal who had blamed the younger boy for the scene, who had impressed on him that he must never again expose his brother to indignity; if Louis spat on his bed he must remember that he did so with royal spittle, and it was not for Philippe to object.

Philippe was sullen; but he could not, of course, blame Louis; he could only be envious of Louis.

Now he remembered this and sullenly took the hand of the little girl, while Louis called to a musician to come and play music that his brother and cousin might dance.

Little Henriette danced with grace, and Louis watched with mild pleasure. The Sun God! he was thinking, and he smiled at the picture of himself. The ballet would be devised to show his perfections; he would have the central part and, when it was over, everyone would fawn on him and tell him that he was no human; he was too perfect; he was divine.

But he would remember La Porte and try not to be too pleased with himself.

Philippe and Henriette had finished their dancing.

'Well done!' said Louis. 'You shall have a part in the ballet, cousin.'

Philippe had languidly dropped his cousin's hand. He said: 'Louis, let us call in the others. Let us call de la Châtre, and the Coslin boys and du Plessis-Praslin ... and de Guiche.'

'Yes,' said Louis, 'have them brought. We will devise our ballet of the Sun God; and, cousin, I have promised you a part.'

'Thank you, Sire,' said Henriette shyly.

The King's playmates came into the apartment. Louis said: 'I have thought of a ballet. I am to be the Sun God.'

Philippe took de Guiche into a corner where they arranged each other's hair and giggled together. Louis' admirers closed about him.

Henriette stood apart. No one was very interested in the thin little girl.

*

Henrietta Maria came to see her daughter. Henriette was faintly alarmed. She knew her mother so well that she guessed some fresh task was about to be given her.

'I have good news for you, *chérie*. Your brother is coming to France.'

'Charles ...'

'No, no, no! Always it is of Charles you think. You have other brothers. I refer to your brother Henry.'

'Henry ... my youngest brother. I have never seen Henry.'

'Then that shall be remedied. You shall see him ere long, for he is coming to Paris.'

'Oh, Mam, I am so pleased.'

'I shall have yet another of my children with me. That pleases me. He is thirteen. I remember well the hot day he came into the world. It was in the Palace of Oatlands and your father . . .'

'Mam, I pray you do not speak of those days. They but distress you, and you must be happy now because Henry is coming.'

'Yes; and there is something we have to do for Henry – you and I.'

'I, Mam?'

'Yes, indeed. You are a fortunate girl. Do you realize that? You came to France when you were but two years old and heresy had scarcely touched you. Your brother has been less fortunate. I fear his immortal soul is in danger. We must save him, Henriette. And in this I shall allow you to help me. You must explain to him what Père Cyprien has taught you so well. Together we will save his soul.'

Henry arrived – a shy boy of thirteen, very happy to be reunited with his family. His mother was loud in her exclamations of pleasure. Her beloved child restored to her; this was one of the happiest days of her life. Then she burst into passionate weeping because Elizabeth could not be with them.

Henry wept with her, and his little sister took his hand and begged him not to cry.

'For you are here, Henry,' she said. 'That is one matter for rejoicing. Let us think of that and nothing else.'

Henry was pleased to do this; he was a boy who had had too much sorrow.

When they were alone together Henriette sought to do what her mother had commanded. She made him tell her of his life with James and Elizabeth and how James had escaped during a game of hide-and-seek. Then he told her of that time when they had lived at Syon House; but he did not speak of that January day when he and his sister had been taken to Whitehall to see their father. Instead he told her of Carisbrooke Castle and how Mr Lovel had been good to him and had been his main companion since the death of Elizabeth; he told her how he had longed above all things to be with his mother again.

'Brother,' said Henriette, 'you are not of our faith – Mam's and mine.'

'I am of the faith of my father.'

'Henry, Mam wishes you to be of our faith. Will you come with me and hear what Père Cyprien has to say tomorrow?'

The boy's mouth grew stern. 'I beg of you, Henriette, do not ask me to do that. I did not tell you, but when we were at Syon House, Elizabeth and I went to Whitehall one day. It was a cold day and the river was frozen. It was the saddest day of my life, Henriette; but I did not know it then. We went to see our father. It was the day before he died.'

'Do not speak of it, Henry,' said Henriette shrilly. 'I pray you, do not speak of it.'

'I must speak of it because I must explain. Our father took me on to his knee and told me that I must remain in the faith in which I was baptized.'

'That is not Mam's faith and mine.'

'No. But it is the faith of my father and my father's country.'

'I see, Henry.'

'Oh, Henriette, tell no one of this, but Mr Lovel has said to me that if our mother had been of our father's faith, if she had not tried to turn him into a Catholic, and our country into a Catholic country, our dearest Papa might be alive today.'

'Is it true then, Henry? Can that be true?'

'It is what has been said . . . not only by Mr Lovel, but by many. I could never turn to a faith which by its very existence was responsible for my father's death.'

'But it is Mam's faith, Henry.'

'I am of my father's faith and I will never be of another. I promised him, Henriette. Oh, you never knew him. It is so long ago, but I cannot think of him without weeping, Henriette. I cannot . . . I cannot . . .'

Henriette dried her brother's eyes with her kerchief.

'Dearest brother, I shall never again ask you to change your faith. I am afraid myself . . . I am afraid of a faith which could bring about our father's death.'

'Perhaps I am wrong, Henriette. Perhaps it is not a faith that could do this. Perhaps it is the way in which people think of their faith. It is not a religion which brings heartbreak and bloodshed; it is something in men which says:

"I think this way and I will kill and torture all those who think otherwise." That cannot be true religion, Henriette. That is pride . . . self-pride and perhaps . . . doubt. I do not know. But do not ask me to change my faith.'

'I will not,' declared Henriette emphatically. 'I promise I never will again.'

*

Henriette had passed her tenth birthday. She was leading a gayer life now than ever before. The royal brothers of France, discovering that, though only a little girl, she could dance gracefully and play the lute, graciously allowed her to take part in the revels. At the ballet in which the King appeared, not only as the Sun God, Apollo, but also as Mars, taking as well the minor roles of dryad, fury and courtier to show his versatility, the Court appeared to grow restive when he was not to the fore. Little Henriette had played the part of Erato, the muse of love and poetry; crowned with myrtle and roses she had repeated verses which she had learned by heart. Such an enchanting figure did she present that the Court was loud in its applause, and Henrietta Maria told those about her that this was one of the happiest moments of her life; she had one grief and it was a great one; her martyred husband could not be here to witness his daughter's triumph. Even Anne of Austria, lolling in her chair, had taken her eyes off her Sun God for a brief moment to study the little girl.

She nodded her head. 'How the costume becomes her,' she said. 'This little girl of yours will be a beauty yet, sister. Louis tells me that he is pleased with her dancing and that she plays the lute with a skill beyond her years.'

Ah yes, that had been a happy day for Henrietta Maria who already saw the crown of France on her daughter's head; but she was not so pleased as she surveyed her youngest son.

Stubbornly he had determined to shut his ears to the truth with which Père Cyprien was trying to save him from perdition.

'But he shall be saved!' Henrietta Maria told herself, tapping her foot. 'He shall! Or I will make him wish he had never been born to defy his mother and God.'

Little Henriette had been delighted with her success. She loved to dance; she had learned her verses more easily than anybody, and Louis himself had been delighted with her. She found that Louis' praise made her very happy. When those large brown eyes were turned on her in appreciation, she felt that she could be perfectly happy if she could go on pleasing him. How different was Philippe! Philippe's dark, long-lashed eyes were quite scornful of her; being a clever little girl and sharper-witted than the two boys, she was aware that neither of them wished to play with a girl as young as she was; the difference was that Philippe was anxious for her to know that they despised her youth, while Louis was anxious to hide this fact from her. Louis was not only handsome; he was kind. Henriette was beginning to think that he was one of the kindest people she had ever known. She was moved because he was a king – a much cherished king – and yet had the kindness to care for the feelings of a little girl. She tried to think of new ideas for ballets, and if Louis liked them she was happy; if his interest was perfunctory – which meant that he liked them not at all – she was desolate and cried a little when she was alone at night because she had failed to please him. Sometimes, oddly enough, if she had pleased him she would cry – but with different feelings; perhaps this was because she wistfully longed to be older and more beautiful, so that he would like her better.

But her excitement in her companionship with the King was spoilt by her pity for her brother. Why could he not be allowed to continue in the faith of the Church of England? It was Charles' faith; therefore it was right that it should be Henry's; and as Henry had promised his father that he would never leave it, why could not Mam be satisfied with one little Catholic in the family?

Charles came to see her and she forgot even her new friendship with Louis. He kissed her affectionately and told her he was going away again. It was to Cologne this time.

'I am a wanderer on the face of the earth, Minette,' he said. 'I am not only a king without a crown, I am a man without a country. I cannot stay long in one place for fear of wearing out my welcome. So I just flit from place to place, never staying long anywhere lest, when I next wish to visit it, my previous visit may be remembered as a very long one.'

'Here we love to have you.'

'You do, Minette, I know. But this is not your home either. However, be of good cheer. One day we shall be together. Then I shall be a king with a crown, and you shall be my companion for ever. How will you like that?'

'Let it be soon, I pray. It is what I should love more than anything on earth,' said Henriette vehemently.

'Oh come, you are happy enough here. They tell me you have done well in the ballet and that Louis himself is pleased with you. There, Minette! You may bask in the rays of the Sun God, so what do you want with a poor wandering prince like me when you move in the radiance of the Olympians?'

'I would rather be in a hovel with you.'

'Nay, Minette, do not say such things. Make the most of your good fortune. Louis is a good fellow. It makes me happy that you have pleased him. And now I must see Mam before I depart, and make her swear not to plague poor Henry.'

Henrietta Maria listened to her son in cold silence before she brought out the old arguments. The King, her husband, she stressed then, had promised that her children should be brought up in her religion.

'Mam! Mam! Why cannot you leave this matter of Henry's religion and concern yourself with the ballet as does our little Henriette?'

'You are frivolous, Charles. It is small wonder that God does not crown your efforts with success. This is a child's soul for which we are battling.'

The King was stern for once. He said: 'Henry has given his solemn word to our father that he will not change his religion. Mam, you astonish me. Would you force the boy to break his word? I speak to you now as your King, Madam. I forbid you to plague the boy. I command that you obey.'

Henrietta Maria pursed her lips together to keep back the angry words.

'My own son is against me,' she complained bitterly to her daughter when Charles had gone. 'It is small wonder that he is an exile . . . small wonder indeed. It is small wonder that God is on the side of our enemies.'

'But *they* are not Catholics either, Mam,' said Henriette gently.

And for once the Queen pushed her daughter away from her; she was in no mood for further argument.

Her mind was made up. Charles was the King and he had commanded her; but Charles was an exile and would soon be far away.

*

Young Henry was bewildered. For so many years he had longed to escape from his father's enemies, to be with his family; and now that he had achieved this end he found that he was tormented as he never had been when he was in the hands of the Roundheads.

His mother gave him no peace. He must read this; he must study that; he must listen to the teachings of older, wiser men than himself. Père Cyprien was at his elbow; so was the Abbé Montague.

To all their talk he remained mute and faithful to the promise he had given his father; his mother did not see his attitude as fidelity; she called it stubbornness.

The little boy was only fourteen. He did not know what he would have done without his brothers and sisters. Charles was not only his brother but his King, and Charles supported him. But Charles had gone to Cologne for a brief spell. His brother James was in Paris, and he supported him.

'Mam is a loving mother,' James had said; 'she is fond of us all, but she has one real passion – her faith; and where that is concerned she is a regular tornado. Stay firm, brother. Those are Charles' commands, and he is the King. You promised our father. You do well to remember your promise, and in this you are in the right.'

He knew that his sister Mary, the Princess of Orange, had placed herself on his side. He was certain that Elizabeth would have supported him had she been alive; Elizabeth would have died rather than break her word to her father.

'And so will I!' declared Henry on his knees. 'And so

will I. I swear it, Papa. I remember. I will remember.'

And when his mother railed against him, he shut his eyes tightly and thought of that man in the velvet jacket and lace collar with the hair falling about his shoulders. 'Never forget what I ask, Henry. . . .' He heard those words in his dreams. 'Papa . . . Papa . . .' he sobbed. 'I will remember.'

Sometimes his little sister Henriette came to his bed and sat beside it, holding his hand.

She wanted him to be happy. She did not know whether she ought to obey her mother and try to bring her brother into the Catholic faith; but when she heard that Charles had commanded his mother not to molest Henry, she knew what she must do.

She soothed Henry; she did not say much – it seemed so wrong to speak against her mother – but Henry knew that his brothers and sisters without exception were on his side; and he continued to hold out.

*

Henrietta Maria was growing impatient. She would sit glowering at her youngest son, tapping the floor with her foot, her eyes hard.

Obstinate fellow! she thought. What an unhappy woman I am! My children will not obey me. They flout me. They are fools. Had Charles become a Catholic he might have stayed here. He might have been helped to regain his kingdom; who knew, Mademoiselle might have married him. But this obstinate clinging to heresy . . . it is ruining my life! What an unhappy woman I am!

It was true that Anne of Austria was protesting against the celebration of the rites of the Church of England in the Louvre; it was true that she was ready to help Henrietta Maria in her battle for little Henry's soul; but no one in France was ready to go to war with the Protector of England to help the King regain his throne. Still, Henrietta Maria liked to believe that this was so.

And now the boy had dared, without his mother's knowledge, to despatch a letter to his brother, the King; that was because she had dismissed his tutor Lovel – an evil influence if ever there was one.

Henrietta Maria now had Charles' reply to Henry in her hands, and she fumed with rage as she read it.

'Do not let them persuade you,' Charles had written, 'either by force or fair promises; the first, they neither dare nor will use; and for the second, as soon as they have perverted you, they will have their end, and then they will care no more for you ... If you do not consider what I say unto you, remember the last words of your dead father which were "Be constant to your religion and never be shaken in it"; which, if you do not observe, this shall be the last time you shall hear from

Dear brother,
Your most affectionate
Charles II.'

Her own family banding against her! It was more than a mother could endure. She would not be treated thus. She would settle this matter of her youngest son's religion once and for all time.

She waited until they had dined that day; then, as they rose to leave the dining chamber, she went to Henry and embraced him warmly.

'My son,' she said, 'how grieved I am that I should be forced to deal so severely with you, but it is my love that makes me do it. You must know that well.'

'Oh, Mam,' said the little boy, his eyes filling with tears, 'please understand. I gave my word to Papa.'

'Please ... please, Henry, don't talk to me of Papa. There are some days when the memory of him hurts me more than others. I knew him more than you did, child. We had years together before you were born. Any grief you have felt for Papa is a small thing compared with mine.'

'Mam ... then ... it is because of him, you understand ...'

'You are weary, my son,' she interrupted, 'of being talked to on this matter. God knows I am weary of it too. Let us shorten the trial. Go to your apartments now and I will send the Abbé Montague to you.'

'Please, Mam, there is nothing I can do. Do understand me when I say ...'

'Go now, my son. Listen to the Abbé, and then give me your final answer.'

'It can make no difference.'

She pushed him gently from her, wiping her eyes as she did so.

He went to his apartment where the Abbé came to him; wearily he listened, and again and again he reiterated his determination not to swerve from the faith in which he had been baptized, not to break his word to his father.

'This is going to hurt your mother, the Queen, so deeply that I fear what the result will be,' warned the Abbé.

'I cannot heed the result,' answered the boy. 'I have only one answer to give.'

So the Abbé left him and went to Henrietta Maria who was with her youngest daughter; together they were stitching an altar cloth for Chaillot.

'Your Majesty,' said Montague, 'I fear I have only bad news for you. The boy remains obstinate. He clings fast to heresy.'

Henrietta Maria rose to her feet, letting the altar cloth fall to the floor.

Her daughter watched the purple blood disfigure her face as, clenching her hands together, she cried: 'Very well! This is the end then. He shall see what it means to flout God . . . and me. Go to him. Tell him that he shall see my face no more. Go at once. Tell him that. Tell him I can bear no more sorrows. I am weary. I am going to Chaillot to pray . . . for there only can I find peace.'

'Oh, Mam!' cried Henriette. 'Mam, what are you saying? You cannot mean this.'

'I do mean it. I never want to see his face again. I want to forget I bore him.'

'But, Mam, he swore to our father. He *swore*. You must understand.'

'I understand only that he wishes to flout me. I shall make him repent this ere long. Go to him at once, Abbé. Give him my message. The ungrateful boy! He is no child of mine!'

Henrietta Maria flung herself out of the room; Henriette slowly picked up the altar cloth; then she sat down on the stool and covered her face with her hands.

Was there no end to these troubles which beset her family?

*

After a while she rose. She must go to Henry. Poor Henry, who had dreamed so often of reunion with his family!

She went along to his apartment. Montague was talking to Henry, whose face was white; he looked stricken yet incredulous. It was clear that he could not grasp what the man was saying; he could not believe his mother had really cast him off.

'Just think what this will mean,' Montague was saying. 'If your mother renounces you, how will you live? How will you supply your table with food? How will you pay your servants?'

'I do not know,' said Henry piteously. 'I cannot understand!'

'Then go to the Queen; tell her that you will be her very good son, and she will have a proposal to make which will set your heart at rest.'

'I fear, sir,' said Henry in a quavering voice, though his lips were determined, 'that my mother's proposals would not have that effect upon me, for my heart can have no rest but in the free exercise of my religion and in the keeping of my word to my father.'

James came into his apartment while Henriette was wondering what she could do to soothe her brother. When James heard the news he was astounded.

'But our mother cannot do this!' he cried. 'I will go to see her. There has been some mistake.'

He strode out of the apartment, and Henriette put her arm about Henry. 'Be of good cheer, Henry,' she begged. 'There has been a mistake. You heard what James said. It *must* be a mistake.'

But shortly afterwards James was back. 'Our mother is in a fury,' he said. 'She declares that henceforth she will show her pleasure to neither of her sons, except through the medium of Montague.'

'Then she discards us both, James,' said Henry. 'Oh, James, I almost wish they had not let me come to France. I was happier at Carisbrooke than here.'

153

'I would there were something I could do,' said Henriette. 'I do not believe Mam means this. She flies into tempers, but they pass. Go to her, Henry. Speak to her. She will soon be leaving for Chaillot, where she is going for Mass. Speak to her before she goes.'

James thought that their mother might be in a softened mood as she was departing for her devotions.

So Henry waylaid his mother; he knelt before her, entreating her not to turn away from him; but she pushed him angrily aside and would not speak to him.

*

The boy was heartbroken and uncertain what to do. James put his arm about him, and together they went to the service which was held in Sir Richard Browne's chapel for the English Princes.

'She'll get over her anger,' James told him. 'Don't fret, brother.'

But when Henry returned to his apartment after the service, he found that all his servants had been dismissed. There was no place for him at the table.

Bewildered, he flung himself down and gave way to bitter weeping. His mother, for whom he had longed during the years of exile, had turned away from him and had declared her intention of looking on his face no more.

*

Gloomily he walked about the palace grounds. He did not know what to do.

The day passed; he returned to the palace. He decided he would go to bed and try to make plans for the morrow. As he entered the palace his little sister ran to him. 'Henry, what are you going to do?' she asked.

'I do not know. I must go away, I suppose. But I do not know where to go.'

'Then you will resist . . . our mother?'

'I must, Henriette.'

'Oh Henry. . . . Oh, my brother! Oh, my mother! What can I do? I shall never be happy again.'

'So you too are afraid of her. She is only kind to you

because you are a Catholic. If you were not, she would be as cruel to you as she is to me.'

Henriette continued to weep.

Her brother kissed her. 'I am going to my apartment,' he said. 'I shall try to rest. Perhaps in the morning I shall know what to do.'

She nodded and kissed him fondly.

He broke down then. 'It is because I so longed to be with her . . . so much . . .'

'I know, Henry. I know, dear brother.'

She turned and fled; and Henry went up to his apartments, only to find that the sheets had been taken from his bed, and that all the comforts had been removed from his room.

His Controller found him there, staring about in a bewildered fashion; he reported that the horses had been turned out of the stables and that he himself had been dismissed and warned that he should expect no wages from the Queen while he remained in the service of Prince Henry.

'But I do not know what to do!' cried the boy.

James sought him out and James had good news.

'Fret no more, brother,' he cried. 'All will be well. Did you think Charles would forget you! He knows how fierce our mother can be when she is engaged in conversions. Charles has sent to you the Marquess of Ormonde who waits below. He has horses and instructions to take you to Charles in Cologne.'

'Charles!' cried Henry, tears filling his eyes. 'I am to go to *Charles!*'

'Charles would never desert you!' cried James. 'He expected this. He wrote to you somewhat sternly because he knew that you would never be at peace if you broke your word to our father. He wished you to hold out against our mother, and he is proud that you have done so. But never think that he would desert you. Be of good cheer, brother. You will find life more agreeable with the King, your brother, than among the monks of a Jesuit college which Mam had in mind for you.'

And that night, after taking fond farewells of his brother James and his little sister Henriette, Henry, an exile from his mother's care, set out to join that other exile in Cologne.

CHAPTER SIX

ANNE OF AUSTRIA delighted to see her son dance – an accomplishment he performed with such grace – and it pleased her often to give an informal dance, inviting just a few members of the highest nobility to her own private apartments in the Louvre. Here she would sit in her dressing gown, her hair hidden under a *cornette* to indicate that the occasion was an intimate one and by no means to be considered a ball. She would have the violins in one corner of the vast room, and her friends about her in another; and in the middle of the floor the young people danced while she gossiped with her friends who must constantly supply her with the latest scandal and compliments on her son's perfections.

To these dances she often invited Henrietta Maria and her daughter.

'Such a pleasure for the little girl!' she said. 'For she grows so charming. How old is she now?'

'Eleven,' said Henrietta Maria. 'Yes, she is growing up. It is difficult to believe that it is eleven years since that terrible day when . . .'

Anne interrupted quickly: 'Louis enjoys dancing so much. Ah, what it is to be young! And as for Louis, he is never tired. There never was such a one.' Anne tittered. 'Why, do you know, I shall soon begin to believe that it was Apollo who stole in on me while I slept and planted his seed within me!'

'You will soon have to think of his marriage,' suggested Henrietta Maria.

'One constantly thinks of his marriage. It will be the most important of marriages. But who, dear sister, *who* will be worthy to mate with Louis? That is the problem.'

'Only the best,' said Henrietta Maria fervently. 'Only the best.'

Anne looked slyly at her sister-in-law. Now if none of these tragic events had occurred in England, she pondered, if young Henriette's brother were safe on the throne, there could be no objection to my son's marriage with her daughter. Of course it would depend on Louis.

Anne spoke her thoughts aloud. 'Louis will make his own choice, I doubt not. I remember once I took him to the Convent of the Carmelites, and when he was in the community room and the nuns spoke to him, he took no notice of them because he was so interested in the latch of the door. He played with the latch and would not have his attention diverted from it. I was forced to scold him. I said: "Leave that latch, Louis." But he frowned and answered: "It is a good latch. I, the King, like this latch." I said: "It is a fine thing for a King to sulk before ladies and not utter a word." Then suddenly his face grew scarlet and he stamped his foot as he shouted: "I will say nothing because I wish to play with this latch. But one day, I shall speak so loudly that I shall make myself heard." Oh, what a bold little fellow he was! Yes, Louis will have his own way, depend upon that.'

Louis would indeed have his own way. So, at the private dances in Anne's apartments, Henrietta Maria could scarcely contain herself as she watched the crescent friendship between her daughter and the King of France.

*

Louis' valet was dressing him for an informal dance in his mother's apartments.

Louis was silent, smiling to himself as he was being dressed, but he did not see the handsome figure reflected in the mirror. He looked like a young god in his costume of cloth of silver and black velvet embroidered with golden lilies. He felt like a god.

Yesterday he had had an adventure. It was an adventure which had seemed to befall him by chance. It had happened last night, and the partner of his adventure had been Madame de Beauvais who had always fascinated him in some strange way. Now he knew why. He had been dancing with her. The night was warm, and something in her expression as she looked at him made him say: 'Madame,

I should like to know you better than I do.' She had laughed and moved closer to him and had said: 'That is a command. Should I come to your apartments or you to mine, Sire?' Oddly enough he had stammered like a nervous boy – he the King! She had laughed, strange, throaty laughter, which made his heart beat faster. 'I'll come to you,' she said. 'The King cannot move without attracting attention. I will be in the antechamber when the guards are sleeping tonight, when all have retired.'

He only vaguely understood; he was very innocent. His mother and Mazarin had determined to keep him so; they did not want him to give rise to scandalous rumours about himself, as his grandfather had done in his early teens. He was astonished that this should have happened. She was old; she was twenty or more; she was plump; she had only one eye; but she had such merry laughter – merry and kind. And the thought of what she might have to say to him made his heart beat quickly.

So he had cautiously joined her in the antechamber. Did any of the guards see him go? Perhaps. But if they opened one eye they would realize from his manner that he did not wish to be seen, and the wishes of Louis Quatorze were always obeyed.

He was remembering now; he had wondered what he would say to her, but there had been no need of words. She wore nothing but a loose robe which fell from her as she approached him. He gasped; this reminded him of the first time he had dived into deep water when learning to swim; he had been tremendously exhilarated and fearful on that occasion, as he was on this.

'So to me comes the honour of leading Your Majesty to the *doux scavoir!*'

He stammered: 'Madame . . . Madame . . .'

And she had said: 'But you are beautiful. I am to mate with a god. I never thought that I should be the one.'

He was bewildered, but she was not. She was the kindest, most tender person in the world.

And afterwards they lay side by side until the dawn came; and then he said he had better leave her, but they would meet again. So he had tiptoed back to his apartments and lain in his bed, mazed, bewildered and enchanted.

He was grown up; the boy-King had become a man.

All that day he had gone about in a dream – a dream of power and pleasure. He could not help knowing that any beautiful woman on whom he cast his eyes would, he dared swear, be ready to share with him such an adventure as he had enjoyed last night with Madame de Beauvais.

This was exciting knowledge.

These were his thoughts as he prepared himself for the dance in his mother's apartments.

As he walked into the room all rose and fell to their knees, except the two Queens who sat side by side. He made his way to them and kissed, first his mother's hand, and then that of his aunt.

'My beloved, how splendid you look!' said his mother. 'These apartments seemed so dull a moment ago. Now you have entered and the sun shines on us all.'

'Your mother but voices the thoughts of everyone present, Sire,' added Henrietta Maria.

Her eyes were on her young daughter. Oh dear, she thought, if only the child would plump up! How thin she thought, if only the child would plump up ! How thin she is ! I would we had more money that she might be ade-Court and that she is not here like a bird of paradise putting us all to shame.

She glanced at her sister-in-law, informal in her brocaded dressing-gown and *cornette*. It was but an informal occasion. She doubted much whether she and Henriette would have been invited had it been a grand ball or a masque, since their favour was not high at Court.

Louis was gazing round the company. Now that he had arrived, the violins began to play, but no one would dance until the King led the way. According to etiquette he must dance with the lady of the highest rank, and since neither of the Queens would dance, Louis would be bound in duty to ask his little cousin to dance first.

But Louis seemed disinclined to dance. The violins played on. He stood there, smiling to himself. He thought: If *she* were here, I would go to her now and ask her to dance with me. I should not care that she is not of the highest rank; I care nothing for rank. That is what I would have her know. I care only for what we were to each other last night, and that is something I shall never forget as long as I live. I will give her estates when it is in my power to do so. I will give her titles ... and all she can desire. For no one could have been so kind as she was, pretending not to notice my inexperience, making of a simple boy a man of experience in one night.

Oh, the ecstasy of that encounter! Again tonight? Why had he come to a stupid dance? He had no desire to dance. He wished only to lie with her in the dark ... in that ante-chamber. Had not that which he desired always been granted?

She was not there, his dear, dear Madame de Beauvais. Perhaps it was well that she was not, for he would not have been able to hide his grateful love. Now he knew – and fresh gratitude swept over him – that for this reason she had stayed away: she did not wish him to betray himself! She understood. She was wise as well as tender; she was modest as well as sweetly full of knowledge.

He looked round the assembly. No! He would not dance with that thin little cousin of his. He was in no mood to talk to a child tonight. His newly-found manhood made demands upon him. Tonight he was in love with women –. all mature women who understood the delights of the *doux scavoir*. He offered his hand to the Duchesse de Mercoeur, who was the eldest niece of Cardinal Mazarin, a young and handsome matron.

Anne gasped. There was one thing which could always arouse her from her torpor – a breach of etiquette.

This was impossible! Louis had overlooked the Princess Henriette.

She rose and went to her son's side. 'My dearest,' she whispered, 'you have forgotten ... Your cousin Henriette is here ...'

The King frowned; now he looked like the little boy who had played with the latch in the Carmelite convent. 'Tonight,' he said, 'I do not wish to dance with little girls.'

Henrietta Maria felt faint with anxiety. The King was slighting her daughter. He did not want to dance with a little girl! Well, Henriette was young yet, and she was so thin – bad, bad child; she would not eat enough! But later on he might grow fond of her. In the meantime this was disastrous. What could she do?

She rose uncertainly and went to Anne and Louis.

'I must tell Your Majesties,' she said, 'that my daughter cannot dance tonight. She has a pain in her foot. It would be too painful for her to attempt to dance. I am sure that His Majesty was aware of this and for that reason asked the Duchesse to dance.'

Anne replied: 'If the Princess is unfit to dance, the King should not dance tonight.'

The King's natural good-temper seemed to have deserted him. There was an ominous silence throughout the apartment. All eyes were on the royal party. Henrietta Maria thought quickly: A scene must be avoided at all costs. This might result in our being banished from Court.

She said firmly: 'My daughter *shall* dance. Come, Henriette.'

Henriette, blushing and miserably unhappy, obeyed her mother.

For an instant the King did not move to take her hand. Why should he – a man as well as a King – be told with whom to dance? Why should he not choose whom he pleased? He was no longer a boy. Madame de Beauvais understood that; all the Court . . . all the world must understand it too.

Then he looked at the little girl beside him. He saw her lips tremble and he noted the misery in her eyes. He realized her humiliation and he was ashamed suddenly. He was behaving more like a spoilt boy than the man he had become last night.

He took his cousin's hand and began to dance. He did not speak to her. He saw that she was fighting back her tears, so he pressed her hand tightly. He wanted to say: it is not that I do not wish to dance with you, Henriette. It is just that I am in no mood for the company of children.

But he said nothing and the dance continued.

That night the Princess Henriette cried herself to sleep.

*

Henriette was with her mother in the great Cathedral of Notre Dame de Rheims. It was an honour to be here, she knew; her mother had impressed that upon her. They were participating in the Coronation of the King of France to which they had been invited, although it seemed that there was very little hope of the royal house of England's ever reinstating itself.

Charles was wandering around Europe, never staying long in one place, now and then daring to hope that there might be a chance of a little help from some important monarch who had reason to dislike the Protector of England. Plans . . . plans . . . plans . . . which never seemed to materialize. Then he would return to his dicing and women. Rumour reached France that the profligacy of the roaming English Court was becoming notorious.

Henriette longed for news of him, longed to see his face again. Each day, she hoped, would bring some news of him. At least, when he idled with his profligate friends, he was not endangering his life.

Once she had found consolation for the loss of her brother in the exciting company of her magnificent royal cousin, but that had changed recently. She and her mother spent most of their time in seclusion now at the Palais-Royal, Chaillot or Colombes, this last being a pretty house on the Seine, which Henrietta Maria had acquired, and where it was pleasant to spend the hot summer months. Life was growing quieter. Henriette was studying a good deal; her education was opening out into a course hardly ever pursued by ladies of her rank. There was little to do but study. She was thinner than ever and growing too quickly. Already she was aware of a slight deformity in her spine. She dared not tell her mother of this. One could not add to the sorrows of *La Reine Malheureuse*. Henriette knew that her mother longed for her to grow plump, with rounded cheeks and limbs. She, the daughter of an exiled family, would have nothing to recommend her as a wife but rank and beauty; and at this stage it seemed that the latter would never be hers.

Sometimes she worked in a frenzy that she might please her tutors and Père Cyprien; her knowledge increased and her wits sharpened; for recreation she played the lute and harpsichord and also practised singing. She improved her dancing, practising often, sometimes alone, sometimes with her women; she wished to excel at that because Louis set such store by it. Her slenderness gave her grace, and she learned to disguise her slight deformity by the dresses she wore, so that only her intimate attendants were aware of it.

She longed to be able to please her mother. She dreamed sometimes that she had become a *bel esprit* of the Court; she devised clever remarks; she imagined that Louis himself laughed heartily at her *bon mots*. It was pleasant dreaming.

Often she was at Chaillot with her mother, and there she was able to please the Queen by waiting at table on the Abbess and her Filles de Marie. They all declared that she was charming, graceful and modest.

And now there had come this invitation to attend the Coronation. Henrietta Maria was delighted.

'So we are not forgotten!' she cried. 'On an occasion they realize, do they not, that it would be a great breach of etiquette to ignore such close relationships.'

It was not as her mother believed, Henriette was sure. Louis had wanted them to be present, for Louis – King though he was, haughty though he could be – was more sorry for them than anyone else at the Court. Henriette remembered how he had danced with her and that the frown on his face had meant that he was sorry he had slighted her. He was ashamed of what he had done. Therefore he would take great pains to be kind. That was the sort of boy Louis was. While he had strong desires, while the sycophants about him assured him that his conduct was as perfect as his person, he yet wished to do what was right in his own eyes.

He was sorry for his thin little cousin; therefore he made a point of graciously inviting her and her mother to his Coronation. That was all. Henriette kept reminding herself of this.

Now they were bringing Louis into the Cathedral.

At six o'clock that morning, two Bishops, preceded by the Canons of the Chapter, had gone to the Archbishop's Palace – where Louis had had his lodging – and up to the

King's bedchamber. The Precentor had knocked on the door with his silver wand.

'What do you want?' the Grand Chamberlain had asked from within.

'We desire the King,' said the Bishops.

'The King sleeps.'

'We desire Louis, the XIV of that name, son of the great Louis XIII, whom God has given us to be our King.'

Then they entered the chamber where Louis had been lying in the state bed, pretending to be asleep. He wore a cambric shirt and red satin, gold-braid-trimmed tunic slit in certain places to allow him to be anointed with holy oil. Over this he wore a robe of cloth of silver, and on his head there was a black velvet cap decorated with feathers and diamonds.

The Bishops and their followers then helped him to rise and conducted him to the Cathedral.

As he entered, between the Bishops, Henriette studied this beautiful boy. All eyes were on him; he was sixteen and the eulogists had not greatly exaggerated when they declared that his youthful beauty was unequalled.

Between the Swiss Guards the procession made its way to the chancel where the King's chair and *prie-dieu*, upholstered in purple velvet decorated with the golden lilies of France, had been placed on Turkey rugs.

As she watched the ceremony, Henriette thought of another man whom she loved very dearly indeed. If he could have been in a similar position, how wonderful that would be! If it were Charles who was being anointed with oil, and this ceremony was taking place, not in France but in England, she told herself, she would have felt complete contentment, for then he would take her home with him, and she would live at his Court where there would be no slights, no humiliations; she need not then be disturbed by her feelings for her cousin Louis; she could give herself up to the pleasure of the King of England's company and forget those incomprehensible longings which were aroused within her by the King of France.

The Bishops were asking those present if they were willing to have this Prince as their King; and the purple velvet sandals were being put on Louis' feet while he was helped into the robe and dalmatica, and the great ceremonial cloak of purple velvet embroidered with golden lilies was placed about his shoulders. Now he looked indeed magnificent. He held out his hands that the consecrated gloves might be slipped over them and the ring placed on his finger; then he took the Sceptre in his right hand and the Hand of Justice in his left, after which the great Crown of Charlemagne was set upon his head, and he was led to the throne, there to receive the homage of the peers.

'Long live the King!' echoed through the Cathedral and the streets beyond.

Louis XIV, the *Roi-Soleil*, had been crowned. It was an inspiring ceremony. Tears dimmed Henriette's eyes. She was praying fervently for the King of England, but the magnificent image of the King of France would come between her and her prayers.

*

How tired one grew of exile! thought Charles. How weary of moving from place to place in search of hospitality! One had to suppress one's finer feelings when one was a beggar.

'Ah,' he said one day, as he looked on the river from his lodgings in the town of Cologne, 'it is a mercy that I am a man of low character, for how could one of noble ideals tolerate my position? From which we learn that there is good in all evil. A comforting thought, my friends!'

He smiled at his Chancellor, Edward Hyde, who had joined him in Paris some years ago and had since been his most trusted adviser. He liked Hyde – a grim old man, who did not stoop to flatter the King in case he should one day come into his own.

That amused Charles. 'Others,' he said, 'wish to ensure their future – not that they have any high hopes that I shall be of much use to them – but flattery costs little. Reproaches cost far more. That is why I will have you with me, Edward, my friend. And if there should come that happy day when I am restored to my own, you shall be well paid for those reproaches you heaped upon me when I was in exile. There! Are you not pleased?'

'I should be better pleased if Your Majesty would not

merit these reproaches. I would rather have the pleasure of praising you now, than the hope of rewards in the future.'

'Would all men had your honesty, Chancellor,' said the King lightly. 'And would I had a state whose affairs were worthy of your counsel. Alas! How do we pass our days? In vain hopes and wild pleasure. What new songs are there to be sung today? Shall we throw the dice again? Any pretty women whose acquaintance we have not made?'

'Your Majesty, could you not be content with one mistress? It would be so much more respectable if you could.'

'I am content with each one while I am with her. Content! I am deeply content. One leaves me and another appears, and then I find contentment again.'

'If Your Majesty would but occupy yourself with matters of state you would have less time for women.'

'Matters of state! They are things to dream about. Women! They are to be possessed. One woman in Cologne is worth a million imaginary state papers in Whitehall.'

'Your Majesty is incorrigible.'

'Nay, Edward, merely resigned. I will tell you this: You have enemies here at my mock Court and they would seek to drive a wedge between us were that possible. Yesterday one said to me: "Your Majesty, do you know what your respected Chancellor said of you? Most disrespectfully he spoke of you. He declared you are a profligate who fritters his time away in vices of all descriptions." And how do you think I answered your calumniator, Edward? I said: "It does not surprise me that he should say that once in a way to you, for he says the same of me to myself a hundred times a week!" '

Charles laughed and laid his arm about his Chancellor's shoulders. 'There!' he continued. 'That is what I think of you and your honesty. I can appreciate other things ... I can love other things ... besides beautiful women!'

'Let us talk of state matters,' said Edward Hyde. 'It would be better if your sister of Orange did not make her proposed visit to Paris to see your mother.'

Charles nodded. 'I see that, Edward.'

'Now that we are entering into negotiations with Spain,

and Ormonde has gone on a mission to Madrid, we do not wish Spain to think that the bond between ourselves and France is being strengthened. The Spaniards will know that your mother and sister are being treated with scant courtesy in France; therefore they will be more likely to favour us. Any who is out of favour with France should readily find favour with Spain.'

'I will speak to my sister.'

'You should forbid her to make the journey.'

Charles looked uneasy. 'I . . . forbid Mary!'

'You are the King of England.'

'A King without a kingdom, a man who would often have been without a home but for Mary. What would have happened to us but for her, I cannot think. Holland was our refuge until, with the death of her husband, she lost her influence. Even now we owe the money, on which we live, to her; but for my sister Mary I should not have even this threadbare shirt to cover my shoulders. And you would ask me to forbid her making a journey on which she has set her heart!'

'You are the King.'

'I fear she will think me an ungrateful rogue.'

'It matters not what she thinks of Your Majesty.'

'It matters not! My dear sister to think me an ungrateful oaf? My dear Chancellor, you astonish me! A moment ago you were complaining because the world looks upon me as a libertine; now you say it is a matter of little importance that my sister should find me ungrateful.'

'Your Majesty . . .'

'I know. I see your point. Ingratitude . . . intolerance . . . are minor sins in the eyes of the statesman. If the outcome of these things is beneficial, then it is good statecraft. But to invite a pretty woman to one's bed . . . in your eyes, Edward, and in the eyes of Puritans, that is black sin; yet to me – if she be willing – it seems but pleasure. We do not see life through the same eyes, and you would be judged right by the majority, so it is I who am out of step with the world. Perhaps that is why I wait here, frittering away my time with dice and women.'

'I should advise Your Majesty to speak to your sister.'

Charles bowed his head.

'And if I were Your Majesty I would not continue to associate with the woman, Lucy Water, who now calls herself Mistress Barlow.'

'No? But I am fond of Lucy. She has a fine boy who is mine also.'

'She is mistress of others besides Your Majesty.'

'I know it.'

'There are many gentlemen of the Court who share your pleasure in this woman.'

'Lucy has much to give.'

'You are too easy-going.'

'I am content to go where my will carries me. There is no virtue in my easy temper.'

'The woman could be sent to England.'

'To England?'

'Indeed, yes. It would be better so. She could be promised a pension.'

Charles laughed.

'Your Majesty is amused?'

'Only at the idea of such a magnanimous promise from a man in a threadbare shirt.'·

'There are some who would help to pay the pension for the sake of ridding Your Majesty of the woman.'

'Poor Lucy!'

'She would enjoy returning to her native land doubtless. If the Spanish project comes to anything, we should leave Cologne. She would not wish to stay here when all her lovers had gone. Have I your permission to put this proposition to her, Your Majesty?'

'Put it by all means, but don't force her to go back to live among Puritans, Edward.'

'Then sign this paper. It is a promise of a pension.'

Charles signed. Poor Lucy! He had ceased to desire her greatly. Occasionally he visited her in indolence or out of kindness. He was not sure which, and he did not care enough to find out. One never knew, when visiting her, whether one would startle her with a lover who might be hiding in a cupboard until the royal visitor had departed. Such situations were not conducive to passion.

But as he signed he was really thinking of Mary, and what he would say to her.

Was it possible that Spain might help him to regain his throne?

There were times when some wild scheme would rouse him from his lethargy, and he would once more be conscious of hope.

*

Mary, the Princess of Orange, had all the Stuart gaiety. She had lost her husband; she was young and alone in a country which did not greatly love her; she was full of anxieties for her baby son; yet when she was with her brother she could fling aside her cares and laugh, dance and make merry.

She was looking forward to going to France as she had not looked forward to anything for a long time.

'Paris!' she cried. 'And all the gaiety I hear is indulged in there! I want to enjoy all that. And most of all, I want to see our mother whom I have not seen for thirteen years, and dear little Henriette whom I have not seen at all. Poor Mother! She was always so tender and loving.'

'To those who do her commands!'

'Charles, you have grown cynical.'

'Realistic, my dear. The longer I live, and the farther I wander, the greater grows my respect for the truth. Ask poor Henry to tell you of our mother's tender love!'

'Poor little Henry! His was a sad experience.'

'And entirely our mother's doing.'

'You must not dislike her because she is a Catholic.'

'It is not her religion that I hate. It is her unkindness to our brother. The boy was heartbroken when Ormonde brought him to me.'

'Well, Charles, you have made up to him for what he suffered at our mother's hands. He may have been disappointed in her, but he is not so in his brother. He adores his King; and is it not pathetic to see how he tries to model himself on you?'

'It is more than pathetic – it is tragic. And so bad for his morals.'

'You might try to prevent that by leading a more respectable life yourself, brother.'

169

'I cannot attempt the impossible – even for young Henry.'

Mary laughed. 'Now you are looking stern,' she said. 'Now you are preparing to pass on Master Hyde's orders to me. You are going to forbid me to go to Paris.'

'Mary, who am I to forbid you!'

'You are the King and the head of our house.'

'You are the Princess of Orange, mother of the Orange heir. I am your out-at-elbows brother.'

'Oh Charles, dearest Charles, you are not a very good advocate for your cause. You are a profligate, they say, and I know that to be true; you are careless; you are idle; but I love you.'

'If the reward of profligacy is love, then mayhap I am not such a fool after all.'

'Are you forbidding me to go to Paris?'

'I forbid nothing.'

'But you ask me not to go?'

' 'Twill offend the Spaniards.'

'Listen to me, Charles. You and our mother have quarrelled over Henry. It is a bad thing in any family to quarrel – in ours it might well be disastrous. I wish to right these matters. For years I have longed to see our mother again.'

Charles smiled. 'Dear Mary,' he said. 'You must please yourself. Go, if that is what you wish.'

'I am sure I am right. I do not believe the Spaniards will help you regain your kingdom. They'll not fight for you. They are just temporarily friendly with you because, for the moment, the French are not.'

'I think you have the truth there.'

'We must not have these rifts between members of our family. Our mother must love you again. She must love Henry. Oh, Charles, there are so few of us left now. Smile on my journey. I could not enjoy it if you did not.'

'Then if my smile is necessary to your pleasure, you must have it, dear sister. Take a kiss to my dear Minette.'

Mary embraced him warmly.

'Yes, Charles,' she said. 'Do you know you're my favourite brother? I would almost go further and, but for a small person who now resides in Holland, I would say you are my favourite man.'

'I really begin to think,' said the King, 'that I am not such a fool as I believed myself to be.'

'You're the wisest fool on earth. I shall take your Chancellor's daughter with me as a maid of honour. She is a pleasant girl, Anne Hyde. And I wish her to make herself very agreeable to our mother whom I would like to see reconciled to the girl's father. She declares Hyde advises you to act against her wishes, you know.'

'You make me wistful. I would that I could go with you on this journey to France.'

'What! Have you a fancy for the Chancellor's daughter?'

'Anne Hyde! Assuredly not.'

'Then I am glad, because I think her father would have a high pride in her virtue.'

'I was not thinking of being with Anne Hyde,' said Charles. 'I was thinking of the pleasure of seeing Minette again.'

*

Lucy was in bed nibbling sweetmeats. She could hear Ann Hill moving about whilst she cleaned the apartment. Lucy had coarsened slightly, but she was still beautiful. On the pillow beside her had rested, until a few hours ago, the fair head of one of the Court gentlemen. She did not know his name, but he had been a satisfactory lover.

Her clothes lay on the floor where she had flung them; Ann had not yet been in to tidy the room. Ann was angry with her mistress. Ann thought her mistress should not receive any gentlemen in her bed except the King.

But Lucy must have a lover; she might sigh for the King, but the King was not always at hand, and there were so many waiting to take his place.

Now she wondered whether the fair gentleman would visit her again this night. If he did not, another would.

Ann had come into the room and was clicking her tongue at the state of the apartment as she picked up the garments which lay about the floor.

'Don't frown!' cried Lucy. 'It makes you look uglier than usual.'

'If this is what beauty brings you to, I'm glad I'm ugly,'

muttered Ann. 'A new man last night! I've never seen him before.'

'He was wonderful!' murmured Lucy.

'What if . . .'

'What if the King had visited me? Oh no!' Lucy sighed and was momentarily sad. 'He is pleasantly occupied elsewhere for the last week – and the next, I doubt not.'

'It's wrong,' said Ann, shaking her head. 'Quite wrong.'

'Is it? I never have time to think about it.'

'You think of little else!'

'It seems that I am thinking of last night's pleasure until it is time to anticipate tonight's.'

Ann said: 'It's depravity . . . and everybody here seems to . . . to wallow in it.'

'It is a pastime in which one cannot indulge alone.'

'For the children to see such things is not right.'

'They are too young to know.'

'Mary may be. Jemmy is not. He begins to wonder. He is nearly seven. It is time you gave up this way of living and settled down to quiet, and thought of looking after the children.'

Lucy stared before her. She loved her children – both of them – but she adored Jemmy. He had such vitality, such charm, and he was such a handsome little boy. Moreover everybody who visited the house – and in particular the King – made much of him.

Settle down and be quiet! Look after Jemmy! As well ask a bird not to sing in the spring, a bee not to gather honey!

Ann went on: 'There are rumours. There'll be another move soon.'

'I dare swear we shall go to Breda.'

'If there is another attempt . . .'

'Attempt?'

'You think of nothing but who your next lover will be. Don't you see they're only waiting here. One day they'll be gone . . . and then where will you be? They'll all be leaving here to fight with the King, and you'll be left with a few Germans to make love to you.'

'You're in a bad mood today, Ann.'

'It's all these rumours,' said Ann. 'We shall be moving soon, I know. I wish we could go home.'

'Home?'

'To London. Fancy being in Paul's Walk again!'

Lucy's eyes were dreamy. 'Yes,' she said. 'Just fancy! Fancy going to Bartholomew and Southwark Fairs.'

'I'd like to walk by the river again,' said Ann wistfully. 'No other place is the same, is it? They don't look the same . . . don't smell the same . . . All other places are dull. They weary a body . . . and make her long for home.'

'To walk down the gallery at the Royal Exchange again . . .' murmured Lucy.

Jemmy came running into the room. He wore a toy sword at his belt; it was a present from his father. 'I'm a soldier!' he cried. 'I'm for the King. Are you for the Parliament? Then you're dead . . . dead . . . dead . . .'

He took out his sword and waved it at Ann, who skilfully eluded him.

'Wars, wars, wars!' said Lucy. 'It is always wars. Even Jemmy dreams of wars.'

'I'm the Captain,' said Jemmy. 'I'm no Roundhead.' He climbed on to the bed looking for comfits and sweetmeats which were always kept close by Lucy so that all she had to do was reach for them. Her lovers kept her well supplied; they were the only presents Lucy appreciated.

Jemmy sat on the bed, arranging the sweetmeats as soldiers and eating them one by one. 'Dead, dead, dead,' he said, popping them into his mouth. 'Is my Papa coming today?'

'We do not know,' said Ann. 'But if you eat more of those sweetmeats you will be too sick to see him, if he does.'

Jemmy paused for a second or so; then he continued to murmur 'Dead . . . dead . . . dead' as he popped sweet after sweet into his mouth. He was remarkably like his father at that moment.

A serving maid came in to say that a gentleman was waiting to see Mistress Barlow.

'Hurry!' cried Lucy. 'My mirror! My comb! Ann . . . quick! Jemmy, you must go away. Who is it, I wonder?'

'If it is my father, I shall stay,' said Jemmy. 'If it is Sir

Henry, I shall stay too. He promised to bring me a pony to ride.' He leaped off the bed. 'He may have brought it.'

The maid said that it was neither the King nor Sir Henry Bennett. It was an elderly gentleman whom she did not know and who would not give his name.

Lucy and Ann exchanged glances. An elderly gentleman who had never been here before? Lucy liked young lovers. She grimaced at Ann.

'I should put a shawl over your shoulders,' said Ann, placing one there.

Lucy grimaced again and pushed the shawl away so that the magnificent bust and shoulders were not entirely hidden.

Edward Hyde was shown into the room. He flinched at the sight of the voluptuous woman on the bed. The morals of the Court – which he would be the first to admit were set by his master – were constantly shocking him. He thought of his daughter, Anne, and was glad that the Princess of Orange was taking her away. He thought: What I must face in the service of my master! And his thoughts went back to that occasion when, seeking to join Charles in France, his ship had been taken by corsairs, and he, robbed of his possessions, had been made a slave before he finally escaped.

'It is my lord Chancellor!' said Lucy.

Edward Hyde bowed his head.

'This is the first time you have visited my apartment,' she went on.

'I come on the King's pleasure.'

'I did not think that you came on your own!' laughed Lucy.

The Chancellor looked impatient; he said quickly: 'It is believed that we shall not be here in Cologne much longer.'

'Ah!' said Lucy.

'And,' went on Hyde, 'I have a proposition to make. Many people remain here because they dare not live in England. That would not apply to you. If you wished you could return there, set up your house, and none would say you nay.'

'Is that so?'

'Indeed it is. And it would be the wisest thing you could do.'

'How should I live there?'

'How do you live here?'

'I have many friends.'

'English friends. The English are as friendly at home as in exile. The King has promised to pay you a pension of four hundred pounds a year if you return to England.'

'It is for Jemmy,' she said. 'He wants Jemmy to be brought up in England; that's it, I'll swear.'

'It would be a very good reason for your going.'

'London,' she said. 'I wonder if it has changed much.'

'Why not go and find out?'

'The King . . .?'

'He will not be long in Cologne.'

'No,' said Lucy sadly. 'He will go, and he will take the most gallant gentlemen with him.'

'Go to London,' said the Chancellor. 'You'll be happier there, and one day, let us hope, all the friends you have known here will join you there. What do you say? Four hundred pounds a year; and you have the King's promise of it as soon as it is possible. A passage could be arranged for you. What do you say, Mistress Barlow? What do you say?'

'I say I will consider the offer.'

He took her hand and bowed over it.

'The serving girl will show you out,' she told him.

When he had left she called Ann Hill to her.

'Ann,' she said, 'talk to me of London. Talk as you love to talk. Come, Ann; sit on the bed there. How would you like to go to London, Ann? How would you like to go home?'

Ann stood still as though transfixed. She was smelling the dampness in the air on those days when the mist rose up from the Thames; she was hearing the shouts and screams of a street brawl; she was watching the milkmaids bearing their yokes along the cobbled streets; she was seeing the gabled houses on an early summer's morning.

And, watching her, Lucy caught her excitement.

*

At the Palais-Royal, Henrietta Maria and her daughter were awaiting the arrival of Mary of Orange. The Queen felt happier than she had for some time; the royal family of France, although they had so long neglected the exiled Queen and her daughter Henriette, were preparing to give Mary of Orange a royal welcome.

'This is an honour of which we must not be insensible,' said Henrietta Maria to her youngest daughter. 'The King, the Queen, and Monsieur are all riding out to meet Mary at Saint-Dennis.'

'It is Holland they honour, Mam, not us,' Henriette reminded her mother.

'It is Mary, and Mary is one of us. Oh, I do wonder what she will be like. Poor Mary! I remember well her espousal. She was ten years old at the time, and she was married in the Chapel at Whitehall to the Prince her husband, who was a little boy of eleven. It was at the time when your father was forced into signing Strafford's death warrant; and the day after the marriage the mob broke into Westminster Abbey and . . . and . . .'

'Mam, I beg of you do not talk of the past. Think of the future and Mary's coming. That will cheer you.'

'Ah, yes, it will cheer me. It will be wonderful to see her again . . . my little girl. A widow now. Oh, what sorrows befall our family!'

'But there is joy coming now, Mam. Mary will soon be with us, and I know her visit will make us very happy.'

'Hers was a Protestant marriage.' Henrietta Maria's brow darkened.

'Please, Mam, do not speak of that. She will soon be here with us. Let us be content with that.'

They heard the shouts and cheers as the party approached.

Mary was riding between Louis and Queen Anne. Philippe was on the other side of his brother. This was indeed a royal welcome for Mary.

So the first time Henriette set eyes on her sister was a very ceremonious occasion; but there was time in between the balls and masques, which the royal family of France had devised for Mary's entertainment, for them to get to know each other.

Henriette discovered Mary to be warm-hearted and delighted to be with her family again. She was merry and quick to joke, and in that she reminded Henriette of Charles; she talked continually of her little boy who was now five years old – her little William of Orange, such a solemn boy, a regular Dutch William! She spoke sadly of her husband. She had been loth to marry him, she told Henriette as they sat alone. 'So very frightened I was. I was younger than you, Henriette; think of that! But he was frightened too, and far shyer than I was, and we soon learned to love each other. And he died of that dreadful pox. It was a great tragedy for me, Henriette, in more ways than one. I could not then offer your brothers the hospitality which I had shown them hitherto; but more than that, I had lost a husband and protector . . . the father of my little Dutch William.'

Henriette shed tears for her sister's sorrow, but more often she was joining in her sister's laughter.

Each day there was some entertainment for Mary's pleasure. Even young Philippe gave a ball two days after her arrival. It took place in the Salle de Gardes, and Philippe himself had spent much time and trouble ensuring that the illuminations should be of the brightest. In the tapestry-decorated *salle*, it was King Louis who opened the ball with Henriette. Mary, of course, did not dance, as French etiquette, dictated by Queen Anne, decreed that widows should not dance at great balls, and only on private occasions should they be allowed to do so.

Louis composed a ballet for her pleasure. It was founded on the story of Psyche, and never, declared the courtiers, had the King danced with greater perfection. Chancellor Seguier gave a fête in her honour, and the galleries which led to the ballroom were lighted with three hundred torches.

Mademoiselle, who was still banished from the Court, invited the Princess of Orange to her country residence of Chilly where she sought to outdo in splendour all the previous entertainments which the Princess had seen.

Mademoiselle, resplendent in jewels, was a dazzling hostess.

'Why, Henriette,' she said to her cousin on that

occasion, 'how thin you are! Worn out, I dare swear, by all this unaccustomed gaiety. You must be rather sad at Colombes and Chaillot and the Palais-Royal. So very quiet it must be for you!'

'And you too, Mademoiselle, here in the country.'

'Oh, I know how to entertain myself. I have my own little Court here, you see, and I have heard that I shall very soon be invited back to Court. I shall go at my pleasure.'

'I am glad of that, Mademoiselle,' said Henriette. 'I know how unhappy it must have made you to feel the King's displeasure.'

'It is not Louis. It is his mother. What jewels your sister has! They rival anything I see here. And Henriette, there is something I would say to you. You should not, you know, go in to supper before me. I should take precedence over you.'

'My mother says that is not so; and you know how important it is that everyone should walk in the right order.'

'In the old days the Kings of Scotland gave place to the Kings of France. Your brother . . . if he had a crown . . . would be a Scottish King, would he not?'

'But also a King of England . . .'

'My dear Henriette, you really should step aside for me to go into supper before you.'

'My mother would never allow me to. Nor would Queen Anne.'

Mademoiselle pouted. 'Such fusses!' she said. 'And over such small details. The Queen gives too much thought to such matters. Well, we shall see who will have precedence. Mark you, I think it would be a different matter if your brother were a ruling king.'

'In the eyes of the French Court he is still a king.'

'Lately, I have wondered. But enough of this. Enjoy yourself, Henriette. My poor child, it must be enchanting for you. You only go to the little private dances at the Louvre now, don't you?'

Mademoiselle left Henriette and returned to her guest of honour.

'And how do you like the Court of France, Madame?'

'I am in love with the Court of France,' Mary told her.

'It is very different from that of Holland, is it not?'

'Indeed yes. Mayhap that is one reason why I have fallen so deeply in love with it.'

'You do not love the Court of Holland?'

'I will tell you this, Mademoiselle: as soon as my brother is settled in his kingdom, I shall go and live with him.'

'Ah! When will that be?'

'I pray to God each night,' said Mary vehemently, 'that his return will not be long delayed.'

'You think you would live in amity with Charles?'

'Any woman could live in amity with Charles. He is the sweetest-tempered man alive.'

Henrietta Maria heard them as they talked of her son, and her eyes sparkled with intrigue. Mademoiselle might be temporarily out of favour at the Court, but she was still the richest heiress in Europe; and badly Charles needed money.

'Ah!' she cried. 'I hear you talk of this poor King of England. So you wish to hear news of him, Mademoiselle?'

'Her Highness offered it without my expressing the wish,' said the insolent Mademoiselle.

'He is foolish,' said Henrietta Maria, 'in that he will never cease to love you.'

'And wise,' said Mademoiselle, 'in that he does not allow this devotion, which you say he has for me, to interfere with his interest in others.'

'He bade me tell you how sorry he was that he had to leave France without saying goodbye to you. Why, Mademoiselle, if you were married you would be your own mistress.'

'But the King, your son, would not give up any of his if I were!'

'You would do exactly as you pleased. He is, as his sister tells you, such a sweet-tempered person. It is impossible to quarrel with him.'

'And you, Madame, have achieved the impossible!'

'It is because he is unhappy that we have quarrelled. If you married him he would be so happy that he and I would be reconciled.'

'If the King cannot live happily with you, Madame, I doubt whether he could with me.'

179

Mademoiselle's brilliant eyes were turned on Louis who had begun to dance.

Henrietta Maria followed her gaze. She could scarcely hold back her anger. It was ridiculous. Mademoiselle was eleven years older than the King of France and Henrietta Maria meant Louis to marry her own Henriette.

Henrietta Maria knew that she must shelve her immediate desires – Charles' marriage with Mademoiselle and Henriette's with Louis. Her daughter Mary was as amiable as her brother and as eager to please and live peaceably with her family. She attended the Anglican church every day; but perhaps it was possible that Henrietta Maria might save her for the true Church.

'Dearest daughter,' she said, 'I want you to come to Chaillot with me tomorrow. I am sure a rest in the tranquil atmosphere there will do you so much good.'

Mary smiled at her mother. Charles was right about her, she thought. She was the most affectionate of mothers when her children obeyed her. But, thought Mary grimly, she shall never make a convert of me.

'Yes, Mama,' she said, 'I will with pleasure come to Chaillot, but I shall not go to Mass there. As you know, I always attend the Anglican church.'

Henrietta Maria frowned. 'One should never shut one's ears and one's heart, Mary. It is well to listen to both sides.'

'That is true enough, Mama. So I hope you will attend the Anglican church with me, as I shall come with you to Chaillot.'

'That is *quite* impossible!'

Henrietta Maria's whole body seemed to be bristling with indignation. Then her eyes filled with tears. 'I always think,' she said, 'that everything would have been so different had your father lived.'

Mary was filled with pity. Poor Mother! she thought. It is sad. She lost her husband and she loved him dearly; she must continually be haunted by the fear that she was instrumental in bringing him to his end. That is why she so fiercely maintains her grief. All her children will disappoint her, I fear. Charles has quarrelled with her. She has sworn she will never see Henry again. James – her favourite – will bring sorrow to her, I doubt not, for he was mightily taken with Anne Hyde when they met. And what will Mother say to a marriage with Anne Hyde, Charles' Chancellor's daughter? But perhaps it will not come to that. Let us hope that she will not disown James as she has Henry, and doubtless would Charles if she dared. I disappoint her because I will not turn Catholic. No wonder she dotes on our little sister. Henriette seems to be the only one who is able to please her. Now I foresee many arguments; she will call Père Cyprien and the Abbé Montague to deal with me. Dear Mother! I am so sorry. But I cannot give up my faith even to please you.

But those arguments did not take place, for within a few days news came that Mary's little Dutch William was ill, and the smallpox was feared.

She was beside herself with grief, and left at once for Holland.

*

Charles was riding to Breda. Another move – and who could say how long he would stay at Breda?

It was more than five years since he had set foot in England. Five wandering years! How many more would he spend – an exile from his kingdom? He was accustomed now to dreaming dreams, making plans which became nothing more than dreams. 'I have had so little luck since Worcester,' he told his friends, 'that I now expect none.'

He had said goodbye to Lucy and his son. They would be in London now. He did not care to think of London; but he hoped Lucy would fare well there. But Lucy, he assured himself, would fare well in any place. She would always have lovers to provide for her. How was he going to pay the four hundred pounds a year which he had promised her? He had no idea. His purse was empty. 'I am a generous man,' he often said. 'I love to give, and if the only things I am able to give are promises with little hope of fulfilling them, then must I give them.'

Lucy had said a sad farewell to him ... and to others; she had wept to leave him ... and to leave others.

He had swung young Jemmy up in his arms, and he knew then that he dearly loved the boy. If he had been the son of himself and Mademoiselle or Hortense Mancini or the now widowed Duchesse de Châtillon – someone whom he could have married – he would have been well content. It was a pity such a fine boy as Jemmy must be a bastard.

'What will you do in London, Jemmy?' he had asked.

'Fight for the King's cause!' had answered the sturdy little boy.

'Ah, my dear boy, you will best do that by keeping those fine sentiments to yourself.'

'I shall do it with my sword, Papa. Dead ... dead ... dead ... I'll cut off Cromwell's head.'

'Take care of yourself, my son. That is how you will best serve your King.'

Jemmy was not listening. He was fingering his sword and thinking of what he would do in London.

'You'll have to curb our young Royalist, Lucy,' Charles told the boy's mother. 'We have talked too freely before him, I fear.'

So they had gone, and here he was riding on to Breda.

His sister Mary joined him in the little town. She had left the French Court in haste on hearing news of her son's illness, but now cheering messages were reaching her. Her little William was merely suffering from an attack of measles, and not the dreaded smallpox as had been feared.

Mary, released from fear, was full of gaiety. She declared she could not come near Breda without meeting her favourite brother.

They embraced affectionately, and Charles made her tell him in detail all that had befallen her at the Court of France. He was particularly eager for news of Minette.

'I wonder who loves the other more – you or your little sister,' said Mary.

'Tell me – is she well?'

'Yes – well and charming; but she grows too fast; and life at the Court is not very happy for her and our mother. Mademoiselle makes herself unpleasant, demanding precedence whenever they meet.'

'A curse on Mademoiselle!'

'I thought you wanted to marry the woman.'

'Mam wanted it, you mean, and as for myself, I would

marry her, I dare swear, if she would have me. I'm not enamoured of her, but her fortune is too great to be turned lightly aside.'

'Poor Charles! Is your purse quite empty?'

'Very nearly.'

'I have brought twenty thousand pistoles for your use.'

'Mary, you are an angel! One day I shall pay you back. That's a promise.' He smiled wryly. 'I would give you a fortune if I had one; alas, all I have to lay at your feet is a promise.'

'One day you will in truth be King of England. I am sure of it, Charles. One day you will be restored to the throne. The people of England are not pleased with Puritan rule. How could they be? You know how they love gaiety. Now the theatres are closed; there is no singing, no dancing, nothing to do but contemplate their sins and wail for forgiveness. It is not the English man's or woman's way meekly to accept such constraint. They love pageantry above all things. They will soon decide to have no more of puritanism. They decided they would have no more Catholic rulers at one time; they will be equally firm, when the time comes, to ban puritanism. The Englishman does not like his religion to interfere with his pleasure.'

'I am beginning to think,' said Charles, 'that I make a very good Englishman.'

'You do indeed. And soon the English will realize this. Then they will implore you to return. They'll go down on their knees and beg you to return . . .'

'They will have no need to. They have but to lift a finger, to throw a smile to poor Charles Stuart, and he will be entirely at their service. Now let us talk of the family. It is so rarely that we meet and can be alone together. Let us indulge ourselves, Mary.'

'I wish it were a happier subject. I am a little disturbed about James and Anne Hyde. Perhaps I should never have taken the girl with me.'

'James . . . and Anne Hyde?'

'He has a fancy for her. She is a good girl, Charles.'

'And James . . . is not so good?'

Mary sighed. 'I can only hope that no ill comes of

it. I think of our mother and what she would have to say.'

'Poor Mam! We do not want her declaring that she will not see *James'* face again.'

'She is so ambitious for us all. She has been plaguing Mademoiselle . . . trying to persuade her to take you.'

Charles groaned. 'No! Not again!'

'And Mademoiselle spoke quite emphatically. I think, Charles, that you have fascinated her a little. If you were not an exile, willingly would she marry you.'

'There are hundreds who would willingly marry the reigning King of England, Mary. It is only when they consider Charles Stuart the exile, that they find him such an unattractive fellow.'

'Never that!' said Mary fondly. 'Threadbare and empty of purse you may be, but you are the most fascinating man in Europe. Mademoiselle's problem is that she would like to marry you, but her pride won't let her.'

'True! And I thank God that Mademoiselle's pride is there to protect me from Mademoiselle.'

'And, of course, our mother has hopes of Louis for Henriette.'

'That is what I would wish for, Mary. It is a cherished dream of mine. Dear sweet Minette . . . the Queen of France! How think you she would feel about it? I should not care to see her unhappy.'

'Louis is magnificent, Charles. He is physically perfect . . . a little stupid perhaps, by Stuart standards.' They laughed together. 'But he is so beautiful and not unkind. I think Henriette is fond of him. In fact I do not see how she could help being fond of him. She compares him with you. I know it. I know of it by the manner in which she speaks of you both in the same breath.'

'Then must Louis' perfections be more obvious than ever!'

'No, Charles. That is not so. In her eyes you are perfect. I said to her: "How perfectly Louis dances!" She answered: "He dances well, but he is not so graceful as Charles." I said: "Louis is surely the most handsome man in the world." She smiled and said: "That may be so. I am no judge. But he has not the wit of Charles." It is always

Charles. It should not be so: a Princess so to love her brother!'

'Dear Minette! She should not. I shall write to her and scold her for loving me too well. But I do not think she loves me one whit more than I love her. If ever I become King I shall bring my family home. We shall all be together. That is what I long for more than anything.'

'But,' said Mary pensively, 'I do not think she is untouched by Louis' charm. Indeed, I think she is very fond of him. He is a charming boy and of good character. He must be, for never was one more flattered, and yet his arrogance is not overpowering, and he always gives the impression of wishing to do what he considers right.'

'I doubt that he would marry Henriette while I am still an exile. Oh, Mary, if I regained my kingdom, what a difference that would make, eh? I doubt not that then my little Minette would become the Queen of France. What an excellent thing that could be for our two countries! What an alliance! For I would love the French more than ever if Minette were their Queen.'

'And you would take Mademoiselle for wife?'

'Ah! I doubt it. I doubt it very much. There is a great obstacle which I feel may prevent Mademoiselle and me from joining hands at the altar. While I am an exile she cannot contemplate marrying *me*; and if I had a crown fixed firmly on my head I could not bring myself to take *her*. Now let us drink to the future. Let us hope that our dreams will come true.'

'Our first step will be to put you on the throne of England, where you belong.'

'Our first step! But what a step! Yet, who knows . . . one day it may come to pass.'

*

When Lucy arrived in London she found that a great change had taken place in the city since she had left it.

Now the clothes of the people were drab, and the people themselves were, for the most part, suppressed and sullen. Those who were not, seemed to wear an air of perpetual complacency. All the ballad-singers had disappeared, and there were no spontaneous outbursts of pageantry which had been a feature of the old days. The only places which still flourished were the brothels, and their inmates still chattered to each other from windows of rooms which projected and almost met over the cobbled streets.

Lucy found rooms over a barber's shop near Somerset House. She was warmly received by the barber and, as she called herself Mistress Barlow, no one knew of her connexion with the King, nor that the bright-eyed little boy was Charles' son.

Ann Hill had taken charge, and told the barber that her mistress was a lady who had been living abroad and been trying for a long time to return to her native country.

They had a little money, and for a few days Lucy was content to lie in the room looking out on the street; but she soon began to long for a lover.

Each day Ann discovered more of the changes which had befallen London. All the taverns were closed; bull-baiting was suppressed; all the pleasure gardens were closed except the Mulberry Garden. There had been no Christmas festivals in the churches for a long time. There was no dancing in the streets on May Day.

'Why did we come back?' wailed Lucy. 'There was more fun at The Hague and in Cologne.'

A few days after her arrival she dressed herself with great care and went out. Everyone stared at her; she was different from other women. She looked like a foreigner. She soon found a lover – a high-ranking soldier of Cromwell's Ironsides; but she did not enjoy her relationship with him as she had with the merry Cavaliers in exile. He was conscious of sin the whole time he was with her, and he felt compelled to make love under cover of darkness, slipping into the rooms over the barber's shop at dusk, and leaving before it was light. Lucy was beautiful, and beauty, she believed, was not meant to be hidden by darkness. She was restive. She was wishing she had not come to London.

Finally, she told her lover that she had had enough of him and his preoccupation with sin, and that he had best take himself off to repentance.

After that it had become her habit to go out and wander disconsolately in the Mulberry Garden; it was not what it had been, of course; but it was still a place in which to sit and watch the world go by, to take a little refreshment under the trees and perhaps pick up a lover.

She did not meet a lover in the Mulberry Garden; but as she sat at one of the tables a woman approached and asked if she might join her.

'I saw you sitting there,' she said, 'and I thought I should like to join you. It is rarely one sees such ladies as yourself in the Mulberry Garden in these days.'

'Ah, these days!' said Lucy incautiously. 'In the old days, it was different, I can tell you.'

'I could tell you too!' sighed her companion. 'The old days! Will they ever come back, do you think?'

'You would like to see them back?'

'Who would not? I was fond of the play. I was fond of a bit of fun . . . a bit of gaiety in the streets. Now it is nothing but prayer-meetings . . . all day and every day. Will you take a little refreshment with me?'

'Thank you,' said Lucy, warming to the company. The woman was rather flashily dressed; she was no Puritan; that much was clear.

They ate tarts with a little meat, which they washed down with Rhenish wine.

'You are a very beautiful woman,' said Lucy's new friend.

Lucy smiled her acknowledgement of the compliment.

'And very popular with the men, I'll warrant!'

'Are there any men left in this town?' asked Lucy ironically.

'Yes. A few. They visit my house near Covent Garden occasionally. You must pay us a visit.'

'I'd like to.'

'Why not come along now?'

'I have a family who will be waiting for my return.'

'A family indeed!'

'A boy and a girl. I have left them with my maid.'

'Where do you live then?'

'Near Somerset House. Over a barber's shop.'

'It hardly seems a fitting lodging for a lady like you.'

'Oh, I have had some fine lodgings, I can tell you.'

'I don't need to be told. I can guess.'

'You would be surprised if I told you where I have lodged.'

'You have been in foreign parts, eh?'

'Yes. At The Hague and Paris. And . . . Cologne.'

'There were Englishmen at those places, were there not?'

'Indeed there were!'

'Real gentlemen, I'll warrant.'

'You would be surprised if you knew.'

'Nothing would surprise me about a beautiful woman like yourself.'

'You are very kind.'

'I but speak the truth.' The woman lifted her glass and said: 'I will drink to the health of someone whose name should not be mentioned.'

Lucy seized her glass and tears shone in her eyes. 'God bless him!' she said.

'You speak with fervour, madam.'

'I do indeed. There is none like him . . . none . . . none at all.'

'You knew him . . . in The Hague and Paris . . .?'

'Yes, I knew him well.'

The woman nodded, then said: 'Do not speak of it here. It would not be safe.'

'Thank you. You are kind to remind me.'

'It is good to have a friend. I hope we shall meet again. We *must* meet again. Will you visit my house tomorrow?'

'If it is possible, perhaps.'

'Please come. Come in the evening. We make merry then. What is your name?'

'Barlow. Mistress Barlow.'

'Mistress Barlow, I hope we shall be great friends. I see we are two who think similar thoughts in this drab place our city has become. My name is Jenny. Call me Jenny. It's more friendly.'

'I am Lucy.'

'Lucy! It's a pretty name, and you have a pretty way of speaking. That's not the London way.'

'No. I come from Wales.'

'Barlow! Is that a Welsh name?'

'Yes. It is, and so is Water . . . my maiden name.'

'Water, did you say?'

'Yes. My name before I married . . . Mr Barlow.'

'Lucy Water . . . recently come from The Hague. You will

come to see me tomorrow, please. I shall look forward to your visit.'

Lucy went home not ill-pleased with her visit to Mulberry Garden. Perhaps she would go to Jenny's house next day. It would be interesting to meet some merry company again.

*

Lucy did go, and it was a merry evening. She awoke next morning in a strange bedroom, and when she opened her eyes she was slightly perturbed.

Ann would guess that she had stayed the night, not caring to face the streets at a late hour, and she would look after the children, so there was nothing to fear on that score; but Lucy's lover of last night had not entirely pleased her. She missed the pleasant manners of the Court gentlemen. Yes, that was it; last night's lover had been too crude for Lucy.

There was another discovery she had made. Jenny's home was nothing but a bawdy house. She had begun to realize that, not long after she had entered it; but already by then she had drunk a little too much and felt too lazy – and, of course, it would have been very impolite – to leave abruptly.

As she lay there she understood that she had not enjoyed last night's lover. Love, such as undertaken in Jenny's establishment, was quite different from that which she had hitherto enjoyed. She had always been fastidious in choosing her lovers; something in them had attracted her or made a strong appeal to her sensuality. This was quite different. This was lust, to be bartered for and haggled over. Lucy was not that kind of loose woman.

Now she knew why Jenny had been so friendly in the Garden, why she had been so eager for her to visit her home. She was glad her companion of last night was no longer with her. She would rise and dress, thank Jenny for her entertainment and slip away, never to see the woman again.

She was dressed when there was a knock at her door.

'Come in!' she cried; and Jenny entered.

'Good morrow to you, Lucy. Why, you look as pretty by morning light as by candle light, I swear. Were you comfortable in this room?'

'Yes, thank you. I was quite comfortable.'

Jenny laughed. 'I notice you took the most amusing of the gentlemen, Lucy.'

'Was he the most amusing?'

'I could see that from the moment you set eyes on him, no other would do.'

'I fear I drank too freely. I am not accustomed to over-much wine.'

'Are you not? It is good for you, and it gives you such high spirits, you know.'

'My spirits have always been high enough without. Now I must thank you for my lodging and be off.'

'Lucy . . . you'll come again?'

Lucy was evasive. She was telling herself that if she had not drunk so much wine, if she had not been so long without a lover, what had happened last night would never have taken place.

'Mayhap I will,' she said.

'Lucy, I'll make you very comfortable here. Those rooms over the shop . . . they must be most unsuitable for a lady used to the comforts you enjoyed at The Hague and Cologne.'

'I manage very well. I have my faithful servant to look after me, and my children to consider.'

'You could bring them all here. I could use a new servant, or you could keep her merely to wait on you. The children would be welcome here. We are a very happy family in this house.'

The woman was breathing heavily. Lucy smelt the stale gin on her breath, and was aware of the avaricious gleam in her eyes. Lucy was not clever, but she now understood that she had behaved with the utmost folly. Doubtless there had been gossip bandied about as to the life Charles led on the Continent, and her name might well have been one of those which were mentioned in connexion with him; and she, stupidly, had betrayed who she was, and perhaps last night had babbled even more.

No wonder this woman was eager to make her an inmate of her brothel! She could imagine what a draw the mistress of Charles Stuart would be.

Then Lucy wanted to get away. She wanted to wipe the

shame of the place from her mind. She wanted to forget that she had spent the night in a brothel. All her love affairs had been so different. She had discovered that last night – half tipsy though she had been.

She drew herself away. 'Well, I will say goodbye now.'

'But you'll come again?'

'I . . . I'll see.'

The woman's eyes narrowed. She was not going to let Lucy escape as easily as that.

*

Ann was reproachful. She guessed that Lucy had spent the night with a man. She said nothing, but she was a little frightened. Glad as she was to be in London, she was quicker than Lucy to realize that, in more ways than one, this was not the same London which they had left more than eight years ago.

Jenny called. She was wheedling, and then faintly threatening. She hinted that one who had come rather mysteriously from across the water and had clearly been a close friend of people who were regarded as the enemies of the Commonwealth, might find it convenient to shelter in the house of a good friend who would protect her.

'I am very comfortable here,' Lucy told her.

'You may not always be so,' retorted Jenny. 'You may be glad of friends one day, and that day soon!'

'I shall not join you at your brothel,' declared Lucy firmly.

Jenny's eyes gleamed. 'You may find there are worse places than my house, Lucy Water.'

'I have never been in one,' said Lucy carelessly.

'You'll change your mind.'

'Never!' cried Lucy, and for once her mouth was set into lines of determination.

The woman left, and Lucy lay thoughtfully nibbling sweetmeats.

Jenny called again on two other occasions; she sought to placate Lucy, but Lucy's determination not to join her household brought more veiled threats.

A few days later two men called at the rooms over the barber's shop. They were soberly-clad, grim-faced men, servants of the Commonwealth. They came to search the rooms and Mistress Barlow's belongings, they said.

'For what reason?' demanded Ann on the threshold.

'For this reason,' answered one of the men. 'We suspect that the woman who occupies these rooms has recently come from the Continent, and that she is a spy for Charles Stuart.'

Lucy rose from her bed, her flimsy draperies falling about her; but these men were not Court gallants to be moved by beauty in distress. They began to search the room, and in a box they found the King's promise to pay Lucy four hundred pounds a year.

One of them said: 'Mistress, prepare yourself to leave this place at once.' He turned to Ann. 'You also. We are taking you all to another lodging.'

Trembling, Ann prepared herself and the children, who were making eager inquiries.

'Where are we going?' said little Mary. 'Are we going for a walk?'

'You must wait to see where we are taken,' Lucy told her.

'Mama,' cried Jemmy, 'do you want to go? If you don't, I'll run them through with my sword.'

The men looked at Jemmy without a smile. Jemmy hated them. He was used to caresses and admiration. He drew his sword from his belt, but Ann was beside him; she caught his arm.

'Now, Master Jemmy, do as you're told. That is what is best for your mother . . . and for us all. It is what your father would wish.'

Jemmy fell silent. There was something in Ann's face which made him pause to think; he saw that his mother was in earnest too. This was not a game.

In a very short time they had left the barber's shop and were being taken towards the water's edge, to where a barge was waiting for them.

Slowly they slipped down the river, and soon Jemmy was pointing out the great grey fortress on its banks. 'There's the Tower!' he cried.

'That's so,' said one of the men. 'Take a good look at it from the outside, my boy. Mayhap you'll be seeing nothing but the inside for a long time.'

'What do you mean?' cried Lucy.

'Just that we are taking you to your new lodging, Mistress, your lodging in the Tower . . . the rightful place for friends of Charles Stuart who come to London to spy for him.'

*

Lucy was ailing. The rigorous life of a prisoner did not suit her. She had been accustomed to too much comfort. She had grown thinner since her incarceration; she would sit listlessly at her barred window, looking out on the church of St Peter ad Vincula, and every time she heard the bell toll she would be seized with a fit of shivering.

Ann looked after her as well as she could, but Ann too was frightened. She remembered the day, over six years ago, when the Parliament had beheaded the King. She wondered if the same fate was in store for them.

Their jailer would tell them nothing. He would bring their not very palatable fare each day, and they would eat it in their cell. There were no sweetmeats for Lucy now; worse still, there were no lovers.

Jemmy often flew into a rage. He was a bold boy and a spoilt one. He demanded that they be set free.

He told the jailor: 'One day you will suffer for this. My father will see that you do. I will kill you dead with my sword, and when my father is King again . . .'

The jailor listened in horror. He had not heard such words since the close of the war, and to think that he had under his care the son of Charles Stuart – bastard though he might be – overwhelmed him with astonishment at the importance and responsibility of his task in guarding these prisoners.

The jailor had a son who helped him in his work – a youth in his teens. Lucy's interest was slightly stirred at the sight of him, for he was a good-looking boy; but her attempts to fascinate him were half-hearted; she missed her ribands and laces, her sweetmeats and her comfortable lodgings. She was almost always tired and listless; there was about her an air of bewilderment. She, who had always been so healthy as to be unconscious of her health, was now made uncomfortably aware of many minor ailments.

All the same she made the young man conscious of her fascination, and when his father was not present he would smile shyly at his pretty prisoner and exchange a few words with her. He even brought in some sweetmeats for her, and a blue riband to tie about her hair.

Ann thought: One night I shall doubtless find him sneaking in to lie on the straw with her. Will she sink so low?

But that did not happen, for it was quickly realized that Lucy was no subtle spy. She was merely one of Charles Stuart's mistresses and, said those in authority, if we are going to keep all such women under lock and key, we shall soon have no room in the Tower for others. What harm can this woman do? She is nothing but a stupid, wanton creature. Why should we waste good victuals on Charles Stuart's mistress and his bastards? Send them back whence they came, and warn them not to come to England again.

So it was arranged, and a few months after Lucy's arrival in England she found herself, with Ann and the children, on the way back to Holland.

*

Henrietta Maria and her daughter had once more retired to the country and only made very brief appearances at state functions.

It was clear that the fortunes of the Stuarts were at their lowest. Cromwell, determined to fight the 'Lord's battles', had sent his Ironsides to join with Marshall Turenne against the Spaniards who, he declared, were 'the underpropper of the Romish Babylon'; which meant that the Protector was fighting with France. How could the royal family of France honour the enemies of their ally, the Protector? All Henrietta Maria and her daughter could do was remain in obscurity, while it was impossible for any of the Stuart men to set foot in France. In desperation Charles, James and Henry joined forces with the Spaniards. Charles had been reported wounded when fighting in Spain, but this rumour had proved to be false. A few months later James and Henry were actually in Dunkirk, which was in the hands of the Spaniards, and was taken after a siege by the French.

During this period Henrietta Maria could do little but lie on her bed and weep bitterly. In vain did Henriette try to comfort her mother. The Queen saw the dissolution of all her high and mighty schemes.

When an invitation came for the Princess to attend the

fête given by the Chancellor Seguier, Henriette was loth to go, but her mother insisted.

'My child,' she said, 'I grow sick and ill, but you must go. What will become of us, I wonder. And, my dearest, whatever has happened, you are still a princess. You have your position to uphold, and the King and Queen will never forget what is due to you; I am sure of that.'

But afterwards Henrietta Maria wished with her daughter that Henriette had never gone to the Chancellor's fête, for Mademoiselle was present and she was determined on this occasion to assert her rights.

As the party left the ballroom for the banqueting hall, very deliberately she stepped in front of Henriette.

This was noticed by many, and the next day the whole Court was buzzing with the news. Etiquette was one of the most serious topics of the day – Queen Anne would have it so; and this seemed a matter of major importance.

Mazarin and the Queen called Mademoiselle to their presence and demanded an explanation.

Mademoiselle was haughty. She was sure, she said, that she had the right to enter a room before the Princess of England.

'She is the daughter of a king, Mademoiselle,' said Anne sternly.

'Your Majesty, the Kings of Scotland always stood aside for the Kings of France, and Charles Stuart is not even a king of Scotland. He is King in nothing but in name.'

'This is most distressing,' said the Queen. 'I am annoyed with you.'

'Your Majesty, I did not wish to make too much of the matter. To tell the truth, I caught her hand as we passed in, and to many it would seem that we walked together.'

Philippe, who had been listening while studying the rings on his fingers, cried out suddenly: 'And if Mademoiselle did step before the Princess of England, she was perfectly right to do so. Things have come to a fine pass if we are to allow people who depend on us for bread and butter to pass before us. For my part, I think they had better take themselves elsewhere.'

Louis, who had been giving only half his attention to the dispute, was startled by his mother's sharp cry of protest.

Louis was not really interested in the question as to which

of his cousins stepped aside for the other. Greater matters concerned him. Since Madame de Beauvais had initiated him into the *doux scavoir* he found no pastime to equal it. He would be grateful to Madame de Beauvais for the rest of his days; he would always feel tender towards her, but his desires strayed elsewhere. There were three beautiful nieces of Cardinal Mazarin: Olympia, Marie and Hortense. Louis, who had been violently in love with Olympia – quickly married off to the Count of Soissons – had now transferred his affections to Marie. He was eager to marry her. She was after all the niece of the Cardinal and she bewitched him. Louis could not think very much about his thin little cousin, who was only a child, when his thoughts and feelings were so deeply involved with the fascinating Marie.

All the same, he was sorry for the little Henriette. She and her mother were out of favour now because of foreign affairs, and it was certainly not the fault of the Princess. Philippe was wrong to speak of her so slightingly, for what he had said would surely be carried hither and thither until it reached the ears of the desolate Queen and her little daughter.

So Louis joined his mother in reprimanding Philippe, who slunk off in some annoyance to go and find his favourite de Guiche and tell him what had happened, to complain that Louis and his mother conspired together to humiliate him, and to receive de Guiche's assurance that he was the most charming and clever of princes even though he had had the misfortune to be born two years later than his brother.

Louis went on dreaming of the beauty of Marie Mancini.

Love! What a pastime! What a pleasure! He would not of course wallow in it as did his cousin, Charles of England. Louis must have more dignity; he had so much to remember, so much to live up to. He was no wandering exile. That was why he would try to persuade his mother and the Cardinal to agree to his marriage with Marie. Then he could enjoy legitimate love, which would be so much more gratifying since it would not involve a lack of dignity.

Marie! Beautiful, charming, voluptuous Marie! But if the occasion arose, and he remembered, he would be kind to poor little Henriette.

*

In his bedchamber at Versailles, Louis awoke to a new day. His first thoughts were of Marie. He intended to plead with his mother to allow him to marry her; he would do so this very day, without delay. Marie was urging him. Marie loved him, but she was also very eager to be Queen of France.

Louis' morning in Versailles involved a ritual. As soon as he awoke he said his prayers and rosary in bed, and when his voice was heard, his attendants would come to his bedside; among them would be the Abbé de Péréfixe whose duty it was to read to him from the Scriptures. Sometimes the Abbé substituted a part of the book he was writing – a history of Louis' grandfather.

When the Abbé had finished his reading, the valets, La Porte and Dubois, would come forward; they would put his dressing-gown about him and lead him to his commode, on which he made a habit of sitting for half an hour. On rising, he went back to his bedroom where the officials of state would be waiting for him; he would chat with them in that charming and easy way which made them all so delighted to be with him. He continued to chat while he washed his face and hands and rinsed his mouth; then prayers began. After that his beautiful hair was brushed and combed amid expressions of admiration, and he was helped into the light breeches and cambric shirt which he wore for his morning physical exercises. At these he excelled, but on this morning he showed less than his usual skill, so that it was clear to those about him that something was on his mind. He did not land on the seat of the wooden horse with his habitual agility, although the usher, seeing his mood, had taken the precaution of not winding it quite so high as usual. It was the same during the bout of fencing; Louis was not displaying his customary good judgement. Even during the drill with pike and musket he was absent-minded. But no one reproached him. Even when he made a fault there came a chorus of admiration. Then followed the ballet-dancing to which he usually looked forward with such pleasure. Now he imagined himself to be dancing with Marie; and although he ignored the instructions of Beauchamp, the foremost master of the ballet in the country, he danced with inspiration that morning.

Sweating from the dance, he returned to his chamber, there to change his clothes before eating breakfast.

After that he went to the apartments of Cardinal Mazarin to discuss state matters.

Cardinal Mazarin! He was quite excited to be with him, for the Cardinal had a special importance at this time, being Marie's uncle.

He wondered whether to approach the Cardinal on the matter of his marriage; surely the great man would be on the King's side and would wish to see his niece Queen of France. All the same, Louis did not entirely trust Mazarin, and dared not speak to him until he had laid his plans before his mother.

He went to her as soon as he had left the Cardinal. It was now eleven o'clock and she was still in bed, for Anne never rose early.

Her face lighted at the sight of her son. Each morning it seemed to her that he had grown in beauty; he was like one of those romantic heroes of whom Mademoiselle de Scudéry wrote so entertainingly; and indeed this was not to be wondered at, for all writers of the day saw in Louis the romantic ideal, and no man could be a hero – even in fiction – unless he bore some resemblance to the King.

This was one of the hours of the day which Anne enjoyed most. To lie in bed and receive the filial duties of her beloved boy; to watch him as he gracefully handed her her chemise; to chat with him while she consumed the enormous breakfast which was brought to her bed; these were indeed great pleasures. She almost wished that he were a small boy again, that she might pop titbits into that pretty mouth.

She was glad he was so physically perfect. What did it matter if he were not a bookworm or if, after he left her, he indulged in sports and devoted but an hour or so a day to books?

'I have something to say to you, dear Mama,' he said.

'You would wish us to be alone?'

He nodded. She waved her hand, and in a few moments her chamber was deserted.

'Now, my beloved?'

'Madame, it is this: 'I am no longer a boy, and it is time I thought of marriage.'

'Dearest, that is true. I have thought of your marriage ever since you were in your cradle.'

'I have now found one whom I would wish to make Queen of France. I love her, *chère Maman*. I cannot live without Marie.'

'Marie?'

'Marie Mancini.'

'My son! But you joke!'

'It is not a joke. I love her, I tell you.'

'Oh yes, you love her. That is understandable. It is not the first time you have loved. But marriage . . . the marriage of the greatest King in the world, my boy, is not a matter to be undertaken lightly.'

'I am not a boy. I am twenty and a man.'

'Yes, you are a man, and marry you shall. But you shall have a wife worthy of you.'

'I love Marie.'

'Then love Marie. She will be honoured to become your mistress.'

'This is a different love, Mama. Marie is too good, and I love her too deeply . . .'

'Fortunate Marie! Now, my son, there is nothing with which to distress yourself. Have your Marie. She is yours . . . in all ways but that of marriage. Why, you demean yourself, Louis! You . . . the King of France . . . and such a King as never before sat on any throne! Why, none but a royal bride would do for you.'

'If I married Marie I should make her royal.'

Anne was so distressed she could not do justice to the delicious cutlets which she so enjoyed.

'Dearest, you love Marie, but you have a duty to your country. Think about this, and, with your good sense, you will see that a marriage between you and Marie Mancini is out of the question. You must have a royal bride. I thought you were going to tell me that you wished to marry your cousin Henriette.'

'Henriette!' Louis' eyes were wide with distaste.

'Do you not like Henriette?'

'She is but a little girl.'

199

'She is fourteen now . . .'

'She is quiet and oh . . . I think of her as a little girl. I do not like little girls. I wish for a woman . . . a woman like Marie.'

'Then we will find you a woman like Marie . . . a royal woman. But if you had wished to marry Henriette, if you had been in love with Henriette, in spite of her brother's exile, we should have been ready to consider the match. For you see, dearest, you are the son of a line of Kings and you must continue that line. Your children must be royal. You understand that, beloved. Henriette is royal. She is a princess, and her grandfather was your own grandfather, great Henri. The people would not be displeased to see you united to his granddaughter, pitiable though the state of her country's affairs may be. But . . . I would not say that was the best marriage you could make. There are other royal houses in Europe which are not in eclipse. If we could make peace with Spain you might marry the daughter of the Spanish King.'

In the King's mind, love battled with his sense of duty. He never forgot for a moment the responsibilities of his position. He was fully aware that he must not make a *mésalliance*. He wished to be perfect in all things; he must not fail in this matter.

'But I love Marie,' he persisted. 'It is Marie whom I wish to marry.'

'But, dearest, you will do your duty, I know. And in a little while you will forget Marie. There will be so many women to love you. Believe me, dearest, the one you marry need not necessarily come between you and your pleasures. Give France royal sons; and give as many sons as you wish to others. You will enjoy the begetting, and there is no woman in France who would not be proud to bear the King's sons, even though they be bastards.'

'Such behaviour seems wrong.'

'What is wrong for ordinary men is right for kings. Never forget, my loved one, your brilliant destiny. You are not to be judged as ordinary men. Oh, my beloved, do not turn from your mother because she cannot give you what you want. How willingly would I give my consent if I could! My one wish is to give you all you ask. There! See how I love you! I have been unable to eat my breakfast.'

He stooped and kissed his mother's cheek.

'Then you do not blame me, dearest?' she said anxiously.

'I understand, of course,' answered Louis. 'But, Mama, I cannot marry Henriette. Do not ask that of me.'

'Why are you so much against her?'

'I think it is because I am sorry for her. I do not like to be sorry for girls. I like to admire, not to pity. And she is too learned. She spends too much time in study. No! It must not be Henriette.'

'How vehement you are against this poor child, Louis. One would think you hated her.'

Louis shook his head. He did not understand his feelings for his cousin. He protected her when he could from slights and insults; but he was determined on one thing; he would not marry her.

Sorrowfully he left his mother and went to the riding school, where he forgot his problems temporarily as he galloped round the school, picking up rings on his lance and holding them suspended during the gallop.

He was an expert at such feats, but as the cheering of his attendants filled his ears that day he began to think of what he would tell Marie; yet he found that it was the tall figure of Henriette which troubled his mind.

*

Shortly after that interview with her son, Anne, in panic, invited to the Court of France the Dowager Duchess of Savoy, a daughter of Henri Quatre. The Dowager Duchess had a daughter. This was the Princess Marguerite, a small, dark-skinned girl, very plain, and, knowing the purpose of her visit to the French Court, very nervous.

Louis received her with all the courtesy he could muster, but it was impossible to hide his feelings of distaste. It seemed to him that, the more he saw of other women, the more he was in love with Marie.

'I shall not marry my cousin Marguerite,' he told his mother. 'I could not entertain the idea.'

'You need see very little of her,' said Anne. 'And you would soon grow accustomed to her.'

'Dear Mother, that is not my idea of marriage.'

201

'You will have neither Marguerite nor Henriette then!'

'Neither,' he said firmly.

The Cardinal would have liked to see a marriage between his niece and the King, but he realized that such an alliance was inadvisable. He knew that if the royal tradition of the house of France was so flouted, not only the nobility but the people would rise against him. They would blame him, as they were always ready to blame him for France's troubles. He remembered the wars of the Fronde, and the unpopularity he had suffered at that time; and he could see that such a marriage would do him more harm than good.

'Sire,' he said, 'if you should persist in making this marriage against my advice, I should have no alternative but to give up my office as your minister.'

Louis was morose; he felt inadequate to deal with the situation. He thought continually of Henriette, because he knew that if he declared he would marry her, there would be no objection.

He wished that he had studied more assiduously; he wished he was more learned. It was all very well to be able to leap and vault to perfection, to outstrip all others in the hunt. But there was more to life than that. If he had had more book-learning, he might have been able to confute the Cardinal's arguments; he would certainly have been able to state his feelings with more clarity; he realized that well-chosen words were weapons which he had never before appreciated.

His cousin Marguerite returned to Savoy, and the Cardinal decided to send his niece away from Court.

Louis did not protest; he knew that what had been done was right for the King of France, no matter how disappointing it was to Louis the man.

He declared himself heartbroken, and then he found a lady of his mother's bedchamber who comforted him with great skill, and he was soon feeling as grateful to her as he had, during a previous period, been to Madame de Beauvais.

*

Court gossip reached Henriette at Colombes. Her attendants chattered about the King's passion for the Cardinal's niece and the arrival of his cousin Marguerite.

'She was small and plain . . . and Louis would have none of her.'

'It would have been such a suitable match,' murmured Henriette.

'Ah yes, but he could not find it in his heart to love her. And he is so handsome . . . so romantic . . . so made for love.'

Henriette pictured that poor plain Marguerite who had failed to charm the King. She was very sorry for her; she knew how the poor child must have suffered.

Henriette wept silently for Marguerite . . . and for herself.

*

Lucy was tired, but she still walked through the streets of Paris. She was frequently ill now; she knew that she had changed, all in a few short months. She grew breathless at the least effort, and worse, she was suffering from an illness which she knew would not allow her many more months of life.

There were times when her mind wandered a little, when she thought she was back in the past, when men and women whom she had known would seem to walk beside her and talk to her.

Her father was often there. He said: 'We shall have to marry that girl quickly.' And her mother nodded and understood.

I was born that way, Lucy told herself. 'Twas no fault of mine. It was something which had to be. It was as natural to me as breathing. If I had been born ill-favoured like poor good Ann Hill, I should have been different. So who should blame such as I? Is it our fault that some of us are born with bodies which demand the satisfaction of physical love with such an intensity that we are not strong enough to deny it? Some have a love of mental exercise, and they become wise and are applauded; others have great skill in the art of war, and they win honours; but those who love – and love is all taking and giving pleasure, for the two go hand in hand – come to this sad end.

She would wander past the new houses in the Place Royale and the Place Dauphine; she did not notice the fruit trees and the flowers which grew in the gardens and nearby meadows. She was looking at the men who passed her by.

They scarcely threw her a look nowadays – they who had once sought her so eagerly. She had sauntered through Paris; she had wandered along the north and south banks; she had strolled from the Place de Carrousel to the Porte St Antoine, from the Porte du Temple to the Porte Marceau, and she found not one man who was ready to be her lover even for an hour.

To this had she sunk.

The roundness had left her face, and her cheeks hung in flabby folds; there were dark shadows under her still beautiful, large brown eyes. Her hair had lost its lustre, and she had no money to buy coloured ribands with which to adorn it.

Her good health had begun to desert her during her stay in the Tower; but her troubles had been slight then. When she had arrived in Holland she had still been a comely girl. There were lovers in Holland, but it seemed to her that one followed another in too rapid succession; they grew a little less courtly, less of the gentleman.

'I dislike this country,' she had declared to the faithful Ann. 'I hate the flatness and the wind.'

By degrees they had made their way to Paris, going from town to town. Ann worked in some of the big houses, sometimes in gardens, often in the fields. Lucy plied the only trade for which she had any aptitude. And eventually they had come to Paris. But how changed was everything! She had hoped to find the King there, for she heard little news during her wanderings. She thought: He will not desert me. He will want to help me, if only for Jemmy's sake.

But there were rumours in Paris. The King of England never came there now. The French were friendly with his enemies. The Queen of England and the Princess Henriette were rarely seen in the capital; they attended few state functions; they lived in obscurity.

And so here was Lucy in Paris, trying to find lovers who would support her and her children, feeling too old and too ill to struggle any longer.

She sat on the bank and stared at the river.

It would have been better, she thought, if I had stayed in London. Jenny, the brothel-keeper, was right. I should have been better off had I followed her advice, for what is there for such as I when we grow old and ill and are no longer desirable!

She sat dreaming of her lovers. There were two whom she remembered best. The first because he *was* the first: she recalled the copse at twilight, the light in the sky, the shouts of Roundhead soldiers, and the sudden understanding of herself. She would never forget her first lover, and she would never forget Charles Stuart.

'Charles,' she murmured, 'where are you now? Yes, the most exalted of them all, would be the one above all others to help me now.'

She thought of the children. What would become of them when she died?

Panic seized her, for she knew that she must soon die. She had known others who had contracted this disease which now threatened her life. She had seen how death came. It was the result of promiscuous pleasure. It was inevitable, mayhap, when one took lovers indiscriminately.

She must get back to her lodgings – the miserable room in a narrow cobbled street; she must get there quickly and talk to Ann. Ann was a good woman – a practical woman who loved the children. When Lucy died Ann must take them to their fathers and make sure that they were well cared for.

She struggled to her feet, and began to walk away from the river. As she neared that part of the town where she had her lodging, a fish-wife, from whom now and then Ann bought scraps, called to her: 'Have you heard the news then?'

'What news?'

'You'll be interested ... since you are English. Cromwell is dead.'

'Cromwell ... dead!'

'Aye! Dead and buried. This will mean changes in your country.'

'That may be so,' said Lucy in her slow, laborious French, 'but I'll not be there to see them.'

She mounted the stairs to her garret and lay exhausted on the straw.

'This will mean changes for *him*,' she murmured.

When Ann came in with the children she was still lying there.

Ann's face fell into the lines of anxiety habitual to it now. She had been excited when she came in, and Jemmy was shouting: 'Cromwell's dead . . . dead. Cromwell is dead!'

'Yes,' said Lucy, 'Cromwell is dead. Ann, there is something I want you to do without delay. I want you to leave at once . . . with the children. Find out where the King now holds his Court. Go to him. Tell him what has befallen me.'

'We'll all go,' said Ann.

'Where shall we go?' demanded Jemmy.

'We are going to the King's Court,' Ann told him.

'To the King's Court?' cried Jemmy. He seized his sister's hand and began to dance round the garret. He was so strong and healthy that the life of poverty had scarcely had any effect upon him.

'Ann,' said Lucy quietly, 'mayhap the King will be going to England now. Who knows? You must find him quickly. You must not rest until you have found him and taken the children to him. He will do what has to be done.'

'Yes,' said Ann, 'he will do what has to be done. Would to God we had never left him.'

'Ann . . . leave soon. Leave . . . now.'

'And you?'

'I think I can fend for myself.'

'I'll not leave you. I'll never leave you.'

Lucy heard Jemmy's shouts. 'Cromwell is dead. We are going to see the King. You are Cromwell, Mary. I am the King. I kill you. You're dead.'

'You have a fever,' said Ann to Lucy.

'Leave tomorrow, please, Ann. It is what I wish . . . for the children.'

'I'll never leave you,' said Ann, and the tears started to run down her cheeks.

Lucy turned away. She said: 'It has to end. All things have to end. It was a happy life, and all will be well for Jemmy and Mary. He will see to that. He is a good man, Ann, a good gay man . . . for a gay man can be as good as a sombre one.'

'There is none to equal him,' said Ann.

'No,' agreed Lucy. 'None to equal him.'

She lay still for a long time; and she fancied he was beside her, holding her hand, telling her not to be afraid. Life had been gay and merry; let there be no regrets that it had come to its end.

She whispered as she lay there: 'In the morning, Charles, Ann will set out to bring the children to you . . . Jemmy who is yours, and Mary . . . who ought to have been yours. Look after Jemmy and see that Mary is well cared for. You will do it, Charles, because . . . because you are Charles . . . and there is none to equal you. In the morning, Charles . . .'

All night she lay there, her throat hot and parched, her mind wandering.

She fancied she heard the voices of people in the streets; they seemed to shout: 'Cromwell is dead! Long live the King! God bless him!'

'God . . . bless . . . him!' murmured Lucy.

And in the morning Ann, with the two children, set out for the King's Court, for poor Lucy no longer had need of her.

CHAPTER SEVEN

IT WAS ALMOST two years since the death of Cromwell, yet the people of England showed no sign of recalling Charles Stuart to his throne, having installed Oliver's son Richard as Protector.

The excitement at the news of Oliver's death had still thrilled the King and his Court, who were then in Brussels, when Ann had arrived with the children.

Charles was silent for a few moments when he heard of Lucy's death. He embraced Jemmy warmly and, when the little girl, Mary, waited with such expectancy, there was nothing he could do but embrace her also.

He laid his hand on Ann Hill's shoulder. 'You're a good girl, Ann. Lucy was fortunate in you . . . more fortunate than in some others. Have no fear. We will do our best to see you settled.'

Ann fell on her knees before him and kissed his hand; she

wept a little, and he turned away because the tears of all women distressed him.

Later he sent for Lord Crofts – a man whom he admired – and said to him: 'My lord, you have this day acquired a son. I command you to take him into your household and bring him up as one of your own. I refer to my son James.'

Lord Crofts bowed his head.

'I thank you with all my heart,' said the King. 'I know I cannot leave Jemmy in safer hands. Henceforth it would be better for him to be known as James Crofts.'

'I shall obey Your Majesty's commands to the best of my ability,' said Lord Crofts.

And so Jemmy was handed over to Lord Crofts to be brought up as a member of his family and to be taught all that a gentleman of high quality should know.

There still remained Mary.

'God's Body!' cried the King. 'That child is no responsibility of mine.'

He sent for Henry Bennet.

'Your daughter is at Court. What do you propose to do about her?' he demanded.

'Alas, Sire, I know of no such daughter.'

'Come,' said the King, 'she is Lucy's girl. You knew Lucy well, did you not?'

'Even as did Your Majesty.'

'I have placed my son in a household where he will be brought up in accordance with his rank. You should do the same for your daughter.'

'Ah, the boy is lucky. It is a simple matter for a King to command others to care for his bastard. It is not so simple for a humble knight.'

'It should not be a task beyond the strength of such as you, Henry.'

'Poor little Mary! They have been brought up together, those two. It is a sad thing that one should have a future of bright promise and the other . . .'

'What do you mean, Henry? They're both bastards.'

'But one is known to be the King's bastard. The other, bastard of a humble knight. A King's bastard is equal to any man's son born in wedlock. It is not such a bad fate to be a

King's bastard. Poor Mary! And, for all we know, she might have been . . . she might have been . . .'

'She could not have been! I have a good alibi, Henry. I know I am far from impotent, but I am not omnipotent. My children are as the children of other parents. They grow as other children . . . before and after birth.'

'Many have thought her to be your child, Sire. You can be sure Jemmy boasted that he had a King for a father.'

'Are you suggesting that I should take upon myself the responsibility of fathering the child?'

'Sire, you have had children already, and there will be many more, I doubt not. Can one little girl make such a difference?'

'You're insolent, fellow! You would shift your responsibilities on to me, when it is a King's privilege to shift his responsibilities on to others. Did you not know that?'

' 'Tis so, Sire!' sighed Henry. 'Alas, poor Mary! The poppet has set her heart on having a King for a father. Your Majesty has charmed her as you charm all others. She is, after all, a woman.'

Charles said: 'Oh . . . put the girl with a good family then. Give her a chance such as Jemmy will have.'

'In Your Majesty's name, Sire? Mary will bless you all her days. She's Jemmy's sister, remember. You know how you love to please the ladies, and this little lady will be but one more.'

'You may get you gone from my presence,' said the King with a laugh. 'First you steal my mistress when my back is turned; and not content with that you cajole me into fathering your daughter!'

He strode away laughing. He had been enchanted with little Mary; he wished she were in truth his child. But as Henry said: What did one more matter? The children would be well cared for, well nurtured; and Lucy – poor Lucy – could rest in peace.

He had thought at that time that his chances of regaining his throne had improved; alas, he had hoped too soon.

He went to Holland, where, on the strength of his hopes, the Dowager Princess of Holland smiled on his betrothal to Henriette of Orange. She was a charming girl, and Charles found it easy to fall lightly in love with her. But the romance was upset for two reasons: Most important, the Dowager Princess realized that Charles was not to be recalled and would doubtless remain an exile; and secondly, even while courting Henriette he had become involved in a scandal with Beatrix de Cantecroix, a very beautiful and experienced woman who was the mistress of the Duke of Lorraine.

Charles left Holland for Boulogne where he planned to journey to Wales and Cornwall, there to gather an army and fight for his throne.

But his plans were discovered by the enemy, and once again they came to nothing.

He decided then to see Mazarin and ask for France's help in regaining his crown.

Mazarin was already in negotiation for a peace with Spain, and Charles was treated with the utmost coldness.

And so it seemed that, nearly two years after Cromwell's death, his position was as hopeless as it had ever been.

*

The French Court travelled south. In the eyes of Mazarin this journey was very necessary. There had been rioting in some southern towns, and a great deal of dissatisfaction had followed the arrest of certain men, some of whom had been hanged, others sent to the galleys.

Mazarin believed that a sight of the handsome King, together with his most gracious and benign manners, would rouse new feelings of loyalty in rebellious Frenchmen.

But that was not the only reason why the Cardinal so favoured this tour.

He was considering a peace treaty with Spain, and his experience had always taught him that the best cement for securing peace was a marriage between the members of the two countries concerned.

Philip IV of Spain had a daughter – Marie Thérèse – and she would be a fitting bride for Louis.

Louis knew of this, and realized the importance of such a match. For two years there had been war between France and Spain; and unless real peace could be made between the two countries, doubtless ere long there would be war again. Marriage was one of a King's first duties, providing it was the right kind of marriage; and Louis was ever conscious of his duty.

When Marie Mancini had been sent away from the Court he had turned to her elder sister Olympia who had married the Count of Soissons. He was soon deep in romantic love again, and gave balls in honour of the lady when he was not gambling in her house until three in the morning.

The Queen and Mazarin watched this friendship. 'There is nothing to fear,' said Anne to the Cardinal. 'She is married, and he is safe with her. It is the romantic attachments to unmarried ladies which bother me. My Louis is so noble; he loves like a boy of sixteen still.'

The Cardinal nodded; he was eager to reach the Pyrenean frontier.

Philippe was pleased because his favourite, the Comte de Guiche, travelled with the royal party.

The Comte was an extremely handsome young man with bold dark eyes and a dashing manner; Philippe had admired him from his earliest days and had commanded that the Comte should be his special companion. De Guiche was clever, witty and very sure of himself. Moreover, being a married man, he seemed knowledgeable in the eyes of Philippe. The young Comte had married – most reluctantly – when he was very young indeed, a child who was heiress to the great house of Sully; he had never had the slightest affection for his young wife, avoided her as much as possible, and was content to be the *bel ami* of the King's brother.

He was of the noblest family – that of the de Gramonts. His father was the Maréchal who enjoyed the affection as well as the respect of the royal family. The young Comte had grace of person; he excelled in social activities such as the ballet, which Louis had made so popular; he knew exactly how to please Philippe, and Philippe declared that he simply could not *exist* without his dear friend.

De Guiche had quickly discovered that one of Philippe's chief wishes was to be told that he was in reality as attractive as Louis. It was clear to the sly young Comte that Philippe had suffered much through his proximity to his royal brother. Louis was tall; Philippe was short. Louis was handsome in a masculine mould; Philippe was almost pretty in a girlish way; he had beautiful dark eyes, long lashed; he was graceful, almost dainty, and he accentuated his good points by means of jewels and cosmetics. Philippe must be constantly assured that he, in his way, was as attractive as Louis, and de Guiche's task was to assure him of this without saying anything which could be construed as disrespectful to the King. This was not easy, and there were occasions when de Guiche grew bold in his confidences with the young Prince.

As they journeyed through Marseilles – that turbulent town which had been more rebellious than most – and the people looked on their young King, those who had been ready to condemn the royal house experienced a quick change of mind. How could they do anything but express their love and loyalty to this handsome Apollo who rode among them, bowing and smiling, telling them that he was their 'Papa Louis', that he was their King who loved them?

Philippe, watching his brother's triumph, scowled. The people did not cheer him as they did Louis; they did not admire him as they did the King. He fancied some of them tittered at his appearance. That was intolerable.

De Guiche knew that his royal friend was in special need of comfort and he wondered how best to give this.

It was a few evenings later, when they had rested at one of the chateaux on their road, that the two walked together in the grounds, and Philippe had his arm about de Guiche's shoulders.

'This journey is not so much in order to soothe these people by Louis' magnificent presence,' said Philippe with a touch of anger as he referred to his brother, 'as that there may be conferences between the ministers of Spain and our own.'

'Monsieur is right as usual,' said de Guiche. 'It is Louis' marriage which is under consideration.'

'I wonder if he will like Marie-Thérèse.'

'I have heard rumours that she is very small and far from well-favoured,' said de Guiche, to please his master.

Philippe laughed. 'He'll not like that. He likes big plump women – matrons – with some experience to help him along.'

De Guiche joined in Philippe's laughter, and Philippe

went on: 'Louis is the most innocent King that ever sat upon the throne of France.'

'He has not Monsieur's quick mind,' said de Guiche. 'That has kept him innocent.'

'You flatter, dearest Comte.'

'It is no flattery. Is it not clear? See how he worships Madame de Soissons. She clearly loves the King because he is the King. And Monsieur de Soissons is so blind because his wife's lover is the King. But Louis thinks it is pure good chance that Soissons should not be in her apartment when he visits her. Louis is so romantic!'

Mayhap he will not feel so romantic when he is married to Marie-Thérèse. She is very thin; she is very plain. Why are all the girls whom princes may marry, thin and plain? Marguerite; Henriette; and now Marie-Thérèse.

'Henriette?' said de Guiche sharply.

'My cousin . . . the Princess of England.'

'She is thin, yes,' said de Guiche slowly; 'but she has a charm.'

'A charm! But she is so very thin . . . nothing but a bag of bones! And so quiet.'

'There are some who are quiet because their discourse would be too profound to interest most of those who are at hand to hear it.'

'But . . . Henriette . . . profound!'

'She has a quality,' said de Guiche. 'It is as yet hidden. She is not fifteen, your little cousin. Wait, Monsieur . . . ah, wait!'

'This is amusing. I think you but seek to make me laugh, dear Comte.'

'No. I speak with great seriousness. She is a child yet, but she is clever. There is one thing: I have seen a certain sparkle in her eyes. She is sad because her life is sad. She has always lived in exile . . . like a plant in the shade. Ah, if the sun would shine on her! If she could let loose her natural gaiety! But she cannot. She is plagued all the time. She is an exile . . . a beggar at Court. Mademoiselle de Montpensier continually seeks to take precedence. Henriette's brothers wander the Continent; she never knows when they will meet their death. She is humiliated at every turn and, being so clever – so full of imagination – she is sensitive;

so she remains in her corner, quiet and pale, and to those who have not the eyes to see, so plain. Do not underestimate Henriette, Monsieur. Your brother is not insensible to her charm.'

'Louis!'

'Ah, Louis knows it not yet. Louis sees her as you do. Poor plain little cousin. "Nothing but bones," he said, and he thinks of his plump matrons. But Louis is romantic. He is a boy in heart and mind. You, Monsieur – forgive me; this sounds like treason, but between ourselves, eh? – you are so much cleverer than the King. You see more clearly. I'll wager this: One day Louis will not be insensible to the charms of little Henriette. Let her brother regain his throne; let her come out of her corner; let her dazzle us with *her* beautiful clothes, her jewels. Then we shall see her beauty shine. Do you remember that, in the ballets, it is she who often says: "Wear this . . . it will so become you." And how often is she right! Have you seen her, animated in the ballet, playing a part? Then she forgets she is the exiled Princess, the little beggar-girl who may be snubbed at any moment. The true Henriette peeps out for a while to look at us; and, by the saints, there you have the most charming lady of the Court!'

'You speak with fervour, de Guiche. Are you in love with my cousin?'

'I? What good would that do me? I do not love women, as you well know. They married me too young, and so I lost any taste I might have had for them. I was merely telling you that the King is not insensible to the charms of his cousin.'

'But he has refused to marry her; you know that.'

'Yes. And she knows it. It has made her quieter than ever in his presence. But you have noticed the softness in the King's eyes when he speaks of her? Poor Henriette! he says to himself. He is sorry for her. He does not understand. He gambols with his plump matrons. He is like a child learning love . . . for he is far younger than his brother. He has spent his time in youthful sports; he is a boy yet. He has now acquired a certain taste for love, but at the moment he likes the sweet and simple flavours. Wait . . . wait until he demands something more subtle.'

'Then you think . . .'

'He will one day greatly regret that he turned away from the Princess Henriette.'

'I cannot believe that, Comte.'

But Philippe was thoughtful; and his mind was filled with memories of Henriette.

*

During the journey of the French Court to the Spanish border, Henrietta Maria and her daughter remained in Paris. Charles took advantage of the absence of the Court to visit his sister.

He came riding to Colombes where they were residing at that time. Unceremoniously he found his sister, and Henriette, giving a little cry of joy, ran into his arms.

She was laughing and crying, looking eagerly into his face, noting the changes, the fresh lines about the eyes and mouth which did not detract from his charm.

'Charles! Charles!' she cried. 'What magic have you? That which makes others ugly merely adds to your charm.'

'I was born ugly,' said the King. 'Those who love me, love me in spite of my face. Therefore they are apt to find something to love in my ill-favoured countenance and they call it charm . . . to please me.'

'Dearest brother, will you stay long?'

'Never long in one place, sister. I merely pay a flying visit while the coast is clear.'

'It is wonderful to see you. Mam will be delighted.'

Charles grimaced. 'We are not the best of friends, remember. She cannot forgive me for taking Henry's side against her, and for not being a Papist. I cannot forgive her for the way she treated the boy.'

'You must forgive her. There must not be these quarrels.'

'It was to see you I came.'

'But you will see her while you are here. To please me, Charles?'

'Dearest, can it please you to displease us both?'

'You would go away happier if you mended your quarrels with Mam. Charles, she is most unhappy. She grieves continually. She thinks still of our father.'

215

'She nurses her grief. She nourishes it. She tends it with care. I am not surprised that it flourishes.'

'Try to understand her, Charles. Try . . . because I ask it.'

'Thus you make it impossible for me to refuse.'

So he did his best to mend the quarrel between himself and his mother. He could not love her; he could not tolerate cruelty, and when he remembered Henry's sorrow he was still shocked. But they did not discuss his brother, and he was able to spend many superficially pleasant hours in his mother's company.

It was not long after his arrival at Colombes that he betrayed to Henriette a secret excitement.

'I will tell you, sister,' he said, 'because if this should fail – as most projects have failed – I should not mind your knowing. Have you ever heard of General George Monk?'

'No, Charles.'

'He was one of Cromwell's supporters, but I do not think my lord Protector ever entirely trusted him. I have heard that once when George Monk was in Scotland, Oliver wrote to him: " 'Tis said there is a cunning fellow called George Monk who lies in wait to serve Charles Stuart. Pray use your diligence to take him and send him to me." You see, Oliver was not without some humour.'

'You speak as though you could even forgive Oliver.'

'Forgive Oliver!' Charles laughed. 'I thank God I shall never be asked to. He has passed beyond my forgiveness. I was never very skilled in judging and affixing blame. It is a matter of great relief to me that the judging of Oliver has passed into other hands. But more of Monk. He married his washerwoman – Mistress Anne Clarges; she must have a strong will as well as a strong arm for the tub, to induce the General to marry her. And do you know, Minette, Anne Clarges gives her support to me. She has a taste, not only for Generals, it seems, but for Kings; and I doubt not that she has urged her lord to favour me, with the same urgency as she once pressed him into marriage.'

'Do you mean, Charles, that there is a General in England who would be ready to help you regain your kingdom?'

'I do, Minette. Aye, and do not speak of him as *a* General. He is the foremost General. He is a man who served the Protector well, but who, since the death of Oliver, has become disgusted with the Parliamentarians' rule. He has come to the conclusion that kings are slightly more attractive than protectors.'

'What is happening? What is General Monk doing?'

'He has drunk in the presence of others to "His Black Boy". That is his name for me. He is reputed to have said that he is tired of the bickering in high places and that, if he had an opportunity of doing so, he would serve me with his life.'

'Oh, Charles! If only it would come true!'

'If only, Minette! There have been so many "if onlys" in my life. The sign of many failures, alas!'

'I shall hope and pray that Your Majesty soon comes to his kingdom. I shall pray that all health and happiness may attend Your Majesty.'

'Come, come, do not treat me with so much ceremony. There should not be so many "Your Majesty's" between us two; there should be nothing but affection.'

She clung to him, her eyes shining. Surely there must be some good fortune waiting for him at last! Surely the exile must soon be restored to his kingdom!

*

Mademoiselle de Montpensier was faintly alarmed.

She had lost all hope of the exalted marriage for which she had longed. It was now common knowledge that Louis was to marry Marie-Thérèse, the daughter of the King of Spain. Negotiations were going ahead. Louis was reconciled to the fact that as a king he must do his duty. It would not be many months before the marriage would take place.

So I shall never be Queen of France! thought Mademoiselle.

There were other offers for her hand. She was still a granddaughter of France if not a daughter, she reminded herself, and she was the richest heiress in the world. A grand marriage was still possible for her. She was fascinated by Charles Stuart, but she certainly would not marry a roaming exile, and she had no wish to leave France. France was her home, and to have lived for years at the Court of France was to know that other Courts could never satisfy. No! Mademoiselle knew definitely what she wanted. She

217

wanted to remain in France, and she wanted to make a brilliant marriage. There was only one other man worthy of her, in her opinion, now that she could not have Louis. A second-best it was true, but it would still be a royal marriage – Philippe.

She and Philippe were good friends. They had been brought up together. She was thirteen years older than he was, but that was not an insurmountable difficulty. She had bullied him in childhood because it was Mademoiselle's habit to bully, but Philippe had accepted her domineering ways and even admired her for them. In the recent dispute over the right of precedence, Philippe had immediately placed himself on her side and demanded to know why people who depended on them for their bread should walk before them.

Mademoiselle was certain that she only had to make her wishes known to Philippe and he would be eager for their marriage.

It was strange how serving-women seemed to know more of what was going on at Court than their masters and mistresses.

It was Clotilde, her maid, who first made her aware of the mistake she might be making concerning Philippe.

As she combed Mademoiselle's hair, she said: 'Do you think Monsieur is serious in his attentions to the English Princess, Mademoiselle?'

'What is this? Monsieur . . . serious?'

'Oh yes, Mademoiselle. He is paying court to the Princess, it is said. He rides over to Colombes very often and . . . he is continually at the Palais-Royal.'

'This is nonsense.'

'It is, Mademoiselle?' Clotilde was silent. None dared contradict Mademoiselle.

'Well?' said Mademoiselle impatiently. 'What else have you heard?'

Clotilde wished she had not spoken. She stammered: 'Oh, 'twas a rumour, I dare swear, Your Highness. It is said that he is enamoured of the Princess Henriette and is spending much time with her.'

Mademoiselle's face was scarlet with mortification. She did not believe it. She would not believe it.

But she was uneasy.

Later, in the ballroom, when she was dancing with the King, she could not refrain from mentioning the matter to him. 'Your Majesty is setting the fashion for marriage, I hear. Is it true?'

Louis raised his eyebrows. 'Is what true?'

'Philippe, Your Majesty. I hear rumours. I wondered if they were true. I have heard that he has become enamoured of that little bag of bones, Henriette.'

Louis smiled. 'Have you then? I doubt not that he will get her. Our aunt has tried in vain for the Grand Duke of Tuscany and the Duke of Savoy. They'll have none of our poor Henriette. I am sorry for that girl. A hard life she has had. If Philippe wants to marry her he is sure to do so . . . for no one else will have her, I fear.'

'But . . . Your Majesty has heard these rumours?'

'Philippe has been thoughtful of late, and that is a sign of love. He rides often to Colombes, I hear; and Henriette is at Colombes.'

'Your Majesty would give your consent to such a marriage?'

Louis hesitated. He would do nothing, Mademoiselle knew, without the agreement of his mother and Mazarin. Louis, for all his magnificence, was a boy in the hands of those two. He now said uncertainly: 'I would her brother could regain his kingdom. If so . . . it would be an excellent match . . . an excellent match.'

'There is little chance of that. And would Your Majesty allow your brother – Monsieur of France – to marry with the sister of an exile?'

'It would be hard to refuse,' said Louis. 'If they were really in love . . . I should find it hard to refuse.'

Mademoiselle wished she could have slapped the sympathetic smile from the handsome face. It was all she could do to prevent herself doing so.

She was enraged. It would be intolerable if she lost not only Louis but Philippe.

*

All Paris was en fête.

This was an occasion beloved by all, for on this hot

August day the King was bringing his bride to the capital.

It might have been said that this year, 1660, was one when the stars of kings shone brightly.

Across the water there had been another great day – an even greater one for England than this was for France.

In London, a few weeks before, the streets had been decked with flowers and tapestries, fountains had run with wine, the citizens had shouted derisive farewells to the old *régime*; the life of pleasure and revelry was back, and there should be, all declared, more merriment than there had ever been before. The Black Boy was back; the Merry Monarch had returned; and his restoration was due to the will of his people – all except a few miserable Puritans.

Such rejoicing there had been that Charles, while he yet revelled in it, while he rejoiced to be home again and to be received with such wild enthusiasm, had stroked his lined face and remarked with a slightly cynical smile that it must have been his own fault he had not returned before, since every man and woman he met now assured him with tears and protestations of loyalty that they had always wished for the King's restoration.

So the exile was an exile no longer. He was back in White-hall, full of gaiety and charm, delighting all who saw him – from the highest nobleman to the lowest fishwife.

The King had come home.

And what a difference the restoration made to his family abroad! No longer were Henrietta Maria and her daughter poor exiled beggars depending on the hospitality of their relations. They were the mother and sister of the reigning King of England.

Now they sat beneath the canopy of crimson velvet on the balcony outside the Hotel de Beauvais, one on either side of Queen Anne. From other windows watched the ladies of the Court. Cardinal Mazarin also was at a window.

The procession passed along the streets – the gilded coaches; the mules with their silver bells; the magistrates in their red gowns; the musketeers in blue velvet with silver crosses; the company of light-horse in scarlet; the heralds carrying emblems; the grand equerry who held aloft the royal sword with its scabbard of blue velvet and golden *fleurs-de-lis*. But all the brilliant colour was eclipsed by the glory of Louis himself. Looking more handsome than even he had ever looked before, he rode his bay horse under a canopy of brocade. His face was benign as he moved forward, and the people roared in expression of their love and loyalty. Here was a King who was indeed a King. He was dressed in silver lace decorated with pearls and pink ribbons; his hat was kept on his head by means of an enormous diamond brooch, and the magnificent white plumes fell over his shoulders.

Behind him rode Philippe in a costume of silver embroidery; and behind Philippe came the Princes of the royal houses led by Condé.

Then came the bride – little Marie-Thérèse – in her coach which was covered with gold lace. She was dressed in gold-coloured cloth and was ablaze with jewels, so that eyes were dazzled as they looked at her. In those gorgeous garments, framed by the gold of her coach, she seemed like a fairy princess to the people of Paris; they cheered and exclaimed at her beauty.

Following her coach, Mademoiselle de Montpensier led the Princesses of France. Mademoiselle was trying to smile and to hide her bitter resentment. *She* should have been the Queen in that gilded coach. This should have been *her* day of triumph. She could smile – a little spitefully – to think of Marie-Thérèse, stripped of her finery. That was how Louis would have to know her, a silly little girl without that charm and wisdom which was an accomplishment acquired by those brought up in the Court of France.

A grand marriage with Spain! Let Louis enjoy it if he could.

Now the King had reached the royal balcony in which sat the two Queens and the Princess Henriette. Louis drew up his horse that he might salute the Queens and the Princess.

Henriette, her eyes dazzled with his beauty, suddenly understood her feelings for this man. She had grown up in that instant. She, a girl of sixteen, knew that she loved this man of twenty-two. Now she understood why she had wept so often after she had been in his company, why she had been hurt by his pity. It was not pity she had wanted from him.

Charles was now King of England; if he had been King of England last year ... But Louis had never loved her; Louis would never have married her. But did he love little Marie-Thérèse?

Louis was looking into her eyes now. He saw the tears there and a faint flicker of surprise crossed his face. Why were there tears? he wondered. She had little to weep about now. Her brother was restored to the throne and it was very likely that Philippe would marry her; and what a suitable match this would be between the brother of the King of France and the sister of the King of England!

How pretty she was! He had never seen her dressed in such a grand fashion. He could realize now why Philippe was falling in love with her. Her beauty was not obvious as was that of Madame de Soissons ... and others; but she had a certain charm, that little Henriette.

Louis was no longer sorry for her, and his pity had been replaced by another emotion which he did not fully understand, and as he rode on to receive the ceremonial congratulations of the Parliament on his marriage, it was not of Marie-Thérèse he was thinking, but of Henriette.

*

Philippe was giving a ball at Saint-Cloud. He was pleased with himself. Saint-Cloud was a beautiful mansion which Louis had recently brought from Harvard, his Controller of Finances, and presented to his brother. Moreover, Philippe's uncle Gaston had died that year, and on his death the duchies of Orléans, Valois and Chartres as well as Villers-Cotterets and Montargis, had fallen to Philippe.

He was young and handsome; he was rich; he was the brother of the King; it was his lot to be courted and flattered. Had he but been born a few years earlier, he would have been completely content.

But he was smiling to himself as, with his special friends about him, he was preparing himself for the ball. His valets loudly proclaimed that they had never served a more handsome master; some of his friends – far bolder – whispered to him that there was no one, simply no one, to equal him in beauty. They did not admire those pink and gold men who excelled at vaulting and the like; they preferred the subtler kind of masculine beauty – agility of mind, rather than body.

Philippe laughed. It was pleasant to be assured that not everyone found Louis more charming than his brother.

His head on one side he criticized the set of his dalmatica. Was the sapphire brooch quite right? Would his dear Monsieur de Guiche decide whether ruby ornaments would be better? He thought after all that he would wear more emeralds.

Tonight was important. He would open the ball by leading the Princess Henriette out to dance. Henriette! He looked slyly at de Guiche. De Guiche was the cleverest man he knew. He saw further than did ordinary men. Henriette was charming. He realized that now. Occasionally he would be treated to those quick flashes of wit; he would see the sudden sparkle in her eyes. The restoration of her brother had acted as a tonic. She was no longer the plain little sit-in-a corner. She had been too sensitive of her position; that was all that had been wrong with little Henriette.

And when he compared her with Marie-Thérèse he could laugh aloud. Marie-Thérèse might be the daughter of the King of Spain, but Henriette was the daughter of a King of England and now sister to the reigning King. There was no difference between the two girls in rank; but there were other differences. And what delight Philippe would enjoy when Louis became aware of the charms of Henriette!

'Come!' he said. 'It is time I was greeting my guests. Do not forget that this is *my* ball. Tonight I am the host to His Majesty my brother, to his Queen and ... the Princess Henriette.'

*

Henrietta Maria was in a flutter of excitement. She dismissed all their attendants and was alone with her daughter.

'My dearest,' she said, 'what joy is this! Sometimes I find it difficult to assure myself that I am not dreaming. Can this be true? Your brother has regained his crown! Oh, would I had been there to see him riding through the streets of London. What joy! If only his father had been there to see him proclaimed their King!'

'Then it would not have been Charles who was their

King, Mam. Oh, I beg of you do not weep. This is too happy a time.'

'Tears of joy, dearest daughter. Tears of joy. I must go to Chaillot and thank God and the saints for this happiness which has come to me. And, dearest, I wish to go to England. Charles wishes us to go. He wants us all to be together for a little while at least. It is his wish. It is his *command* – as we must say now.'

'Oh, Mam! To go to London. That would be wonderful.'

'To be received in London as a Queen, and to remember how I fled from England all those years ago!'

'Mam . . . I beg of you, look forward, not back.'

'Yes, I must look forward. Dearest, you are the sister of a King who is indeed a King. You know that there has been talk of your marriage?'

'Yes,' said Henriette, and her eyes as well as her voice were expressionless.

'It fills me with pleasure. It is a wonderful match. Few could be better.'

'Philippe . . .' said Henriette slowly.

'Yes, dearest Philippe. The little playmate of your childhood. Oh, how happy you will be! Think, dearest. You will spend the rest of your life here . . . in great honour. You will be "Madame" of the Court. You do not realize the extent of your good fortune. Your face tells me that. Do you know that there is no Court in the world to equal that of France . . . for elegance, for culture, for luxury? I can think of none other at which I would care to live except . . .'

'Except at home . . . at Charles' Court,' said Henriette.

'Foolish child! How could you live at your brother's Court unless you remain unmarried? That you surely would not wish to do.'

'Mam, I think I should like to live my life as Charles' sister.'

'Holy Mother of God! What nonsense you talk! You should love your brother, it is true, but verily I believe you and he would carry to excess this affection you bear each other. Charles himself is delighted with the prospect of your marriage. I have heard from him on this matter.'

'What . . . said he?'

Henrietta Maria came closer to her daughter. 'He says

he knows that if you marry Monsieur he will always have a friend at the French Court, one who will never forget the interests of England – and the interests of England are Charles' interests. He says it will be as though his other self is at the Court of France while he is in England. He says he will always love a country of which his dear sister is the Madame. He says he sees peace between France and England through a union which he would rather have for you than any.'

'So he says all that?'

'He does indeed. And he is right. What an opportune moment this is! What glory! Why, had they kept him out of his kingdom another ten years, what would have become of us? What sort of a marriage would you have been able to make? Philippe is the most desirable *parti* in France. There is only one I would have rather seen you marry. And, mark you, if your brother had regained his kingdom a little earlier, who knows . . .'

'Mam . . . Mam . . . please do not speak of that.'

'Why not, foolish one? We are alone. Moreover it is clear to any who give the matter a thought. Everyone knows that, while it is a good thing to be the wife of the King's brother, it would have been more desirable to have been the King's.'

Henriette turned away.

Her mother must not see that she was too emotional to speak. How could she explain to Henrietta Maria that she longed to be Queen of France, not for the glory of that title, not for the honours she would enjoy, but because as Queen of France she would also have been Louis' wife.

*

Louis was conscious of his brother and Henriette. They were an attractive pair, he murmured to his wife.

She did not understand, of course. Her knowledge of the French language was limited.

He was smiling at everyone in his usual friendly manner; he accepted the congratulations on his marriage; he showed the utmost deference to his bride, and he would not admit, even to himself, that he was miserably disappointed in her. Louis was not given to frequent analyses of his feelings. Marie-Thérèse was his wife; she was the

225

daughter of the King of Spain; his marriage was highly desirable. Mazarin considered that he had achieved a diplomatic feat of great importance to France by bringing it about; his mother had assured him that one of her dearest wishes was fulfilled. Louis must be pleased with his bride.

But how rigid was Spanish etiquette! And what a scrap of a thing was Marie-Thérèse, divested of her robes of state – small and brown and, it must be admitted, far from beautiful. Louis, who had enjoyed the luscious charms of more desirable and desiring ladies in his pursuit of the *doux scavoir*, could find little to attract him in his politically admirable match.

Marie-Thérèse never put ceremony aside, even in the bedchamber. During the day she seemed to wish to do nothing but eat, play cards and go to church. She was very greedy. In spite of her rigid adherence to etiquette, her table manners disgusted him. He would see those little black eyes watching the food; and when her own plate was filled she would still have her eyes on some favourite morsel in the dish, terrified lest someone else should be given it before she could announce her preference for it. There was another thing which was worrying Louis; shy and reluctant as she had been during the first night of their nuptials, she was fast overcoming her shyness and with it her reluctance. Often he would find her eyes fixed on him as though he were a dainty morsel in the dish.

She was going to fall in love with him and, as she did so, he was going to find her more and more repulsive.

But at present Louis would not admit this.

The Spanish marriage had been a good thing for France; therefore it was an admirable marriage. And the next marriage in the family should be between England and France. Two brilliant marriages – and so good for the state policy of Mazarin.

Philippe . . . and Henriette!

She had changed since her brother had regained his throne, and Louis was glad of it. She was less shy. Silly little Henriette, to have cared so deeply because of the humiliation she had suffered! He remembered the occasion when he had not wished to dance with her; he now reproached himself bitterly for that crude behaviour.

Dancing in her blue gown, which was decorated with pearls, she was a charming sight. Philippe looked handsome too – and how ardent he was! Philippe ardent . . . and for a woman! It seemed incredible, but it was true.

He glanced at his bride. She looked well enough in her cloth of silver and multi-coloured jewels. He tried not to gaze in Henriette's direction; but his mother, sitting beside him, had noticed his interest in his cousin.

'Philippe and Henriette!' she said. 'What a good match!'

'The best Philippe could make,' replied the King.

'So he can be sure of Your Majesty's consent?'

Mazarin and his mother had already given it, Louis knew; but he kept up the pretence that he himself made all the decisions affecting the policy of France.

'I see no reason why such a marriage, so advantageous to France, should not take place.'

'Philippe was afraid he might not have your consent,' said Anne.

'He need not have been,' snapped Louis, and his sudden rush of anger astonished him. 'He'll get Henriette. Why, no one else would have her.'

'That was before her brother's triumphant return. She is a more desirable *partie* now, my beloved.'

'She . . . she has changed in more than her status.'

'It has made a great difference to her and her mother, and I rejoice to see it. I never thought Henriette so charming before. She seems almost beautiful; and she is so frail, with such a look of innocence. Quite charming. Philippe is eager for the marriage, and it is small wonder.'

Louis said in a mood of unaccustomed ill-temper: 'Philippe should not worry. He shall marry the bones of the Holy Innocents.'

Anne looked at him in amazement, but he was smiling fondly at Marie-Thérèse.

*

Mademoiselle was furious.

The King was married; Philippe was to marry Henriette, and she had always thought that, if she lose Louis, Philippe would be hers for the taking.

What had come over her young cousin? This passion

for Henriette had sprung up so suddenly. It was only a little while ago that he was taking sides against her.

Mademoiselle was no longer young. She was past the time for marriage. If she were not the granddaughter of France and its richest heiress she would be alarmed.

She must marry, and her marriage must be one which would not bring shame to her proud spirit.

There was one marriage which would please her more than any – except perhaps with Louis. Yet when she compared the two marriages she thought she would prefer the one still open to her. She would have wished to be Queen of France beyond anything, she supposed, because France was her native land and the Court well known to her; it would have been completely satisfying to spend the rest of her days in France. But to be the Queen of England – married to that fascinating rake, Charles Stuart – would be an exciting adventure.

Had she known he was to come into his kingdom, she would have married him ere this. But it was not yet too late, for he was still unmarried.

She went to his mother and, after kissing her hand, asked permission to sit beside her. Henrietta Maria graciously gave that permission.

No longer an exile! thought Mademoiselle. She is almost condescending to me now. I shall have to let these Stuarts know that I consider it my privilege to walk before their daughter, for the girl is not yet Madame of France.

Henrietta Maria's fond eyes were on Henriette now.

'A triumphant day for your daughter, Madame,' said Mademoiselle.

'I rejoice to see her so happy.'

'Is she happy? She does not seem entirely so. Do you think she is as eager for this marriage as . . . others?'

'She will be. She is but a child. Philippe is eager . . . very eager.' Henrietta Maria stole a malicious look at her niece. 'He is as eager to marry her as others are to marry him.'

'Let us hope she will be happy.'

'Who could fail to be happy in such a match, Mademoiselle?'

'There will be matches in plenty in your family now, I doubt not.'

'I doubt not,' said Henrietta Maria. 'My son, the King, will not hesitate now.'

'She will be a happy woman whom he chooses.'

'There was a time, Mademoiselle, when you did not consider his wife would ever be in such a happy position.'

'Nor would she have been had he remained in exile.'

'He will remember the days of his exile, I doubt not. He will remember his friends of those days . . . and those who were not so friendly.'

'Here at the French Court there have always been many to offer him sympathy and friendship.'

'He owes much to his sister Mary.'

'A charming princess. She reminded me of Charles.'

'So you found Charles charming then?'

'Who does not?'

'Many did not during the days of his exile. But I doubt not that the charm of a king – to some – is more obvious than that of a wandering beggar.'

Mademoiselle was growing angrier. Was the Queen suggesting she was too late? Had she forgotten the vast fortune which Mademoiselle would bring to her husband! She had heard that the King of England still suffered from a lack of money.

Henrietta Maria was remembering it. She wondered what Charles would feel about marrying this woman. She must curb her impetuosity; it would not do to offend one who might become her daughter-in-law.

She turned her gaze on Henriette, and was soothed. *There* was one who was to make the best marriage possible – since Louis was married.

Mademoiselle followed her aunt's gaze, and her anger was turned to something like panic.

Too late for Louis; too late for Philippe. Could it be that she was too late for Charles?

*

Henriette and her mother were ready to leave France on their journey to England. Henriette was longing to see her brother; but she was bewildered. Too much had happened to her in too short a time. The step from girlhood to womanhood had been too sudden. The thought of marriage alarmed her although as a princess she had been prepared for it, and she had been long aware that love played little part in the marriages of royal persons.

She liked Philippe; she continually told herself that. There had been one or two quarrels when they were children, but was not that inevitable? He had not always been kind to her; but he had been only a boy, and all that would be changed now that he was in love with her. She could not doubt his love; he made it so evident. His eyes scarcely left her and he was obviously proud of her. It was touching to see the way in which he looked at his brother as though he were comparing Henriette with Marie-Thérèse, to the disadvantage of the Queen. How ridiculous of Philippe! And yet she found it to be rather charming and very pleasant, after all the humiliations she had received, to be so loved by such an important person.

She would not wonder whether Louis was happy in his marriage; she would not think of Louis. Happily she was going to England and there it might be possible to talk with Charles, to tell him all that was in her mind and ask his advice.

She sought her mother, but when she reached the Queen's apartments she found Henrietta Maria lying on her bed, weeping bitterly.

'What is wrong?' cried Henriette in great alarm. Her thoughts had gone at once to Charles. Had he lost the kingdom he had so recently regained?

'Leave me with the Queen,' said Henriette, and the women obeyed.

The Princess knelt by the bed and looked into her mother's face. The small dark eyes were almost hidden behind their swollen lids, but Henriette knew at once that her mother's grief was caused more by anger than sorrow.

'Can you guess what is happening in England?' she demanded.

'Tell me quickly, Mam. I cannot endure the suspense.'

'There is danger of that woman's being received at Court.'

'What woman?'

'That harlot . . . Anne Hyde!'

'You mean . . . Anne . . . Clarendon's daughter?'

'Yes, I do mean that rogue's daughter. That fool James

has married her. Your brother has dared ... without my consent ... without the consent of his brother, the King, to marry her in secret!'

'He ... he loves her.'

'Loves her! She has tricked him, as she would well know how to do. He married her just in time to allow her bastard to be born in wedlock. And he ... poor simpleton ... poor fool ... acknowledged the child to be his.'

'Mam, it may well be that the child *is* his.'

'My son ... to marry with a low-born harlot!'

'Marriage with James will make her Duchess of York, Mam.'

'If you try to soothe me I shall box your ears! I'll not be soothed. Thank God we can go to England to prevent further disaster. Can you believe what I have heard! Your brother Charles is inclined to be lenient over the affair and will receive the woman at Court as James' wife!'

'Yes,' said Henriette, 'I can believe it. It is what he would do.'

'Charles is soft. There will always be rogues to get the better of him.'

'No, Mam. He is kind. He says: "They love each other; they are married; they have a child. So ... let us all be merry together!"'

'For the love of the Virgin, daughter, let me not hear such nonsense from you. I thank the saints that we shall soon be in England and that I may be able to stop this folly.'

'Mam, if Charles wishes to receive James' wife at his Court ...'

'He must be made to see his folly. Does he want to lose that which he has just gained?'

Henriette shook her head sadly. How could she say to her mother: Nay. It was you with your bad temper, with your insistence on having your way, who lost your crown. Charles' kindness will make him popular with the people.

One did not say such things to Henrietta Maria. One let her rave and rant, and if one were like Charles, one avoided her as much as possible.

How regrettable this was! It seemed as though the visit to England would be spoilt. There would be trouble with

James; and Henriette had been wondering what would happen when her mother and her brother Henry met again.

'Ah, it is high time I was at your brother's Court,' continued Henrietta Maria. 'I have had this news from your sister Mary. She and I see eye to eye in this. She is incensed that that Hyde girl . . . *her* maid of honour . . . should have dared marry your brother. She blames herself. She remembers that she brought the girl with her when she visited us. She remembers that it was in her retinue that your brother first set eyes upon her. She knew they were meeting; but she – considering the girl's lack of rank – thought her to be but the mistress of a few weeks. But to marry the girl . . . to legitimize her bastard!'

'Please, Mam, do not speak of them. Let us wait and see what Charles has to say. It is his Court after all. He will finally decide what has to be done.'

Henrietta Maria's eyes narrowed. 'He was never one to listen to his mother's advice.'

'Mam,' said Henriette, 'I have been thinking of my brother Henry.'

Henrietta Maria's face grew darker still. 'You may consider you have a brother of that name. I have no son called Henry.'

'But, Mam, you cannot at such a time continue to turn your face from him.'

'I swore that I would not look at his face again while he persisted in his heresy. I have no reason to believe that he has discarded it.'

'Please, Mam . . . he is but a boy. He swore to our father the day before he died, that he would not change his religion. You *must* receive him. You *must* love him. You must remember that he is young and eager for the love of his family . . . and in particular he would wish his mother to love him.'

'Then he knows what to do.'

'He was separated from you for so long. He looked forward so eagerly to be with you and then . . .'

'You make me angry, Henriette. I do not want to be disappointed in *all* my children. Would you have me break my vow?'

'Would you have him break his vow to his father?

God would forgive you, Mam, if you broke your vow in order to make him happy.'

'You horrify me, daughter. Have my nuns of Chaillot ... have Père Cyprien and the Abbé Montague not taught you better than that?'

'Are we not told by God to love one another?'

'You think strange thoughts, child. Listen to me. I have sworn I will never look on Henry's face until he changes his religion. I shall keep my word.'

Henriette turned away. Was the stay in England going to be so happy after all?

She need not have worried about the future of her brother Henry. They were on their journey to Calais when a message concerning him was brought to them.

Henry, Duke of Gloucester, had died the day before. He had been ill with the smallpox and had seemed to take the sickness lightly, so that all had hoped for a speedy recovery. He had been in the care of the King's doctors, who did all they could for him; he had been profusely bled and assiduously attended; but in spite of their efforts – or perhaps because of them – his illness had ended in death.

Henriette went to her mother, who was staring blankly, before her.

This is terrible for her, thought Henriette, for she will be unable to forget the last time she saw Henry.

She threw herself into her mother's arms and they mingled their bitter tears.

'Mam, you must not grieve,' cried Henriette. 'What you did you did for your Faith. You believed you were right, and perhaps we cannot be blamed for doing what we believe to be right.'

Henrietta Maria did not seem to hear her. 'So ...' she said slowly, 'I have lost my son. My daughter Elizabeth ... my son Henry ... They are both lost to me, and they both died heretics.'

Then she burst into bitter weeping, moaning that she was indeed *La Reine Malheureuse*.

It may be, thought Henriette, that her regrets will make her lenient with James.

But this was not so. Henrietta Maria could not regret that she would never now have an opportunity of breaking

233

her vow; she saw her action as the right one, the only one a good Catholic could take. All human emotions were subdued in her quest for converts. Now she wept, not because her son had died, but because he had died a heretic.

*

James met them at Calais with a squadron of ships – the first outward sign of the glories which awaited them. Henriette anxiously watched her mother's greeting with her son, but it was formal and affectionate. The Queen had no quarrel with James; providing he would repudiate Anne Hyde she was ready enough to forgive him.

James was a good seaman, but in spite of his prowess they spent two days in crossing the Straits on account of the calm; and when they arrived at Dover, Charles, with a brilliant retinue, was waiting to receive them.

Henriette looked into his face and saw the difference which the restoration of his kingdom had made to him. He was jauntier than ever; but the cynicism with which the years of exile had endowed him would be with him for ever; he was very affectionate with his dearest Minette, warning her that, even as a King returned to his throne, he would not tolerate too many 'Your Majesty's' from her.

To his mother he was graciously polite and showed all that affection which was demanded of him. The people, who had gathered to watch the royal meeting, were a little cool in their reception of Henrietta Maria; the population of Dover was largely composed of Puritans and Quakers, and they looked with distrust on the King's Catholic mother; but the young Princess they thought charming, and they cheered her loudly, much to the delight of Charles.

'You see how my people wish to please me in all things,' he whispered to her. 'It seems they know that their appreciation of you pleases me far more than that which they have for any other.'

He led his mother and sister into Dover Castle, where a great banquet was prepared for them. Charles placed his mother on one side of him, his sister on the other.

'This gives me great happiness,' he whispered to Henriette. 'Soon Mary will join us and then we shall all be together.'

Later Henriette expressed the wish that Henry could have been with them.

'If he were here,' said Charles, 'we should have Mam turning her back on him.'

'How did he die, Charles?' she asked. 'Was he heartbroken? Did he long to speak to Mam before he died?'

'I was with him, Minette. I persuaded him not to grieve. You see, I am a profane man, and I said to him: "If you side with Mam, you break your word to our father; if you do not break your word you are banished from our mother's favour. Side with yourself, brother. Do nothing that can offend yourself, and then, surely, in God's eyes, you have taken the right side." '

'You are a good man, Charles – the best in the world.'

'You joke, Minette. I am the world's biggest rake – or one of them. I doubt whether there is a man living who could compete with me. Now were my grandfather alive . . .'

'You are the world's kindest man, and it seems to me that kindness is one of the greatest virtues.'

'If I am kind it is due to my laziness. That can scarcely be called a virtue. Nay, I beg of you, sister, do not see me as a better man than I am, for one day there may be disillusionment. Love me for my faults; for that is the only way in which a man such as I may be loved.'

'What of James' trouble?'

'Trouble? James is in love, and his wife loves him. Can that be called trouble?'

'Mam will make trouble of it.'

Charles groaned.

'She always hated Chancellor Hyde,' went on Henriette. 'She says if his daughter enters Whitehall by one door, she will leave by another.'

'Poor Mam!' said Charles. 'So she is bent on making trouble. Does she never learn? Have the years of exile taught her nothing then?'

It seemed not, for while they were at Dover – in that Puritan stronghold – she insisted that High Mass be celebrated in the great hall by Père Cyprien de Gamaches, whom she had brought with her.

Charles was in a dilemma. To forbid it would mean trouble; to allow it would be to offend the people.

Henrietta Maria, that diminutive virago, opposed to the Puritans of Dover! He smiled wryly. He feared his mother more, and hoped that in the excitement of the royal visit, in the pageantry so new to them after the years of Puritan rule, the people would overlook his mother's tactlessness. So he decided that it would be wiser to risk offending the people of Dover than to cross his mother, who must somehow be reconciled to James' marriage.

*

In spite of the death of Henry, which cast a shadow over her pleasure, in spite of the apprehensive fears of the marriage which lay before her, this period seemed to Henriette the happiest of her life. In the grand entertainments which her brother had prepared for her she endeavoured to forget the past and shut out thoughts of the future.

She discovered that she was like Charles; she could banish unpleasantness from her mind. She was very sorry for the Duchess of York, whose father was keeping her a prisoner in his house because the King's mother had been so furiously enraged every time her name was mentioned. But she was able to forget her in the joy she found in her brother's company.

Mary, the Princess of Orange, had arrived in England, and there were special balls and fêtes to honour her. She was almost as fierce in her denunciation of Anne Hyde as Henrietta Maria was; and Charles, although his sympathies lay with his brother, was too lazy to enter into long arguments with his strong-minded mother and sister. It was easier to shelve for a while the matter of the Duchess's banishment and give himself and his family the pleasure he had always promised this reunion should bring them.

Scandal spread about the Court concerning the Duchess. She was a harlot, it was said; the Duke was not the father of her child; it seemed there was nothing too bad that could be said of the Duchess. Henriette shuddered; but she did not know that there was scandalous gossip concerning herself and Charles. She had no idea that sly gossips were asking each other: 'What is the nature of this affection between the King and his sister? Is it not a little too fond to be natural?'

There would always be scandals where there were Stuarts to provoke them.

If the King knew of these rumours he did nothing to refute them. He was too lazy for one thing, too wise for another. He often said that one could not alter people's thoughts, and to protest too strongly was often construed as evidence of guilt.

Henriette was fast passing out of childhood. One of those who hastened her steps in that direction was George Villiers, Duke of Buckingham. Almost as profligate as the King, he declared his infatuation for the young Princess and did all in his power to seduce her. He was sixteen years her senior, well versed in the art of seduction – having had plenty of practice – as cynical as his master, though lacking his lazy tolerance. Buckingham immediately recognized in the Princess that which had attracted de Guiche and so guided the attention of Philippe towards her.

She was not plump like most Court beauties, who looked so much alike, who were ready with the catch-words of the moment; she was ethereal, dainty and slender; her laughter was gay yet innocent; her wit was growing sharp. All the Stuart charm, which had been latent, was suddenly apparent. She danced with enthusiasm; she was as gay as any; she had grown vivacious and amusing. This was a new Henriette.

'By God's Body!' declared Buckingham. 'She is incomparable, this little Princess. Having seen her, I find it difficult to see perfection in other women.'

But all his practised gallantry, all his polished charm, failed to move Henriette. She saw him as a rake and a libertine; Charles was as bad, she knew; but Charles was her beloved brother, and nothing she discovered about him could alter her love for him. But she was not ready to fall in love with a pale shadow of her brother. In love she demanded different qualities. There was one who possessed all that she would demand in a lover. He must be good to look upon, but he must be of high integrity; he need not be supremely witty, but he must be good-natured and kind at heart. She had met such a one, but she must not think of him, for he was not for her.

So she amused herself by listening to Buckingham's protestations of affection, flirting with him while making it perfectly clear that his desires concerning her would never be fulfilled.

' 'Od's Fish!' said her brother in high amusement. 'You are leading poor old George Villiers a merry dance.'

'Then it will do him much good to dance, as he has doubtless made others dance.'

'I am sorry for poor George.'

'I am sorry for his wife.'

'I doubt not that Mary Fairfax can look after herself.'

'To think it is only three years since she married him! How sad she must be to see him pursuing other women!'

'Three years!' cried Charles. 'It is an eternity . . . in marriage.'

'Would you not ask for three years' fidelity in a wife?'

'Dear Minette, I would not cry for the moon!'

'You are all very cynical here, and you, Charles, set the pace.'

'That may well be. But don't fret for Fairfax's daughter. She was promised to Chesterfield, you know, and after the banns were published she eloped with Buckingham. We might say "Poor Chesterfield!" There were those to say it once. Nay! Do not waste pity on others in this game of love, Minette. Only take care that there is none to say "Poor Henriette!" '

'Charles, I am reminded that I must marry soon.'

'It is a good match, Minette. There is none I would rather see you marry, now that you cannot have Louis.'

'I am unsure.'

'We are all unsure at such times, dearest.'

'I cannot understand why Philippe so suddenly should want to marry me.'

'You are very attractive, Minette, as well as being the sister of a King – one who has now a throne. You are a worthy match for Philippe, as he is for you.'

'I wish I could love Philippe.'

'Some would say "That will come". But we do not allow fictions to exist between us, do we, Minette? No. You should not think of love in conjunction with husbands. I do not, in connection with wives.'

'You are being cynical again, Charles.'

'There are some who turn from the truth when it is not pleasant and call it cynicism. Do not let us be of their number, Minette. Face the truth and you will find that if you study it well you may discover that there is some part of it which is not as unpleasant as you thought it.'

'Must I marry Philippe, Charles?'

'It would be unwise not to.'

'But could I not wait awhile? I am young yet.'

'Mademoiselle de Montpensier told herself she was young yet, and now she is . . . not so young.'

'She would give much to marry you now, Charles.'

'And you see she comes too late. Do not follow Mademoiselle in that, Minette. Marry Philippe. We shall not be far apart then. We shall visit each other often. It is the best marriage you could make.'

'Is it what you wish?'

'I dearly wish it.'

'Then I will marry Philippe.'

'And I will give you a handsome dowry – 40,000 jacobuses and 20,000 pounds, that you may not be a beggar when you come to your husband. I wish all the world to know that, though I am the most inconstant man in the world, there is one to whom I am constant for ever – my sweet Minette.'

'Thank you, Charles. But, I pray you, let us talk no more of my marriage. Let us be gay and happy while we are together.'

So she danced and was happy; she forgot Henry; she forgot the Duchess of York; she forgot that soon she must return to France where she must marry one royal brother while she loved the other.

*

The King insisted that his mother and sister should not leave England until after the Christmas festivities. Christmas was celebrated with more gusto in England than in any other country, and this year's celebrations promised to be more exciting than ever, for under the rule of the

Protector such revelries had been considered a sin. All Englishmen were going to make England merry once more; they were determined on it, and during that December there was high excitement in the streets of the capital.

The Princess Mary had thrown herself into the preparations with enthusiasm. There were to be ballets and masques.

'We must not fail Charles,' she said to Henriette, 'for he wishes his Court to rival that of Louis. We can help him achieve this, I am sure, although the English do not dance with the grace of the French.'

Henriette agreed. She began feverishly planning the ballet. There would not be Louis to dance so gracefully, to enchant the spectators with his commanding presence; but she fancied they could give the English Court something it had never seen before.

As she and Mary sat together talking of the costumes they would wear, and the dances they would arrange, the verses which would have to be compiled, Mary said suddenly: 'You look sad, sister.'

And Henriette said in a rush of confidence: 'It is this talk of the ballet. It reminds me of others. It reminds me that soon I must go back to France, and that . . .'

'Is it your marriage of which your are apprehensive?'

'Yes, Mary.'

'We all are when our time comes. Our marriages are arranged for us, and we have nothing to do but obey. Oh, Henriette, you are more fortunate than many. At least you will not go to a stranger.'

'Mary, sometimes I think that Philippe is almost a stranger.'

'But you have known him from childhood.'

'Yes. But it seems I knew a different Philippe.'

'It is because he seemed then but a boy to you, and now he is the man who is to be your husband. I remember my own marriage. I was very young, but in time I came to love my husband.'

Henriette turned to look at her sister. 'It is such a comfort to have a family,' she said. 'I often think what a wonderful life ours might have been if everything had gone well for our father, and we had all been brought up together ... Charles, James, you, Elizabeth, Henry and myself. I never knew Elizabeth. I saw very little of Henry ... and now they are both dead.'

'The rest of us must be good friends ... always,' declared Mary.

'And be happy together,' said Henriette. 'James is not very happy now, is he, Mary?'

Mary had put her hand to her head. She said: 'I feel too tired to talk further, sister. I think I should like to rest awhile.'

Henriette felt saddened, suspecting Mary was making excuses. Mary was as obstinate as their mother, over the affair of Anne Hyde.

Mary stood up. She swayed slightly and it occurred to Henriette that she really was feeling ill, so she helped her sister to bed and told her attendants that their mistress wished to rest.

'You have had too much excitement, Mary,' she said. 'You'll feel better in the morning.'

But in the morning Mary was not better; and the news spread through Whitehall. The Princess of Orange was smitten with the smallpox, that dreaded disease which, so recently, had carried off her brother.

*

Henrietta Maria was beside herself with anxiety. Henry dead. Mary ill. Smallpox in the Palace. Frantically she commanded her daughter to prepare to leave at once.

'Who will nurse Mary?' asked Henriette.

'Not you! You are to leave Whitehall at once. That is the King's command. I shall send you to St. James's Palace, and there you must remain.'

The King himself joined them. His face was grave. He took Henriette into his arms and kissed her solemnly.

'It is as if there is a blight on our family,' he said. 'First Henry ... now Mary. Minette, I want you to leave Whitehall at once.'

'I think Mary would wish to have some of her family about her.'

'Mary is too ill to recognize her family, and you, my

dearest, shall certainly not come within range of contagion.'

'You are to leave at once,' commanded Henrietta Maria. 'I have arranged for you to leave in twenty minutes.'

'And you, Mam,' said the King, 'must go with her.'

'My place is at my daughter's bedside, Charles.'

'Your daughter is sick. This is not the time for your conversions.'

'A sick bed, Charles, is the place for conversions.'

'Mary is very weak. She has been bled many times. Several of my doctors are with her. She is in no state to listen to your religious advice.'

Henrietta Maria looked sternly at her son, but she knew him well enough to recognize the obstinate line of his mouth. Here was the little boy who had refused to take his physic. He was slack; he was easy-going; but suddenly he could make up his mind to stand firm, and then none could be firmer.

For a few seconds they glared at each other, and she gave way.

He was too good-hearted to make his victory obvious. He said: 'Stay and look after Henriette, Mam. We should never forgive ourselves if aught happened to her.'

'It may be you are right,' agreed the Queen.

And she was thinking: Later, when Mary is a little better, I will talk to her; I will make her see the truth.

She left with Henriette and in the Palace of St. James's eagerly they awaited the news.

It came. The Princess of Orange was improving. The doctors believed that the bleeding had proved efficacious.

Henrietta Maria made her youngest daughter kneel with her.

'Let us thank the Blessed Virgin and the saints for this recovery. It is a miracle that she is now on the road to good health. My prayers have been answered. I said: "Holy Mother, I cannot lose two children . . . and so soon. I cannot lose them both in so short a time, and both to die heretics." And, Henriette my child, my prayers have been answered. "Give me my Mary's life," I said, "and I will give you her soul!" When she is well enough . . . a little later on, I will go to her and tell her that her life has been saved through prayer, and that she owes her soul to God.'

Henriette, kneeling with her mother, was not listening to the Queen's words. The tears ran slowly down her cheeks.

'Thank God,' she murmured. 'Thank God we have not lost Mary too!'

*

The King was at Mary's bedside. She had asked for a cordial that she might have the strength to receive the sacrament.

Charles could not keep back his tears. He knew that Mary was dying.

Only yesterday they had believed her condition to be improved, but they realized now that they had been too quick to hope.

'Charles,' said Mary. 'Are you there, Charles?'

'I am here, Mary.'

'You should not be. It is dangerous.'

'I am a tough fellow, Mary.'

'Oh, Charles . . . my favourite brother . . .'

'Don't talk,' he said. 'Keep your strength to fight for your life.'

'It is too late. The fight is over. You are weeping, Charles. Pray do not. We are an unlucky lot, we Stuarts. We don't live long, do we? Elizabeth, Henry, and now Mary. Only three left now. Three and poor Mam. Father went . . . long ago.'

'Mary, I beg of you, save your breath.'

'I'm not afraid of death, Charles. I regret dying only because of my boy. Charles, be a father to him.'

'I will, to the best of my ability.'

'My little Dutch William. He is a solemn boy.'

'Have no fear. All shall go well with him.'

She lay breathless on her pillows. Her glazed eyes looked up at him. 'Charles . . . Charles . . . you should not be here. And you the King!'

'I have seen so little of you, Mary. I cannot leave you now.'

'There will not be long for us to be together. I was cruel to James' wife, Charles.'

'Do not think of that now.'

'I cannot help it. I wish so much that I had been kind. She was my maid of honour. She was a good girl and I . . . in my pride, Charles . . .'

'I know. I know. You thought no one good enough for royal Stuarts.'

'You are fond of her father, Charles.'

'Aye! A good friend he has been. I am fond of his daughter, too.'

'You will have her recognized. Charles . . . you will make our mother understand how I feel now. Any day her time may come too. Don't let her feel as I do now. It is a terrible thing to have wronged someone and to come to your death-bed without setting that wrong right.'

'I'll set it right, Mary. Think no more of it. I shall speak to Mam. I'll set that matter right. And Anne Hyde shall know that at the end you were her friend.'

'Thank you, Charles. Thank you, my favourite brother.'

He could not bear to look at her. He dashed the tears from his cheeks. They were giving her the sacrament, and she took it eagerly.

Afterwards she lay back on her pillows and quietly she died.

*

That Christmas at Whitehall was a sad one, and arrangements were made for the return to France of Henrietta Maria and her daughter, for Philippe was urgently requesting that his marriage should be delayed no longer.

The King sought his mother in private audience soon after Mary's death; his face was stern, and Henrietta Maria was quick to notice the lines of obstinacy about his mouth.

'Mam,' he said without preliminary ceremony. 'I have come to ask you to accept James' wife as your daughter-in-law.'

The Queen set her lips firmly together. 'That is something I find it hard to do.'

'Nevertheless you will do it,' said the King.

She looked at him, remembering the stubborn boy who had taken his wooden billet to bed and refused to part with it, not with tears of rage, as most children might have done, but with that solemn determination which made him hold

244

the piece of wood firmly in his small hands and look at those who would take it from him as though he was reminding them that he would be their King one day. He was looking at her like that when he said: 'Nevertheless you will do it.' She remembered that he had settled her yearly allowance and that she depended upon him for much. She knew that she would have to give way.

He was ready, as ever, not to humiliate her unduly. He did not want acknowledgement of his triumph. He merely wanted peace in his family. He said: 'The rumours concerning poor Anne have been proved to be false. James loves her. They have a child whom I have proclaimed heir-presumptive to the crown. There remains one thing; *you* must receive her.'

Henrietta Maria still did not speak.

'In view of all that has gone before,' Charles continued, 'it will be necessary for you to make public recognition of her. We are too unlucky a family not to be happy when we can be together. Fate deals us enough blows without our dealing them to each other. Mary realized that. On her death-bed she wept bitterly for the hurt she had done Anne Hyde. There will be a farewell audience at Whitehall before you leave, and during it James shall bring his wife to you. You will receive her, and do so graciously. I would have it seem that there has never been ill feeling between you.'

Henrietta Maria bowed her head; she was defeated.

But she knew how to accept defeat graciously – in public at least, and when Anne Hyde was brought to her, she took her into her arms and kissed her warmly, so that it was as though there had never been aught amiss between them.

*

The next day they left for France. As their ship tossed on the stormy seas, Henriette grew frightened – not of the death which the roaring winds and the angry waves seemed to promise, but of marriage with the Philippe who had become a stranger to her.

The visit to England had been a connecting bridge between childhood and womanhood. She had known it, and she was afraid of what was waiting for her.

245

Tossing in her cabin, she felt that her body was covered in sweat as she lay there, and suddenly it seemed to her that she was not in a boat at all. It seemed that she was flitting from one scene to another, and always beside her were the two brothers, Louis and Philippe. Philippe was embracing her, laughing slyly at her because she had believed he loved her; and Louis was turning away from her, looking with eager eyes at Madame de Soissons, Madame de Beauvais, Olympia and Marie Mancini – and dozens of others, all beautiful, all voluptuous. He was turning away from her, refusing to dance, and she was afraid because Philippe was waiting to seize her.

'Charles!' she cried. 'Charles, save me, and let me stay with you.'

Charles was somewhere near, but she could not see him, and her cries for help could not reach him.

Her mother was calling to her. 'Henriette, my dearest. They have turned the ship. Thank God we have come safely in. You had a nightmare. We are back in England now. The Captain dared not continue the journey. My child, are you ill?'

Henriette closed her eyes and was only vaguely aware of being carried ashore. For fourteen days she lay at Portsmouth close to death.

*

But she did not die. She refused to be bled as her brother and sister had been, and her malady proved not to be the fatal smallpox but only measles.

As she grew well she seemed to come to terms with life. She must marry. All royal persons must marry, and Philippe was a good match. The real Philippe was quite unlike the creature of her nightmare.

As soon as she was well enough to travel, they crossed the sea on a calm day, and on the way to Paris they were met by a royal party, at the head of which rode Philippe.

Henriette was received in Louis' welcoming embrace without betraying her feelings. She knew that her visit to England had not changed her love for him; growing up had but strengthened that.

She overheard him mention to his mother that poor Henriette was thinner than ever.

To her he said: 'Now that you are in Paris, we shall soon have you strong, Henriette. We have some royal entertainments ready for you. I have a new ballet which I myself prepared for your return. Would you like to know the title?'

He was like a boy, she thought – youthful, eager to be appreciated, hoping that on which he had spent so much pains, would give her the enjoyment he had intended it should.

'Your Majesty is gracious to me,' she told him with tears in her eyes.

'Well, you will be my sister in a few short weeks. It is fitting that I should welcome my sister on her return. The ballet is about lovers who have been separated too long and yearn for reunion. I have called it *L'Impatience des Amoureux!*'

'I am sure it will be very entertaining,' said Henriette.

And the King was satisfied.

*

The dispensation had arrived from the Pope; the wedding was arranged; but there was a postponement because of the death of Mazarin. Louis and his mother insisted on two weeks' Court mourning, during which time it was impossible for a Court wedding to take place. Buckingham, who had accompanied the Princess and her mother from England, was too obvious in his attentions to Henriette, and Philippe showed his jealousy. The Court was amused; so was Louis. It was amazing to see Philippe in love with a woman, and that woman his future wife.

Philippe insisted on Buckingham's being recalled to England, and Charles complied with his request. And all the time Henriette seemed to be in a dream, hoping that something would happen again to postpone the wedding.

But this time all went smoothly, and at the end of March the contracts were signed at the Louvre, and later that day at the Palais-Royal the betrothal took place before the King and Queens Anne and Henrietta Maria. All the nobility of France was present and, although owing to the recent

247

deaths of the bride's brother and sister and the bereavement the royal family of France had suffered in the loss of Cardinal Mazarin, there were no balls and pageants such as were usually given to celebrate a royal wedding, the country showed itself delighted with the union, for all felt sure that it would bring peace between England and France, and moreover, the little Princess with her romantic story had always been a favourite in the land. La Fontaine wrote verses in which he told the story of her escape from England and the years of exile which had culminated in this brilliant marriage.

Charles was delighted; so was Louis. Philippe seemed completely happy; only the bride was filled with foreboding.

*

So she was married. She was no longer the Princesse d'Angleterre, a shy young girl to be ignored and humiliated; she was Madame of the French Court and, after the little Queen Marie-Thérèse and Anne, the Queen Mother, she was the most important lady of France.

Terror had seized her when it was necessary for her to leave her mother and go with Philippe to the Tuileries.

He had been tender and by no means a demanding lover. She believed she had to be grateful to Philippe. He was kind during those weeks of the honeymoon; he had begged her not to be afraid of him. Did he not love her?

She reminded herself that all royal princes and princesses must face marriage. It was a duty they were called upon to perform. If there were love in their marriages they were indeed fortunate; it did not happen to many.

Philippe, she sometimes thought, was more in love with himself than with her. He liked her to admire his clothes and jewels. She believed it would not be difficult to live with Philippe. He was not very much older than she was, and she began to think she had been childish to feel so fearful.

Sometimes she would find his eyes upon her – alert, watchful, as though he were searching for something, as though he found her fascinating in a way he could not understand.

Once he said: 'My lovely Henriette, you are charming.

But yours is a beauty which is not apparent to all. They must look for it. They must seek it out. And then they find how very charming it is, because it is so different, so enchanting that the voluptuous beauties of the Court seem merely fat and vulgar when compared with you.'

She said: 'You are fond of me, Philippe, and thus you see perfection where others see what is imperfect.'

He smiled secretly and after a while he said: 'Now that all these perfections are mine, I should like others to see them and envy me my possessions.'

She grew gay during those days of her honeymoon. She felt she had made an important discovery. There was nothing to fear from Philippe; he was kind and not excessive in his demands for a love she could not give him. It was as though, like herself, he accepted their intimacy for the sake of the children they must beget. She was no longer to suffer humiliation. He talked of the entertainments they would give as Monsieur and Madame of France; and she found herself waiting eagerly to begin the round of gaiety he was proposing.

'You were meant to be gay, Henriette,' he told her. 'You have suffered through living in the shade. Now that the sun will shine upon you, you will open like a flower. You will see; others will see.' He went on: 'We should not stay here in solitude too long. We must not forget that we are Monsieur and Madame, and there is one whom we must entertain before all others. I refer, of course, to my brother. Let us plan a grand ball and decide on whom we shall invite. The list will not include the Queen. Poor Marie-Thérèse! Her condition is just what the country would wish it to be, but I'll swear she looks plainer than ever. We'll have to provide another lady for Louis. That should not be difficult. Who shall it be? Madame de Soissons? Perhaps ... But enough of Louis. This is your first appearance as Madame, and I wish it to be remembered by all who see it. Your gown ... what shall it be? The colour of parchment, I think. That will show your dark eyes. And there shall be slashes of scarlet on it ... again for the sake of your *beaux yeux*. And in your hair there shall be jewels. Remember, Henriette, you are no longer an exile. You are Madame ... Madame of the Court, the first lady of the ball; for my mother will not come, nor will yours; and poor little Marie-Thérèse must lie abed nursing the heir of France within her!'

'Philippe, I have rarely seen you so excited.'

'I think of your triumph. How proud I shall be! Henriette, make me proud. Make all men envy me.'

She laughed and threw herself gleefully into the preparations. There should be a dazzling ballet for the King's enjoyment. She and Philippe would dance together. Their first entertainment for the King should surpass all that had gone before.

She was gay. She wrote verses; she practised the singing of them; she practised the dance; her gown would be the most becoming she had ever possessed. For life had taken a new turn, and she was going to assume that gaiety which was her birthright and which had lain slumbering too long.

Philippe watched her, smiling, clapping his hands, kissing her lightly.

'All men will envy me this night!' he declared. '*All* men!'

*

Animated, and vivacious as none had seen her before, she greeted Louis on his arrival, gracefully curtseying as he extended his hand for her to kiss.

He had said good-night to his wife before he had left for the Tuileries; and he had thought how plain and sallow she was.

She was lying back in bed playing cards with her women, her greedy eyes turned from the dish of sweetmeats which were on the bed. She looked at him as though he were one of the sweetmeats, the biggest and the most succulent; and he had felt sick and angry because the daughter of the King of Spain did not look like Madame de Soissons.

Now Henriette stood before him. Such radiance! Such beauty! He had never before seen her thus. All his pity for his poor little cousin was swept aside and there remained feelings which he did not understand.

He said: 'It shall be my privilege to open the ball with you, cousin . . . nay, you are my sister now.'

He took Henriette's hand.

She thought how handsome he was, and she was momentarily wretched because it was his brother and not himself who was her husband. But now he was looking at her as he had never looked before, when the violins began to play and the dancers fell in behind them.

'You have changed,' said Louis.

'Is that so, Your Majesty?'

'Marriage has changed you.'

'Your Majesty knew me for a long time as the sister of an exiled King. Now Your Majesty sees me as the sister of a reigning King and . . . your brother's wife.'

'Henriette,' he whispered, 'I'm glad you are my sister.'

Her eyes filled with sudden tears, and he saw them.

Then suddenly understanding came to him. So many women had loved him; here was another.

He was silent as they continued the dance, but she was no longer silent. She was beautiful and vivacious tonight, and she knew that this was the beginning of a new life for her. She knew that all in the vast room watched her and marvelled at the change in her. She could almost hear their voices, see the question on their lips: Is this little Henriette, the quiet little Princess who was so shy, so thin, so ready to hide herself in a corner? Has marriage done this? So all that charm and gaiety was hidden beneath those quiet looks!

Louis was enchanted. He did not notice Madame de Soissons. He could not bring himself to leave Henriette's side; and she felt recklessness sweep over her. She had been unhappy so long because he had failed to find her attractive.

Now she was happy; she could live in the moment. At last Louis had looked at her and found the sight a pleasing one.

He said to her: 'Now that the Queen is indisposed, there is much you can do to help me. We shall need a lady to lead the Court. My mother has felt the Cardinal's death sorely, my wife is indisposed . . .'

'I shall do my best to prove a good substitute,' she murmured.

'Substitute!' said Louis. 'Oh . . . Henriette!'

'Your Majesty finds me changed. Have I changed so much? I am still thin.'

'You are as slender as a willow wand.'

'Still the bones of the Holy Innocents! Do you remember?'

'You shame me,' cried Louis. 'I am thinking what a fool I was. Henriette, what a blind, stupid fool!'

'Your Majesty . . .'

'I think of what might have been mine, and what is. I might have been in Philippe's place. I might . . .'

She broke in: 'Your Majesty, what would I not have given to see you look at me thus a year ago!'

'So you . . .'

'Do you doubt that any who look upon you could fail to love you?'

'What can we do?' said the King. 'What a tragedy is this! You and I . . . and to know this . . . too late!'

She said: 'We are princes, and we have our duty. But that will not prevent our being friends. It is enough for me to be near you and see you often.'

'Yes, often. It shall be so. Henriette . . . you are the most perfect being of my Court, and you are . . . Philippe's wife!'

So they were together and Madame was gay that night.

This is the happiest time of my life, she told herself.

Philippe watched his wife and his brother with immense satisfaction, for at last he had that which Louis coveted. Here was his revenge for all the boyhood slights.

Louis wanted Henriette, and Henriette was Philippe's wife.

CHAPTER EIGHT

HENRIETTE BEGAN TO be happy as she had never been happy before.

Louis loved her; he sought every opportunity of being with her. She was to reign over the Court with him; he reproached himself a hundred times a day because he might have married her, but had been a blind fool; he realized that he had never been indifferent to her, that those stirrings of pity which she had aroused in him had, in fact, been true love. He saw himself as a simpleton, a man who had never thought for himself because there had been others to think for him, a man who had never explored his own mind, because there were so many to tell him he was perfect, more god than man. He had never been given to self-analysis. Why should he? He had been told he was perfect. He had been taught to vault and ride, to show off his physical perfections rather than to study and use his brains.

He saw himself for the first time as a man who had been duped by his own simplicity. Beside him, loving him, had been the perfect companion, and he had failed to see in her more than a sad little cousin, worthy of his pity.

If Henriette had changed, so had Louis. He was no longer the puppet King. Mazarin was dead, and he intended to be the true King of France. He had grown up through the realization of his love for Henriette; he was a simple boy no longer; he was a man who would also be a King.

Now he began to show his mother that she could no longer lead him. He, Louis, would decide.

He seemed to increase his stature. He was at least three inches taller than most men at Court, but he seemed more than that in his high heels and his wig of stiff frizzed hair which rose straight up from his brow adorned with the broad-brimmed plumed hat. He was a magnificent figure, the leader of the Court, as he had never been before.

In those weeks it was enough for Louis – as it was for Henriette – to know themselves loved by the loved one. Their relationship seemed to them the more perfect because, as they saw it at this time, it could never reach its natural climax. It was romantic love which seemed to gain beauty from the fact that it could not reach that climax and therefore would go on for ever at the same high level. Both Louis and Henriette were too well-versed in the etiquette of the Court to believe that Henriette could ever be his mistress – not only because of their marriage vows, but because of the close relationship which Henriette's marriage with Philippe had brought about.

Fontainebleau made a perfect setting for their romance. There in the gilded salons, Louis whispered to Henriette that he loved her; he told her the same thing as they wandered through the gardens. He enjoyed establishing an unceremonious rule at his beloved Fontainebleau, at this time his favourite palace. He would be there with Henriette, the Queen of his intimate Court; he would walk among his friends, joining their games of billiards and piquet when the fancy took him. Always Henriette was beside him, his hand resting lightly on her arm, his candid eyes alight with affection; they would discuss together the rebuilding of Versailles, planning the long gallery with its border of orange trees to be set in boxes of silver and to be lighted by candles in rock crystal lustres. Through the shrubberies and groves they wandered when they wished to be alone; under trees and past bushes which they planned to take from these woods of Fontainebleau to beautify the gardens of Versailles and make a charming setting for its statues and its water-works.

And most vivid of all, it seemed, were the figures who moved about in this perfect setting. Jewels flashed; silks and satins rustled; blue, green and scarlet feathers drooped over shoulders and the air was filled with perfume. Fans were of brilliant colours and exquisite design; gloves were elaborately embroidered; swords were diamond-hilted; spurs were of gold. In the centre of all this magnificence were the royal lovers – Henriette, so different from others because she was frail and slender, yet vivacious and gay as she had never been before. She was able now to give expression to her natural elegance and good taste in clothes, and it was she who set the fashion. Louis, in cloth of gold, with black lace, in silks, velvets and satins, jewels adorning his handsome person, diamonds flashing in his hat, towered above them all – a fitting King of this paradise.

He could not honour Henriette enough. He must make up for all the years of neglect. He would have her take the Queen's place on Maundy Thursday in the hall of the Louvre at the ceremony of washing the feet of the poor. At the grand fêtes, he would open the ball with Henriette. 'Where the King is,' said the Court, 'there is Madame.'

She was just seventeen; she was romantically in love. Louis, in all his manly beauty and with his new authority, was all that she would ask in a lover. She did not seek sexual satisfaction; her experiences with Philippe had not made her desire to extend her knowledge in such matters. This was the perfect love; romantic, idealistic, untouched by the sordid needs of daily life.

She had a great influence over him. At her instigation he was turning to more intellectual pursuits. They wrote verses together and often read them aloud, when they were vociferously applauded by the courtiers.

Sometimes Henriette and her women would drive out to bathe in a stream in the forest; the King would ride through the trees to greet her returning from her bathe that she might have an escort back to the palace. She was more beautiful than she had ever been; and she had always looked well on a horse, in her gold-laced habit with the brilliantly coloured plumes in her hat shading her face. At the head of the retinue she and Louis would ride side by side.

Often there were picnics under the trees. She had inspired in him an appreciation of the arts, and sometimes musicians would play to them as they went along the river in a gondola decorated with purple velvet and cloth of gold. They would plan the entertainments for the next day as they sat side by side or rode through the forest. For Henriette that was an enchanted summer. Hunting was continued into the night, and Henriette and the King often went for long walks through the moonlight alone through the forest. If they did not meet each other every day they would write notes.

She had introduced to his notice many of the artistic personalities of the day. Lulli, the musician, must compose the music for his ballet; Molière must write the lyrics. Louis was reading the romances of Madeline de Scudèry and the dramatic pieces of her brother Georges. Because Henriette wished writers to be encouraged, Louis followed her lead, and, much to his delight, he found that a new world full of interest was opening to him.

The Court was changing; it was becoming more intellectual, and so more elegant than it had been for many years. 'We are returning to the days of François Premier,' it was said. 'He loved writers more than any other men. He also loved his sister!'.

It was impossible for this new relationship to pass

unnoticed. There were sly glances and shaking of heads when the King was not present.

'So Madame is his newest mistress?' ran the murmurings. 'What a situation! And, Monsieur! What does he think of his honeymoon's being interrupted?'

Philippe was more quickly aware of the sly looks, the whispered comments. All had worked out as he had been told it would. De Guiche had been right in his hints. Louis was in love with Henriette and had been for a long time, only he had been too simple to know it. The King of France envied his brother. That was quite satisfactory to Philippe. But it was not turning out quite as he had wished. Louis was not tormented by jealousy; Louis was indulging in a romantic love affair, and, it seemed, was content with life. Therefore Philippe was dissatisfied.

He walked in the gardens of Saint-Cloud with his dear friend de Guiche. He should have been contented. This palace was delightful, especially since those excellent architects, Lepante and Girard, had improved it that it might be ready for Philippe on his wedding. The beautiful parks and gardens had been designed by Le Notre himself, and the fountains, which equalled those of Fontainebleau, were the work of Mansart. From the terraces could be seen the river winding its way to Paris. Clipped yew hedges, arbours, palisades and parterres planted with orange trees and embellished with statues of Greek gods and nymphs, were an added glory. Saint-Cloud was indeed beautiful, and he was proud to possess it. Madame could spend as much time with the King as she liked – so he had thought – he would not object. He had his own friends to amuse and flatter him, and – constant gratification – Louis envied him his wife and compared her with the plain Spanish woman.

But it was not quite as he had planned.

'You were right,' he said to his friend. 'Louis was certainly in love with her. He needed her marriage to me to show him that.'

'She has changed, has she not?' said de Guiche quietly. 'Who would recognize her as the little Princess she was before her marriage? Now . . . she shows great charm. She has her brother's wit, I am glad to say, but not his looks – I am equally pleased to add. She is the natural friend of the most intellectual people at the Court. She has shown the Court that there is more to beauty than layers of fat. Henriette happy, is not only the most elegant, she is the most desirable woman at Court; and to be elegant and desirable – those are higher attributes than mere beauty.'

'You speak as though you yourself are in love with my wife. If I did not know you so well, I should say you were. But it is not as I wished it to be – this love my brother has for my wife. They revel in it. She is changing him; she is ruling the Court. Now we do honour to those artists of hers. That fellow Molière would seem to be an intimate of the King ... because Madame wishes it. Those de Scudèrys ... this fellow he has taken from his band of violins ... what is his name ... Lulli? Old Corneille is made much of; and this young fellow, Racine ... They surround the King; they swamp the King; he spends much time listening to their verses and their music. And it is at the command of my wife! It would seem to me that in marrying Henriette, I have made her Queen of France.'

'A worthy Queen!' said de Guiche.

'I shall have to remind my brother that Henriette is Madame – not Queen – of France.'

'You will dare do that?'

'I shall speak to my mother. She never cared for scandal which touched her own family – much as she loves it concerning others. She will make my brother see that there must be an end to these amorous talks tête-à-tête, these moonlight rambles, these dainty perfumed notes they send each other. I shall bring Madame back here to Saint-Cloud. She must be made to understand that she is not – although she and my brother may wish she were – the Queen of France.'

'Alas! Madame makes an enchanting Queen!'

Philippe looked sharply at his friend.

If I did not know him so well, and that he does not love women, I should say he was in love with Henriette, thought Philippe.

But he did not entirely know his friend.

*

Anne of Austria asked that she might see her son alone.

257

'Louis,' she said, 'my beloved, this is a delicate matter of which I must speak to you. Forgive me, I know that it is merely idle gossip which I repeat, but there must not be gossip concerning our great King.'

'Gossip!' cried Louis. 'What is this?'

'It concerns you and Madame.'

'Who speaks this gossip? I will have him brought before me. I . . .'

'You cannot punish the whole Court, dearest. You will, I know, be your wonderful, reasonable self and, although there is no cause for this gossip, you will remove all excuse for it.'

'What has been said of me . . . and Madame?'

'Merely that you are always together, that you treat her as your Queen, that you neglect the real Queen, that you write notes to each other if you are parted from her for a few hours at a time; in short, that you love your cousin who is the wife of your brother.'

'This . . . this is monstrous!'

'It is true that you spend much time in her company?'

'And shall continue to do so. Tell me who brought this news to you!'

'It was not one. I heard it from many. I beg of you be discreet. Do not give rise to such rumours. Have a mistress if you want one. Why should you not? And particularly while the Queen is indisposed. But let it not be your brother's wife. Philippe is jealous.'

'Philippe! Let him return to his boys!'

'Henriette is his wife. It is the future we must think of, dearest. If she had a child . . . and it was believed to be yours . . .'

'This is foul!' cried Louis. 'This is scandalous! That any should dare talk thus of Henriette!'

He strode from his mother's apartments and went to his own. He paced up and down, waving away all attendants. So they were talking about his devotion to Henriette! They were whispering sly things! They were besmirching his beautiful romance! It would never again be quite the same for him.

*

Henrietta Maria tapped her foot and looked at her daughter.

'You must be more discreet. What an unfortunate thing this is! If Louis had but felt towards you a short time ago as he does today, what a wonderful thing that would have been! What glory! My son King of England; my daughter Queen of France! But this will not do. They are calling you the King's mistress.'

'It is not true,' said Henriette.

'Of course it is not true!' Henrietta Maria's arms were about her daughter, and Henriette received one of those suffocating embraces. 'My daughter . . . so to forget herself . . . no! It is not true. But there must be no scandal. You and the King! Your husband's brother! You can see what scandal there could be! What if you were to have a child? We shall have them saying it is the King's! That would be intolerable.'

Henriette said coldly: 'These rumours are false. The King has never been anything but a good brother to me.'

'Then I beg of you curb your affection for one another. You are too ostentatiously affectionate. You are too often in each other's company.'

'I am tired,' said Henriette. 'I can listen to no more. I will do my best, I assure you, to see that you suffer no anxiety on my account.'

She went to her apartment and asked her women to draw the curtains about her bed, shutting her in.

So . . . they were watching her and Louis! They were spying on their love.

It was true that she was going to have a child – Philippe's child. If only it had been Louis'!

Now she knew that she had passed the summit of her happiness. She knew the romantic idyll was less bright than it had been. She had been aware that it could not last for ever. She buried her face in the silken cushions and wept.

*

Louis sought her out. They did not always have to be asked to be left alone; discreet attendants withdrew. That was a sign, they both realized now, of the construction which was being put on their relationship.

He said: 'Dearest, they are talking. There is scandal concerning us.'

'I know it, Louis,' she answered.

'My mother has warned me.'

'Mine has warned me.'

'What must we do?'

'We must never be alone together; we must give up our moonlight rambles. You must select a favourite and spend much time with her. You must treat me more as a sister.'

'I could not do it, Henriette. Loving you as I do, I could not pretend not to do so.'

'Yet it must be done.'

'How I hate myself! We should have been free to make the most perfect marriage ever made by King and Queen . . . if I had been less of a fool!'

'Do not speak of yourself thus, Louis. If you were not exactly as you are, how could I love you? To me you are as perfect as your courtiers tell you you are – not because I think you are the wisest man in France, not because I think you write better verses than Molière and Racine, but because I love you. I love you as you are, and would not have one little part of you changed.'

He kissed her with passion. In future there must be no opportunities for such displays of feeling. They were both a little afraid of where such displays might lead them; they had both been brought up in the French Court by two mothers who had never failed to impress upon them the importance of their royalty. Etiquette was second nature to them and neither of them could act without being conscious of their royalty.

He released her and cried: 'What are we going to do, Henriette? What shall we do, my love?'

It was to her that he had always turned for suggestions.

'There is only one thing we can do,' she said. 'We must make everyone believe that the affection we have for each other is pure . . . as pure as we know it to be. We must see each other rarely and never without others present.'

'That I'll not agree to!'

'Then, Louis, you must come to see me, but it must appear that you are not interested in me, but in someone else.'

'Would anyone believe that?'

260

'I have some pretty maids of honour.'

He laughed at the suggestion and, taking her hands, kissed them fervently. 'Henriette,' he demanded, 'why should we care? What should our positions matter to us? Has there ever been love such as ours? Why should we not ignore all those about us! Why should we not follow our inclinations! Life has cheated us.'

'Nay, Louis,' she answered sadly, 'we have cheated ourselves.'

'The fault is mine.'

She stroked his face gently as though she longed to remember every detail of it. 'I'll not have you blame yourself. The fault was mine. I was too proud. I was too conscious of my beggary. I hid myself away; I was shy and gauche.'

'And I was blind.'

'Nay, Louis, it is not true. I was there, but I was not awake then. I was only a child – a shy, proud child. I was not the person I am today. Nor are you. You, too, have changed.

'We have grown up, dearest. We have left childhood behind us. Why should we not be happy together?'

'I am trying to think of a means whereby we might continue our happiness. At the ball tonight we shall present the *Ballet des Saisons*. All the most beautiful women of the Court will either be among the spectators or taking part in the ballet. You must pretend to be mightily interested in one of them. There is a charming girl, Frances Stuart, one of the loveliest girls I ever saw.'

'She will not seem lovely to me. I shall not see her.'

'Dear Louis, you must see her . . . or one of them. There is young Marie-Anne, the youngest Mancini girl. She is charming.'

'I shall dislike her. She will remind me how foolish I was with her sisters.'

'There is a quiet little girl – only just sixteen. She is very shy, but she seems quite pretty at times. She would be enchanted if you but smiled at her. She will be carrying your Diana's train.'

'I shall have eyes only for Diana.'

'Please spare a glance for little Louise de la Vallière. She will be overcome with delight at the honour; and if you pay some attention to her, it will be said that Madame no longer draws to herself all the King's attention.'

Then he held her against him and she clung to him. She had a feeling that there would be so few opportunities in the future.

'Dearest Louis,' she said, 'do not be jealous if you see me showing some civility to a friend of Philippe's, for I shall have to play my part. The Comte de Guiche will be to me as little Louise is to you; and you need not feel any jealousy, for he is one of Philippe's friends, and you know they have no interest in women.'

'So . . . we must disguise our love. We must pretend to care more for others. . . .'

'It is the only way, Louis. You may trust me with de Guiche, and I shall trust you with the little Vallière.'

*

It was the most elaborate of all the fêtes, and the ballet, most appropriately, took place out of doors. The stage had been set on the lawn near the lake, and torches lighted in the avenues of trees.

The Queens Anne and Henrietta Maria were seated in state, surrounded by those members of the Court who were not taking part in the ballet.

First came beautiful nymphs, scattering roses on the grass as they sang and danced, and their songs were eulogies of the qualities of Diana the huntress. Then the curtain was drawn to show Henriette. A gasp of delight came from the spectators at the sight of her. She was clad in fine draperies and her hair hung loose about her shoulders; the silver crescent was on her brow and in her arms were the bow and quiver.

About her were green-clad beauties, and two of these were young girls whom Henriette had recommended to Louis: Frances Stuart who, it was clear, in spite of her youth, would be a great beauty, and the much less noticeable brown-haired girl, Louise de la Vallière.

The seasons of the year entered to pay tribute to Diana, and, dressed as Spring, in green and gold and ablaze with diamonds, came the King himself. He knelt before Henriette and lifted his eyes to her face. The chorus was singing verses in praise of Spring with such passion and verve that, if any had failed to recognize Louis in his verdant robes, it would have been known that Spring could only be the King.

Louis was not listening to the verses. He was looking at the young girl who stood with downcast eyes, not daring to glance his way.

Louise de la Vallière was very shy, and obviously in agony because she feared she would forget her words. Now came her cue to join Diana's handmaidens in a song, and Louise missed it.

She looked at the King and the King was looking at her; she blushed hotly and a wave of tenderness swept over Louis. Poor child! She was shy because she was taking part in a ballet with him, and he himself had seen that she was not so clever at the acting and singing as some of the girls.

He smiled, and he saw that it was all she could do to prevent herself falling on her knees before him. He raised his eyebrows. His lips formed the words: 'I am not now the King; I am merely Spring.' They seemed like part of the ballet. La Vallière smiled, tremulous and adoring; and Louis, accustomed as he was to admiration, was well-pleased.

*

They walked about the gardens of Fontainebleau, the ladies and gentlemen of the Court. Henriette had changed Diana's draperies for a gown of cloth of silver and scarlet. Until today the King would have been beside her. With feelings of mingling relief and regret she saw that he was with a group which included La Vallière. It was as they had planned, but how she wished he had refused to carry out their plan! She imagined his coming to her and saying: 'I care not for their gossip. I wish to be with you, and with you I shall be.'

Armand, the Comte de Guiche, was beside her. 'Madame,' he said fervently, 'may I congratulate you on a wonderful performance?'

'You are kind, Monsieur le Comte.'

'It is you who are kind, Madame, to allow me to speak thus with you.'

'Oh come, monsieur, we do not stand on ceremony on

such occasions. Those are the King's orders. See how he himself mingles with his guests.'

'It has been so difficult to speak with Madame,' said de Guiche. 'Usually the King is at her side. I am delighted to have this opportunity.'

'The part you played in the ballet was considerable, Comte. You were a great success.'

'I shall treasure such praise, coming whence it does.'

'You have an air of melancholy. You have not quarrelled with Monsieur, have you?'

'No, Madame.'

'Then is anything amiss?'

'Amiss, Madame? I am the victim of a hopeless passion. I love a lady, the most delightful in the Court, and I have no hope that my passion will ever be returned.'

'I am sorry to hear that. I did not know you cared for ladies.'

'I never did until I saw this one.'

'I am sorry she will have none of you. Have you courted her long?'

'I have seen her often, but there has been little opportunity for courtship. She is far above me. She is elegant; she is slender; and she is quite different from the plump beauties of the Court.'

Henriette smiled. 'Then I can only wish you the good fortune of falling out of love, since you cannot win this woman. Now, Monsieur le Comte, will you conduct me to the King? I wish to hear whether he himself is satisfied with our entertainment.'

She was thinking: I cannot bear to be away from him. He has shown the arranged interest in La Vallière, and I mine in de Guiche; we have done our duty for this night, and we must not break away too suddenly.

She noticed how Louis' face lighted as she approached, and in that moment Fontainebleau was a very happy place for Henriette.

*

Philippe faced his friend and demanded an explanation of his conduct. 'You ... flirting with Madame! What means this?'

264

'You have been misinformed.'

'My eyes do not misinform me. I saw you. You were mincing along beside her, complimenting her like a young fop bent on seduction!'

'Does Monsieur think Madame would look my way?'

'It appears that she did.'

'Only because . . .'

'Never mind why she smiled on you! Why did you smile on her?'

'She is enchanting.'

'Armand!'

'Of what use to deny it?' said the Comte. 'Of course I am in love with Madame. I was in love with her before anyone else saw how delightful she really was. I have always watched her; I have always understood her . . . known more of her than anyone. . . .'

'How dare you stand there and tell me you love my wife . . . you who are *my* friend!'

'Monsieur . . . Philippe . . . I am sorry. I love you. I have loved you since we were boys. This is different. It should not come between us. You, as her husband, should understand that.'

'What has that to do with you and me?'

'You know her . . . how charming she is. I feel that I have helped to make her what she is today. I have helped to tear away that shyness, that *gaucherie* . . . but to me, even that was charming.'

'Armand! I will not have you talk thus before me. Do not imagine that my favour is for you alone. There are others who would be only too ready to take your place in my affections. You may go away for all I care. And, in fact, if you are thinking of making love to Henriette, go you certainly shall! Do not imagine you can make me jealous by preferring my wife!'

De Guiche threw up his hands in a gesture of despair. 'I see this is an impossible situation. I shall leave the Court, I shall go to the country. I cannot stay here any longer.'

'Then go!' cried Philippe. 'I have other friends to fill your place.'

So Armand de Guiche retired to the country, and all the

265

Court whispered that he did so because Monsieur had discovered his love for Madame.

*

Louis had kept his part of the bargain. He had sought out the little Vallière. He enjoyed being kind to her because she was such a frightened little thing and over-awed to have the attention of the King focused upon herself. She could not understand why, until other maids of honour told her that he was falling in love with her.

'It is impossible!' cried the little Vallière. 'The King would never fall in love with me, when there are so many beauties of the Court all sighing for him.'

But Louis continued to seek her out. He would be by her side when the Court rode together; he would join in the dance with her, for she was present at those informal occasions at Fontainbleau; he would say: 'Come, Mademoiselle de la Vallière, come and watch the piquet.'

Sometimes he himself would play, and when everything he did was applauded, La Vallière would clasp her hands together and her big brown eyes would be wide with adoration.

Louis thought: Poor child! She seeks too much to please. Oh, Henriette, if we could but be together! If only you were with me now!

The Queen was near her time. She spent much of the day lying in bed playing cards, in which she took great delight, still eating a great deal – far too much, it was said, for the good of the child.

Louis visited her as rarely as he could without calling attention to the fact that she bored him.

His mother was delighted because he was no longer constantly in the company of Henriette. She did not appear in public as frequently as before; she was content to leave state matters to Louis and his ministers. Like her daughter-in-law, her chief interest was in food and cards, although she had a love of the theatre; she was content to keep certain ladies with her to gossip in her *ruelle* every night and bring her the latest scandals.

It was evening, and Louis was strolling through the

grounds of Versailles with a little party of noblemen and ladies. Among the group was La Vallière.

The conversation was by no means profound; there were no literary allusions as there would doubtless have been had Henriette been present. The jokes were trivial and obvious, and everything the King said was greeted with hilarious laughter. He felt a longing to have Henriette beside him, to be free of these empty-headed sycophants.

Then he looked into the face of La Vallière who was close beside him. He knew that she was in love with him, and he was moved because of the sincerity of this young girl who could not hide her devotion; she was like a young fawn, fascinated yet apprehensive.

Louis realized that he had been faithful to Henriette ever since he had discovered that he loved her. He had had no mistress since then, and from those days when Madame de Beauvais had initiated him into the pleasure of the *doux scavoir* such delights had been a frequent need. He felt sexual desire upon him then like thirst in the desert or hunger after a long fast. It came to him as he stood there in the scented gardens with La Vallière beside him.

He looked at the girl, and felt pity for her. Pity! He had first felt that for Henriette, and in some ways this girl reminded him of Henriette – not as she was now, not Madame, but the shy Princess Henriette with whom he had once refused to dance.

He was unaware of the silence which had fallen about him, his large eyes had become a little glazed, and he was still looking at La Vallière.

He said, and although his voice sounded normal to him, it seemed to those about him – accustomed as they were to anticipating his moods – that it held a note of high-pitched excitement: 'Mademoiselle de la Vallière, have you seen the new summer house I have had built near the ornamental grotto?'

La Vallière stammered, as she always did when directly addressed by the King: 'N . . . no, Sire. Why . . . yes . . . I believe I have, Sire.'

'Then let us go and make sure that you have.'

By the time they reached the grotto the party which had accompanied them had lingered here and there, and there was none left but La Vallière and her King. They went through into the new summer house where were set out gilded chairs and a velvet-covered couch – scarlet, and decorated with golden *fleurs-de-lis*.

'So . . . you see it now,' he said, and taking her hands he drew her to him and kissed her.

La Vallière trembled. The frightened fawn . . . the eager fawn . . . thought Louis. It is Henriette whom I love, but she is my brother's wife, and this timid little Vallière is so eager to be loved.

*

Armand de Guiche soon returned to the Court. He found that his longing to see Henriette forced him to return. So he asked Philippe's pardon, which was graciously accorded him, and he became again the close friend of Henriette's husband in order that he might not be banished from Henriette's presence.

Henriette had an opportunity to speak a few words in private with the King while they danced together.

She said: 'So we have produced the desired effect. There is talk of you and the little Vallière.'

'Is that so?' said Louis.

'And I have heard my name is mentioned with that of de Guiche.'

'I like that not,' said Louis.

'Nor do I like to hear it said that you are in love with La Vallière.'

'You could not believe that I would love anyone now . . . that I ever could, after I came to love you!'

'I hope not, Louis. I hope your love for me is like mine for you.'

'Mine is infinite,' declared the King; but he avoided meeting her eyes. He wished that he had not fallen into temptation with La Vallière. He wished that he did not keep remembering her little fluttering hands, her cries of protest and pleasure.

It should not happen again; he had promised himself that. He had not meant it to happen that second or third time, but it had been almost impossible to avoid it; she was so ready, so shy, so adoring. It would have been churlish not to. It was not love he had for the little one, he assured himself; it was pity . . . and the desire to honour her.

Henriette said: 'Armand de Guiche came to my rooms this day, disguised as a fortune-teller. He is very bold. I had forbidden him to come near me. I thought there had been enough scandal, and I had no wish for more. Montalais, one of my maids of honour, came to me and said there was a teller of fortunes without, who had great things to tell me; and when I had him brought in I discovered it was de Guiche. I recognized him when he raised those mournful eyes to my face. I sent him off at once. I was thankful that none of the others present knew who my fortune-teller was.'

'The insolent fellow!' exclaimed the King.

'Do not be hard on him, Louis. We chose to make use of him, remember.'

Louis, heavy with the guilt of his affaire with La Vallière, found that he was feigning anger against de Guiche which was greater than he felt. But Henriette was smiling tenderly; she felt it was wonderful to know that Louis could love her so much.

*

In the streets they were singing songs about the amours of the Court. Madame was loved by Monsieur's *bel ami*; the King was neglecting his wife for one of Madame's maids of honour.

Mademoiselle Montalais, who loved to make mischief and knew more of her mistress's affairs than Henriette realized, whispered to her one day: 'La Vallière is absent-minded these days . . . They say it is her preoccupation with the King. She is afraid because she has surrendered her chastity to the King and, like all the pious, she seeks to justify her actions and tells herself that it would have been worse to have been a disloyal subject and refused him than to offend the laws of the church by lying with him in the summer house.'

'There is always gossip,' said Henriette.

'There is some truth in this, I'll warrant,' said Montalais. 'I have heard La Vallière saying her prayers. She asks for courage to resist when the next time comes, and then in the same breath she seems to be asking that the next

269

time may come soon ... I could never endure pious harlots.'

'I cannot believe this of . . . La Vallière!'

'Madame, it is true. The whole Court knows it. Though doubtless it is kept from you on account of your friendship with His Majesty.'

Henriette dismissed the woman. Could it be true? Little La Vallière ... the last person worthy of him, and yet her very timidity might make an appeal to Louis! She, Henriette, who loved him, knew him well.

Henriette hesitated to face the truth, yet she could not bear to remain in ignorance. She sent for La Vallière, and when the girl stood trembling before her, she said: 'Mademoiselle de la Vallière, I have heard gossip concerning you. I do not want to believe that it is true. In fact I find it hard to believe, but I must ask you to tell me the truth. You are – as one of my maids of honour – in my care, and I should not wish to think that you had behaved wantonly while in my household.'

Before the girl was able to speak she had revealed the truth to Henriette. First a wild anger possessed her – anger against Louis, against this girl, against herself for being such a fool as to recommend the girl to his notice, against Fate which had been so cruel to her.

She stood trembling, her face pale, her hands clenched together; she could not look at the girl.

La Vallière had thrown herself at Henriette's feet and was sobbing out her confession.

'Madame, I did not mean it to happen. I could not believe that His Majesty would ever care for me. I know that I have done wrong ... but His Majesty insisted and ... I could not refuse.'

'You could not refuse!' cried Henriette, pushing the girl from her. 'You lie! You ... you lured him with your seeming innocence. You feigned shyness ... modesty ... reluctance ...'

'His Majesty is so ... so handsome,' stammered La Vallière. 'Madame, I tried hard, but I could not resist him. No one could resist him once he had made up his mind. Even you ... you yourself ... could not have resisted him ... had you been in my position.'

Henriette cried in anguished fury: 'Be silent, you wretched girl! You lying, hypocritical wanton, be silent!'

'Madame, I implore you. If you will speak to the king. If you could ask him to explain how it happened . . .'

Henriette laughed. 'I . . . speak to the King . . . about you! You are of no importance to His Majesty. You are one of many . . . many!'

Henriette was trying to shut out of her mind pictures of Louis and this girl together; she could not. They would not be shut out. She saw Louis – passionate, eager, refusing to be denied.

Oh God, she thought, I cannot bear this. I could kill this silly girl who has had that for which I so longed. I hate her . . . I hate Louis for deceiving me. I hate myself for my folly. What a fool I have been! I gave him to her.

But she must be calm. All her life she had had to be calm. No one must know how she suffered. She must not be the laughing stock of the Court.

She said coldly: 'Get up, Mademoiselle de la Vallière. Go to your apartment. Prepare to leave. I will not allow you to remain another night in my household. Not another night, I tell you. Do you think I shall let you stay here, corrupting others! You . . . with your sham humility! Prepare to leave at once.'

La Vallière raised her tear-filled eyes to Henriette's face. 'Madame, where shall I go? I have nowhere to go. Please Madame, let me stay here until I can see the King. Please see His Majesty yourself. He will tell you how he insisted . . .'

Henriette turned away; she was afraid that the girl would see the anguish in her face. 'I have said Go!' she told her. 'I never want to see your face again.'

La Vallière rose, curtsied and hurried from the room.

When she had gone, Henriette threw herself on to a couch. She did not weep; she had no tears. There was no happiness left for her in the world. She had been brutal to La Vallière but her jealous fury had commanded her to be so. She hated herself and the world. She understood that Louis could not maintain their rarified devotion; he was not made for such idealism; he was young and lusty; he needed physical satisfaction. It was wrong to blame La Vallière, but how could she bear to see the girl daily!

'I wish I were dead!' she murmured. 'I can see that life has nothing to offer me.'

Her restless fingers plucked at the golden lilies embroidered on the velvet of the couch, but she did not see them; she saw nothing but Louis and La Vallière, locked in a lovers' embrace.

*

Montalais brought her the news.

'The King is distracted, Madame. He has heard of the flight of La Vallière. He has himself gone in pursuit of her. Who would have thought that His Majesty would have cared so much for our silly little Vallière!'

'So,' said Henriette, 'he has gone in pursuit of her!'

'He is determined to find her,' continued Montalais. 'He is urging all his friends to join in the search. There will be rewards for those who uncover the hiding place of His Majesty's little inamorata.'

'His Majesty has not mentioned the girl's flight to me.'

'Has he not, Madame?' said Montalais, not without a trace of malice. 'That is indeed strange. One would have thought you might have been able to tell him something of the girl's possible whereabouts, considering she was in your service.'

Henriette said: 'Doubtless the matter slipped his memory when he was with me.'

'Doubtless, Madame,' said Montalais.

They know! decided Henriette. They all know of my love for the King. They know he has turned from me to my maid of honour!

*

A *calèche* drew up outside the Tuileries. From it alighted a man in a long concealing cloak and hood, and with him was a shrinking girl. The man demanded audience of Madame.

There were some who wanted to know how he dared storm the Tuileries at such an hour and peremptorily demand to see Madame d'Orléans.

But when the man threw back his hood and revealed his features, those who had asked the question fell on to their knees before him. They hastened to Madame's apartment to tell her that the King was on his way to see her.

Louis was already there, and Henriette saw that the shrinking creature who accompanied him was La Vallière.

Louis waved aside ceremony as Henriette would have knelt. He took her hand, looking earnestly into her eyes. 'I have found little Mademoiselle de la Vallière,' he said. 'She was in a convent near Saint-Cloud whither she had taken refuge. Poor child! She was in a state of great distress. I know you will help me, Henriette.'

'I . . . help Your Majesty!'

'I ask you to take her back into your service, to look after her as your maid of honour. I want it to be as though she has never run away.'

He turned to La Vallière, and Henriette felt as though her heart was breaking as she saw the tender looks he bestowed upon the frightened girl. Louis was so frank; he was incapable of deceit; he could not hide from her the fact that he was in love with this girl.

This is too much to be borne! thought Henriette. It is more than I can endure. Can it be that he has no understanding? Can he be as obtuse as he seems?

'Your Majesty,' she said, steeling herself to speak calmly, 'I cannot take this girl back. She admits that she has been guilty of an intrigue with a gentleman in a high place at Court.'

'It was no fault of hers,' said Louis.

'Your Majesty, I did not understand that she was the victim of rape.'

Louis' eyes were full of anguish. He loved Henriette; she was the perfect woman, he told himself. If she could have been his wife he would have asked nothing more of life. But she was the wife of his brother; and between them there could never be the kind of love which was so necessary to him. His eyes pleaded with her: Understand me, Henriette. I love you. Ours is an ideal relationship. It is unique. You are my love. And the affair with this girl . . . it is nothing. It happens today and is forgotten tomorrow. But I am fond of her. She is so small and helpless. I have seduced her, and I cannot desert her now.

Poor Louis! He was so simple, so full of the wish to do right.

273

Help me, Henriette, said his pleading eyes. I beg of you show me the greatness of your love for me by helping me now. Surely love that exists between us is beyond the pettiness of an affair like this.

How I love him! thought Henriette. I love him for his simplicity. He has not yet grown up. Our great Sun God is but a child.

'Louis . . .' she murmured brokenly. 'Louis . . .'

He laid his hands on her shoulders and gently kissed her cheek. Then he turned and, drawing La Vallière towards him, put an arm about her.

'Have no fear, my little one,' he said. 'You should not run away. Do you think you could hide from the King?'

Even as he looked at her, his desire was apparent.

What can she give him that I cannot? Henriette asked herself. The answer was clear: All that is so necessary to a man of his appetites.

'Madame is the kindest and greatest lady in the world,' Louis was saying. 'I give you into her care. She will love you and cherish you . . . for my sake.'

Henriette said: 'It is my one desire to serve Your Majesty.' And she thought: I can do this for him . . . even this . . . so much do I love him.

*

She did not sleep; she could eat very little. A great melancholy filled her.

Her mother visited her and was shocked by her appearance.

'What has happened?' she demanded. 'You look so tired, and you are thinner than ever. And what is this I hear about your refusing to eat? This will not do, my child. I see that you need your mother to look after you.'

Henrietta Maria was seriously disturbed. She could not forget that in a comparatively short time she had lost three of her children. 'You are coughing too much!' she cried. 'How long have you coughed thus?'

Henriette wearily shook her head, but the sight of her angry mother, the quick rebukes, the tapping of the little foot, the bright darting eyes, had the effect of unnerving her. She, who had not shed a tear during all the weeks of jealous heartbreak, now burst into bitter weeping.

Once again she was held in her mother's suffocating embrace. Of all her children, Henrietta Maria loved best her youngest daughter. Henriette had been her darling since she had been brought to France from England and had become a Catholic.

'Oh, Mam . . . Mam . . . I wish we could go away together . . . you and I . . . just the two of us . . . to be together as we used to be. Do you remember, when we were at the Louvre and I had to stay in bed because it was too cold to be up? Oh, Mam, I wish I was your little girl again!'

'There, my love, my dearest,' crooned the Queen. 'You shall come with Mam. We will be together, and these hands shall nurse you, and this Queen, your mother, shall wait upon you. There has been too much gaiety . . . too many balls, and in your condition . . . ah, in your condition . . . But Mam will nurse you, my darling. You shall be with Mam and no one else. Not even Philippe, eh, my darling?'

'No, Mam. No one but you.'

So Henrietta Maria sent for a litter and had her daughter conveyed from Saint-Cloud to the Tuileries, and there she nursed her.

During those weeks Henrietta had no wish to see anyone but her mother. She thought often of Charles. Her other love! she called him to herself. Charles . . . Louis! How different they were, those two men whom she loved beyond all in the world. Charles so adult, Louis such a boy; Charles the ugliest, Louis the most handsome King in Christendom; Charles clever and subtle, Louis so often naïve for all his grandeur, a man with a boy's mind, a man who had not yet grown up mentally.

There is only one thing which could make me happy now, she mused. To go to England . . . to be with Charles.

During her illness he wrote often. His letters were a source of great delight; he alone could make her laugh.

He wrote: 'Do you suffer from a disease of sermons, as we do here? 'Od's Fish! What piety surrounds us! Dearest Minette, I hope you have the same convenience that the rest of the family has, of sleeping out most of the time, which is a great ease to those who are bound to hear them. But this sleeping has caused me some regret. South – he's an outspoken fellow, that one – had occasion to reprove Lauderdale when preaching last Sunday's sermon. Lauderdale's a man who can snore to wake the dead, and South stopped in the middle of his sermon to rouse him. "My Lord," he cried in a voice of thunder, "you snore so loud you will wake the King!" ' '

Oh, to be with him! thought Henriette. Oh, to hear his voice again!

Her child – a daughter – was born prematurely. She had so longed for a son, and so had Philippe. Marie-Thérèse had borne a Dauphin; Philippe would be jealous now because Louis had a son while he had a daughter.

Perhaps, thought Henriette, my little daughter will one day marry Louis' son. In the years ahead mayhap I shall find peace, and these turbulent years will seem of no importance then.

It was thinking of Charles that made her aware of the compensations life had to offer. She longed to be with him, to hear his merry laughter, to listen to his witty comments on life, to enjoy that cynicism which veiled the kindest heart in the world.

*

A few weeks after the birth of her child, Montalais came to Henriette to tell her that the Comte de Guiche was begging for an interview with her. His father, the Maréchal de Gramont, had arranged for him to be given command of the troops, and he was required to leave the Court at once.

Henriette, who had found the handsome young man a cultured companion, declared herself sorry that he was leaving, and received him.

He fell on his knees before her and kissed her hand.

He told her that he had been desolate when he had heard of her illness. He was saddened because he was ordered to leave the Court, and he knew this had been brought about by his enemies on account of his friendship with her. He would have her know that wherever he went he would carry with him the memory of her goodness and graciousness, and that he would never cease to love her beyond all others.

To Henriette such devotion came as balm in her humiliation. She was constantly hearing rumours of the growing passion of the King for La Vallière. It was even rumoured that the shy maid of honour was with child by the King.

So Henriette could not help listening with sympathy and some pleasure to the declarations of the Comte.

He left her, protesting eternal devotion; but there were spies in Henriette's household, and it was not long before Philippe came to tell her that he had heard from his mother that she was very angry with her daughter-in-law. 'It has come to her ears that you are receiving young men in your apartment.'

'Young men!'

'De Guiche was seen leaving by a private staircase.'

'This is ridiculous, Philippe. De Guiche is a friend of yours.'

'But more of yours, it would seem.'

'That is not so. He merely sees in me the wife of his beloved friend.'

'So it is not true that you and de Guiche are lovers?'

'It most certainly is not true. Were I the wife of any but you, he would pay me no attention.'

'Has he said so?'

'I believe it to be so,' said Henriette.

Philippe smiled. 'Poor de Guiche! To be banished from Court! He is desolate. Well, he will soon return, and it will be a lesson to him. Henriette, you are a very charming woman. I begin to think I am fortunate in my marriage. It is good to be a father. Though I would we had a son.'

'You do not care that Louis should have what you lack, Philippe?'

'Louis!' he said. 'The Queen is a plain creature. He loathes her. And La Vallière . . . she is no beauty either! It may be that he turns to her because he desires one other whom he dare not attempt to make his mistress. He has a son . . . but mayhap one day soon . . . I shall have a son. I have the most charming wife at Court. Why should I not have a son also? Eh, Henriette?'

He smiled at her and she shrank from him.

She thought: Oh, Charles, my brother, if I could but be with you at Whitehall!

CHAPTER NINE

HENRIETTE LAY ON her bed. She was in need of rest, for she was pregnant again.

During last year she had plunged more deeply into the gay life at the Court; there had been a great need to hide the hurt she suffered. Louis was still devoted to La Vallière. In spite of his mother's protests he had refused to give her up, and even when she had been far advanced in pregnancy she had remained at Court.

But not the Queen, nor the King's mistress, had been the leader of the fêtes and ballets. It was Henriette who had been the centre of the wildest amusements; she who had been more daring than any. She had taken the savants under her protection. Molière had dedicated his *L'Ecole des Femmes* to her. Certain holy gentlemen had declared that the playwright should be burned at the stake when *Tartuffe* had been produced, but Henriette had laughed at them and insisted on the King's attending a performance of the play at Villers-Cotteret. She gave audience to Molière, delighting in his conversation. She laughed heartily when he told her that he had named his hypocrite Tartuffe because one day he had seen two devout priests, palms pressed together, eyes raised heavenwards, when a basket of truffles was brought into the apartment wherein they were performing their religious duties. They went on praying, reminding God and the saints how they had subdued their earthly appetites while their eyes were on the truffles and the saliva ran down their chins. At length they could not stop themselves crying aloud: 'Tartuffoli! Tartuffoli!'

Racine had dedicated *Andromaque* to her, declaring that but for her protection in his struggling days he could never have produced the work. La Fontaine had also received her patronage.

She was the benefactress of artists and, while she reigned with Louis ostensibly as his Queen, there was more culture in the Court of France than in any other in Europe, and again people recalled the days of François Premier and his sister Marguerite.

Charles wrote that he wished she could be with him to reign as Queen over his Court. He had married a wife from Portugal. She was no beauty, he admitted to his sister, but he had the good fortune to be able to compare her favourably with her maids of honour who accompanied her – six of them, all frights, and a duenna who was a monster. He was amusing himself, he told her, playing the good husband and, somewhat to his astonishment, not misliking the role. He had the plays of Wycherley and Dryden with which to amuse himself, and Sir Peter Lely to paint the beauties of his Court. He lived merrily but there would always be one thing he lacked to make his contentment complete – the presence of his beloved sister at his Court.

News came to Henriette of the troubles between his mistress-in-chief, the brazen Castlemaine, and his Queen Catherine. Charles and Louis were alike in one thing, it seemed.

She had tried to be content, lacking two things which would have assured contentment: Louis and Charles as her constant companions; for these two she loved beyond all else in the world.

She had not come unscathed through the scandals which had surrounded her. There were many stories circulating concerning her and de Guiche.

De Guiche had been wounded in Poland and had almost met his death. The story was that a case, containing Madame's portrait, which he carried over his heart, protected him from a bullet which would otherwise have cost him his life.

There had been many to notice the charms of Henriette, and since these scandals and her gay method of life suggested she was not inaccessible, many came forward to seek her favours. Among them were Monsieur d'Armagnac, of the house of Lorraine and Grand Ecuyer de France, and the Prince de Marsillac, son of the Duc de la Rochefoucauld. All were charming, all amusing, all certain that Madame could not prove continuously and tiresomely virtuous; but all were disappointed.

Then there was the Marquis de Vardes. Henriette

found him more cultured, more amusing than any; and as a gentleman of the King's bedchamber, he had won Louis' regard, so she found herself often in his company.

He was a rake, but an extremely witty one, a companion of writers, artists and musicians; at this time he was the most popular man at Court. He had been involved in love affairs with Madame d'Armagnac and the Comtesse de Soissons, but he had now set his heart on the conquest of no less a person than Madame herself.

Henriette was at first unaware of this; indeed she believed him to be still involved with the beautiful Madame de Soissons who, since the King's favour had turned to La Vallière, had accepted him as her lover.

As she lay in her bed, Henriette was thinking of Louis. She had seen little of him for some weeks and then only in the company of others; those pleasant confidences which were the delight of her life were no longer offered. There were times when she fancied his glances were more than indifferent; they were cold.

He had turned against her.

She felt wretched and alone. Her mother had gone to England and was residing at Somerset House. She missed her sadly, although Henrietta Maria, disturbed by the gay life her daughter led and the fact that she had incurred the displeasure of Anne of Austria, had lectured Henriette so incessantly that she had longed to escape. If she could have explained to someone, how much better would she have felt! But how could one explain to Henrietta Maria? How could the fiery little Queen ever understand this passion of her daughter's? Henrietta Maria would never love as her daughter loved – secretly brooding, hiding her misery. Henrietta Maria had to parade hers that all might see it and commiserate with her.

Why had Louis suddenly turned against her? She had asked herself that question a hundred times. He had grown tired of their relationship and now he was not even taking the trouble to conceal that fact.

What satisfaction was there for her in the rounds of balls and fêtes? What did it matter if all complimented her on her elegant attire, her dancing in the ballet, her conversation? Louis had turned from her. He was not merely tired of her; he was beginning to dislike her.

And as she lay there, one of her women came to her and said that the Comtesse de Soissons, who was ill and seemed to be near death, wished to speak to her. Would she be so good as to go to the Comtesse's bedchamber, as the Comtesse could not come to her?

Henriette rose from her bed then and followed the woman to the Comtesse's apartment.

It was difficult to recognize the beautiful Olympia Mancini, the woman who had enslaved Louis before her marriage and had been his mistress after it, in the thin wasted woman who now lay on the bed.

Henriette, full of sympathy for the sick since she herself did not enjoy the best of health, touched the Comtesse's hot forehead and begged her not to agitate herself.

'There is something I must tell you, Madame,' said the Comtesse.

'Later will do.'

'No, Madame. Later will not do. I feel so ill that I believe death to be near me, and I must warn you while it is in my power to do so.'

'Of whom is it that you would warn me?'

'De Vardes.'

'De Vardes! But he is my friend and your lover!'

'He was my lover, Madame. That was before he was determined to make you his mistress. When that determination came to him he vowed he would let nothing stand in the way of its fulfilment.'

'It seems that I stood in the way, Madame de Soissons.'

'Yes, Madame, you stood in the way. It is he who circulated the scandals about yourself and Monsieur de Guiche. He has carried these tales to the King.'

'I . . . see,' said Henriette.

'He believes that you love de Guiche, and has sworn to ruin you both.'

'And how . . . does he propose to do this?'

'Madame, he has the ear of the King.'

Henriette put her hand to her heart in a sudden fear that the violence of its beating might be betrayed to the sick woman.

'Does he think that the King would turn his favour from me if he believed I loved Monsieur de Guiche?'

'No, Madame.' That answer hurt Henriette more than one in the affirmative would have done. 'No, Madame; it is not the scandals he has uttered against Monsieur de Guiche. It is . . . the letters you receive from your brother.'

'The letters of the King of England!'

'He says he has seen some of them.'

'It's true. They are often witty. I remember being so amused with something my brother wrote that I showed the letter to de Vardes.'

'Madame, de Vardes has accused you of betraying French secrets to your brother of England.'

'But this is impossible!'

'Nay, Madame, it is true.'

'And the King believes that . . . about me!'

'He knows how you love your brother. If Charles asked you to do little things for him it might be hard for you to refuse him.'

'So Louis thinks I am my brother's spy! He thinks I would betray him to Charles!'

'He thinks you love your brother dearly.'

Henriette turned her head away, but Madame de Soissons was stretching out her hand. 'You will forgive me, Madame? You see, I loved the King . . . and then de Vardes. I should have told you how de Vardes determined to ruin both you and de Guiche. I should have told you before.'

Henriette turned back to the sick woman. 'You have told me now. That will suffice.'

'Then, Madame, I have your forgiveness?'

Henriette nodded; she hurried from the sick room.

She must see Louis as soon as possible. Those doubts and suspicions must not be allowed to remain between them.

*

But before she saw him her child was born. This time it was a boy.

As she lay with the child in her arms, she felt that the boy would, in some measure, make up for all she had suffered.

Philippe was delighted; the King sent his congratulations

and promised the boy a pension of 50,000 crowns. Anne of Austria declared her satisfaction at the birth of the boy, since the Dauphin was but a sickly child and his sister had recently died. Henrietta Maria was filled with more delight than she could express. As for Charles, he himself was suffering from a chill, having taken off his wig and pourpoint on a hot day, and was unable to write until almost a week later. Then he wrote of the extreme joy he felt because she had a son. Nothing, he said, could give him greater pleasure than that news.

She wanted to reply, telling him that she had fallen into disfavour with the King, and how unhappy this made her. She doubted whether he would understand. He would call her devotion to the King, folly. He loved easily and lightly – not one but many. Here again, Charles, perhaps, showed his wisdom.

It was not until she was up from her bed that she was able to secure the desired audience with Louis.

'I must,' she insisted, 'speak with Your Majesty alone.'

Louis bowed his head in acknowledgement of her request, and she noticed with dismay how cold his eyes were.

As soon as they were alone, she cried out: 'Louis, there has been a terrible misunderstanding, and I must make you see the truth.'

He waited impassively.

She continued hurriedly: 'It is quite untrue that I have conspired with my brother against you.'

He did not answer, and she went on imploringly: 'Louis, you cannot believe this to be so?'

'You are very fond of your brother.'

'That is true.'

'The affection between you has been marked by many.'

'I know it.'

'Brothers and sisters should have a certain regard for each other, but this affection between you and the King of England is unusual in its intensity, is it not?'

'I admit we are very fond of each other.'

'I have talked freely to you of matters of state ... state secrets ... because I have admired your lively mind. I did not think you would so betray me as to discuss such matters with the King of another country, even though that King was your brother.'

'You have been misinformed.' She had broken down suddenly. The tears had started to stream down her cheeks. She stammered: 'It is not so much that you should think these evil thoughts of me . . . it is that you should look at me so coldly.'

Louis' pity was immediately aroused. She looked so frail after her recent ordeal; he went to her and laid his arm about her shoulders. 'Henriette,' he said, 'if you have erred in this, mayhap it was due to thoughtlessness.'

'I have never erred. I would never betray your secrets. Cannot you understand that my only wish is to serve *you*?'

'And to serve Charles.'

'I love him, it is true. But he would never seek to embroil me in trouble. He would never ask me to do that which my regard for you would not allow me to.'

'You say you love Charles,' said Louis. 'I know it. But what of Louis?'

'I love you both.'

'Can one person love two others equally?'

'He is my brother.'

'And I, Henriette?'

'You . . . you are the one beside whom I should have been content to live all the days of my life . . . had that been possible.'

'Most women would love such a one more than a brother.'

She did not answer, and he kissed her cheek gently.

'I have misjudged you, Henriette. Those who have slandered you shall not escape my displeasure. It may be that one day you will have an opportunity of showing me how much greater is the love you bear for the King of France than that you have for the King of England.

'I hope that day will not come.'

He had taken her hands and was kissing them fervently. 'It would be infinite joy for me to know that I held first place in your heart,' he said. 'Who knows . . . mayhap one day I shall ask you to prove that to me.'

*

For a long time after that Henriette was apprehensive.

284

The Comtesse de Soissons recovered, and seemed to regret her confidences. Louis had not redeemed his promise to punish de Vardes, and the man was still at large. Henriette knew that together he and the Countess planned to harm her in the eyes of the King; de Vardes because he knew that now she hated him and there was no hope of her becoming his mistress, the Countess because she was so infatuated with de Vardes that she was glad to help him in any way he wished.

Henriette realized how little Louis trusted her, and that he still believed she was in secret correspondence with her brother. It seemed to her that the most important thing was to win back Louis' faith and trust.

De Guiche had returned to Court. Louis had only allowed him to come back on condition that he did not attempt to see Henriette; but the foolish man could not resist writing to her, and de Vardes, feigning to be his friend, offered to deliver this to Henriette.

It was only a few weeks after the birth of Henriette's son, the little Duc de Valois, that she received a message from de Vardes. He assured her that he had been the victim of a terrible misunderstanding and implored her to grant him a short interview.

Disturbed and desirous of getting to the bottom of these intrigues which were in progress to turn the King against her, Henriette agreed to see de Vardes and hear what he had to tell her.

De Vardes accordingly planned to visit her, but before going to Saint-Cloud he sought an audience with the King. He begged His Majesty's pardon for the intrusion, but if the King would walk with him the length of the gallery, he would show him something which would convince him that he, de Vardes, had been misjudged.

Louis frowned but said testily that he would grant the interview; and the two strolled off together.

De Vardes said: 'Sire, I have been misjudged with regard to Madame.'

'I have no wish to speak of Madame.'

'Your Majesty, I beg of you, allow me to defend myself.'

'On what grounds?'

'When I uncovered the perfidy of Madame in her

relationship with her brother, my one thought was to serve Your Majesty. Your Majesty did not believe me, preferring to trust Madame.' De Vardes bowed. 'I can do no other than accept Your Majesty's decision. But Monsieur de Guiche has returned to Court, having promised on his honour not to see Madame again.'

'You suggest that they are meeting?' demanded Louis.

'I have this letter – a profession of his undying devotion. He knows full well that he disobeys Your Majesty's command.'

'He is a man in love,' said Louis musingly.

'And Madame? Is Madame a woman in love?'

Louis was hurt and angry. It was true that La Vallière was his mistress whom he desired passionately, but for Henriette he had cherished an ideal love. If, while professing to love him, she was receiving a lover, it was more than he could bear. She had sworn to him that there were no lovers; she had in her way reproached him for lacking her own fidelity. And mayhap now she was laughing at him with de Guiche.

He said: 'Take this letter to Madame. I will come with you, but you shall go to her and I shall remain hidden until you have handed her the letter. If she is my good friend – as she swears she is – she will not read the letter, which she knows comes to her in flagrant disobedience to my commands.'

De Vardes bowed.

Louis took de Guiche's letter, read it and knew great jealousy.

He thought: I have been deceived. I have told myself that if I could have married Henriette, I should be the happiest man alive. I have idealized her; but if this man is her lover, she is unworthy of idealized love.

It was typical of Louis, openly unfaithful himself, to expect fidelity in others. Henriette had always known this side of his nature; but did she love him for his virtues? No more than she loved Charles for his.

And so the letter was brought to her, and the King was secreted in a closet to see and hear her reception of it.

When she saw what her visitor had brought, she turned away from him. 'You bring me that which I have no wish to receive,' she said. 'I pray you take it back to him who gave it to you and tell him that he breaks the King's command by writing to me thus.'

De Vardes fell on to his knees; he tried to take her hands; he exerted all his fascination, to the potency of which there were so many women at Court to bear witness, in an effort to make her betray some weakness to the watching King.

But Henriette had no love for either de Guiche or de Vardes, although she entertained a certain fondness for the former.

'Pray leave me,' she said. 'I wish to hear no more from either of you. I wish only to be left in peace; you have done me too much harm already.'

De Vardes left and immediately Louis joined Henriette. She was shocked to realize she had been spied upon; but it was a great relief to know that Louis was her friend again.

'Now I have heard with my own ears and seen with my own eyes how you spurn these fellows. Can you forgive me for accepting their word against yours? I was jealous, Henriette. Oh, what an unhappy state is this in which we find ourselves!'

'If I may see you often,' she said, 'if I may enjoy your friendship, I could be happy.'

'We shall be together as we were before. My favour is yours as it ever was. Henriette, we love and our love is a sacred passion . . . above more earthly loves.'

Then she felt it was as it had been when they had first made that wonderful discovery regarding each other.

But still he did not carry out his threats to punish de Vardes; and he remained jealous of Charles.

*

One of the noblemen of the Court was giving a masked ball, and as the King was not present on this occasion, the principal guests were Monsieur and Madame.

There was a great deal of excitement, as there always was at these affairs; flirtations were conducted under cover of wigs and masks. Henriette was glad of the anonymity.

She and Philippe went by coach to the nobleman's mansion – not in their own coach, which would have betrayed them, but in a hired one. Philippe scarcely spoke to his wife nowadays; he had ceased to show any great interest in her. He was pleased that she had given him a son who seemed to be more healthy than the Dauphin; he was pleased also that their daughter lived, although the King's had died. Henriette knew that such rivalry would always exist between them. Anne of Austria and Mazarin had perverted Philippe's mind during his childhood, when he had always been compelled to remember that his brother was his King.

When they arrived at the house Philippe gave his hand to the nearest lady, and a man immediately came forward to escort Henriette.

As she laid her hand on his satin sleeve she was aware of his excitement.

She said: 'Have we met before, Monsieur?'

He answered: 'Madame, we have.'

'Then you know my identity?'

'Who could fail to recognize the most elegant and beautiful lady of the Court? Madame is like a slender lily compared with weeds.'

Then since you know me, I pray you keep my identity secret. Remember this is a masked ball.'

Then glancing down she caught sight of his hand, and she remembered hearing that, in the recent battle in which he had taken part, de Guiche had lost several of his fingers. The hand of this man was maimed.

Henriette caught her breath. How could she have been mistaken? He had a distinguished air, this de Guiche. He had a recklessness, something of the adventurer in him. He was taller than most men – though not as tall as Louis; now she saw that the large mask did not entirely conceal the well-shaped nose and sensitive mouth.

She thought: So he has dared to seek me out in this way! This is folly. If Louis were to hear of our meeting he would believe that I have been guilty of conspiring to bring it about.

'Monsieur,' she said, 'I wish you to leave me when we reach the top of the staircase.'

'Madame . . . dear madame . . . I had hoped to be your companion for longer than that.'

'You are a fool!' she cried. 'I know who you are. So will others. And as you recognized me . . . so will they.'

'Madame, I had to speak to you. I had to find some way. I could not endure those days without a sight of you.'

'Monsieur de Guiche, you know you disobey the King's orders. If you have any regard for me, bring no more trouble on yourself . . . or me.'

'It is not only to give myself the joy of seeing you and speaking to you which has brought me here. I know that to be dangerous. But I have to warn you; I do not believe you understand to the full the treachery of de Vardes and his mistress.'

'I think I understand full well how those two have tried to harm me in the King's eyes.'

'I beg of you, listen to me. De Vardes is determined to ruin us both. Madame de Soissons is jealous, not only of the King's regard for you, but because de Vardes desired you so passionately. De Vardes is not in high favour with the King, but Louis always has a soft spot for his mistresses, and Madame de Soissons has his ear. She has this day told the King that, in secret correspondence, you have suggested to your brother that you take possession of Dunkirk in his name; also that this is my plan, and that I am ready to place my regiment of guards at your disposal.'

Henriette caught her breath. 'But this is madness.'

'The madness of jealousy . . . envy . . . and those determined on revenge. The King already suspects you are more ready to serve your brother than to serve him. Madame, beware.'

Philippe, who had reached the top of the staircase, had turned and was watching them.

Henriette whispered: 'He knows you. He has recognized you. He has never forgiven you for turning from him to me. He too suffers from his jealousy. I beg of you, Monsieur de Guiche, as soon as we reach the top of the stairs, leave me. And leave this ballroom. It is unsafe for you to be here.

And when they reached the top of the stairs, she turned hastily from him and started to walk towards Philippe. In her haste her foot caught in her gown and she tripped and fell. It was de Guiche who leaped forward to catch her.

There were gasps of horror from those about her. Someone said in a loud voice: 'Madame has fainted!'

Henriette realized that she was recognized, and in de

Guiche's arms. She hastily disengaged herself; but as she did so she was aware of de Vardes' cynical voice beside her.

'There is no mistaking Madame. That beauty ... that elegance cannot be hidden by a mask. But who is her saviour? I think we may be forgiven a little curiosity on that score.'

He stepped towards de Guiche and with a swift movement tore off his mask.

There was a murmur of: 'De Guiche!'

'Our gallant soldier!' said de Vardes mockingly. 'It is no great surprise that he should be at hand ... when Madame needs him.'

With great dignity de Guiche cried: 'Monsieur de Vardes, my friends will be calling on you tomorrow.'

De Vardes bowed: 'Monsieur, they will be most welcome.'

De Guiche then turned and walked haughtily through the press of courtiers and out of the ballroom.

Philippe, white-lipped with anger – for never had it seemed to him that de Guiche looked more handsome – gave his arm to his wife and led her away.

All through that evening, behind their masks, guests talked of this affair; and Henriette knew that, before the night was over, news of what had happened at the masked ball would reach the ears of Louis.

*

She had implored the King to believe her guiltless. He was kind. He agreed on the villainy of de Vardes, but still he allowed him to go free. In her heart, Henriette knew that he did not entirely believe in her innocence.

Was there no one to whom she could appeal? There was only one person in the world whom she could entirely trust, and he was on the other side of the water.

At last she decided to ask for Charles' help, and she wrote to him:

I have begged the Ambassador to send you this courier that he may inform you truly of the affair which has happened about de Vardes. This is a matter so serious that I fear it will affect the rest of my life. If I cannot obtain my object, I shall feel disgraced for ever that a private individual has been allowed to insult me with impunity, and if nothing is done to punish this man, it will be a warning to the world in future how they dare attack me. All France is interested in the outcome of this affair. Out of your love for me, I beg you ask the King for justice. I am hoping that the consideration in which you are held here will settle this matter. It will not be the first debt I have owed you, nor the one for which I shall feel the least grateful, since it will enable me to obtain justice in the future.

She knew that her cry for help would not be in vain. Charles answered at once that she could rely on his assistance.

Two weeks later de Vardes was lodged in the Bastille.

*

As for de Guiche, it was clear that he must not be seen at Court again. His father, the Maréchal de Gramont, advised him to beg one last audience with Louis, during which he must convince the King that he served no other master; after that he must depart and never see Henriette again.

This de Guiche promised to do, but he could not deprive himself of one last farewell. He dared not seek her in her apartments, so he dressed himself in the livery of one of the servants of La Vallière that he might see Henriette pass in her chair from the Palais-Royal to the Louvre.

This was the last he saw of her before he left for Holland and a brilliant military career.

The affair of de Guiche and de Vardes was closed, the King implied; but he continued to ponder on the relationship between Henriette and her brother.

CHAPTER TEN

A YEAR HAD passed since the imprisonment of de Vardes and the banishment of de Guiche.

Louis was often in the company of Henriette. Always he was deeply affectionate, although at times she was aware of those suspicions which would return to his mind, and they always concerned her brother Charles.

Now that Louis was coming into his kingdom, now that he had made himself true ruler of France, he began to realize that he could use Henriette's influence with her brother in negotiations between the two countries. Moreover, Henriette's quick mind was as good as that of any statesman he possessed; and Louis was shrewd enough to know that a woman who was in love with him would make a better servant than anyone who worked for his own fame and glory.

There was only one doubt which arose now and then in his mind: Did the affection of Henriette for her brother exceed that which she had for himself?

He could not be entirely sure. It was a matter of great fascination and importance to him. This love between himself and Henriette was of greater interest to him than the more easily understood passions which he felt for La Vallière and her new rival, Madame de Montespan.

His mother, Queen Anne, was very ill, and he was aware that she could not live long. As he danced with Henriette, La Vallière or Montespan, his thoughts went often to his mother. He was fond of her, although lately she had interfered too much in his affairs, and she could not forget that he was her child, and continued to look upon him as such.

'Poor Mama!' he often murmured. 'How she loves me! But she never understood me.'

In the Palais-Royal, the great gallery of which was hung with mirrors and brilliant with torches, the new play by Molière, *Médecin Malgré Lui*, was performed for the first time, after the banquet.

Louis, with Henriette beside him, laughed loudly at the wit of his favourite playwright, and forgot his mother.

He was happy. He enjoyed such occasions. It was good to have a quiet little wife who adored him. She was not here tonight to admire him in his suit of purple velvet covered in diamonds and pearls, because she was in mourning for her father. He was glad she was absent, for the sight of his mistresses always distressed her, and La Vallière was pregnant again. It was good to have such a meek and tender mistress as La Vallière and such a bold and witty one as Madame de Montespan. And all the time he was enjoying a love affair on a higher plane with his elegant and clever Henriette. He enjoyed the pathos of their relationship; he did not see why it should not endure for ever. Tonight she had arranged this entertainment for him; all the most brilliant fêtes, masks and ballets were arranged by Henriette for the pleasure of her King. If only he could have been entirely sure that her affection for him obsessed her completely, he would have been content.

But he was for ever conscious of the dark witty man on the other side of the water, in whose capital city men were now falling like flies, stricken by the deadly plague.

*

About the bedside of the dying Queen Mother of France were her children, Louis and Philippe, and with them stood their wives, Marie-Thérèse and Henriette.

All four were in tears. Anne had suffered deeply, and her death was by no means unexpected. The beautiful hands, now gaunt and yellow, plucked at the sheets, and her eyes, sunken with pain, turned again and again to the best loved of them all.

Louis was deeply moved; he was on his knees recalling that great affection which she had always given him.

Philippe was also moved. She had loved him too in her way, but, being a simple woman, she had not been able to disguise from him the fact that almost all the affection she had to give must go to her glorious first-born.

Philippe took the hot hand and kissed it.

'Be good, my children,' murmured Anne.

Henriette turned away because she could no longer bear to look on such suffering. She wished that she had not flouted Anne's advice; she wished that there were time to tell the dying Queen that she now understood how foolish she had been in pursuing gaiety, and so giving rise to scandals such as those concerning de Guiche and de Vardes. But it was too late.

'Louis . . . beloved . . .' whispered the Queen.

'My dearest Mother.'

'Louis . . . be kind to the Queen. Do not . . . humiliate her with your mistresses. It is sad for a little Queen ... so young ...'

Marie-Thérèse, who was kneeling by the bed, covered her face with her hands, but Louis had placed his hand on her shoulder.

'I ask your forgiveness,' he said, the tears streaming down his cheeks. 'I ask both of you to forgive me ...'

'Remember me when I am gone,' said Anne. 'Remember, my dearest, how I lived for you alone. Remember me ...'

'Dearest Mama ... dearest Mama ...' murmured the King.

And all four about the bed were weeping as Anne of Austria ceased to breathe.

*

Very soon after Anne's death, gaiety was resumed at Court. Louis was now free from all restraint. He planned a great carnival; it was to be more magnificient than anything that had gone before.

Henriette arranged the ballet.

The Queen came to her at the Palais-Royal, and when they were alone together she wept bitterly and told her sister-in-law how galling it was for her to see La Vallière and Montespan at Court.

'La Vallière is at least quiet,' said Marie-Thérèse. 'She always seems rather ashamed of her position. It is a different matter with Montespan. I believe she deliberately scorns me.'

'Have no fear,' soothed Henriette. 'Remember the death-bed of the Queen Mother. Louis has promised to reform his ways. There will certainly be a part for you in the ballet.'

'I am no good at dancing.'

'There will be little dancing for you. You will be seated on a throne, magnificently attired to receive homage.'

'It sounds delightful.'

'And La Vallière and Montespan will find that there are no parts for them.'

'You are my good friend,' said Marie-Thérèse. 'I am glad of that, for you are a good friend of the King's, I know.'

They embraced, and Henriette looked forward to her new friendship.

Through the window at which she sat with Marie-Thérèse she could see Philippe in the garden with his friend the Chevalier de Lorraine, who was a younger brother of Monsieur d'Armagnac. Lorraine was very handsome and Philippe was enchanted with him. They strolled through the grounds, their arms about each other, laughing and chatting as they went.

Henriette did not like Lorraine; she knew that he was determined to make mischief. He was insolent to her and it was clear that he wished to remind her that as Monsieur's *bel ami* he was more important to him than his wife. He was also the lover of one of her maids of honour, Mademoiselle de Fiennes, and scandalously he used this girl to make Philippe jealous. It was an unpleasant state of affairs.

Sometimes, thought Henriette, I feel I am married to the worst man on earth. What is the use of saying: If only I had married Louis, how different, how happy and dignified my life would have been!

Louis himself called at the Palais-Royal next day.

He was angry and did not bother to command a private audience. He came straight to her.

'I see, Madame,' he said, 'that there are no parts in the ballet for Mademoiselle de la Vallière and Madame de Montespan.'

'That is so, Sire,' answered Henriette.

'But you know our wish that these talented ladies should have parts.'

'I understood from your promise to the Queen, your mother, that you had decided no longer to receive them at Court.'

'Then you misunderstood my intentions, Madame.'

Henriette looked at him sadly. 'Then there is no alternative but to rearrange the ballet,' she said quickly.

'Thank you, sister. That is what I would have you do.'

'Mademoiselle de la Vallière is now scarcely in a condition to appear in the ballet, Sire.'

'Let her take a part where she may sit down, and wear such a costume that shall disguise her condition.'

'There is the Queen's part . . .'

'Yes, the Queen's part. Let that be given to Mademoiselle de la Vallière.'

'But the Queen?'

Louis looked at her testily. 'The Queen has no great love of the ballet.'

Henriette's thoughts went to the sad little Queen who had wept so much because she must stand aside for the King's mistresses. She thought, too, of poor little La Vallière, who would soon be outshone by the more dazzling Montespan; it would be no use hiding in a convent then, for, if she did, Louis would not hasten to find her.

There he stood – magnificent even when peevish. Woe to those who love the Sun King! she told herself soberly.

Louis was saying: 'There is another matter of which I would speak to you. It concerns my son.'

'The Dauphin?'

'No. Mademoiselle de la Vallière's son. I would have him brought up at Court . . . perhaps here at the Palais-Royal or at the Tuileries. He should not live in obscurity since he is my son. He should enjoy royal honours. It is my wish that he should do so.'

Henriette bowed her head. 'I will do all that you command for him,' she answered.

She saw now that the Queen's death was having its effect, even as had that of Mazarin.

Louis was in complete control now. La Vallière, large with child, should be in attendance on the Queen. La Montespan, brazen in her accession to the King's regard, would become Queen of the Court.

*

Henriette was anxious. Charles was at war with Flanders, and relations between her brother and brother-in-law she knew to be very strained.

The Hollanders were holding out tempting promises to Louis; she, who was in his confidence in these matters, knew that a state of war between France and England was threatening.

Henrietta Maria, who had returned to France at the time of the great plague, was, with her daughter, horrified at the idea of hostilities between France and England.

The Queen and her daughter spent many hours together

talking of state matters, and it seemed possible that Henriette's anxiety brought about her miscarriage.

The Queen nursed her daughter through her illness; she herself was ageing fast and suffered from a weak heart and sleeplessness. She was scarcely the most cheerful of companions, talking as she did continually of the old days and how her stay in England had revived her memories.

The news grew worse. Louis decided that Charles was no longer his friend, and French troops were sent into Holland against England's ally, Christian Bernard von Galen, Bishop of Münster.

Never in her life had Henriette been so wretched.

Her brother, whom she loved dearly, and the man whom she had longed to marry, were enemies, and each was expecting her to be his friend.

'Now,' said Louis, 'you have to decide between us. Which is it, Henriette?'

She looked into his handsome face. She said: 'He is my brother, and nothing could make me do anything but love him. But I love you also, and you are my King.'

Louis was well pleased with that answer. She would be useful when he made peace with England.

These warlike conditions between the two countries did not long persist, and by the May of that year both Kings were ready for peace. Henriette and her mother had done much to bring about this state of affairs.

'I hope and pray,' said Henriette, 'that I shall never see you two at war again.'

Louis kissed her hand. 'You will be loyal to me always, Henriette. That is so, is it not? You will remember our love, which is beyond earthly love, the noblest affection that was ever between two people.'

'I will remember,' she told him firmly.

She wished that she could have stayed at Colombes with her mother, and that there was no need to go back to Philippe.

*

Sitting on a raised dais Henriette, exquisitely dressed, her white and tan spaniel, Mimi, in her arms, was the central figure in the Ballets des Muses. She listened to the chanting of verses written by Molière; she watched the graceful dancing; and, as usual, her eyes rested on one figure, taller, more magnificent than all others – Louis, gorgeous and a-glitter with jewels, his velvet dalmatica sewn with pearls, his high heels accentuating his height so that he stood above all, the Sun King, the Sun God, beautiful as Apollo himself.

She looked about and saw Mademoiselle de Montpensier, who was no longer Mademoiselle of the Court now that Philippe had a daughter to assume that title. Poor Mademoiselle! She was less proud now than she had been in her youth. None of those glorious marriages, whose worthiness she had doubted, had come her way. Now it was rumoured that she was passionately in love with Lauzan, the dashing military commander, but a marriage between them would never be permitted.

Surely Mademoiselle was feeling sorry for herself, and yet perhaps even more sorry for Henriette. She had said that she would rather have no husband at all than one such as Philippe.

La Vallière was at Court again, recently delivered of a daughter, not entirely happy. She was very jealous of Montespan and greatly feared her rival. In protest she had retired from Court and gone into a convent; this time the King sent for her but did not go after her in person. Poor La Vallière! It seemed possible that her days as King's favourite were numbered.

And as Henriette sat there with the dancers circulating about her she did not see them. She was thinking of Charles and the terrible fire which, following the plague of last year, had ravaged his capital.

There was a great deal of misery in the world.

She stroked Mimi's silky ears. Even Mimi suffered; she had her jealousies and could not bear to see her mistress's attention turned to anyone or anything else. She would run away and hide out of very pique, if Henriette as much as picked up a book.

Roused from her reveries, Henriette noticed that one of the women was trying to catch her eye. Something was wrong.

She was glad when the ballet was over and she was free to listen to the woman.

'Madame, it is the little Duc de Valois. He has had a re-lapse.'

*

So she left the ball and drove with all speed to Saint-Cloud where her children were lodged.

The little boy's eyes lighted up when he saw his mother, but his appearance shocked her. She sank down by his bed and gathered him into her arms. In the service of the King, with the continual entertainments and ballets, she saw less of her children than she could have wished.

It was obvious that the little boy had a high fever and she turned appealingly to those about the bed.

'But his teeth came through quite well. I was told there was no longer need to worry. How did this happen? Why was I not informed?'

'Madame, the fever came on suddenly. The little Duc de Valois was playing yesterday with his sister. Then ... suddenly he was in the grip of fever. The doctors have bled him continually. Everything has been done.'

She was not listening. She was holding the precious child against her, rocking him to and fro.

I am weary of this life, she mused. I have had enough of balls and masques. I will nurse him myself. I will cease to be the slave of Louis. I will live differently ... quietly. When I have nursed my boy back to health I will spend long hours with my children. I am tired. Each day I grow more quickly weary.'

But while she thought thus the child's breathing grew more difficult and he did not recognize his mother.

Later she was aware of gentle hands that took the dead boy from her.

After that there arose the need to have another son. There was a return to the hateful life with a Philippe who was becoming more and more dominated by that vilest of men, the Chevalier de Lorraine.

*

There was continual friction between Henriette and Philippe. Philippe seemed to be filled with hatred for his wife. To him it was a matter of great annoyance and envy that Louis should discuss with her those secret matters of state which concerned England.

Often he would cry: 'You would have secrets from me? Is that the way in which to treat a husband? Tell me what passed between you and my brother.'

'If he wished you to know he would tell you,' Henriette would reply. 'Why do you not ask him?'

'Is it meet that my wife should spend long hours closeted with my brother?'

'If the King wishes to command that it should be so, it *is* right.'

'What is happening between our country and England? Should these matters be kept from me, yet imparted to my wife?'

'That is for the King to decide.'

Philippe would fling away from her in a passion and seek out his dear friend Lorraine, who would console him and tell him that he was unfortunate indeed to be married to such a wife.

*

At Saint-Cloud a new situation had arisen. One day Henriette asked for Mademoiselle de Fiennes, whom she had noticed was not amongst her attendants. She was told that the woman had gone away.

'Gone away? By whose permission?'

The answer was: 'At Monsieur's orders. She did not wish to go, but Monsieur drove her from the house.'

Henriette went to her husband's apartments. The Chevalier de Lorraine was sprawled insolently on his master's bed. Philippe sat in a window seat.

Neither rose when she entered. Lorraine was polishing a magnificent diamond on his finger – one of his latest presents from Philippe.

She was angry, but with admirable courage restrained herself from as much as glancing at her husband's favourite.

'Why have you sent Mademoiselle de Fiennes away?' she asked Philippe. 'I found the girl useful.'

'So did I, Madame,' said Lorraine with a laugh.

'Monsieur de Lorraine, I know you are completely without the social graces of a gentleman in your position, but,

I beg of you, do not address me until I speak to you.'

'If I am to be treated in this way I shall leave,' said Lorraine.

'I am glad you have given me an indication of how I may rid this place of your presence.'

'But it is the house of Monsieur, Madame. Have you forgotten that?'

'Philippe!' cried Henriette. 'Why do you sit there and allow this creature to behave thus to me?'

'It was you who were unpleasant to him in the first place,' said Philippe sullenly.

'You may pamper the creature. I shall ignore him. I repeat: Why did you send Mademoiselle de Fiennes away?'

'I will tell you,' cried Lorraine. 'Yes, Philippe, I insist. *I* did not wish the girl to go. I liked her. I like women at times, and she was a pretty girl. It was Monsieur who sent her away. Monsieur could not endure her. It was because he thought I liked her too well.' The Chevalier de Lorraine burst into loud laughter, and Philippe scowled.

'Do you expect me to endure this state of affairs?' demanded Henriette.

'You have no choice in the matter,' answered Philippe. 'And I will tell you this now: We leave for Villers-Cotteret tomorrow.'

'*We* leave?'

'You, I and Monsieur de Lorraine.'

'You mean you will carry me there by force?'

'You will find that you must obey your husband. I am weary of your spying servants. Our daughter's governess dared go to the King and complain about Lorraine and me, saying that we did not treat you in a becoming manner.'

'At least she spoke the truth.'

'And my brother has dared to ask me to mend my ways. And this, Madame, is brought about through your servants. Therefore we shall go where we shall not be spied on.'

'I will hear no more.'

'Hear this though. We leave tomorrow.'

'I shall not come.'

'Madame, you will come. The King does not wish an open break between us. And have you forgotten our need for a son?'

Henriette turned and left the apartment. She shut herself in her bedchamber and paced up and down.

What had she done, she asked herself, to deserve the worst husband in the world?

*

Solitude was the happiest state she could hope for at Villers-Cotteret. Often she wept bitterly during the night.

If she had a son she would insist on breaking away from Philippe; she would no longer live with such a man. She wept afresh for the loss of her little boy.

It was fortunate that Philippe and Lorraine were soon tired of the solitude of Villers-Cotteret, and they returned to Court.

It was Christmas time and a round of festivities was being planned. Now she was able to find new pleasure, for there came into her presence one day a tall, handsome young man who brought a note from her brother. It ran:

'I believe you may easily guess that I am something concerned for this bearer, James, and therefore I put him in your hands to be directed by you in all things, and pray use that authority over him as you ought to do in kindness to me. . . .'

Henriette looked up into the dark eyes so like Charles', and embraced the young man.

James, Duke of Monmouth, had been sent by her brother to visit her. Charles was proud of his son; perhaps, could Lucy Water see her Jemmy now, she too would be proud.

Henriette knew that Charles had received him at the London Court, that he had given him a dukedom and that he loved him dearly; but this was the first time she had set eyes on him.

Now she became gay again; it was the best way of forgetting those humiliating days at Villers-Cotteret; and how easy it was to be gay with Charles' son!

In some ways he reminded her of Charles, but he lacked her brother's wisdom, that gay cynicism, and perhaps that underlying kindness. How could she have expected it to be otherwise? There was only one Charles in the world.

'James,' she cried, 'you must tell me about my brother.

You must give me news of him. You must tell me every little detail: What time he rises ... how he spends his days ... Please, all these little humdrum things that take no account of state affairs. Talk to me ... talk to me of my dearly beloved brother.'

So James talked, and Henriette often drew him aside to hear the news of her brother's Court. She would have him show her the dances prevailing there, those quaint folk dances which seemed so strange to the French; but best of all she liked to hear news of Charles.

Lorraine seemed to grudge her even this pleasure.

'They talk in English,' he pointed out to Philippe. 'She is half in love with this handsome nephew of hers.'

'Nonsense!' said Philippe. 'He is but the son of the brother she loves so well.'

'She loved the brother too well, some say. Now she loves the brother's son. These are the ways of the Stuarts ... all know that.'

So Philippe taunted his wife, and their life together became more intolerable than ever. Even the Duke of Monmouth's visit was spoiled for Henriette.

*

In the June of that year Marie-Thérèse gave birth to a son. There was general rejoicing throughout the country. The Dauphin, though sickly, still lived.

Henriette was expecting a child in two months' time. She prayed for a son. If she had a boy she was determined to leave Philippe. She would speak of these matters to the King, once her child was born; and surely Louis would understand that no woman of her birth could endure to be treated as she was.

She was worried about her mother, who had aged considerably since her return from England. She had become ill through her anxiety when there had been trouble between England and France, and had spent many sleepless nights wondering about the future relationship between her son and nephew.

Henrietta Maria came to see her daughter at Saint-Cloud because at this time the birth of Henriette's child was imminent, and she herself could pay no visits. They did not speak of the state of friction between the two countries, nor of their private affairs; these subjects were too unhappy to be talked of. Henrietta Maria knew of her daughter's treatment at the hands of her husband – indeed the whole Court knew. So they talked of the child who would soon be born, of their hopes for a boy, and the Queen's malady.

'I do not know what it is that ails me,' said Henrietta Maria. 'But perhaps it is not a good thing to complain. I have always thought that to complain of illness did little good, and I do not care to be like some ladies who lament for a cut finger or pain in the head. But how I wish I could sleep! I lie awake and brood on the past. It parades before me. I fancy your father speaks to me . . . warns me . . . that I must curb the levity of Charles.'

'Charles is popular, Mam. I should not worry about him. It may be that subjects like their Kings to be gay. It may be that they wish for these things. They grew tired of Cromwell's England.'

'But the women at his Court! It is not that he has a mistress . . . or two. It is a seraglio.'

'Mam, Charles will always be Charles, whatever is said of him.'

'And no son to follow him! Only James Crofts . . . or Monmouth, as he now is.'

'A charming boy,' said Henriette.

'And likely to become as profligate as his father and mother.'

'Lucy Water!' pondered Henriette. 'I saw her once. A handsome girl . . . but with little character, I felt. Well, Charles loved her and he has kept his word to care for her son; and the little girl is well looked after, although many say that Charles is not her father.'

'He is ready to accept all who come to him and accuse him of being their father.'

'Dearest Charles! He was always too good-natured. Mam, I beg of you, cease to worry. I will send my physicians to you to prescribe something for your sleeplessness.'

'My child, may the saints bless you. May they bring you through your troubles to happiness. May you have a happier life than your poor mother.'

'I always remember that you had a good husband who

304

was faithful to you, Mam. It would seem to me that that made up for so much.'

'Ah, but to have such a one . . . and to lose him . . . to lose him as I did!'

Mother and daughter fell into silence, and after a while Henrietta Maria left for Colombes.

Four days later Henriette's daughter was born. Her mother did not come to see her; by that time she was feeling to ill to leave Colombes.

*

Henrietta Maria lay in her bed while the physicians sent by her daughter ranged themselves around her.

'It is sleep Your Majesty requires,' said Monsieur Valot. 'If you could rest you would regain your strength. We shall give you something to ease your pain, Madame.'

Henrietta Maria nodded her assent. She, who had complained bitterly of her unhappy life, bore pain stoically.

Monsieur Valot whispered to one of the doctors: 'Add three grains to the liquid. That will send Her Majesty to sleep.'

Henrietta Maria, hearing the talk of grains, raised herself on her elbow. She said: 'Monsieur Valot, my physician in England, Dr Mayerne, has told me I should never take opium. I heard you mention grains. Are those grains you spoke of, grains of opium?'

'Your Majesty,' explained Valot, 'it is imperative that you sleep. These three grains will ensure that you do. My colleagues here all agree that you must take this sleeping draught, for you cannot hope to recover without sleep.'

'But I have been strictly warned against opium on account of the condition of my heart.'

'This dose is so small, and I beg of Your Majesty to accept the considered opinion of us all.'

'You are the doctors,' said Henrietta Maria.

'I shall then instruct the lady in attendance on Your Majesty to give you this dose at eleven o'clock.'

Henrietta Maria felt a little better that day. She was able to eat a little, and soon after supper her women helped her to bed.

'I feel tired,' she said. 'I am sure that, with the aid of my sleeping draught, I shall sleep well.'

'There are two hours yet before you should take it, Your Majesty,' said her ladies.

'Then I shall lie and wait for it in the comfort that a good night's rest is assured me.'

Her ladies left her, and two hours later one of them brought in the draught. The Queen was then sleeping peacefully.

'Madame,' said the woman, 'you must wake and drink this. The doctor's orders, Your Majesty will remember.'

Half awake Henrietta Maria raised herself and drank. She was too sleepy to question the wisdom of waking a sleeping person to administer a sleeping draught.

When her attendants came to wake her in the morning, she was dead.

*

Henriette held her child in her arms. Another daughter. Did this mean she must resume marital relations with Philippe? It was too much to ask. She would not do it. She hated Philippe.

Her woman came to tell her that Mademoiselle de Montpensier was on her way to visit her.

When Mademoiselle came in there were traces of tears on her face; she embraced Henriette and burst into tears.

'I come from Colombes,' she said.

Henriette tried in vain to speak. Mam . . . ill! she thought. But she has been ill so long. Mam . . . dead! Mam . . . gone from me!

'She died in her sleep,' said Mademoiselle. 'It was a peaceful end. She had not been able to sleep; the doctors gave her medicine to cure her wakefulness, which it has done so effectively that she will never wake again.'

Still Henriette did not speak.

*

Louis came to Saint-Cloud. He was full of tenderness, as he could always be when those for whom he felt affection were in trouble.

'This is a great blow to you, my darling,' he said. 'I know

306

how you suffer. My brother's conduct is monstrous. I have remonstrated with him . . . and yet he does nothing to mend his ways.'

'Your Majesty is good to me.'

'I feel I can never be good enough to you, Henriette. You see, I love you. When I am with you, I am conscious of great regret. I have a wife . . . and there are others . . . but you, Henriette, are apart from all others.'

'It warms my heart to hear you say so.'

'You and I are close, my dearest . . . closer than any two people in the world.'

He embraced her tenderly. She was frailer than ever.

'I know you love me,' went on the King. And then: 'Your brother is asking that you may visit him.'

She smiled, and jealousy pierced Louis' heart, sharp and cold as a sword-thrust.

'He says that it is long since he saw you. He says that the grief you have both suffered makes you long to be together for a short while.'

'If only I might go!'

'I have spoken to Philippe. He is against your going.'

'And you, Sire?'

'Philippe is your husband. His consent would be necessary. It might be that we could force him to give it. Henriette, I wish to speak to you of secret matters. I know I can trust you to work for me . . . for me exclusively.'

'I am your subject, Louis.'

'You are also an Englishwoman.'

'But France is my country. I have lived all my life here. You are my King.'

'And more than your King?'

'Yes, Louis. You are my King and my love.'

He sighed. 'I wish to make a treaty with your brother. It is a very secret treaty. I think he may need . . . a certain amount of persuasion to make him agree to this treaty.'

Henriette's heart was beating fast.

'There is none who could persuade him . . . as you could,' Louis went on.

'What is this treaty, Louis?'

'I could only disclose it if I thought that you were entirely mine. There are few who know of its contents, and I trust you, Henriette. I trust you completely.' He was looking into her eyes. She saw that his were brilliant – as brilliant as when they rested on one of his potential mistresses. But what was happening now was seduction of a different kind: mental seduction. He was as jealous as a lover, but he was jealous of her love for her brother; he was demanding her complete surrender, not to be his mistress but his slave – his spy.

She was overcome by her love for him; the love of years seemed to envelope and overwhelm her.

She knew that if she failed him now, she had lost him; she knew that, if she gave herself to him in this way, they would be bound together for ever, that what he felt for his mistresses would indeed be light compared with what he felt for her, that what they could give would be as nothing, compared with her service. She had something which she alone could give: her influence with her brother. He was demanding now to know the extent of her affection for him, how great it was compared with that which she had for Charles.

She felt as though she were swooning. She heard herself say: 'Louis . . . I am yours . . . all yours.'

*

There were quarrels at Saint-Cloud. Philippe was furious with his wife.

The King had had the Chevalier de Lorraine arrested and sent to the Bastille. He had insulted Madame, and that, in the King's eyes, was a sufficient reason.

Madame was the King's favourite now. It was as it had been in the old days. Where Louis was, there was Henriette. They walked through the groves and alleys of Fontainebleau and Versailles, Louis' arm through that of Madame. They spent hours together with one or two of the King's ministers. Madame was not only the King's dear friend, it seemed; she was his political adviser.

Philippe came upon them once, poring over a document, which was put aside as he entered. His rage was boundless.

'What does the King talk of with you?' he wanted to know. 'Answer me! Answer me! Do you think I will allow myself – the King's brother – to be pushed aside!'

She replied coldly: 'You must ask the King. He will tell you what he wishes you to know.'

'Holy Mother! You are now such a minister of state that you shall ask for the release of Lorraine.'

'I shall do no such thing.'

'You will . . . you will! It is to please you that he has put my dear friend away. And the only way you shall live with me, Madame, is to live with him as well. We will be together – the three of us – and if you do not like that, you shall endure it!'

'I will endure no such thing. The King has not yet released him, remember.'

'If you do not have him released, I will not allow you to go to England.'

'The King wishes me to go to England.'

'You shall not stay long, though.'

She turned away, shrugging her shoulders.

'I shall divorce you!' he cried.

'That is the best news I have heard for a long time.'

'Then I shall not divorce you. I shall make you live in hell . . . a hell upon Earth.'

'You have already done that. Nothing you do to me in the future can be worse than you have done in the past.'

'You are ill. Anyone can see that. You are nothing but a bag of bones.'

'I know I cannot hope to compete in your eyes with your dear little friends, Monsieur de Marsan and the Chevalier de Beuvron.'

'It is true you cannot.'

'Then I hope they console you for the loss of your dear Lorraine!'

Philippe flung out of the room. His rage had brought him near to tears. It had always been the same, Louis always in the ascendant. The same story now, as it had been in their childhood! He wished he had not married Henriette.

*

Henriette could not sleep.

Now she knew the terms of the treaty. She knew that for Louis' sake she must persuade her brother to do something which she knew it was wrong for him to do.

Sometimes she would whisper to herself: 'I cannot do it.' She recalled her father's terrible end. He had gone against the wishes of his people. Was Louis asking Charles to do the same?

She repeated the terms over to herself. Charles was to join Louis in the invasion of Holland. The French were not popular in England, and that would be a difficult thing for him to arrange; but it was not that clause which gave her the greatest anxiety.

Charles was to make a public confession of his conversion to the Roman Catholic faith. Louis would pay him a large sum of money on his signing the treaty, and would give him men and ammunition to fight his fellow-countrymen, should they object to their King's decision.

Louis had said: 'I hold that only with a Catholic England can we have a true alliance.'

'But if the English will not accept a Catholic King?'

'We must see that they do.'

'This could make tragedy in England.'

'My dearest, we are concerned with France. Your brother was brought up to be more French than English. He is half French, and it is more natural for him to follow our faith. I have heard that he – as well as your brother James – has a fancy for it.'

'But the people of England . . .'

'As I said, we must think of France first, England second, eh? Your brother will know how this may be arranged. We do not ask him to proclaim his conversion at once. He may do so at his own leisure. The time to announce it will be for him to decide. There will be great advantages for him.'

But still she did not sleep.

'I love them both,' she whispered. 'I love France; I love England. I love Louis; I love Charles.'

But she knew she was placing the safety of England in jeopardy for the sake of France, for she was going to beg Charles, whom she loved, to risk his crown for the sake of Louis, whom she loved even more.

*

So with great pomp she arrived at Dover. There was one young girl in her suite whose freshness and beauty delighted

Henriette. She kept the girl beside her, for it was pleasant to see her childish delight in all the sights and ceremonies. She was the daughter of a poor Breton gentleman, and her name was Louise de Kéroualle.

It was a wonderful moment for Henriette when her brother and Monmouth came on deck to welcome her to England.

She was held fast in Charles' arms, and she saw the tears in his eyes.

'Minette . . . it has been so long. And how frail you are, my dearest, my darling!'

After the ceremonial greetings, the banquet given in her honour, she found herself alone with him. He told her he was grieved to see her so frail. He had heard of her suffering, and that her married life was by no means a felicitous one. He had heard the rumours concerning Lorraine. He would like to lay his hands on that gentleman, he said.

How close they were in those hours!

He learned the terms of the secret treaty. She watched his lean, dark, clever face. Charles understood her anxiety; he understood everything; she might have known that she could keep nothing from him.

Moreover, he was aware that she understood what she was asking him to do in signing this treaty; he knew, therefore, that she was working not for him, but for Louis. It was characteristic of him that he should understand this. His mind was alert. He had said that if he were less lazy he would be a good statesman, and if he could feel as enthusiastic about state matters as he could about a woman's charms, he would be a better King but a far inferior lover.

So it was clear to him that Louis had sent Henriette on this mission because Henriette loved Louis.

Charles was momentarily angry. This was not because she had failed in her love for him – he was but her brother and there was certain to be another whom she must love more – but because of what she had suffered in France. He knew her proud spirit; he knew of the humiliations she had endured at the hands of Philippe. He knew that she must soon leave him and go back to France. There, her position would only be tolerable if she were the King's favourite. Charles loved her; he loved her far more than she loved him.

A poor statesman, I! he thought. But a good lover.

He took her face in his hands and kissed it.

'I am entirely yours, Minette,' he said.

His quick mind was working. If I sign, I shall receive Louis' pension. That is a good thing. I may declare my conversion at any time I wish. Also a good thing.

My grandfather said Paris was worth a mass. Is not the happiness of my dear sister – she whom I believe I love beyond all things – worth a signature to a treaty?

Then he held her against him.

'My dearest Minette,' he said, 'you must go back and enjoy your triumphs. Louis is your friend. You can never have a better friend in a country than that country's King – providing he knows how to keep his crown. And you, my sister, have two who love you. When you return to France with my signature on that treaty, the King of France will indeed love you. But I do not think it can be said that he will love you more than does the King of England. Fortunate Minette, to be so loved by two Kings!'

He would not release her. He did not wish to see her tears, nor her to see his.

Minette now had what she had come for. As for Charles, he would find his way out of this awkward situation, as he had on other occasions.

*

The treaty was dispatched to France. Then the entertainments began. Charles was determined to show his sister that the Court of England was as full of wit and luxury as that of France. But the most wonderful thing in the world was, as he told her, for them to be together.

The days passed quickly and it was soon time for her to leave.

'I will give you a parting gift, Charles,' she said. 'I will give you something which will remind you for ever of this meeting of ours.'

She called to little Louise de Kéroualle to fetch her casket, that the King might select a jewel. But when the girl came, the King's eyes were not on the casket but on her.

'Pray choose, brother,' said Henriette.

Charles laid his hand on the arm of the girl. 'Give me this

beautiful child,' he said. 'Let her stay at my Court. She is the only jewel I covet.'

Louise's beautiful eyes were opened wide; she was not insensible of his charm.

'Nay,' said Henriette. 'I am responsible to her parents. I cannot leave her with you, Charles. Come ... take this ruby.'

But Charles and Louise continued to exchange glances, and before Henriette left for France he had managed to kiss the girl.

'I shall not forget you,' he said. 'One day you shall come to me.'

On a hot June day Henriette took her last farewell of Charles; and those about them wept to see their sorrow at this parting, for, never, it was said, had royal brother and sister loved each other as these two did.

*

Louis received her back in France with great warmth. She was his dear friend; now he would trust her for ever; never again would he doubt to whom her love was given.

There should be balls, masques, fêtes, ballets; and the Queen of his Court should be his Henriette.

She was gay for a while – two short weeks. She enjoyed her triumphs; but at night she would think of the dark, clever face which she loved so well, and she knew that he – past master in the art of loving – had proved the better lover. He had signed for her sake, and for love of Louis she had made him sign. He understood, as he would always understand; as he would have said: 'To love is not only a pleasure, it is a privilege.'

He had written in the verses he had shown her:

"... I think that no joys are above
The pleasures of love.'

Yet she had betrayed him, and because of that she knew she would never be happy again.

Now those about her noticed the effect of the sleepless nights. She was too thin, too fragile for a young woman barely twenty-seven years of age.

Philippe worried her continually. Her influence with the

King was great, he reminded her; she must bring about the return of Lorraine; he would make her very sorry if she did not.

She turned wearily away from him. He forced her to go alone with him to Saint-Cloud where he continued to make her life miserable, and only the command of the King could induce him to bring her back to Versailles; but as soon as possible he forced her to return once more to Saint-Cloud.

There she must endure his company, his continual complaints, and this she suffered, together with the reproaches of her own conscience.

She was coughing a good deal, and there were times when she felt almost too weary to care what became of her.

One evening, only a few weeks after her return, she was dining with Philippe and her ladies when she felt a strange lassitude come over her. When the meal was over she lay down on some cushions because, she said, she felt unusually tired. The day had been hot and she now slept, and while she slept she dreamed. She dreamed she was sailing towards Dover, and her brother was holding out his arms to her, but that she was turning away and crying because she was ashamed to go to him.

Coming out of her dream she heard voices. 'How ill Madame looks! Do you see?'

Then she heard Philippe: 'I have never seen her look so ill.'

'It is the journey to England which has done this. She has not been well since she returned.'

'Ah, that journey to England!' said Philippe. 'I was a fool to allow it.'

Henriette opened her eyes and said: 'I want a drink.'

Madame de Gourdon, one of her ladies, hurried away to bring her a glass of iced chicory water, which she drank; but no sooner had she done so than she was seized with violent pains in her side.

She cried out in agony: 'I have such pains! What was in that glass? I believe myself to have been poisoned.' As she spoke she fixed her eyes on Philippe, who had hurried to her side.

Her ladies unlaced her gown as she fell fainting on to her cushions.

314

She opend her eyes at length and murmured: 'This . . .
pain. I cannot endure it. Who has poisoned me?' Once
more she turned to Philippe. He fell on his knees beside her.

'You must get well,' he said. 'You will get well, Henriette.'

'You have ceased to love me, Philippe,' she said. 'You
never loved me.'

Philippe covered his face with his hands and burst into
tears.

One of the ladies sent for her confessor; another saved
the chicory water that it might be examined.

'Madame,' murmured one of the women, 'the doctors
will soon be here.'

'I have greater need of my confessor,' she answered.

The ladies were looking at her with concern. Henriette,
through the haze in her mind which was the result of pain,
was aware of their suspicions of her husband. They were
sure that she had been poisoned, and they suspected
Philippe of murder.

*

A few hours passed. Philippe showed great distress, but
Henriette was sceptical. She said to herself: 'He has then
tried to rid himself of me as he threatened he would. Did
he plot this then . . . with Lorraine?'

'Madame . . . Madame . . . take this soup,' begged one of
her ladies. 'It will make you stronger.'

'Nothing will make me stronger now. I shall not be here
by morning. I know it.'

'She closed her eyes and thought: Nor do I want to be. I
do not want to live continually to reproach myself.

After a while she said: 'There is one who will be heartbroken when he hears the news of my death. Do you know
who that is? Do you know who loves me more dearly than
any? It is my brother of England.'

'Madame,' she was told, 'the King is on his way to see
you.'

*

When Louis came she was lying back exhausted, and he
could scarcely recognize her; she looked so small in her
nightdress which had been loosened at the neck to allow her

to breathe. Her face was deathly pale, her beautiful eyes sunken; already she appeared to be more dead than alive.

She found it difficult to see him. He seemed to swim before her eyes – tall, commanding, the most handsome man in the world.

'Louis . . .' Her lips managed to form the words.

'Henriette . . . my dearest.'

'Louis . . . I am going . . . I am going fast.'

'Nay!' he cried; and she heard his sobs. 'Nay, you will recover. You must recover.'

'The first thing you will hear in the morning is that I am dead.'

'It shall not be. It must not be.'

'Oh Louis, you are the King and accustomed to command, but you cannot command death to stay away when he has made up his mind to come for me.'

Louis turned to the doctors. 'Will you let her die without trying to save her?'

'Sire, there is nothing we can do.'

'Louis!' she cried. 'Louis, come back to me. For the last time, hold my hand.'

His eyes were so blinded with tears that he could not see her. 'Henriette,' he murmured, 'Henriette, you cannot leave me. You cannot leave me.'

'I must leave you . . . both you and Charles . . . you two . . . whom I have loved so much. Louis, there will be many to comfort you . . . I grieve for Charles. I grieve for my brother. He is losing the person he loves best in the world. Louis, you will write to him. You will tell him of my end? Tell him how at the end I spoke of him. Tell him that . . . if in any way I wronged him . . . I loved him . . . I always loved him.'

'I shall send word to him. I shall send him comfort. I shall send him that Breton girl who was with you . . . You told me how he wished her to stay. She will comfort him . . . She will remind him of you. I shall send her to his Court with my wishes for his comfort.'

Henriette tried to shake her head. She understood the meaning behind those words. He would send the girl to do what she had done – spy for France.

'Louis . . .' she gasped. 'No . . . no!'

'But you will get well,' persisted the King stubbornly. 'I command you to get well. You cannot leave me. I'll not allow it.'

The Curé of Saint-Cloud arrived, bringing the Host with him. She received the Viaticum and asked for Queen Anne's crucifix to hold in her hand as she left this world.

All knew now that she could not live long.

Men and women, courtiers and servants, were crowding into the great hall, for the news that she was dying had spread through the Court.

And there at her bedside stood the King, the tears falling and great sobs racking his body.

'Kiss me, Sire, for the last time,' whispered Henriette. 'Do not weep for me, or you will make me weep too. You are losing a good servant, Louis. I have ever feared the loss of your good graces more than anything on earth ... more than death itself ... and if I have done wrong ... so often it has been that I might serve you. Louis ... remember me ...'

He kissed her tenderly. He knelt by the bed and covered his face with his hands.

*

Charles was stunned by the news. Henriette, who had been with him a few weeks before, dead!

Minette, his beloved sister, who had seemed to be ever present in her letters to him! Minette, whom he had loved beyond all others; for his passion for his mistresses was fleeting, whereas his love for his sister had endured all through his life. Minette ... dead!

Rumours spread that she had been poisoned. Philippe and the Chevalier de Lorraine were suspected.

Charles, in indignant rage, demanded the satisfaction of an autopsy. Louis was only too glad to grant this.

'It is a sorrow we share,' he wrote to Charles. 'If a foul deed has been done, I am as eager to find and punish her murderer as you are.'

The chicory water had been examined and even drunk by others, who suffered no ill effect; at the autopsy no poison was found in her body; it was remembered that it was long since she had enjoyed good health.

317

Were there not always rumours of poisoning when notable people died?

Charles was unable to control his grief. He could not bear to speak of her; he shut himself away from the pleasures of his Court.

Never has the King shown such grief, it was said.

Then there came to his Court one who, the King of France felt, would, while she reminded him of his sister, bring some comfort to Charles. She was the jewel he had coveted, said Louis, and it would have been Henriette's wish that her brother should possess this coveted jewel. It was hoped that the King of England would show his sister's maid of honour 'a piece of tenderness' and cherish her at his Court.

In the lovely young Breton, Louise de Kéroualle, both Kings saw a substitute for Henriette.

Louis saw her as his spy at the court of England, who would serve him as Henriette had done. Charles delighted to see her again and, in his appreciation of her fresh young beauty, was able to subdue his grief. He would show her that 'piece of tenderness', and she would remind him of Henriette, even as Lucy's boy – Monmouth – reminded him of Lucy.

There was pleasure in love, he had always said, and for him there always would be. There were many years ahead for him and for Louis, to indulge in the pleasures of love. There would be many women, the memory of whom would become as hazy as his hours with Lucy had now become; yet as long as he lived he would cherish the memory of his sweet Minette.